You Can Say You Knew Me When

Books by K.M. Soehnlein

THE WORLD OF NORMAL BOYS

YOU CAN SAY YOU KNEW ME WHEN

Published by Kensington Publishing Corporation

You Can Say You Knew Me When

K.M. SOEHNLEIN

KENSINGTON BOOKS
http://www.kensingtonbooks.com

This is a work of fiction. Names, characters, places and incidents either are the product of the author's imagination or are used fictitiously. Any resemblance or relationship to characters or events, living or dead, is purely coincidental.

KENSINGTON BOOKS are published by

Kensington Publishing Corp.
850 Third Avenue
New York, NY 10022

Permission to quote from *Palimpsest* by Gore Vidal (1995) is by courtesy of Random House.

Library of Congress Card Catalogue Number: 2004113880
ISBN 0-7582-0798-0

First Printing: September 2005
10 9 8 7 6 5 4 3 2 1

Printed in the United States of America

The book is dedicated to my father,
for not being the father in this book,
and to Kevin Clarke,
who was there from day one.

In the end, the hardest thing is learning to tell a secret from a mystery.

—Gary Indiana, *Horse Crazy*

THE SON

1

It had been five years since I'd visited Greenlawn, and as soon as I stepped off the bus from Newark Airport, it was clear the only thing that had changed was me.

Many of the same family-owned shops that had been here when I was a kid still stood: the pet store, the hardware store, the place selling musical instruments, the one that made custom-ordered curtains. There was even Georgie's Sweet Shoppe, where I worked one summer during high school, mixing ice cream and chocolate in the basement, putting twenty pounds on my teenage frame. Each of these stores was housed in brick, all warm hues and weathered corners, so that the main street resembled a single, long storefront, sturdy and timeworn. In San Francisco, where I lived, brick was nearly nonexistent; brick walls collapse during earthquakes. The old brick warehouses that I biked past every day on my way to my boyfriend Woody's apartment were all being retrofitted with massive steel beams in X formation along the weight-bearing walls. The effect was something like seeing a brace put on a leg before any bone has broken: The buildings were stronger, but you were newly aware of how vulnerable the original structure had been.

Growing up, I saw Greenlawn, New Jersey, as the epitome of American suffocation and conformity. Now here it stood, a pleasant little village preserved in amber. The brickface was part of this, and beyond that, the fact that there were almost no chain stores on the main street. I looked across the intersection to the town park, whose Veterans Memorial and white gazebo had seemed to my rebellious teenage self symbols of oppression, but which now simply seemed old-fashioned; not *Amerikkka*, but Americana.

My father loved living in Greenlawn. As I stood at the bus stop, waiting for my sister to arrive—luggage at my feet, a lit cigarette in my mouth—I repeated that sentiment in my head, a platitude at-the-ready for meeting and greeting relatives during his wake and funeral in the days to come. *It's good that he died here, in this place that he loved.* This was bullshit, of course: He'd died too young, in the hospital, after a painful deterioration, and for those involved the whole thing was suffused with tragedy. That I wasn't one of those involved was the reason I needed to rehearse platitudes at all. I needed something to say, a way to be and behave during this visit.

A screech of tires, a blur of silver in the winter air: a minivan arcing sharply through the street in front of me. For a split second I imagined it roaring over the yellow-striped curb and plowing into me—I saw the headline, ILLEGAL U-TURN ENDS IN DEATH—but instead it slid efficiently to the curb. At the wheel was my sister, Deirdre. The passenger window lowered halfway, and her voice carried over from the driver's seat: "I know I'm late. Put your bags in the back."

I took one last drag off my cigarette, glancing at the clock on the First Jersey Bank across the street. 10:05. "In my world, five minutes late is early," I said.

I turned to lift my luggage into the back of the van. Staring across the backseat was a small boy bundled in winter clothes. My nephew, AJ. I hadn't seen him since he was born, and what I caught in his wide brown eyes, gazing out from below a snowflake-patterned ski cap, was equal parts anticipation and suspicion. Distracted, in mid-swing, I banged my forehead on the edge of the roof, letting out a pained "Fuck!" I'm all too famous for this kind of klutzy move.

AJ's eyes widened.

"Pretend I didn't say that." I sent him a wink. As I circled back to the front seat, he twisted beneath his safety belt to keep a watch on me.

I hopped inside and leaned across a topography of gray leather to give my sister a greeting: a no-contact kiss near the side of her face and an awkward shoulder pat meant as a hug. She remained more or less motionless through this, her hands firmly on the steering wheel. "How was your flight?" she asked. Her face was thinner than I remembered, tight around the jaw. Or maybe it was the severe way she'd pulled back her hair into one of those clip-combs. When she pressed her burgundy-painted lips together, the effect was one of strain.

"The flight was fine," I said. "No, actually, it was awful. I was in and out of sleep. I'm sort of stiff all over."

"Can't remember the last time I flew anywhere," she said as she pulled the van into the street.

I was contemplating how much accusation I should insinuate from her tone—*I haven't flown anywhere because I've been here, taking care of our dying father*—when AJ interrupted from the backseat.

"Was I ever on a plane, Mommy?" His voice was New Jersey through and through: *evva onna plane.*

"Ayj, you know you weren't," she replied. "Did you say hello to your uncle Jamie?"

"No."

"Why not?"

"He said the F-word."

Deirdre exhaled wearily. "Off to a great start."

"It was self-defense!" I threw my arms apart, exaggerating a plea for mercy, trying to keep things light. "I was attacked by the rear end of this high-octane death machine." I turned around and looked at AJ. "Come on, kid. Don't give your mother any ammunition against me."

Deirdre sighed again. "Just watch your mouth around him, Jamie."

AJ had already grown since the Christmas photo Deirdre and her husband, Andy, had mailed me; dressed in a shirt and a tie and framed by an evergreen wreath, he'd seemed prim and well behaved. He looked more playful in person, rolling a multicolored rubber ball from hand to hand, but I guessed he was kept pretty tight under Deirdre's thumb. "You can fly on a plane to California. That's where I live," I said to him.

"I don't know if I'm allowed."

"You can go when you're ten," Deirdre said.

"That's two times my age," AJ protested.

"He has Andy's knack for numbers," Deirdre whispered.

"Five years is a long time. We'll work on her, AJ." His eyes twinkled back—a lovely moment, a little reward for my efforts to befriend him, but one that evaporated quickly as Deirdre spoke again.

"You're still smoking."

"I've cut back quite a bit," I said.

"*Cut back* isn't the same as quit." She sounded like a mother lecturing to a teenager—like our mother, who'd once caught us sneaking cigarettes in the attic. How old were we then? Mom died when I was seventeen and Dee was fifteen; this would have been a couple years before. I'd taken the heat that day, "confessing" that I'd pressured Dee, when in fact it had been little sister who wanted to get in on big brother's bad habit. The whole episode had ended in some kind of punishment for me when Dad got home.

"Look, I'm a very civilized smoker," I said. "I sit next to an open window when I smoke in my own apartment. I'm not some *chimney* you have to tolerate under your roof."

"You're not staying under my roof."

"Where am I staying?" But I knew before I'd completed the question: at my father's house. About a half mile ago we hadn't turned right at the middle school, which would have taken us to where Deirdre, Andy, and AJ lived on the other side of Greenlawn. Instead we had continued straight on, toward the house where we grew up.

"I need you to keep an eye on Nana," she said.

Our grandmother had been living with our father, her only son, for the past few years, taking care of him through his illness. I had no idea what state I'd find her in, what kind of help she needed. I tried to remember the last news I'd gotten about Nana, in one of Deirdre's monthly phone calls. "How is she?"

"Well, she's eighty-five years old, and she just watched her son die," she said, turning the van into the driveway. "Think about it."

A tightness took hold of my stomach, the awful feeling of returning to a place reverberating with old hostility. The yard looked barren. The spindly oak tree that had stood near the sidewalk was gone, opening up the view to the house—two stories and an attic covered in pale, sooty shingles. The place had always looked its best in the summer, surrounded by green grass, leafy oaks, flowering honeysuckle and azalea bushes. In the winter it resembled some kind of Gothic rooming house, all cold doorknobs and creaky floorboards, a block of grayish white not so different from the grayish white winter sky above it. I thought of what I'd find inside: canned beer in the fridge, a thermostat not turned up high enough, lights flipped off in every empty room. The thrifty way Teddy Garner kept house. Then I remembered what I wouldn't find: Teddy—my father—at the center of it.

For years everyone had referred to my father's condition as Alzheimer's, though it wasn't exactly that. He suffered from a particularly virulent form of what the doctors labeled nonspecific dementia, akin to Alzheimer's but ultimately not diagnosable without a brain biopsy—something my father, with his fear and loathing of the medical establishment, did not allow. The label made no difference; the nerve connections corroding inside his brain, nonspecifically, from the time he was in his mid-fifties, made all the difference in the world. He was dead before he turned sixty.

I had ceased contact with my father five years earlier. Had cut him off. Deirdre periodically pressured me to come home. Her most recent plea came ten days before, when she warned me that this hospitalization would likely be his last. But he was brought in just before New Year's, 2000, the turn of the millennium, a time when even the most rational people were spooked by dire apocalyptic scenarios: computer networks powering down, electricity fritzing off around the globe, passenger jets falling from the sky. No one was flying then. I'd personally stocked up on batteries, canned food and bottled water, just in case. It was a distracting time—neurosis on a mass scale. *Y2K.* A compelling reason to stay away.

But even if I had simply taken the first available flight to New Jersey, stood alongside my sister and brother-in-law, my grandmother and my aunt, claimed my belated membership in the vigilant inner circle, it wouldn't have changed one basic fact: My father lacked the faculties to recognize me. The moment for restorative visitations had passed long ago. Woody had urged me to hurry back for my own sake, for *a sense of closure,* but I didn't take much stock in this. "The case has been closed for years," I told him. For five years, to be precise, since my father and I had our last argument—what I decided would be our final argument.

Deirdre's call had come during an unlit early-morning hour while I was deep in sleep. "It's over," she said, sniffling through tears. "You didn't get to say good-bye." I couldn't tell if she was angry or felt sorry for me.

I propped myself up, half awake, tented in blackness, fumbling for something to say. All the usual sentiments seemed wrong, inappropriate to our family's situation, our strained relations. "What happens now?" I asked.

"There's a lot to do," she said. "I'm going to need your help."

I found myself struggling to recall if I had any freelance work lined up for the next couple days; how difficult it would be to meet with Anton, my pot dealer, before I left San Francisco; which of my overburdened credit cards had room for a last-minute cross-country airfare. "I'll probably need a little time to get myself together," I told her.

"Sure, just take your time," she said, sobs sucked up into steely sarcasm. "See if you can fit it into your schedule, you know, before he's fucking buried."

This caught me off guard. I can see now that it shouldn't have; estranged or not, he was my father, this was his funeral. But on the spot, I thought, I hoped, that I could just show up at the last minute, shake a few hands, and move on—like any other far-off acquaintance. I was wrong.

When we were children, Deirdre and I used to push past our parents and race each other up the stairs of the apartment building in Manhattan where Nana lived. We'd find our grandmother standing ramrod straight in the doorway, wearing an apron over a fancy dress, a potholder in her hand. We'd throw ourselves at her, and she'd always say, in her heavy Irish brogue, "Smelled the cooking, did you?" as she shooed us inside to eat something hearty like baked ham and boiled potatoes. The ritual changed over time—we got older and less demonstrative, and Nana spent far fewer hours in the kitchen after her husband, who we called Papa, died—but I still thought of her that way. Welcoming.

There was no sight of her as I lugged my bags from the minivan into the house. Instead I found her sitting in the kitchen, her eyes fixed on a TV perched atop the refrigerator. I went to her side and wrapped my arms around her. Even in the old days, Nana had been more of a back-patter than a hugger; along with her stiff posture came a certain emotional rigidity. But this time, as I felt the nubs of her vertebrae and the hard lines of her shoulder blades, I got absolutely nothing in return.

I asked her how she was feeling. She shrugged, nothing more. As I slunk back toward the counter she said, "Make yourself a cup of tea, Jimmy."

The name halted my steps. No one had called me Jimmy since high school, and I'd more or less forgotten that anyone ever had. *Jamie* was the name I'd given myself when I left home. (No one ever, ever, used the name on my birth certificate, James, though the stoners I hung out with in college liked to call me Rockford, after the TV detective played by the actor whose name I shared.) When members of my family used *Jimmy,* I felt them clinging to a me who no longer existed. To Nana I would always be the boy racing up four flights of stairs to greet her.

I was starting to take off my coat, thinking about a nap, when Deirdre called from across the room, "Don't get too comfortable."

She was scanning a clipboard and repeatedly clicking the end of a ballpoint pen, *snap-snap, snap-snap,* a tic that pressed whiteness into the tip of her thumb. I noticed her manicured fingernails, maroon like her lipstick. She used to bite her nails, right down to the skin. "Follow me," she said, waving toward the stairs, whisking me into the centripetal force of her plans.

The first task was to haul our father's mattress off his bed. One, two, three, *lift*: The waft of urine, infection and medicinal powder, faint but unmistakable, spiraled into the air between us, and I felt bile bubble up from my travel-addled guts. "This is nothing," Deirdre said, seeing the expression on my face. "You should have been here two weeks ago."

Or two months ago, I imagined her thinking. Or two years. "I'm about five seconds away from puking up airplane food," I said.

"One thing I've learned—you can get used to *any*thing." On her face I could see the toll of getting used to this: worry lines around her mouth and eyes, a tendony tightness to her neck. She was younger than me—she wasn't yet thirty—but she'd started to look like my older sister.

We lugged the mattress, which was bowed at the center and blotchy with stains, out into the damp January air and wedged it into her minivan. It came to rest on top of the seat backs. "It's kind of like a loft bed," I wisecracked. "You might want to use it as a guest room."

"Great, now I know where we can put you," she said dryly. She was dangling the car keys in the air between us. "You remember how to get to the dump?"

"You're kidding, right?" She was not kidding. "Isn't there some service that can take this away?"

"Yeah, it's called Big Brother's Moving Company." She pressed the keys into my palm.

"Don't I have a say in this?"

"Not really." Then, softening just a touch: "Please, Jamie. It's your turn."

Years ago I'd been part of the group that cleared out my friend Paul's apartment after he died from AIDS, and his mattress was the very first thing we got rid of. Deirdre had put off this wretched task for two days, or three, whatever it had been, even with Nana living here and Andy around to lend muscle power. Why? Because it was my turn, my punishment? I knew how easy it was to slip into an argument with her; I wondered if she'd actually welcome it.

But I'd sworn to myself I'd get through this visit without incident. I took my place behind the wheel.

Coping with the smell was easy enough—I opened the windows, gladly enduring the cold air; I lit a cigarette and blew smoke across the dashboard—but the specter of my father wasting away on the mattress now bobbling behind my head was another matter entirely. He'd been a sturdy, almost stocky man—five feet eleven inches, nearly two hundred pounds—but illness would have shrunken him. Again I thought of Paul on the eve of his death, the skin-and-bones appearance; his shallow, dry breathing; the medicated glaze of his eyes as he held on longer than any of us thought he would, longer than we'd hoped was possible. My brain morphed them together, the friend I loved and the father I did not, until a sickly vision floated up behind me—the slate blue of my father's eyes bulging out from a skeletal face, his cracked lips rasping out one of his characteristic truisms: *Responsibility breeds respect. Respect comes from responsibility. Show me one, Jimmy, and I'll show you the other.* Even in death, a lecture.

My foot fell heavier on the gas, and I sped along the residential streets, gunning through a yellow light, honking at a slow-moving subcompact. I flipped the radio to an all-talk station and tried to lose myself in the angry pitch of political debate. Caller and host were arguing about whether or not Al Gore should distance himself from Bill Clinton in order to win the presidency. I joined in: *Yes, distance yourself. Don't get dragged down by the last guy's mistakes. Be your own person!*

At the dump I was the third minivan queued up. I killed the engine and watched one, then another, middle-aged woman extract a withered Christmas tree from her vehicle's rear door, drag it across the frozen ground and, with a scattering of dead needles, heave the barky skeleton into an enormous gray compactor. It was all rather efficient, a time-worn January ritual at which I was some kind of interloper. When my turn came, I felt like the punch line to a comedy sketch: soccer mom, Christmas tree; soccer mom, Christmas tree; gay guy, dirty mattress.

I held my breath as I catapulted his death-bedding into the compactor's jaws, grunting "Rest in peace" as it slipped from my sight. I was answered by an uprising of dust that hovered high above before disseminating on the wind, carrying toward me a last gasp of pine.

* * *

I wanted so badly to sleep, but when I got back to the house I was conscripted into other projects. First, the arranging, and frequent rearranging, of living room/dining room/family room furniture according to Deirdre's orders, in anticipation of the visitors who would stop by after the wake the next night. Given the number of cobweb-caked folding chairs we dragged up from the basement and wiped clean, it seemed that she was expecting half of Greenlawn. Then we took the van to Big Savers, one of those enormous concrete warehouses where everything is sold extra-extra-jumbo size, a place so antithetical to the town's Mom-and-Pop main street that it wiped away all my quaint illusions of Greenlawn. Here were the locals en masse—teenage employees speeding by on forklifts, overweight retirees in motorized wheelchairs, four-year-olds scurrying among the free samples as one mother after another shouted "Jacob, put that down" and "Emily, I said *no.*" I was glad we'd left AJ behind with Nana.

I straggled alongside Deirdre, who commandeered a shopping cart so large an average supermarket cart could have fit inside it. She loaded it up with restaurant-size packs of paper products, cases of carbonated soda, loaves of bread the sizes of roasting pans, boxes of shrink-wrapped guacamole, gallon jars of salsa and all manner of mass-produced snacks, each labeled to sound upscale: Mesquite Chips, Fancy Cookies, Four Cheese Tuscan Pizza.

"Could we maybe buy something besides junk food?" I finally asked, watching another chunky ten-year-old gobble up samples of Turkey Jerky.

"It's just for people to nibble. Nana's making a roast." She handed me a laundry-detergent-size box of Gourmet Party Mix.

"Do you even know what's in this?"

"AJ loves it. You gonna tell me how to feed my son?"

I put on a Big Savers mom-voice and wagged my finger: "Deirdre, I said *no.*"

She paused a moment. Was I joking? Was this worth a fight? "Some fruit would be good," she said finally, returning the offending snack food to the mile-high shelves.

The quiet of the house started to spook me. I had moved my bags into a small room at the end of the upstairs hall that had once been where our mother sewed the clothes Dee and I wore as kids. I pictured Mom staring out the window into the backyard—the weedy lawn, overgrown bushes and tall evergreens—guiding inexpensive poly-cotton fabrics under the needle as she hummed one of the German songs of her childhood. Her Singer sewing machine, with its varnished wood table and brown-plastic foot pedal, was long gone, probably donated to the Salvation Army after her death.

My mother's death had been the inverse of my father's: quick, shocking, unbearable. She'd gone into the hospital suffering sudden, debilitating chest pain and died a day later, after twelve hours on the operating table. The postmortem diagnosis blamed a defective heart valve that had gotten infected, flooding her bloodstream with toxic microorganisms. My father spent the rest of his life suing the hospital and various members of its staff for malpractice. He became a self-taught medical expert, obsessed with figuring out what had gone wrong in surgery, sure that this could have, should have, been averted, and it had made him as crazy as any single-minded crusader.

I was seventeen when she died, a junior in high school, already a troublemaker—chain-smoking, breaking curfew, drinking until I puked. Mom's death turned me into a sort of runaway, hopping between overnights with friends, piling up unexplained absences, infuriating my father. I could no longer stand to be in this house, which was, back then, so clearly hers. Not only had she been home more than the rest of us—she worked part-time as a lab technician in the same hospital where she died—but she kept our family in equilibrium, mediating arguments, offering compromises. I'd been identified as the problem child a decade earlier, a smarty-pants always talking back, and at the same time a confrontation avoider, a late sleeper, a dawdler. My mother had patience for my restlessness. *One day you'll outgrow this,* she'd say, her English so perfect it revealed no trace of her German upbringing. My father was the pessimist. *A wiseass never wins*. We were two stubborn red-haired males, always at odds—though before my mother died we at least had someone to run interference for us.

This was the most I'd thought about her in years.

This sewing room was now a guest room, big enough for only an end table, a twin bed and an enormous wicker planter sporting a dusty bouquet of fake peacock feathers. The wallpaper had a leafy green, vaguely jungly pattern; the bedspread, in contrast, was midnight blue and swirled with stars and galaxies—the same one beneath which I'd agitated as a teenager. The mattress might have been my teenage mattress, too. It was so broken-in I couldn't get comfortable.

Nearly thirty hours had passed since Deirdre's call cut off my last deep sleep, but I was wide awake. Is there anything more enervating, short of chronic physical pain, than not being able to sleep when you're clearly exhausted? I tried reading the book I'd packed and watched pages turn while words went unabsorbed. I opened up the notebook I carry around as a journal, wrote down some thoughts about brick storefronts, dirty mattresses and the dystopia of Big Savers, but then gave up when I tried to put into words what I might be feeling about the reason I had come here. It was too soon; I was too freshly in it. I tried jacking off but couldn't shake the vehemently non-sexual cloak of death hovering in the air, not to mention the image of my grandmother in the next room. The muffled bass tone of her TV rumbled through the wall.

Finally, I got up and phoned Woody at work.

"I'm missing you, Wormy," I told him. "This is pretty hard."

"Must be hard for you there. Is everyone really sad?"

"Not so much sad as—I don't know—tense. Nana's avoiding me. Deirdre's bossing me around."

"What about you, Germy?" (That's right, Wormy and Germy, the private us.)

"Painfully tired. I can't sleep, I'm so traumatized by the sound of Deirdre's cracking whip. You'd be proud of me, though. I haven't started any fights."

I told him I wished he was here with me. This was sidestepping the truth: I hadn't invited him to come along. There was no way to pull him from his fifty-hour-a-week dot-com job, went the official reasoning for his absence, but the fact was, I just couldn't cope with a boyfriend in the midst of the family reunion. The irony of this wasn't lost on me: While my father was alive, my boyfriends weren't welcome.

On my last trip back, a couple months after AJ was born, I'd been hopeful. AJ's birth was a big deal, something to pull us, once and for all, out of the gloom of Mom's death. Change was in the air, and spirits were high. Dad organized a big summer party, inviting friends from all corners of the past along with the whole extended family. Deirdre and Andy had married quickly, and quietly, after she got pregnant, but they'd been dating for years, and everyone was ready to celebrate. This would be the wedding reception my father had been deprived of.

The sun blazed strong that day, the humid air thick with barbecue smoke, cut grass and honeysuckle, the yard trampled with the carefree steps of guests getting drunk. Deirdre wore the tired-but-smiling face of the new mother; Andy was fast growing into the part of proud papa, boasting that AJ's big hands were a sign he would play for the New York Mets some day. Dad had lorded over the grill all afternoon, a whiz with spatula and tongs, his voice booming greetings across the yard, his new apron announcing him as the WORLD'S BEST GRANDPA.

That night, I cornered him in his bedroom for a talk that I'd nervously rehearsed ahead of time. I told him that I had wanted to bring David—the guy I was seeing back then—to the picnic, but that I hadn't because I didn't think Dad would approve. My father, without hesitation, said, "You were correct." The conviction of his voice, its done-deal tone, squeezed the air out of me. "I thought you'd changed," I said, and he replied, "As always, I prefer that you keep your private life private." To which I said, "Then I prefer to not come home anymore."

That's the headline-news version. The actual conversation was lengthy and insulting and loud. I called him a bigot in a dozen different ways. He took great issue with my timing: I was *stealing Deirdre's spotlight*; I was *ruining a joyful occasion.* "You're looking for attention," he told me in his calm, clenched voice. "You've always craved attention." I tried to notch it down, to take the anger out of my voice, to sound as rational as he did, but I wasn't able: It hurt. It hurt because we'd been through this before, when I was a teenager and he'd first discovered my sexuality; after I got out of college, finally able to admit to myself what I was; when I decided to move to San Francisco, hoping he'd understand; and then long-distance, over the phone, in smaller doses. I'd been "coming out" to him for most of my adult life.

That night I told him he wouldn't hear from me until he'd changed his mind. What I actually said was "Until you stop being so fucking closed minded."

All this came roaring back to me after I got off the phone with Woody. I was sitting in a nook in the upstairs hallway, in an armchair next to a small wooden table—the "telephone table" we called it, a name that had always sounded sophisticated to me, something out of a Rosalind Russell movie. I glanced toward my father's bedroom. An eerie, vertical slice of darkness floated between the half-open door and the frame, beyond which I could see our penultimate argument in pantomime: me, pacing uneasily, wearing shorts made from cut-off Army fatigues, a sleeveless T-shirt emblazoned with a random high-school sports logo (WOLVERINE WRESTLING), silver rings on my fingers, silver hoops in my ears, a fresh tattoo inked around my bicep, the whole look an ironic pastiche of the very masculinity that he embodied. I must have appeared so adolescent to him. Clownish. *Gay.* Sitting tensed on the bed, he was intimidating and solid: freshly showered, his clean white T-shirt snug across his barrel chest, his freckled and furry arms, his clenched fists. I saw each contour so clearly. He was dead, but his presence was stronger than it had been for years.

I walked to the bedroom door, pushed it open, flicked on the light. Medical supplies—pill bottles and swabs and a thermometer—cluttered the dresser. The bed frame, devoid of its mattress, sat empty in the center of the room, a fuzzy coating of dust on the brown rug beneath. In a span of five years, my father had been transformed from that imperturbable figure arguing rationally from the foot of his bed to an emaciated shell withering away under the covers. Perhaps he was already heading into dementia the night we'd fought—plaque forming along his nerves, the viral conspiracy to bring down his brain fomenting deep within.

A couple of months after that, he called me in San Francisco to chat. Literally, just to chat. For small talk. When I brought up *the subject,* he seemed perplexed, as if things between us hadn't gotten so heated. "I consider that matter settled," he said, as if reviewing a policy dispute with a co-worker. It was all I needed to end contact, once and for all.

But now I wondered, when he'd made that call, had he literally forgotten the previous argument? Was he, in general, beginning to forget? It was only six or eight months later that Deirdre first started reporting Dad's strange behavior—how he'd begun repeating himself, misplacing things, losing his sense of direction and time.

Her reports continued, always worsening, and Deirdre began urging me to come home. She had always been like our mother in her willingness to compromise for him, to build a game plan around his inflexibility. "You're his son," she would inevitably say. But I couldn't come home. I wouldn't. I had stopped caring, had stopped making myself crazy because my father disapproved of me, and this stopping had unburdened me. Case closed.

Long before my father died, I'd made peace—not with him, but with our estrangement.

And yet.

2

Nana woke me the next morning with a hand on my shoulder, an urgent whisper in my ear. "Up, Jimmy, up!"

The sky was still dim outside the window. Nana had a sympathetic, silvery glow about her. "Mass is at eight. You'll take me, then?"

"What time is it?"

"Seven. But the driveway's covered in snow. It could use a good shovel."

"Okay," I groaned. "Will you make me coffee?"

"Of course," she said. "A fair trade."

Maybe not so fair—Nana's coffee was percolator-burnt, the charcoal taste lingering on my tongue. She really was slipping; I couldn't remember Nana cooking anything that wasn't just right. The night before, she'd microwaved a lasagna and a freezer-pack of vegetables, all of it bland, and during the meal she'd hardly spoken. When Andy tried to draw her into the conversation by asking about her girlhood in Ireland, she responded tersely, with a gaze in my direction, "We didn't have much, but we took care of each other."

She was born Margaret Carey and had come to the United States as the bride of John Garner, a boy from a neighboring West Irish farm; they'd always been Nana and Papa to me. They raised my dad and his sister, my aunt Katie, in an apartment in Hell's Kitchen, back then still an immigrant ghetto on Manhattan's West Side. A few years after Papa died, Nana took a lump sum from her landlord, who was condo-converting the building, and moved to a nondescript garden apartment in Hackensack to be near her children. Three years ago, she moved again, to Greenlawn, taking charge of my father's care. The side-by-side bedrooms that were once Deirdre's and mine were transformed for her into a floral-print-covered sleeping area and a tchotchke-filled TV room. She'd always seemed strong enough to survive anything—her husband had died, then my mother, then Uncle Angelo, who was Aunt Katie's husband—but perhaps this, the death of her only son, Edward, was just one blow too many.

She was already dressed for church, sitting in the kitchen, once again glued to the TV, watching one of those courtroom entertainment shows. A female judge narrowed a hawkish brow and wagged her finger. "Sir, sir, just a minute, sir. This is *my* court. You speak when I tell you to."

Out the window, day was breaking, revealing the shocking brilliance of icy tree branches and white rooftops. "I haven't woken up to snow since forever," I said. "I forgot how beautiful it is."

"The roads will be slippery," she said. "Your father keeps the shovel in the garage."

Father had a dull magnetic force to it, drawing her gaze from the TV and mine from the window. Between us vibrated some combination of bond and rift; the thing that tied us to each other was also the place where we were worlds apart. In the bitter gloom on Nana's face I glimpsed her years as Dad's caretaker—feeding and washing and changing him like he was an infant again. I was reminded of gay guys I'd seen survive their lovers or their best friends; death offered no real relief, no catharsis, just the cold reality of inevitable demise. Nana bore the same kind of battle fatigue.

I felt my face getting hot. "This must be hard for you," I offered.

Something sharp flickered across her face, but all she said was, "He's no longer suffering, thank God."

Years ago, I had talked to Nana about the tension between my father and me, about the reasons behind it, about who I was. We were at her apartment in Hackensack, and she'd cooked me lunch and made a rhubarb pie for dessert. I remember the queasiness I felt as I ate, preparing to break a silence, unsure of what to expect. When the moment came, she listened without interrupting, and then told me, "You'll always be my grandson." At the time this had seemed like a great generosity, but when I asked her to talk to Dad on my behalf, she replied, "When Edward had words with his father, I kept out of it. I'll stay out of this one, too." I had tried not to hold this against her. She was old, even Old World; I could hardly expect her to wave my flags.

But why wouldn't she cut me any slack now? Was it so hard for her to understand my reasons for staying away? Was I really so unforgivable?

Outside, the air was so crisp my cheeks felt slapped. I used a shovel that had been in our family for as long as I could remember, its handle worn smooth, its blade gouged in two places. Each push left behind snaky parallel trails of powder on the black driveway, a sight that had the force of déjà vu: the teenage me clearing this same path with this same faulty shovel, my father examining the work and scolding me for not scooping it all up: *Everything you leave behind will be ice by tonight.*

I drove Nana to St. Bartholomew's in Dad's boxy Chrysler K-Car. Before she got out, she asked, "Will you come to mass, then?"

"I don't go to church, Nana."

"This is a time for prayer."

"Say one for me while you're at it."

"Well, then," she sighed, lifting herself from the car.

I drove through the slushy streets of Greenlawn, to the Athenaeum, the Greek diner where I'd spent a lot of time as a teenager. I took a seat at the counter, read the *New York Times* and slowly came to life over bottomless cups of strong coffee and single-serving boxes of cornflakes. Amid the red vinyl booths and faux-marble tabletops, a memory ignited from fifteen years earlier: sitting here, across from Eric Sanchez, deliberately pressing our knees together under the table, while around us our friends complained about how life *majorly sucked*, how *totally stupid* teachers and parents were, how *so fucking boring* it all was. Eric and I passed a cigarette back and forth, his dark bangs rising upward with the force of each exhale, our eyes stealing time with one another's, sending wordless messages.

I returned to find Nana already waiting for me on the sidewalk, complaining about the cold. She presented me with a list of places she needed to go: a rotation of doctors, then the pharmacy, then Coiffures by Diane, where she had a standing appointment with Diane Jernigan, the older sister of a girl I went to high school with. Nana was very proud about her hair, still thick and full, and though she rarely left the house for anyone to see it, she kept it dyed a deep brown, like stout, like wet earth. It took years off her looks.

"Jimmy Garner!" Diane exclaimed when she saw me. Through Nana, Diane already knew about my father, and her sympathy commingled with reports of other dead parents, dead siblings, dead spouses, the accumulated losses of our high school peers as we left our youth behind. While Diane went to work on Nana, I listened to updates on people I hadn't thought about in years, their marriages and divorces, the births of children, descriptions of the houses they'd bought. A remarkable number of my former classmates still lived in the area, their lives still knowable, without the mystery of departure. I thought of Deirdre among them, caught in this grind, an item of gossip for the Dianes of the world.

"Do you know what happened to Eric Sanchez?" I asked.

Diane paused above Nana's dye-slick head. "Barbara's brother?" she asked. "The one who went into the Navy?"

"Yeah, yeah, that's right."

"I think he's married and living in Maryland or something."

"Really? Married?"

"Barbara was living in Paramus for a while, but she moved a few years ago . . ."

As Diane continued on, I tried to imagine Eric at thirty-three, a husband, probably a father. The head of a household. Eric, who taught me how to kiss—slowly, with anticipation, with all the right pauses—in the backseat of Barbara's Galaxie 500. Eric, who told me he loved me *so fucking much* a week before high school graduation, punching his fist into a wall until the skin broke, until I pulled him by the wrist into an embrace, promising him, *You know I totally feel the same*, asking him, *How can I prove it to you* (as he had to me, in blood)? Eric, who whispered, *If we love each other we should try more stuff*. Eric, whose swollen cock was in my mouth at the moment my father, home early from work for some unremembered, fateful reason, entered my bedroom to find me on my knees, in the midst of worship, surrender, *proving it*—the kind of moment, explosive and unequivocal, that separates everything into before and after.

It went like this: My father's eyes sweeping from me on the floor, wiping my mouth, to Eric, yanking up his jeans, the clasp of his belt rattling as he turned his face away. My father shouting "What the hell are you doing?" though I could see he knew exactly what this was. I tried to throw it back at him: why did he push the door open, why didn't he knock? "No way," he bellowed. "No, no, no, no *way,*" negation repeated like a chant, disapproval and denial in equal measure. *No way* could this have happened, *no way* would it happen again, *no way* is my son this kind of boy. Eric was banned from our house—the official punishment—but worse than this was the scornful silence that descended like a sudden downpour.

"I love him," I said.

"There's no way you can," said my father.

We didn't talk it out; there was no way we could, or so it seemed to me.

I managed to see Eric a few more times that summer before I went to college and he to the Navy—furtive, tongue-tied encounters at the edge of group activities. Each locked gaze was more wrenching than the last, until we learned to avoid each other's eyes, to fake indifference, as was needed, to get away from each other and the mess we'd created. At some point, Deirdre asked me, "How come you aren't hanging out with Eric?" and what I told her was, "We were getting on each other's nerves."

My father never saw me the same again. Before, I'd been a problem child—one to boss around, bargain with, try to fix. After, I ceased to be a child at all. Just a problem—permanent, irreparable. Before, I'd thought it possible to fall in love with a boy. After, I lived with the knowledge that genuine love didn't spark revulsion in others. My first month in college, I got myself a girlfriend.

"Jimmy?" Diane was waiting for an answer. "What about you?"

"Sorry—what?"

"Girlfriend? Someone special?"

I looked at Nana, who sat stiffly under Diane's kneading hands. My relationship with Woody wasn't a secret from her; still, it wasn't something she probably cared to see dropped into the boiling vat of Diane's gossip-stew. "Someone special," I replied, and left it at that.

Ryan's Funeral Home had apparently decided that mourning went down easier in pastel: mint-green cushions, rose-flocked wallpaper, a beige rug. The chairs, cream colored, had been lined up in a semicircle around the coffin, as if the deceased might rise up and recite to the crowd. Most of the guests hovered in the back, near the door, or in the hallway, conversing. The surprise was the music, all old, cool jazz, which my brother-in-law, Andy, had compiled from my father's CD collection. "I forgot he liked this stuff," I said to Andy as we stood side by side beneath a wall-mounted speaker amplifying a melancholy version of "My Funny Valentine." Andy was an accountant. His suit was an accountant's suit, his haircut an accountant's haircut. Years ago, my friend Colleen had dubbed him Average Andy.

"It was all I ever heard him listen to. This is Chet Baker," he said. In Andy's voice I heard a hint of pride, as if my father's connoisseurship had rubbed off on him.

"I think he only started listening to jazz after Mom died," I offered.

"No, he told me he liked jazz when he was young."

"Oh, right." I dimly recalled my father tell of seeing Thelonious Monk play live, in San Francisco, where my father had lived for a handful of months at some point between high school and marrying my mother. We'd hardly ever spoken of his time there; what might have been something that bonded us to each other became just another point of contention. *A lousy place to make a life,* he'd said, writing off his entire SF experience, and by association, mine, as wasted time, a youthful lark. A dart of jealousy pricked my chest as I pictured Andy and my father together: Andy listening earnestly while Teddy's baritone boomed out a point-by-point exegesis on early-sixties jazz.

The casket loomed up front, its glossy brown lid emphatically shut. According to Deirdre this was how my father wanted it, though I suspected it was her own choice. "Looking at a dead body is just creepy," I heard her whisper to one of her friends as I drifted through the room, doing my best to keep conversations brief and superficial. As relatives and friends of the family, none of whom I'd seen since the barbecue for AJ's birth, shuffled forward, one after another spoke to me in the apologetic language of grief. *I'm sorry, I wish I knew what to say, I'm so sorry.* My five-year withdrawal didn't matter. All that mattered was that I was the son, so I got the sympathy.

At one point Deidre pulled me into the hallway, away from the crowd. "I'm a little freaked out," she said through clenched teeth.

I patted her on the shoulder, tentative. "You're doing great."

"When I got here this morning, I got a look at Dad."

"In the coffin? Is he embalmed?"

"Of course he's embalmed. He's all fixed up. You can look, after everyone leaves."

"No, I don't want to," I said, absolutely clear on this.

She wagged her hands, frustrated. "Why I'm freaked out is, he's not wearing his wedding ring." She explained to me that he never took that band off his finger. Though maybe, in the end, in his bedroom, or in the hospital, it had been removed. Or fell off. Or was taken.

"It's probably just misplaced," I said. "Who would steal something like that?"

We were interrupted by a gust of frigid air from the door, whisking in Aunt Katie. She paraded to the viewing room in a full-length fur coat, her frosted hair swept up dramatically, her pumps sporting heels treacherously high for an icy winter night. An entourage fanned out behind her: her son, Tommy; his wife, Amy, cradling a baby; and their three other children, all under twelve. Deirdre and I watched as Katie took the aisle and marched straight to Nana, swallowing her up in furry hugs and air kisses. I let Deidre join them before I made my way toward their conversational pantomime.

"Aunt Katie." I was unsure if I should lean in for an air kiss of my own.

She stood stiffly, eyeing me up and down. "I was just saying to your sister, 'Where's your brother? He better have shown up.' "

"Here I am," I said, bowing my head deferentially.

"I said, 'Don't tell me Jimmy didn't show.' "

"I showed."

She raised her chin. "What's that? You don't shave there?"

"A little San Francisco style," I said, rubbing the arty triangle of auburn hair—the *soul patch*—growing under my lower lip.

Nana said, "You look scruffy."

"At least he got rid of the earrings," Aunt Katie said. "Remember that? When he came home with the earrings?"

"Haven't had earrings for years," I said, my face burning up.

"And that tattoo, with the snakes." She visibly shuddered.

"Aw, leave the guy alone, Ma." From around her side, Tommy extended a beefy paw.

I shook his hand. "How's it going, Tommy?"

"Can't complain. Never does any good."

"Jamie got in a couple days ago and he's really been helping out a lot," Deirdre said to no one in particular.

"I've been helping, too, Mommy." AJ was suddenly there, tugging on the hem of her skirt and looking shyly at his cousins.

"Yes, you have. All my boys are being very good."

Katie sighed—so drawn out it was nearly a hum—her eyes still glued to me. She stepped closer, uncomfortably close. Maybe she'd comment on my breath, smoky from the cigarette I'd sneaked in the parking lot. "Let me tell you something," she said, swallowing hard before continuing. "Your father deserved better."

I sucked in air, backed away reflexively. This was the judgment I'd been dreading, though I'd started to think I would get away unscathed. My head ricocheted with response lines—everything from *I'm sorry* to *Back off, bitch*—but I held my tongue and withstood Aunt Katie's hex, my face flushed but, I hoped, inscrutable. Finally, Deirdre, bless her, took command, helping Katie out of her coat and passing it to me. "Jamie, give this to the guy in the hall. Not you, AJ. It's too big for you."

Walking away, hauling fifteen pounds of raccoon fur, I averted my eyes from the crowd. Who in the room had seen what just happened?

I turned around and found Tommy behind me, passing a pile of coats to the attendant. Tommy Ficchino stood out in this room, a swarthy half-Italian in the midst of a lot of pasty Irish stock. As a kid, his hair had been light brown, like wood varnish, but it was almost black now, with little flecks of gray. He wasn't quite as handsome as his father, Uncle Angelo, had been, but Tommy's face had the same big, expressive features: a wide nose, dark eyes, a rosy mouth surrounded by the perpetual shadow of a beard. Angelo had died of a heart attack about six years ago. I'd come back for that funeral, too—a southern Italian affair, lavish in its grief. A wailing Nonna Ficchino had to be carried out of the church, her tight black shoes fumbling along the carpet as her grandsons bore her weight.

The Ficchinos and the Garners had been neighbors in Hell's Kitchen. Angelo and Katie were high school sweethearts, a few years older than my father, whose nickname in those days was Rusty. I'd grown up listening to their stories of taking Rusty on dates with them, then telling him to *beat it* so they could have their privacy. There was the time a cop caught them necking in the back of Angelo's car. The time Rusty got lost in Central Park for an afternoon. The time they crossed paths with Joe DiMaggio and he shook my father's hand. The stories were so recycled, even I, who hadn't heard them for years, could recite them in detail.

Tommy's hands were rising in front of him, palms up. I knew this gesture, which all the men in his family shared: He was preparing to speak without quite knowing what to say. I scrambled to fill the silence. "I guess this must be tough for you, Tommy. You've already been through this, with your father."

With a shrug of his shoulders, he replied, "Aw, whaddaya gonna do?" I had to bite my lip to hold back a smile.

"Any time you got a death's lousy," he went on. "My dad died too young, but I got no regrets there. You and your dad—that's another story. You being, you know, the black sheep."

I nodded cautiously. "We had our difficulties."

"Jesus, he was pretty tough on you, right? Pretty tough, period. Gotta be a lot of mixed emotions here." He patted his belly.

I felt my eyes dampen—not from grief but from gratitude, like a patient receiving a diagnosis after previously being told it was all in his head. "One day at a time," I said.

"Right. Today, tomorrow. Little here, little there, that's how it goes. Whaddaya gonna do?"

"Hell if I know," I said, letting the smile break through this time. He nodded with finality, and we stood together for a moment, silently perusing the crowd.

"So how's it out there, you know, in San Fran?"

"Crazy times, lots going on. The Internet. The dot-coms." Tommy's accent was contagious. I heard myself saying *dot-calms.*

"We gonna hear you on NPR again?" he asked.

"Sure, sure. Someday."

"You got anything coming up?"

"Not right now. Things have been a little quiet."

In fact, my career in radio had been very quiet. About six months earlier I'd lost a regular producing job for San Francisco's public radio station, and since then I'd worked freelance. Barely. The show I'd produced, *City Snapshot,* a daily report on offbeat cultural events in San Francisco, was one I helped create, and I took its cancellation—its *rebranding,* as the station manager dubbed it—personally. Before that show, I had produced a handful of reports for National Public Radio. Tommy had heard one of my segments on *All Things Considered* and called to congratulate me, and since then I'd been the "NPR guy" to him and all the Ficchinos. I didn't bother to correct this; the lack of a permanent professional affiliation always took too much effort to explain to people not in my field. There were plenty of things I couldn't remember about Tommy's life, too, like were he and his brothers still running the refrigeration and air-conditioning business their father had passed on to them? Judging from Tommy's expensive-looking suit and the fat Rolex on his wrist, he had moved on to something more lucrative.

Tommy went chasing after one of his daughters, who was making a break for the front door, and I slipped back into the main room. I leaned against a wall and watched my sister in action. Deirdre carried herself with great presence, like an event planner, one of those take-charge corporate types who stands in the middle of the action, wearing a matching skirt and suit jacket (this one was black, with padded shoulders), and with precise orders keeps everyone else moving. She and Andy were both performing just fine as far as I could tell, juggling guests, accepting mass cards from well-wishers, keeping AJ out of trouble. Up at the coffin, Aunt Katie was on her knees, dabbing her eyes. On either side, in sharp black suits, knelt one of her dark-haired sons—Tommy's older brothers, Mike and Billy—looking like Secret Service agents assigned to protect her. All around me swirled this big family, everyone performing his or her role just so, a portrait glowing with tradition: functional, ritualized, structured to endure the dark storm of death. I saw myself as they must surely see me, standing apart from the crowd with my alien facial hair and my thrift-store suit, displaying no obvious emotions, and I wondered what I was doing here, why I'd set myself up for this kind of scrutiny. *Most of the trouble that comes along is trouble we cause ourselves.* My father again, his voice ringing out from the past: a lecture delivered one night after I'd been picked up by the cops in the passenger seat of a parked car. At the wheel was a tipsy Eric Sanchez, whom I was trying to persuade to hand over the keys. *You could have walked away,* Dad had said, and he'd been right. But for all my ambivalence about my family, I had never been one to walk away from a friend.

And then, unbidden, another memory: a fishing trip we made with some of his co-workers and their sons, a cluster of men and boys on the shore of a lake in upstate New York. My father stood behind me, his arms encircling me and his hands covering mine, guiding me through the proper way to cast. My discomfort at this physical closeness melted as he helped me reel in my first catch. I couldn't have been more than twelve, but I caught three fish that day, more than anyone else. They were small, none bigger than his outstretched hand, but that didn't stop us from hauling them home and insisting my mother fry them for dinner. And where the memory ends is here: me recounting for her the story of each catch while he looked on, soaking up my little triumphs, taking none of the credit. The weightlessness that came from having made him proud, and the knowledge, confusing even in the moment, that the key had been to put myself in his hands, to not resist.

A rumble was building up in my stomach; I suddenly was sure I would vomit. But when I locked myself in the bathroom, what erupted from my mouth was laughter—loud, giddy, cathartic howls of laughter that I couldn't contain and couldn't stop. I slid down to the tiled floor, and I flushed the toilet again and again, imagining Deirdre scowling on the other side of the door. I thought of Aunt Katie's ostentatious fur, of Tommy's *Whaddaya gonna do,* of those three puny fish twenty years ago, shrinking in the frying pan until they were hardly even there, and I laughed some more, until my stomach tightened and the muscles in my face ached. The frantic laughter only *mixed emotions* can bring.

Back at the house, I filled a plate with food and moved toward the back porch, an enclosed room off the kitchen where I could blow cigarette smoke out the window. The room wasn't insulated, but putting up with the winter chill was preferable to hanging out in the living room, dodging Aunt Katie. Tommy saw me heading out and quick-stepped behind me. "Hurry, before Amy decides there's something I should be doing right now," he joked. "Let's make a break for it."

Tommy and I were the same age, and as kids we liked to slip away from his bullying brothers and go off on our own, coming up with gentler alternatives to the older boys' games: bike riding instead of ball playing, gin rummy instead of "I Dare You!" Over the years, on those rare occasions when we were both at a family gathering, we usually found ourselves, without quite planning it, one on one. That day, I had a bottle of vodka and a bottle of tonic at my feet, and Tommy was soon matching me drink for drink and cigarette for cigarette. We made small talk—real estate on Long Island, where he lived, versus in San Francisco—and caught up on each other's lives—the refrigeration business had indeed been sold, and Tommy was working for a venture capital firm in Manhattan. We even talked a little about the wake. "Don't pay no mind to my mom," he said, lowering his voice. "She's just broken up about it, is all."

"She's pretty hard to ignore," I said. "If looks could kill—"

"If it was you in that coffin, Deirdre would be lookin' for someone to take it out on, too. You know?"

"Yeah, I know." It was true, my sister was loyal. Wasn't that why she had done the hard work of caring for our difficult, declining father, and why she was so frosty with me now—because I'd stayed away? We weren't always like this. We were allies through high school, hanging out with some of the same kids, bitching about the same teachers, helping each other with homework (she had a head for math, I was better at English). Then Mom died, and Dad sued the hospital, and Dad found me with Eric, and I went off to college, freaked out and heartbroken—and I couldn't tell you what Deirdre was doing during any of this. In most families, a mother's death draws the survivors closer, but when we looked at each other, we saw our wounded selves reflected back, and we kept our distance. Years later I finally told Deirdre about Eric. About me. She was more accepting than anyone in the family had been, but I was already living a separate life in New York, while she was dating Andy in New Jersey, pitching her tent in the camp I had fled. I no longer saw her as my ally but as my father's; her proximity to him seemed a judgment against me. *You and your sister push each other's buttons,* Woody would say, listening in on my end of a phone call with Dee that had gone suddenly brittle. I knew I shared the blame; I knew she wasn't blameless. What I didn't know was what was left between us.

My conversation with Tommy was interrupted by Amy, poking her head through the back door to complain about his absence. "I'll be in when I'm in," Tommy told her.

A few minutes later their eleven-year-old, Brian, showed up at Tommy's elbow. "Mom wants to know if you're still smoking."

Tommy looked at the cigarette in his hand. "Whaddaya gonna tell her?"

"I don't know." Brian looked to me for help. I just shrugged.

Tommy roped his arm across Brian's shoulders. "Let me ask you something. Who took you to see the Islanders last weekend?"

"You."

"Right. And who picks you up after basketball?"

"You."

"And who took you and your friends to see *The Matrix?*"

"Yeah, okay, Dad—you."

"So next time your mom tells you to go do her dirty work, to bug your dad, your pal, whaddaya gonna do?"

"I don't know."

"You're gonna ignore her." *Ignaw huh.*

"Okay," Brian said agreeably. "So, can I try your cigarette?"

"I ever catch you smoking I'll smack your mouth," Tommy said with a quick swat at the air. Brian darted back inside.

"Wow," I marveled. "You rule the roost, don't you?"

"It takes everything I got, lemme tell ya," Tommy said through a weary exhalation of smoke. "I work hard. I pitch in around the house. I keep Brian and Lorrie out of the way when Amy's taking care of the babies. She plays this game, though. Gets them to side with her. She can be a real ballbuster."

"Maybe you should stop having kids?" I offered tentatively.

"It's Amy who wants 'em. She wants five. But I'm through. The only times I've had sex in the last five years, out pops a kid." He took a big swig, burped faintly and whispered, "Only time I had sex with *her.*"

"Whoa, Tommy." I peered around to see if anyone had been in earshot.

"Oh, come on. You understand. You're a gay guy. You know what it's like to mess around."

"You think so?"

"Look, I work in Manhattan. I know about this stuff. The fags at work—sorry, gay guys—they get a lot of sex. Even the ones in relationships."

"It's a testosterone thing. No female hormones to balance things out."

He looked over his shoulder to see if the coast was still clear. "I use an escort service. A call girl. Classy. Clean. She meets me at a gentlemen's club, I buy some drinks, go back to a hotel. I'm home by one a.m., a satisfied customer. I'll tell you the truth, Amy's better off with me blowing off a little steam."

"So she doesn't know."

"I deny it when she asks. You understand."

"Hey, I'm in a monogamous relationship."

"Yeah? You make some kinda vow?"

"Not quite," I said, wondering what that would be like—taking a vow, making public expression of what had previously been a private arrangement. The forever of it, the weight. "Woody's a great guy, but he's one-hundred-percent opposed to cheating. I don't want to screw it up. Based on the way I've played around in the past, it hasn't always been easy."

"Trust me, you got it easy," Tommy said. "Being married to the opposite sex is work."

A moment later, Amy reappeared, flashing him a look that said *enough already,* and this time Tommy extinguished his cigarette and headed back into the living room. I lingered in the cold air until my fingers started to feel numb, and then I, too, went back inside, a little tipsy now, a little less anxious facing the gathered clan.

The next day, after the funeral mass had come and gone, after a trip to the cemetery and another round of food and drink and sneaked cigarettes, Tommy reached past my hand, extended for a farewell shake, to pull me in for a hug. "Don't be a stranger," he whispered in my ear. "Family is family." And for the second time in two days he moved me right to the edge of tears.

"You ever come to San Francisco, Tommy?"

"I'm working on a couple of West Coast accounts, so who knows."

I smiled at the idea, imagining Tommy making a little time for his black sheep cousin before heading out for a lap dance. "Sure, come for a visit," I told him. "We've got plenty of places to blow off steam." He gave me a knowing wink and headed down the shoveled walkway to the street, where Amy had their minivan warming up and the kids corralled, all of it waiting for him.

But first: The night of the wake, drunk on vodka after everyone had left, I was enlisted by Deirdre to find my father's wedding ring. "Find it where?" I asked.

"Search the house. The hospital doesn't have it. The mortician doesn't have it."

AJ was asleep in her arms. He was too big to be carried, I could see that in the strain of her muscles. Or maybe not. Maybe five isn't too big to be lifted into bed by your mother. What did I know? There were no children in my life. "Will you promise me you'll look?" she asked.

"Sure."

"I mean it, Jamie. We need it in the morning, before the funeral mass."

"I'll look, I'll look."

I did look. I went back upstairs into his bedroom, which still smelled medicinal, the antiseptic fumes a kind of ghostly presence, a reminder of the failure to hold back death. I moved furniture, and pushed aside clothes on hangers, and got on my hands and knees to root through my father's closet. I found a jar filled with pennies, nickels and dimes. A few boxes of receipts that went back years. Some old hats. A years-old, dusty plaque from his employer—an office furniture company for which he spent the last twenty years writing marketing brochures, catalog copy and annual reports—commending him for perfect attendance. No sick days for Teddy Garner.

Then, buried deep on a shelf, I found a short stack of *Penthouse* magazines, five or six in all, dated from the 1980s. I glanced over my shoulder, worried that Nana might be standing in the doorway, catching me with this pornographic contraband. I tucked them under my shirt and tiptoed back to my tiny bedroom. *Penthouse* had been my porn of choice as a teenager because the "Forum" section, made up of supposedly true stories from readers, was good for at least one bisexual story per issue—my first exposure to man-on-man sex. Sure enough, I opened one of my father's and immediately found a "letter" from a big-breasted woman recounting the day the pool guy seduced both her and her home-early-from-work husband. The money shot: The stud fucks her husband as he's ramming his wife. Everyone orgasms together. Crude, but very sexy. Did my father, so revolted by gay sex, actually read this story? He must have, at least once. But it was nearly impossible to imagine: Teddy, in his bedroom, the very room where he told me to keep my private life private, letting his own private thoughts unfold, taboo story in one hand, family jewels in the other.

The next morning I woke and shaved my face clean, watching the brown and orange bristles, my *scruffy* soul patch, slide down the drain. In the mirror, to my own eyes, I looked not so much like a new man as an impostor, trying to pass myself off as the son I was supposed to be. The day was as glacial as any since I'd been back, and the newly shorn spot under my lip seemed to attract the cold the way an open window draws in a draft. All day long, at every step along the ritual path from funeral parlor to church to cemetery, the damp air was an icy kiss pressed to my face, a mark only I knew was there.

I served as a pallbearer, feeling the tremendous weight of the coffin in every muscle as I joined my cousins lifting the heavy box into the hearse, working hard to keep my balance on the ice-streaked sidewalk. No eulogy was delivered at St. Bart's, but the priest gave a homily in which my father was referred to as *a fighter, a family man, and a son of a bitch.* I mean, *a son of God.* "Son of a bitch" was what I wrote in my journal that night, scribbling furiously, without remorse, trying to fill up the pit in my guts, a throbbing hollow that had grown since I'd gotten here and that now threatened to subsume me.

I never did find his wedding ring. He was buried without it.

* * *

In the days after the guests were long gone, the last of Nana's roast eaten and the last can of carbonated soda guzzled, the folding chairs stowed and the ashtrays emptied, Deirdre kept buzzing with projects. "Take a break," I urged, but she insisted she was better off.

"Know your strengths and work with them," she told me. "That's my motto."

"You're too young to have a motto," I said.

"Jamie, we're not kids anymore. I have a child of my own."

"Yeah, I remember."

I hadn't spent much time with AJ, so one morning I drove to Deirdre's house with the plan to take him to kindergarten. I found him alone in the kitchen. The microwave was beeping four high-pitched signals, and AJ was climbing up on a chair to retrieve some kind of plastic-encased breakfast food. "I have to split it open and let the steam out," he explained to me. "I can wait three minutes for it to cool down."

Three minutes. The kind of precise instruction Deirdre had no doubt been giving him all his life.

"So, where's your mom?"

"Having her morning time."

"What's that?"

"In the morning she closes her door and I don't bother her for five minutes."

Five minutes went by, then six, then seven. AJ kept count. I went upstairs to her bedroom to let her know I was here. From behind the door, I heard her crying and talking to herself, though I couldn't decipher the words. I imagined her crying over that never-found wedding ring, but of course it was more than that. Mourning in the morning.

Quietly, I retreated to the top of the stairs, then called out, "I stopped by to take AJ to school."

She yelled out a strangled, "Oh, hi. Okay, just a minute."

I microwaved myself a bowl of instant oatmeal—the cinnamon scent brought me right back to long-ago winter mornings in Greenlawn. AJ was pouring himself orange juice from a container, the *glug-glug* of it sending splashes all over the table.

"Here, let me show you a trick," I said. I grabbed a knife, poked an air slit in the top, then poured a glug-free stream into my glass. "Ta-da!" I swept my arm wide, clumsily backhanding my oatmeal, which went flying to the floor.

The crash echoed. My eyes met AJ's worried stare. "So you see, AJ, that's how you keep from spilling orange juice. You throw your oatmeal on the floor!"

He melted into giggles. We cleaned up the mess together, making a promise not to tell Deirdre.

After dropping him off, I returned to find Deidre leaning over her clipboard, snapping her pen. The radio was on, and she was singing along to a pop song I'd never heard. She'd emerged from her crying jag looking as pulled-together as ever.

"You think it's okay for me to take Dad's car to the city?" I asked.

"When?"

"Today. I figured I'd look up some old friends."

"Well, actually—" She presented me with the clipboard. "Here's your do-list."

"Not *to do?* Just *do?*"

"Yes, as in *will be done*," she said firmly.

Beneath my name, she'd written a list: "Attic. Garage. Dad's closet." I felt myself wilting. "I need to get out of here, Dee. I'm going stir-crazy."

"Come on, Jamie. There's so much."

"Not today. I'm not in the right headspace."

"Well, excuse me, but you're going back to California in a couple days, and then what? We have to sell Dad's house. If you want anything at all, you better call it, or it's going to wind up in the dump."

I looked at the list again. I considered mentioning the porn in the bedroom, but I held back; let it be a secret between him and me. "I don't have anything in the attic anymore. I cleared out all my stuff when I left for San Francisco. And I don't want any furniture. I live in a tiny one-bedroom. Plus, I don't have money to ship anything."

"Fine. I'll just throw everything away. Our whole family history. What do you care, anyway?" Her voice cracked and dropped off.

"Okay, okay." I lowered my head into my hands, willing myself to do the right thing. "I can go to New York another time. No biggie. Really."

"It would be a huge help," she said. "So, you'll start with the attic?"

"Sure. Just tell me one thing: Who died and left you in charge?"

She froze, and then, catching my smile, shook her head. "You know, you're an asshole."

"It's the most reliable part of me," I said. "I know my strengths. I work with them."

3

Unlike a city apartment, a house with an attic means never saying good-bye to anything. The Garner family attic swelled with the past: boxes of moth-eaten clothing, much of it sewn in that little room at the end of the hall, and the sewing machine itself, which hadn't been donated to the Salvation Army after all but sat here surrounded by boxes of patterns; the small plaster replicas of the *Venus de Milo* and Michelangelo's *David,* once displayed on end tables in the living room, and the end tables themselves, carved from an ugly mustard-tinted wood; the electric typewriter, flecked with Liquid Paper, on which I'd tapped angsty poetry in high school; an outdated stereo system that my father always called the hi-fi; a German knife set that I suspected might have some value. How difficult could it be to let go of a card table—a cheap piece of junk when it was bought and now an actual piece of junk, wobbly, broken, its veneer peeling off? Or a faddish appliance—a fondue set, a Crock-Pot, a carpet broom? How about a plastic Christmas tree, originally a convenience for parents of small children but over time a tacky embarrassment?

The more I took in, the more I understood the difficulty: Everything bore my mother's imprint. Each worthless item was something she'd chosen, no matter how long ago, or had used, no matter for how short a time. Or else it contained a dormant memory that needed only the focus of my attention to activate: the time Dee and I dressed those statuettes in Barbie doll clothes—Malibu Venus, David in madras—then waited for Dad, sighing through his nightly perusal of the newspaper, to notice our alteration, the two of us finally erupting with so much suppressed laughter that Mom dashed in to see what was wrong. Or the time a birthday party devolved into a food fight as my friends used cheese and chocolate fondue for spin art on the kitchen table. Mom was furious at first but eventually relented, flinging a forkful of wet chocolate into my hair.

I came upon a stack of boxes, each labeled, in black Magic Marker, LEGAL, and used my fingernail to slit one open. Inside was everything related to the lawsuit my father brought against the hospital where my mother had died. I pulled out a few manila folders and scanned the contents: research into heart disease, photocopies of my mother's medical history, correspondence between doctors and lawyers. Medicine and law, two languages good at obfuscating meaning. I dug some more, not even realizing what I was looking for until I found it: a file folder marked SETTLEMENT. I read a memo from my father's lawyer, spelling out the situation. After weighing all the evidence, the judge in the case was prepared to decide against him, to give him nothing. My father was advised to accept a settlement of one hundred thousand dollars, enough to pay his attorneys and the private investigators they'd hired and have a little left over for himself, and to promise, in exchange, to drop any threat of appeal. A hundred thousand dollars was more money than I'd earned in my entire life, but considering the many years he'd spent on the case, and the fact that he'd once spoken confidently of *millions of dollars in damages*, my father must have seen this as next to nothing. I couldn't quite believe it had collapsed this way, a decade-long odyssey abandoned with the scrawl of "Edward Garner" on the bottom line. The lawsuit had never been about the money for him, but about getting someone to take blame for his wife's death. And no one had.

I hadn't thought about any of this in years—the shock of her death, the way it extinguished in him what little mirth he'd had. (Never again would he laugh at something as silly as the *Venus de Milo* in a bikini.) I felt an ache behind my eyes, along my neck, and a pressure pulsing in the air around me. I should have gone to New York like I'd wanted. I could have been ambling in and out of galleries, shopping for cheap sunglasses on St. Mark's Place, smoking a joint with old friends while we reminisced about the shit we stirred up in our twenties.

You have to own your issues. This was Woody's voice, the therapeutic language he relied on, which drove me crazy but tailed me everywhere. He'd spent years in therapy, not because of any particular catastrophe, but to develop a protective coating against life's unexpected twists. *You have to deal,* he liked to say, *and you have to be ready*. I thought of my family as having been dealt a lousy hand, one with the Death card smack in the middle; we had never figured out how to play our cards. When I left my family, I left my *issues* behind. Now here I was back at the table. Okay, I would stay a little longer, long enough to feel these old aches, admit to them, *own* them, then get back to the home I'd made for myself, where I could put them to rest, once and for all.

The sun slid past the tiny windows under the eaves. I pushed past the legal files, dragging a floor lamp on an extension cord, and found other items that had been my father's—not my mother's or theirs together, but his alone. A bowling ball and shoes (he'd played in the town league), his Army uniform (he'd done a few years of peacetime duty in Germany, where he'd met my mother), a tuxedo that might have been the one he was married in (no wedding ring in the pockets). I had my eye out for that unexpected something that would ignite the proper emotional epiphany; I would carry this home to Woody to show him that I'd done the work.

After uncounted hours, I didn't find much. My father was a pack rat, something I realized I shared with him. My father had never gotten over my mother, something I already knew. My parents' tastes were tacky in a mid-seventies kind of way—something of a badge of honor for a thrift-store hound like me. I could search here all day and never achieve the desired epiphany. I stood up quickly, steadied myself against the wall while the head rush flooded in, shook the pins and needles out of my limbs. I grabbed the case containing the German knives, which would make a good gift for Woody, who never put any effort into stocking his kitchen. I turned to leave.

Then my sights landed on a taped-up shoebox marked SAN FRANCISCO. It sat atop a dresser near the door; I must have walked right past it on the way in. I stopped and picked it up. In smaller print was written JUNE '60–JUNE '61. Another reminder that my father had once lived in my adopted city.

What had he told me about that time? If I remembered correctly, he chose San Francisco because he had a friend there, and because *back then, we all thought we wanted to be beatniks.* He worked odd jobs but never made much money. He saw Monk play live. And, oh yes, his most dubious claim: He had encountered Jack Kerouac, King of the Beats himself, at a bar in North Beach. They had a brief exchange of words; Kerouac was embarrassingly drunk and hostile to his young fan's enthusiasm. Not long after that, my father returned to New York, broke and disillusioned with all things *beatnik*. That's all I knew. A sketch, barely an outline.

Even years ago, when I was still making the occasional phone call to my father, I never bothered to find out more about his time in San Francisco. Our calls always flared into harsh verbal volleys—him lecturing, me reacting—and after each one, with nothing but scorched earth left between us, we retreated a little farther from the heat. The Kerouac story is a good example. I never believed it had happened because of the way he'd used it against me: a cautionary tale about the perils of rebellion, individualism, artistic freedom. Eyewitness testimony to *the harder they fall.*

How strange to discover that he had saved things from those long ago, much disparaged days. How curious.

I looked again at the dates on the box. My father had stayed only a year in San Francisco. I'd lasted a decade. When I first moved there, he called it Never-Never Land. He was certain I would retreat back East, just as he had. Had I stayed so long just to prove him wrong? As I stood there, surrounded by the full sum of his life—the domestic clutter, the orderly boxes, the failed lawsuit—this seemed like a real possibility. If so, then I guess I'd won. I'd held out. He was gone, and I was Peter Pan.

I heard another voice, that of my friend Brady, who edited the radio show I'd produced: *It's all material, dude.* Freelance producers are always on alert for the next story, an item to be exploited. When something of so-called human interest drops into your hands, you're obliged to notice. To take interest. See where it leads.

When I left the attic, I took the box marked SAN FRANCISCO with me.

That night after dinner, Deirdre sat me down, with Andy at her side, and told me that they were going to move Nana to a nursing home. Not a nursing home—something for people more active than that. *Senior housing.* They'd worked it all out. There was a place just one town over. Nana could stay there all week, with people her own age, and she'd be able to leave on weekends and visit with Deirdre.

"She can't be by herself all day," Deirdre said. "She's not that strong."

"But she used to stay here alone with Dad," I said, "and she managed for both of them."

"With a lot of help from your sister," Andy interjected, patting her hand protectively.

Deidre said, "You haven't seen how she slips sometimes," then paused to exhale, clearly trying to remain calm. "I want to go back to work. I talked to Carly Fazio and she said her company needs someone in human resources."

"Who the hell is Carly Fazio?"

"From high school."

Right: a dark haired girl at the periphery of Deirdre's social life, that little gang of girls occupying our living room every afternoon, watching *General Hospital*, drinking diet soda and French braiding each other's hair. I couldn't summon up a face, much less where she worked, but here she was, Carly Fazio, playing her tangential role in our family drama. I'm sure Diane Jernigan knew all about her.

"What does Nana have to say?"

Deirdre averted her eyes. "We haven't talked to her yet."

"There's money for this," Andy added. "I've been investing Teddy's settlement money in tech stocks—software, search engines, portals. The money these start-ups are making! It's incredible."

"How much did he leave behind?" I asked.

"Two hundred and fifty thousand," Andy said. "More or less."

I hadn't given a thought to my father's estate, but as this astronomical number hovered in the air, I found myself instantly calculating my share. I lived check to check, only a few hundred bucks in savings, and I had student loans to pay, and credit card debt piling up because I rarely covered more than the monthly minimum. I'd been treading water financially since college. Even a tenth of this money would make a world of difference to me.

Andy talked at length, and proudly, about his *investment strategy*. Online trading was his new religion. His day job at the payroll company where he'd worked for eight years offered little room for advancement. "And the office politics," he said, "could drive a guy berserk." Andy was upstanding—he spent time with AJ, followed the Mets religiously, shunned hard liquor because he *just didn't like the taste*—but I harbored a kernel of resentment toward him. He'd knocked up my sister at age twenty-three, before she'd figured out who she wanted to be in the world, before she and I could form an adult friendship. According to this scenario, Andy had created the Deirdre of today, with the minivan and the do-list and the membership at Big Savers, as opposed to the Deirdre who once sneaked my cigarettes, who might have followed me down the path of rebellion. Now Average Andy controlled my father's two-hundred-and-fifty-thousand-dollar portfolio. As Deidre returned from the kitchen with three bottles of Bud Lite and took a seat, almost deferentially, at his side, I saw him for what he was: the new head of the family.

"Care to tell me what the terms of his will are?" It was terrible to hear my money hunger exposed, no matter how indirectly I'd tried to phrase the question.

Andy explained that most of the money was earmarked to take care of Nana, some of it was set aside for AJ's education, and the rest of it went to Deirdre and me. Well, mostly to Deidre. "If you want," he said, "I can invest your share. With the way the market's working, I can grow it fast."

Deidre sat quietly, but I felt her watching me. When I raised my eyebrows, telegraphing a question to her, she said, "Ten thousand dollars. That's what he left you."

"Well." I took a long slug from the bottle. I don't even like beer, much less watery shit like this, but in that moment I couldn't drink enough of it. I wanted it to flush away the hope I'd let myself feel. "What is that, about two percent? Seems about right."

Andy cleared his throat. "I wish there was more for you. We both do."

"Don't worry, Andy."

"No, I got to say, it's sad to me, you know?"

"Seriously. I'm surprised I got anything."

"But you and him not getting along? As a father myself, I can tell you nothing would get in the way of being close to my son."

"Well, talk to me the day you catch AJ sucking off his boyfriend."

His face froze.

Deirdre yelped my name. "You are unbelievable."

"Sorry," I said. "But you never know."

"Guess not," Andy said, his voice almost hoarse. Poor guy. I could see the wheels spinning behind his eyes, his thoughts trapped helplessly by the muddy image I'd set forth. Finally, he shrugged. "I guess a guy doesn't want that for his only son. I mean, I can't lie to you. I don't want that for AJ. You want your kid to not be different, not get pushed around. You want grandkids some day, and so forth. That's natural, right?"

"Actually, I think it's learned." I paused to figure out how much I wanted to get into this. "With me and my father, Andy, I don't think it was about grandkids."

"Jamie, Dad was in denial about everything," Deidre said, her voice nearly a wail. "Look at the lawsuit! Look at the way he treated Andy at first! It wasn't until AJ was born that Dad could even admit we were married."

"But with me, he never *admitted*—" I cut myself off and lowered my voice. "Why should everything have been so tough for him? The rest of the world knows how to change. But he never did."

"He was scared," Deidre said.

"Of what?"

She shrugged, gave her hair a shake. The mystery at the core of our father.

After a long pause, Andy lifted his beer and said, "He's in a better place now."

"He found it in his heart to leave his faggot son a little something," I said. They both flinched, but I just raised my bottle. "Let's drink to that."

That night I sat cross-legged on the bed, the San Francisco shoebox open in front of me. Inside was a stash of souvenirs: a collection of bar coasters advertising long-forgotten brands of beer, a map of the city, a tourist guidebook, a *San Francisco Examiner* announcing John F. Kennedy's election. I flipped quickly through a small notebook filled with crude pencil sketches—eucalyptus trees, Victorian architecture, the Golden Gate Bridge—and scrawled handwriting, little fragments of a diary. I read one at random. It described an afternoon spent riding around with someone named Don Drebinski: *Seems like Don knows every madman and pants-wearing chick in Frisco, and he's introducing me to all of them*. I skimmed a handful of letters from Aunt Katie, chatty with news of her engagement to Angelo, then sat transfixed over a single page written to my father from a woman named Ray Gladwell—a married woman with whom he, and evidently a couple of other guys, too, had been having an affair. *I believe in the freedom of the individual,* she asserted, spelling out her reasons for dumping him.

My father had gone to California to follow his beatnik dream, and remarkably, he seemed to have succeeded. Nothing in this box indicated the disdain with which he'd always spoken of his time there. After just thirty minutes I was light-headed with astonishment. This was indeed *material.*

And there was more. Buried beneath an old, rippled paperback edition of *On the Road* was a photo, an actor's head shot, the carefully lit and formally composed image of a beautiful man's face. Beautiful in a sparkling, pretty-boy style—dark, inviting eyes, thick lashes, glossy hair, full lips in a full smile—like Frankie Avalon or Sal Mineo, an *ethnic* pretty boy, softened at the edges to make teenage hearts race. The name DEAN FOSTER was imprinted at the bottom. A message was scrawled on the photo in black ink:

Rusty—
You can say you knew me when
—Danny, Los Angeles, 1961

To dip into the vernacular of Los Angeles, 1961, Dean Foster was a dreamboat, a pinup. And he was someone my father once knew. At the bottom of the box I found a dozen photos bound in twine, pictures of my father and this guy, snapped in the old neighborhood: blowing out sixteen birthday candles; dressed in suits and ties, squiring a couple of dolled-up girls to a dance; posed in front of a shiny Chevrolet, arms over each other's shoulders. This dazzlingly handsome actor was at my father's side for every childhood milestone. Dean Foster. *Danny.*

One photo was so striking I gasped out loud. It was an image of departure, dated on the reverse side, in my father's half-legible scribble, April 18, 1960. The rear of the Chevy fills the frame, the car showing signs of wear—a broken taillight, a dented fender. Dean/Danny clutches the handle of a suitcase he's hoisting into the trunk. His arms and the suitcase blur with motion. His heavy-lashed eyes, meeting the lens just as his image is captured, reveal annoyance. Even so, his face is spectacular, its natural Mediterranean beauty more seductive here than in the doctored studio shot. I wanted to know where he was going in April 1960. Perhaps to Los Angeles, ready to transform himself into a Hollywood actor. Or maybe to San Francisco; he might have been the *someone* my father said he knew there.

You can say you knew me when. But as I tried to remember if Dad had ever said anything about a Danny or a Dean, I came up empty.

* * *

The next day, I found my grandmother in the kitchen. "Nana, do you remember this guy? A friend of Dad's?" I held up the photo of the boys in front of the Chevy.

She'd been rinsing dishes in the sink—she never used the dishwasher, considered it *money down the drain*—but suddenly she stopped and dried her hands on a towel. She took the photo from me. "Angelo's brother."

I thought she misheard. Danny did look a bit like Uncle Angelo, Tommy's late father, but—"No, this isn't Angelo. This is someone else. I think his name was Danny."

"Yes, Danny, the brother of Angelo."

I was unprepared for this. If Danny was Uncle Angelo's brother, that made him a Ficchino, practically family—my uncle by marriage—which made it all the more surprising that I'd never heard a thing about him. "Is he alive?" I asked.

"He went to California."

"And never, ever visits? Or calls?"

She shrugged. "I don't keep track."

I held up Dean Foster's head shot. "I also found this one."

She stopped wiping and came closer for a look. "Dear, yes." Her stare softened. "He was going to be a movie star. We saw him once, in a picture. We all went to Times Square when it opened. Everyone from the neighborhood."

"That must have been exciting."

"Sure, and we dressed in our Sunday best. Danny came out of a limousine, wearing a white tuxedo jacket, with an actress on his arm." In her broadening smile, the first I'd seen on her all week, I understood the pleasure of the memory, the trickle-down glamour of the spot-lit movie premiere, everyone dressed up to celebrate a local boy made good. "It was a picture for teenagers, one of those beach movies. He was in a bathing suit, with a surfboard. We were so excited when he came on the screen."

"I'll bet," I muttered. Visions of dreamy Dean Foster: shirtless and sun-drenched.

"Mrs. Ficchino yelled, 'That's my son!' You remember Mrs. Ficchino? She sure had the gift of the gab."

"I remember her. But what happened to him? Danny?"

The sound of the car in the driveway intruded. Deirdre returning from grocery shopping.

"There was some trouble. With the police, maybe." Nana narrowed her eyes, as if peering into a dark corner. "You could ask Katie."

Deirdre entered, arms heavy with stuffed paper bags. I tried to squeeze in one last question. "Do you think he's still alive?"

Before Nana could answer, Deidre asked, "Who are you talking about?"

"Danny Ficchino."

Her eyes did some kind of mental search. "Oh—him."

"You know who he is?"

"Yeah, sure. Uncle Angelo's brother."

"How come I've never heard of him?"

"You probably weren't around when it came up." Her gaze moved past me to Nana, trying to determine, I think, if I'd said anything about our conversation last night. She maneuvered from cabinet to fridge to cupboard, a blur of dyed-blonde hair and Old Navy primary colors, putting everything in its place, all the while recounting the successes and failures of her shopping trip. "They didn't have the ______ so I got the ______ instead. The such-and-such was on sale. The whole place was a zoo." At some point during her masterful navigation of the kitchen, she glanced down at the head shot and then back up at me, and I saw something in the set of her expression that reminded me of our father's brand of silent disapproval.

"I found it in the attic," I said, but she only looked away.

AJ was moving through the doorway, struggling under a grocery bag loaded with bottled juice. I stepped toward him to help, but he was determined to go it alone. "I can carry one bag at a time," he announced with the pride of someone granted an honor.

"There's more where that came from," Deirdre said to me. "Get to work."

I shuffled off obediently to make myself useful.

My last night in New Jersey. Deirdre came over to say good-bye and to find out what progress I'd made on the do-list.

I poured her a drink, made her sit down. I told her about the San Francisco box, the photos, my conversation with Nana. I asked her what she knew about Danny Ficchino. She said that Dad had mentioned him only once or twice, general stuff about running around the neighborhood with Danny and losing touch with him after Danny became an actor. He'd hinted that Danny might have had *a run-in with the law,* which led to a falling out between Danny and the Ficchinos. Deirdre wondered if it had been over money. "It sounded to me like one of those Italian things," she said. "*You're dead to me now*. You know what I'm saying?"

"I know it firsthand," I said, with a gulp of the strong cocktail I'd poured.

"Oh, please, Jamie. No one disowned you."

"Dad basically did. Why can't you admit that?"

"I've never denied that he was closed minded." She looked down into her glass, clinking ice in a shaky grip. "But you stopped trying."

"He didn't want anything to do with me!"

"Well, you definitely returned the favor."

"But he sure got the last word. Ten thousand dollars just about says it all."

We tried to keep our voices down, aware of Nana upstairs, but each recrimination was louder than the last. It wasn't a new quarrel—we'd swiped at each other over the phone for years, she insinuating that I'd abandoned her to Dad's illness, me insisting that she never stood up for me—but it was more ferocious than usual, the situation more desperate. I was leaving the next day, and who could say when I'd be back? She wanted to know why I wasn't staying longer, why I hadn't done what she'd asked me to do, why I was dredging up *ancient history* when there was so much going on right now. She complained that I'd taken no interest in AJ; I replied that she'd taken no interest in anything in my life. Deirdre: "You have no concept of what it takes to raise a child." Me: "You have no concept of anything else." Dee: "You're the most judgmental person I know." Me: "You're turning old before your time."

We amped each other up and wore each other down until we were both crying. That is, she was crying, wiping fat tears as they spilled, and I was struggling with dry mouth, a tightened-up throat, eyes burning at the tear ducts—as close as I get to crying in front of anyone else.

Over and over she said, "I can't think. I can't think. I can't think."

I stared into the fireplace, which hadn't been used in years, though it was always roaring when we were kids. It was our mother's domain; she was the only one who could really get it going, and after she died, it sat cold. Its square black mouth seemed, in this moment, to be the very medium through which she'd been sucked away from us; and him, too. The long corridor to the underworld.

I moved nearer to Deirdre, and I said I was sorry. I'm not exactly sure what I was sorry for. Not for my accusations, which I felt, at their core, were true. More for upsetting her—for just being me, I guess, insensitive, defensive, emotionally retarded me.

Deirdre slumped toward me, and I let my arm fall tentatively around her. Having just fought, this physical nearness was unnerving. I smoothed her hair, which at the roots was a nondescript, mousy brown, so plain compared to the fiery red of mine. Slowly she emerged from her tears. Soon enough we were telling old stories, and laughing a little, remembering funny things about Dad and his bearing in the world, like the way he used to insist he was six feet tall, though he fell short even in shoes, or the way he shined those shoes every Sunday night, lecturing me on the importance of starting the week *with your best foot forward.* She told me how the dementia, before it got terrible, actually made him docile, even sweet, in his dependence. We talked about how much he loved our mother, how she had protected him from the world, how he had never gotten over her.

"Since he's died," Deidre said, "I've missed her all over again."

"I can't let myself," I said. "I sometimes forget I ever had a mother."

She looked at me with puzzlement, then blew her nose one last time and threw a damp, crumpled tissue onto the coffee table, where it bounced against the crumpled tissues already there. I walked her to the front door, and we said good-bye awkwardly, like strangers on a descending airplane who'd spoken too intimately and would never meet again.

"I do wish you could stay longer," she said.

"I'll make a point of coming back soon, to help out with Nana and the house." I doubted either of us believed this.

Standing alone in the hallway, listening to her minivan move down the street, I felt myself very far away from all of them—physically far away, even from Nana, asleep upstairs. I phoned Woody, but got only voice mail; I phoned Brady, Ian, Colleen—my closest San Francisco pals. I left messages for them all: "Get the margaritas ready. I'm coming home."

Back in the sewing room, I lit a cigarette and blew smoke out the window while I packed my bags. It didn't take long; I hadn't brought much with me, and the only thing I was adding to my load was the knife set. And, of course, that shoebox.

I shuffled through the box one more time, mesmerized by the photos. Rusty and Danny, in front of that Chevy: my father, pale skinned and broad chested, pulled in close by his impossibly good-looking friend. Two boys with nothing but adventure ahead. I heard the click of the ignition, the roar from under the hood, a doo-wop song on the radio.

And that head shot: Dean Foster's eyes beckoning, his lips drawing sensuous curves into his skin. Eyes and lips working in tandem, conspiring to ignite desire. My reporter's instinct felt it as a dare: the primal male friendship of my father's life, covered in secrecy, a forty-year silence so total there had to be a good reason for it. How to reconcile this discovery with the memory of my father as he'd lived, a man I'd never known to have close friendships with other men, who had failed to find any connection with his only son, who'd always been, to use Woody's words, *emotionally unavailable?* A shiver skipped down my spine, like a stone disturbing the surface of deep water, and in the second it took to shake off the sensation, I knew what I would do: I'd look for Danny Ficchino. If he was still alive, I'd find him. I'd find out why he had been erased from our family's history.

I found myself wishing I had tried harder to interest Deirdre in this. Her curiosity would make things easier; she could go through the rest of Dad's belongings in the attic. Plus, we'd have something new in common, a project to get excited about together. This wish—that his death might afford us common ground again—flared at the edge of my thoughts like a shard of glass catching a beam of light. Flared, then dimmed. My sister's needs, I knew, were more practical right now. She had a husband, a child, a house to manage; she had our grandmother's future to consider; she had Carly Fazio in human resources ready to sign her up. If I truly wanted to be closer to her, I would have come home last year, not last week. If I wanted to delve into an obscure year from our father's past, I would have to go it alone.

ANTISOCIAL

4

I was so excited to see Woody again, to get away from New Jersey and that house crammed full of the past, the money talk and the old arguments. Riding to the airport I was giddy with anticipation, not to mention making choices based on my impending inheritance—springing for a seventy-dollar car service rather than a thirteen-dollar bus ride to Newark.

The flight was delayed because of winter weather. I called Woody to break the news, and then I did what I always did when stranded in airports: I cruised the restrooms. It's an old habit left over from when I lived in Jersey City with my boyfriend Nathan. Back then—this was 1990 or '91, and I was only a year out of college—I used to lurk in the men's room in the underground transit station at the World Trade Center. The World *of* Trade Center, Nathan dubbed it, because of all the white businessmen in suits sucking off rough-trade Latinos wearing wife-beater tank tops. Nathan and I were nearly obsessed with one another, a love marked by demonstrative gestures (he was once arrested for spray painting NO ONE LOVES JAMIE MORE THAN NATHAN on a subway-platform billboard) and public displays of drama (the spray paint was to mark the spot where we'd had a screaming match a week earlier). But we were in our early twenties, so naturally we were always itching for sex with other people, too. Sometimes we granted each other *permission slips* for a night or a weekend. Young and queer, why should we limit ourselves? But inevitably one of us got jealous—usually Nathan, a brooding, wild-haired, motorcycle-riding college dropout with a Slavic gloominess—and we'd argue for a day, or two, or seven. I was proficient in foot-stomping retreats and door-slamming exits. He called me the Red Tornado. Détente would come in the form of sweaty makeup sex. Permission slips were revoked, new limitations imposed. Having strayed and reunited, fought and fucked, we'd sing our own praises, young enough to see our love as different than, better than, all other love. Nathan would write me a poem. Or seven.

And then it would start all over again.

After high school, after Eric, I had avoided the touch of men. College was relatively sexless for me—a couple of girlfriends, a couple of furtive liaisons with boys. By the time I got to New York, I was ready. I discovered that pale blue eyes, freckled shoulders and red hair were a currency with an appeal that ran deep, if not necessarily wide. I learned how to court admirers. I figured out how to *work it*. Nathan was less of a prowler than I, but not blameless. He preferred going home with someone he'd met at a bar, which I thought of as unnecessarily entangled—you had to converse, and spend money on alcohol, and exchange phone numbers, and in the end you were more likely to let emotions seep in, perhaps deciding this new someone was more interesting than your boyfriend. I preferred the quick and anonymous; no talking beyond *Thanks a lot, man. That was hot.* I wanted bodies, not biographies. For a while the World of Trade men's room was unbelievably hopping, with sex acts so blatant you'd feel bad for the poor commuter who had stumbled in needing to pee.

The day I was flying back to San Francisco, I'd been coupled with Woody for over a year and a half, a year and a half of monogamous nesting. I'd been a model partner. Woody's previous boyfriend had run around behind his back; cheating was the one thing Woody couldn't abide. I didn't even flirt with other men in front of him. Plus, having emerged from my slutty years without contracting HIV, it seemed ungracious to tempt fate.

So what was I doing in Newark Airport Terminal C, lingering a little too long at a urinal, looking over my shoulder at every guy who walked in, hoping one of them would make eye contact?

I zipped up and splashed cold water on my face. Before anything could happen, I got away from the temptation conjured up by the piss-and-ammonia stink of a public toilet.

In my carry-on luggage was my father's copy of *On the Road.* Its cover was frayed, its pages jaundiced, but it was dated 1958—an original paperback edition. As Nana would say, it was *the genuine article.*

I'd read the book before, or rather I tried to read it, in college. I never finished; too rambling, too episodic, a self-indulgent string of adventures. Back then I was reading contemporary fiction—*Bright Lights, Big City*; *Less Than Zero*—the self-indulgent, episodic books of my own generation. And after college my reading list tended toward old-guard gays: James Baldwin, Frank O'Hara, Gore Vidal. With time to kill, and curious about what sent my father west, I decided Kerouac was worth a fresh look.

Ten minutes later I had plowed through two chapters, utterly absorbed. The beginning of *On the Road* recounts the narrator's introduction to Dean Moriarty, an ex-con who blazes into New York full of wild energy, charming the intellectuals and the junkies alike. I knew the basics of the Kerouac legend, knew that his books were thinly fictionalized versions of his real life, and that Dean was based on Neal Cassady, who'd been a muse to the young writer. But that summary only hinted at what Kerouac must have felt for Cassady. From the moment Dean answers the door "in his shorts," rambling on about sex, "the one holy and important thing in his life," one idealized, sensual description after another piles up: thin and trim hipped and blue eyed and golden, "a sideburned hero of the snowy West," "a western kinsman of the sun." Dean can't even park a car without being described as a "wrangler." The Kerouac stand-in who narrates the book goes on at length about his "heartbreaking new friend"—heartbreaking!— describing him as a long-lost brother with a "straining muscular sweaty neck" whose "dirty workclothes clung to him so gracefully." I'd never heard anyone depict a *kinsman* so ecstatically. Sure, there are mentions of Dean's wife, but she's labeled a "whore" and dispatched pretty quickly. Sure, Dean and Sal make an attempt at a double date, but the girls never show and the guys don't seem to care. Right there in the first few pages of Kerouac's most famous book—the one that inspired a billion red-blooded boys, my father among them—an undeniable erotic current pulsed along the surface.

When I finally looked up from the book, my eyes landed on a guy staring at me from the next table. He was my age, maybe a couple years younger, dressed in an Abercrombie & Fitch T-shirt and a baseball cap. His gaze was strong and direct as I took in his features—brown skin and black eyebrows, eyes a bit close together, big nose. Indian or Arab, perhaps. I looked away and then back. This time, he raised his eyebrows and pressed his lips into a smile. The nod I sent back to him was very cool, but inside, I was already percolating.

"Kerouac?" A Midwestern accent: *care-whack.*

"Yeah. *On the Road.* Just checking it out." I heard the hint of apology in my voice, caught reading a book I'd once dismissed.

"I've read all his stuff." He stood up and moved toward my table, lugging along an enormous backpack, a fleece pullover and the Lonely Planet guide to Nepal. He wore tan cargo pants with zippered pockets staggered down the legs and those newfangled hiking boots, the ones that look like basketball sneakers crossbred with the brown-suede Earth shoes of my childhood. So maybe this wasn't a cruise. He was just one of those perennial backpackers, happy for the excuse to converse with a stranger.

He shook my hand firmly, asked my name, told me his. I wrote it down in my journal later, but I couldn't quite make out my scrawl—it was either Rich or Rick. He asked if he could sit down, and I said yes, not sure it was such a good idea because as soon as he dropped himself into the seat across from me, he launched a monologue about his round-the-world exploits. He'd say, "Then I went to Micronesia. Have you been there? Jamie, you have to make a point to go. It's unbelievable," and continue on about a cavern, or a reef, or a ravine that was "the best example of its kind in the whole world." Personal history came next. He'd been working on an MBA but ditched the program to create a business plan at a dot-com start-up, "installing servers for the B2B segment—that's business-to-business?" I didn't understand the specifics. Mention business and my brain shuts down. He said, "I saved a substantial amount of income, and then I said good-bye."

"Cashed out your stock options?"

"No, I didn't wait that long. The writing is on the wall. All those geeks will live to regret it, working sixty hours a week, waiting around for the big payoff. Get the money now, Jamie, 'cause the Internet honeymoon is quickly drawing to a close."

"You sound pretty sure about that," I said, thinking about Woody's job at Digitent, a little San Francisco company also funded by venture capital, also providing B2B services I didn't particularly understand. They were gearing up for their initial public offering. I hated the long hours that Woody spent at their chaotic, cubicle-pocked office, but he was firm in his plan to work hard now and cash in later.

"Jamie, I'm telling you—do you work for a pre-IPO?" There was something disconcerting about the way Rick kept using my name, all the while keeping his eyes intently locked onto mine. I decided to cast out a lead.

"No, but my boyfriend does."

"Oh." A pause. Something had registered. "Trust me, Jamie. Tell him don't wait around. There'll be a lot of disappointed wannabe millionaires any day now." Then he leaned forward and lowered his voice. "You guys should just get out there and travel together. It's better to travel with someone, anyway. It gets lonely. You can imagine."

"It's a lonely planet, right?"

He smiled at me. "You're a fun guy."

"But I'm not much of a traveler. I've been in San Francisco lockdown for years."

"San Francisco's a *fun* city." His voice had now, most certainly, gotten flirtatious.

I responded in kind. "I have a lot of *fun* there."

"Yeah? You like to have fun?"

"Who doesn't?"

"I bet you and I could have some fun, Jamie."

I cleared my throat. "Planning on visiting?"

"Yeah, actually. In a few months." He leaned in even closer. "But we could seize the moment."

"This moment?"

"What do you say?" He looked around, lowered his voice. "I need to use the bathroom. How about you?"

Bingo.

We stood at side-by-side urinals, blocked by a metal divider, though I knew he was pulling on his cock just like I was. As soon as the room cleared, we both stepped back and showed each other what we had. His was longer than mine, skinnier, uncut. He looked at me through narrowed eyes, nodded his head slowly and mouthed "Nice," no longer the conversationalist, suddenly Mr. Sex. It seemed funny that I'd ever thought him to be straight. He had the gay-pornspeak down pat. He stopped stroking for a moment and let his cock lay swollen on his open palm to be examined like something on a deli scale. "I'd sure love for you to take care of this," he whispered. "I'm going to be traveling for a long time."

"Sounds good, buddy," I said, speaking the 'speak, too.

He quickly checked over his shoulder, then motioned me into a stall. We squeezed in and locked the door and were immediately upon each other—no kissing, just a lot of groping. Frenzied and clumsy. Beyond the metal stall door I heard footsteps and voices. I thought about my bags, unattended out by the sink, with my father's keepsakes inside. I imagined a quick-handed thief making off with them, or an anxious airport security guard calling in the bomb squad.

Rick stepped onto the toilet seat so that only one pair of our legs would be visible—a ploy I remembered well from my World of Trade days. He crouched and leaned forward, sucking my dick into his mouth with an audible slurp, one hand on my ass, the other on his own cock, which he was pumping madly. I shoved from my hips, hoping to get hard again in his mouth, which was dripping saliva into my pubic hair. I thought about the time my friend Ian got gonorrhea in his cock, transmitted from the back of someone's throat. I thought about having to sit through a six-hour plane ride with a damp crotch. I wondered if Rick's flight was delayed, too, or if he was in a rush, needing to finish this off quickly. Voices shot over from the urinals, two men speaking in an Asian tongue, Vietnamese maybe. I wondered if they could hear the slurping and heavy breathing. I wondered if Rick had ever been to Vietnam.

A wave of regret hit me, and I gasped for air. If I was going to cheat on Woody, couldn't I summon up some pleasure, make this worth the guilt? But the guilt was in charge, a hidden overseer keeping my mind full of chatter and my dick at half mast. Rick finally pulled away from me, letting my cock—fluffed, but definitely not hard—bob out of his mouth. He looked up at me, his too-close-together eyes questioning, and I shrugged my shoulders. He pointed at his hard-on, and then back at me, mouthing, "You suck me?"

I shrugged again. "Okay. Sure."

What I should have done was leave, get out while I could still salvage some sense of having resisted, but that didn't seem fair to Rick. Of course, staying and continuing wasn't fair to Woody, but there you have it: the inverse logic of infidelity.

So I crouched on the toilet seat, positioned as if taking a crap in the woods, and I let Rick guide his skinny brown cock down my throat. Out by the urinals it was silent again, and I guess Rick felt safe enough to speak. He said, "Jamie, this might be the last blow job I get for months," and there was something so earnest, so grateful, in his voice that, unexpectedly, I was galvanized. I stopped thinking about confiscated luggage and delayed flights and STDs, and I stopped worrying about whether or not I was going to tell Woody about this, and I gave Rick some grade-A head, something he could remember when he was jacking off in Nepal a month from now, a lonesome traveler out on the road.

"Here it comes," he hissed.

I pulled my mouth away, but not quick enough. My lower lip took the first big blast, my shoulder the second. I managed to redirect the rest toward the floor. I threw my attention to my own hard-on, which somewhere along the line had decided to join the party, and finished myself off. *Sploop, sploop, sploop* onto the tile. When I looked up, Rick's eyes were full of admiration. He leaned down and sucked his cum right off my shirt, then off my chin. Without warning he kissed me on the lips, and I tasted his spooge on my tongue, viscous. I'd be worrying about STDs after all. But the kiss felt good, and I let it linger.

"Thanks, buddy," he said.

"Happy trails," I said.

Alone again, I wanted a cigarette. Or a sleeping pill. I wanted to call Woody and confess, I wanted him to absolve me. But that was as ridiculous as hoping the clock would spin backwards so I could rewrite the last hour.

I had a window seat and a pillow, but even after two cocktails I couldn't sleep. I couldn't get back into Kerouac, either. The book felt tainted by its association with Rick. So I pulled my father's San Francisco souvenirs out of my bag.

Among the items I'd salvaged was a slim, hardback book called *How to Enjoy 1 to 10 Perfect Days in San Francisco.* I found an inscription from Aunt Katie inside the front cover:

> December 1960
>
> Dear Rusty,
>
> I am sending this book in case there are some corners of the city, you haven't discovered yet, and as well, it is a Christmas gift. Plus, the writer is from New York, so, you can trust him! With this $5.00, I suggest, an all you can eat prime rib dinner at House of Prime Rib, which you can read about, on page 30. Or use it for a long distance phone call, or two! Mother says don't spend it on liquor! Thanks

for writing, because we miss you, and everyone wants to be sure you are well. (Even Papa.)

Love,
Your sister, Katie

Squeezed into the space at the bottom of the page was another note:

If you hear from that brother of mine tell him if he don't want a good swift kick in the keester tell him he better write soon, before Mama has a heart attack from worrying.

From,
Angelo

I turned to page thirty to confirm the House of Prime Rib description, but what caught my attention was a description of the city's nightlife on the facing page:

If you have ever visited New York's Greenwich Village, you will take San Francisco's Beatnik Land in your stride. One suspects that the bohemians of the Village in the '30s produced more genuine talent and creative accomplishments than today's beatnik community. This is probably because the really creative beatniks have long since disassociated themselves from the over-organized movement. In fact, by the time you visit San Francisco, Beatnik Land might be completely relocated in Venice, California.

In the margin, my father had written defiantly, "Says You, Square!"

Clearly this was not a book of any use to a twenty-year-old with *hepcat* ambitions of his own. (Poor Aunt Katie, all good intentions and misplaced commas.) I was touched by this youthful defensiveness—no, *touched* isn't strong enough. It was remarkable to me: my father as defender of the San Francisco underground.

After flipping through the book, I discovered, wedged inside the back cover, an unmarked, sealed envelope. It was literally stuck there, as if the binding glue had softened and then reset around it. I tugged it free and sliced it open.

It was a letter, written in my father's hand.

November 1, 1960

Dear Danny,

Or should I say, "Dear Incredible Vanishing Friend?" Just pulling your leg, but I sure hope this letter gets forwarded to wherever you are, otherwise I won't get to say Happy Birthday, pal!

The news here is good-bye "Rusty." See, nobody calls me Rusty here. They call me "Teddy." It just happened, when I first met Don Drebinski, the guy who runs the Hideaway, I said my name was Edward and he said, How about Teddy? And that's how he introduces me to everyone. Guess I'm ready to be "a new man." You should be here instead of mopping floors in Los Angeles. You could be anyone you want to.

I have it in mind that I'll be a painter. But not as they say a "Sunday Painter" which is what a fellow called me at a party. I went with Ray, remember I wrote about her, the Jewish brunette with the Natalie Wood face and the damn husband. I thought about keeping away in case the old guy shows up with a shotgun, but she's irresistible! I could eat her for breakfast, lunch and midnight snack. She's a painter, and planted the bug in me, having seen my sketches and knowing I was very moved by the Richard Diebenkorn paintings last year. She showed up at my door Saturday to lure me out into the night and I said, "I got to fix my hair first," and she said, "No, don't, you look funk." Which melted me like wax. Funk being hep language for what we would call "cool" on the West Side. We got a lift in Mike Kelsey's T-bird convertible. This is reason for jealousy, because he's another young fool like myself under the spell of the married beauty, but a heck of a nice guy so as its hard to feel meanness and rivalry toward him, and who can resist the convertible? It is a glorious way to travel under the Frisco night sky, where the fog turns orange from city light reflecting up.

In the car we drank whiskey and drove all the way from my place near the ocean to North Beach (which isn't a beach at all, or anywhere near the beach). Ray is between us on the seat and telling stories of all the great characters we will meet tonight, possibly some Negro musicians fond of that smokable tea. But wouldn't you know when we get there Ray disappears with her gang of lady painters which includes the supposedly famous Jane Chase, a tough broad never seen without her own jug of liquid brown poison. My rival Kelsey is smoking a damn pipe which smells like Irish Uncles sitting around telling stories and stinking up the house. I'm eventually drunker than a Roman at an orgy, except alone, when some creep says, "Ray claims you're a Sunday Painter." And the one next to him says, "A real plain air type." I know an insult when I hear one so I tell him "Watch it, I can knock you on your behind." One of them called me "Bruiser" and the other one nearly died laughing. So I swung at them. More like I stood up and fell onto them. I was damned drunk and bang, down I went.

Ray came running over and I said "What's the idea talking bad about me to those jokers" but she just gave me a kiss and said forget about them. She made Kelsey drive me home, and he practically killed us driving in the wrong lane on California Street and making some poor stiff swerve spectacularly to avoid death for all concerned. We cursed Ray and every woman to ever tempt a guy and leave him loveless, then he got me up the stairs and we drank some more booze and had a swell time, just a couple of fellows. After he left I took a shower to cool off. (First I got hot and bothered by thoughts of Ray, her helping me off the floor and holding my head so sweetly as she passed me over to Kelsey, so I had to Take Care of That Need, which I'm sure you know what I'm referring to, my oldest true friend.)

I couldn't sleep so I told myself, Write it down for Danny. Because you're the only one who would live the whole thing out with me if you could. That's why these sentences are a bit wobbly though I hope it all makes sense. The truth is, I like painting out in the plain air but I don't only paint on Sundays, so those guys can kiss my Irish ass.

A long dumb story of your friend in Frisco, hopefully entertaining for you on your birthday because you deserve a good laugh and more than that too. Send the new postal address and news of yourself.

Your friend, Teddy
(Though still Rusty if that's the way you want it)

There was almost nothing about this letter that didn't astonish me, starting with its imitation Kerouac veneer. Phrases like *I could eat her for breakfast, lunch, midnight snack* sounded like my father, the kind of goofy-embarrassing Dad I remembered from long ago—long ago being shorthand for before Mom died. But could I remember him ever saying that he was moved by anything, much less a Diebenkorn painting? Had he ever mentioned that he'd once aspired to be a painter? Was this just folly, nurtured by his lust for a beautiful woman, or did he actually take a stab at painting *plein air*? And what about Ray, this married woman luring younger guys out into the night to parties marked by drunken brawls and pot smoke?

The letter had never been sent, perhaps because it had gotten stuck in the binding and forgotten. Or maybe because Danny was already out of touch, not only with his brother back home but with his old pal Rusty up in San Francisco, too. I felt a rare stab of empathy for my father, or at least for this younger version of him: his obvious affection for Danny, the nearly desperate need to pour his heart out, his drunken humiliation, his late-night masturbation. Was there more of this kind of thing back in the attic in Greenlawn? Would Deirdre find it, and if she found it, would she know to save it? Or would it get thrown away, just another bit of ancient history best forgotten?

As soon as I spotted Woody's smiling face above the crowd and heard him call my name, the guilt-stricken drama I'd set myself up for faded away. He hadn't even told me he would be here. Now I was getting a strong hug, a public kiss, a ready arm to relieve me of an overstuffed carry-on.

"Careful with that," I told him. "There's Garner family treasure in there."

"You brought the family fortune with you?"

"The family baggage, so to speak."

In his other hand he dangled keys to a car borrowed from his friend Annie for the night. My hero. Neither of us owned a car, and the airport was chaotic because of winter-storm delays. Somewhere in that moment I let go of the notion that I would confess my men's-room misadventure. I'd write it off as a *slip* and move on.

"I'm still half asleep," I told him. "You talk first."

He got me up to speed on our friends: Ian's computer crashed while he was uploading his webzine, and Woody spent two nights restoring his hard drive; Brady was informed that the warehouse where he lived had been sold and would be refurbished as an office park; Colleen attempted to dye her hair pink and was flipping out at the results. They'd all been leaving messages with Woody, asking if he'd heard from me, though he hadn't called any of them back because he'd been so busy at work. He had the usual dot-com sweatshop complaints—the extra-long hours, the urgent projects foisted on him without advance notice; the daily meetings that amounted to little more than jargony pep talks; a constantly shifting corporate mission. (Digitent had started out as an *e-commerce website*, but was now defining itself as something called a *wireless service portal*.) Worst of all was what he'd dubbed "digital daycare": supervising a stable of young programmer-dudes who had no clue how to function in an office. Woody, at thirty-one, was one of the oldest of the bunch. He'd been hired as a web designer but was quickly shifted to management because unlike everyone else, he had real work history.

His eyes were bright and active while he talked. He had beautifully shaped eyebrows that wiggled like inchworms when his speech got animated. Woody was the first fair-haired, fair-skinned guy I'd been involved with. If I have a *type* at all it's on the Danny Ficchino end of the spectrum, dark and Mediterranean, a clear contrast to what I see in the mirror. Woody comes from the neighboring Northern European gene pools, Scandinavian-Dutch-Scottish: light brown eyes shot with gold, fair cheeks that pinken when he exerts himself, thin lips made thinner by his wide smile. Since I first saw him I'd adored his ringlet curls, which in the sunshine seemed to be woven from straw and in dim light became mutt-brown, so much so that it seemed a lie that he'd labeled himself blonde on his driver's license.

He was two years younger than me, but I often responded to him as someone older. His therapeutic mindset made him deliberative about plans, levelheaded with problems. I had always charged heedlessly into my life. My career started off as a lark in college; my move to San Francisco was an impulsive attempt to escape Nathan; plans I'd once made to leave were aborted after I met Woody; my close friendships all grew out of infatuation, a pursuit of those who sparkled. There was a trend swelling right around then among Christian teenagers, the wearing of little bracelets marked WWJD: *What would Jesus do?* Answer that question and you would walk the righteous path. Those days, I often asked myself, *What would Woody do?* He wasn't my messiah, but I looked up to him.

Oh, and the most obvious way I looked up to him: with my eyes. He's six-foot-four, almost six inches taller than me, all limbs, with the forward-curving shoulders typical of the tallest guy in the room. Strangers were forever asking him if he played basketball. (The answer: No, tennis. When he stretched up to serve it was like a swan craning its neck before flight.) To me he was adorable as only a gangly guy who takes himself a bit too seriously can be. He was my golden, gawky, smiling swan.

While we waited at the baggage claim, I rushed through a description of what I'd found in the attic, what I'd read on the plane. I told him how eager I was to know more about my father's year in San Francisco and his friendship with Danny Ficchino, to satisfy my curiosity, but also because there might be something here for a radio project. I told him I'd have to visit New Jersey again, this time talking to my grandmother, and maybe even Aunt Katie, with my tape recorder in tow.

"Hey, I just got you back," Woody said, resting a hand on my shoulder. "Why don't you just take a deep breath. You've got a lot of important stuff waiting for you here."

"But this is the top priority now."

"Okay, okay." He patted my shoulder where his hand had been resting, attempting to impart some calm. I have an easy-to-read face, I'm told—my moods are obvious even when I think I'm displaying neutrality. This must have been one of those moments, because Woody was responding to me the way I imagined him talking to the frazzled dudes at Digitent when they were in their twelfth hour of being radiated by their computer monitors. Then his gaze focused on my shoulder. "What is that?"

I peered down at a streak of encrusted spooge. "Fucking clumsy stewardess," I hissed, trying to rub it out. "Great, now my shirt is stained."

"It's not that noticeable," he offered. "I shouldn't have even mentioned it."

"Yeah, well, you did."

I was overdoing it—the culprit's attempt to deflect the evidence—and feeling hot in the face, on the spot. I took off on a lap around the baggage carousel, trying to regulate my breathing as Woody had suggested, trying to will myself a clear conscience. When I got back to his side, I mumbled an apology.

San Francisco's airport was in the middle of an enormous construction project, building a new international terminal: scaffolding, cranes, dismantled concrete, big signs with yellow flip-letters redirecting traffic, all of it disorienting for a travel-addled brain. On this night the upper roadway had been closed to drivers. Curbside was pure chaos—no lines, just masses of people jostling wheeled suitcases past each other, competing for taxis. If Woody hadn't shown up with transportation, I'd have been fending for myself. Once inside the car, I leaned over and kissed him on the lips, grateful. When I pulled back I was rewarded with one of his winning smiles.

"I really am sorry for acting like a maniac," I said. "I'm just fried by the trip."

"Not to mention that your father just died."

"Yeah. That."

He reached over and rested his hand on my thigh. "Whenever you want to talk about it."

I nodded and put my hand on his.

We drove the freeway into San Francisco. Tendrils of fog moved across the night sky, made orange and spooky *from city light reflecting up.* It was the same wide sky Teddy Garner had witnessed forty years ago, drunken and lovelorn in the passenger seat of a convertible, at the start of an adventure that wouldn't last.

5

At the end of my block—a little Mission District street called Manfred Alley—in a dingy storefront, was a knife-sharpening business. The faded sign in the window read THE STRAIGHT BLADE. The place was closed more than open, though on certain afternoons and weekends, the guy who ran it, Anton, could be found on the sidewalk behind an easel, painting scenes of everyday life on the block: punk-rock girls dragging their pit bulls toward Dolores Park, homeless men dozing on the steps of garish Victorians, elderly ladies in conversation, their shopping bags resting on the sidewalk. He sometimes sold these pictures, the paint barely dry, to passersby.

He also sold some of the best pot on the planet. For this reason, whether or not I needed knives sharpened, I visited Anton once a month—about as often as I frequented my other favorite neighborhood establishment, a full-service, two-chair beauty salon that shared its storefront with a pet store. Oddball businesses like these were a tonic for the shiny new boutiques and bistros taking over the Mission. When I first moved here, I was almost mugged at 16th and Valencia, but the only danger to find me lately was instigated by a guy driving a sports utility vehicle, talking on a cell phone and U-turning toward a precious parking space. He cut so close and fast to me, pedaling in the bike lane, that I lost my balance and crashed shoulder-first onto the pavement. I wound up in the emergency room.

A few days after my father's funeral, I brought Anton the knives I'd taken from the attic. He buzzed me in and emerged from the back of the store, squinting into the streetlight behind me. It took a moment for the reflexive paranoia around his eyes to dissolve into his greeting, "Hey, brother." In the eighties, he'd spent a couple years in jail on an

LSD rap, and since then he was forever expecting the DEA to come walking through his front door, ready to bust up his operation.

The interior was neglected in a way that few businesses are anymore: unidentifiable clutter, mismatched furniture, light-faded news clippings taped to the wall. Not *shabby chic,* just shabby. Posters commemorated decades of free concerts and protest rallies in Dolores Park—VIVA LA RAZA, EMBARGO SOUTH AFRICA NOT NICARAGUA, TAKE BACK THE NIGHT, NO NUKES! Everything was curled and yellowed, sort of like Anton, with his tangle of wiry gray hair, his dingy clothes, his stale breath.

I handed him the velvet-lined knife case. "I want the full treatment, Anton. Cleaning, sharpening, oiling, tightening, whatever you can do." He slid the heaviest blade from its slot and examined it through the bottom of his spectacles, letting out an impressed little whistle. "Sturdy stuff. Valuable. Ivory handles."

"I'm going to give them to Woody," I said.

"I dig that," he said, nodding intently. *I dig that* was a tried-and-true Antonism, one he often used when I talked about Woody. Anton was very serious about *digging the struggle of his gay brothers.* He told me once he was thinking about changing the name of his shop because The Straight Blade sounded homophobic. I'd replied that we were living in an age of irony and he should keep it. The sign had stayed, but mostly, I think, out of inertia. Nothing in Anton's world ever changed.

"Anything else today, brother?" Anton asked, one frizzy eyebrow arched.

"Some of your other product," I said.

He flipped the sign on the front door to CLOSED and led me to the back room. Behind a stack of paintings was a locker, from which he extracted several freezer bags crammed with green bud, along with a scale and a couple of scoops. Singing the praises of each strain, he presented my options: indoor versus outdoor, low stem versus top leaf, sticky versus shake. I took the usual, a forty-five-dollar baggie containing an eighth of an ounce—organic, homegrown, sticky—nurtured in a sunlit glen amid the redwoods of Humboldt County. "Excellent choice," he said. "Grown in bat guano."

Ritual demanded that we smoke some of what I bought. I had spent a lot of time in this room over the years, listening to Anton's tales. He was almost, but not quite, a friend. After a voluminous inhale, he asked, "So what's new, brother?"

"My father died," I blurted out.

"Whoa, heavy. Did he live here?"

"No," I said. "New Jersey. Though he lived here once, like, forty years ago."

"I've been here forty years myself." He cocked his head and squinted. "Is that right? Yeah, 1959. Forty-one years. Hitchhiked from Billings."

"You came here to be a painter?"

"No, no, that was later. There were three of us, see. All of us ranchers' sons in Montana. We grew up herding cattle on motorbikes. We had plenty of room but nowhere to go. So we did what you did back then. Hitched to San Francisco." He drifted off and began reloading. I guess I'd struck a chord; usually Anton packed only one bowl per visit.

"I just started reading *On the Road,*" I told him. "It's weird. I'm looking at it as history."

"It is, man. It's *historical.* It was a migration, another gold rush, except we were panning for the truth. Kerouac, Cassady—that was something you could aspire to. You thought, I could be one of those guys." Another staggeringly long inhale, and then: "Mostly we just wanted to be antisocial."

"Antisocial?"

"Yeah-ahhh." Extended exhale, a passing of the pipe. "See, there was this conspiracy of niceness. You wanted to subvert it, man. The cupboards were full—you know, prosperity—so, like, everyone believed it. Everyone believed the big story, the money story. You were supposed to be happy about it."

Another Antonism: "the (fill in the blank) story."

He shook his head. "You forget now, but World War Two was a tragedy. They've been glorifying it for fifty years, man. Back then, every one knew someone who'd been slaughtered. Kids in your school, the ones a few years ahead of you. So afterwards—well, like I'm saying. Everyone wanted to believe the big, nice story." He smiled wide, a kind of mischief in his bleary eyes. "But some of us didn't want to pretend."

Back then, we all wanted to be beatniks. I registered Anton's confused expression and realized I'd spoken these words aloud. "My father came here the same time as you. Did you know him? Teddy Garner?"

I could see the dulled mental machinery trying to pull a name from the clouds. "I've known a lot of folks in my day," he said finally.

"He was only here for a year, 1960 to '61, so the chances are pretty slim." I raced through a short version of the story—Dad's past, my uncovering of it—not sure how deeply Anton was absorbing it, but suddenly wildly optimistic, as pot sometimes makes me, that Anton might be of help. *Stoned hopeful,* as my friend Ian calls it. "I'm trying to do a little research," I concluded. "To find out about his life. There are a bunch of people whose names are in his letters. Maybe you knew one of them." Anton gave me a scrap of paper, a stray crimson brushstroke on one side, and I wrote out a list for him: "Danny Ficchino (aka Dean Foster), Ray Gladwell (female), Mike Kelsey, Don Drebinski."

A short while later Anton and I stood outside of his shop, my fingers rubbing the baggie of dope deep in my coat pocket, my eyes adjusting to the dimming sky. The building next to his wrapped around the corner to Valencia, where a new three-star restaurant had recently opened. We could see the dressed-up crowd already gathering on the sidewalk, near the valet-parking stand, where swift, uniformed boy-men clutched car keys and kept away the junkies. Not long ago, this place held a secondhand furniture store and a women's community meeting space.

"Not much antisocial behavior going on there," I sniffed.

Anton just shrugged. "You think this place is changing because there's valet parking on the block," he said. "But I thought it was changing when you showed up."

I could still taste Anton's pot on my tongue as I made my way home, could still hear his voice in my head. Perspective is everything: The way a place is when you arrive is the way you want it to stay, the way you believe it's always been. Anything new that comes along you see as alarming. It's hard to remember that you're just a visitor, too. It's hard not to be bitter.

Stoned and hopeful, I put in a call to Brady. "I think I have an idea for a project," I told him.

"Sweet," he replied.

I knew Brady Liu from KQED, where he worked as an audio engineer. Years ago, when I started producing local programming for the station, Brady edited my segments; we went on to create *City Snapshot* together. In that stressful, light-deprived, budget-crunched environment, Brady was my better half, the only person I ever wanted to spend time with outside the job. We would get high in the alley after work and take long, detouring bike rides home, or go to indie-rock shows and drink beer and talk politics. We were unlikely friends in some ways: he was straight, outdoorsy, half Chinese and all Californian, the first person I befriended who'd been born and raised entirely in the Golden State. Words and phrases exotically dude-ish to me, like *right on* and *rad* and *sweet* (pronounced sah-*wheat*) fell naturally from his lips; he took it for granted that winters were for snowboarding and summers for backpacking, and of course you were a vegetarian and composted your organic peels. But under the mellow exterior, he was a true neurotic. He suffered greatly, my boy Brady, because he couldn't, on one hand, live up to the ideals passed on by his (white) Buddhist-feminist-anticapitalist mom, who worked at a nonprofit in Berkeley; and, on the other, he didn't have enough ambition to please his father, a gruff, task-oriented chemist with a long list of professional accomplishments for whom Brady's decision to spend years in public radio was a waste of his talent. In the last conversation I'd had with Brady, he spent far too much time agonizing over whether shifting his voter registration to the Green Party was a valiant or a foolish course of action. "I want to vote my conscience," he'd said. "But on the other hand, if I vote Democrat, I'll at least cancel out my father's vote for the Republicans." It was on the subject of fathers that Brady and I had the most in common.

Which is why I was so surprised to find him lukewarm about my idea to build some kind of report around my father's secret year in San Francisco. "So, like a personal story? Like a father-son thing?" he asked me on the phone that night. "Because, no offense, dude, but you've got to have a real *angle* for something like that to work."

"That's where the beatnik thing comes in. How he was part of this wave of people who came to SF in the late fifties."

"Right on," he said, then added, "though that's also pretty familiar turf."

"Yeah, of course, sure," I said quickly. "You're right. I'm still looking for the angle." It had been a while since I'd floated a creative idea to Brady, or to anyone, for that matter, and I was breaking rule number one: Know your story before you pitch it.

"You might just want to give this some time," he said. "Let the dust settle."

"What dust?"

"Um, your dad dying? You might be, you know, too close to this material?"

I could hear him picking his words carefully. I felt transparent. "No, it's not like that," I said. "This has been a long time coming. I already have distance on it."

"Well, let me know what you come up with. You know I can't wait to start something up with you again." Brady and I had always worked together effortlessly, the way automobile drivers merging into a single lane know when to pause and when to proceed, but over the past six months, we'd been on completely different paths. After *City Snapshot*, Brady, a station employee, jumped right into another show; as a contracted employee, I was let go. We had big hopes for our next collaboration—national hopes, *This American Life* hopes—once we, once I, figured out what shape this might take. Before we got off the phone, Brady told me how *crazy-busy* his life was, not just at KQED, and not just because he and Annie were looking for a place to live, but also because of a new side project, working with some guys I'd never heard him mention before, helping them set up a music website. "Streaming audio content. Indie stuff from all over North America. It's very right now," he said. "It could be huge."

That next morning I woke feeling the weight of every bone, zonked-out from smoking too much of my new purchase the night before. Getting myself out of bed took some convincing. The world was expecting exactly nothing from me. I lumbered around my kitchen, spilling a bag of coffee beans on the floor, jarring my elbow on the countertop as I swept up the mess, later knocking my first filled mug across the table. I remembered AJ laughing when I knocked over my oatmeal. I was a one-man danger zone.

My apartment was only four small rooms (one with a couch and desk, one with a bed and dresser, a kitchen with a table, a bathroom with a good-sized tub), but I found endless distractions within these walls—one of my curses as a freelancer. That morning, I watched an hour of housewifey TV. I unpacked the luggage still parked outside my closet. I pruned and repotted houseplants, looking neglected after my time away. I made myself balance my checkbook, the pathetic bottom line reminding me that my last freelance job, producing a few promotional spots for the smaller of San Francisco's two public radio stations, had ended before Christmas.

So I called Bob Flick. When I was hard up for money (that is, more hard up than usual), I took temporary assignments with a company called New World Transcripts. Bob was the manager there, a gregarious, efficient dork. I liked him, but I hated the work—transcribing videotaped interviews for various market-research firms, listening for hours to earnest consumers trying to put into words exactly what they sought in a cordless phone, a breath mint, a cheese-flavored cracker—but since I typed ninety-five words a minute, it was easy money. Bob said he would send some work my way—a new client who had combined shampoo and conditioner in one bottle. "You rinse out the first application," Bob explained, "and leave the second one in." Woo-hoo! Well, it was something to tide me over until my brother-in-law sent that ten-thousand-dollar check my way.

The clock read 11:50 when I finally remembered Colleen. Friday at noon was our standing lunch date. We would meet at Café Frida, in the Mission, where neither the food nor the coffee was especially good, but the boy-watching could be compelling: scrappy, shaggy-haired hipsters wearing tiny, ironic T-shirts, absentmindedly scratching their bellies while reading Noam Chomsky. We'd been meeting like this for over a year, ever since Colleen left her job as a graphic designer for Levi Strauss. These days she worked at a little South of Market shop run by a gay couple who made cheap, outlandish clothes, perfect for drag queens and club kids (and no one else, really). Colleen managed the store and promoted their events, though what she really wanted to do was design her own clothing line. One of the owners had a crystal meth habit and the other was prone to depression—we called them Up and Down—but working for them, she said, was better than answering to a chain of corporate department heads.

I rushed into the café, sweaty from the ride over. She rose to hug me. Her head was wrapped elaborately in a colorful silk scarf that hid her hair and made her features seem larger: her caramel-brown eyes more expressive, her lips wider, her slight overbite more pronounced. She gave me the once-over, taking in my three-day stubble, my ripped sweatshirt, my damp brow. "So you've given up hygiene for the new millennium?"

"And you've started chemo?"

"Ha ha." She dropped back down into the chair. "I'm in Hair Hell."

"Woody said it was very pink."

"He got my message? I've been absolutely paralyzed without your advice, Jamie."

"Pink can be cute."

"This is not cute. It's a disaster."

"Cotton candy?"

"Duller than that. Orangey pink. Salmon. Tongue."

"Labia?"

"Labia!" she screeched. "My hair is the color of my pudenda. This is so not-okay."

"Can I see?"

"I will not flash my pudenda at Café Frida."

Hair dye gone wrong was nothing particularly new for Colleen. Since I'd first met her, back when we both lived in New York, I'd seen her try out blue, green, red and purple, sometimes wearing it proudly, sometimes erasing the whole thing with platinum and starting over. Once upon a time it was a punk thing—she'd had a *riot grrl* phase when she first got to San Francisco, not long after I moved here, when she wore combat boots with vintage dresses and dated a girl who played bass for a band called Hillary's Pills. For the last few years, working for the Man, she'd limited her color to streaks and stripes. The pink, she explained, had been meant as a reaction to all the neutral tones she saw everywhere in San Francisco: khaki pants, brown shoes, beige sweaters. Charcoal gray T-shirts, fifty dollars at Banana Republic. Not to mention a reaction to spending a week with her own family at Christmas. "My cousin, the sleazy lawyer? She had the exact same amber streaks," Colleen explained. "That was the final injury."

We settled on black, deep dark inky black. Sort of mod, sort of new wave, with chopped-up bangs so no one would mistake her for trotting out that tired old Louise Brooks bob. Colleen seemed calmer once we came up with a plan. Me, too. I was back in my world, a place where I was expected to solve problems rather than cause them.

"Here, Pinky, this will cheer you up." I pulled a little bundle out of my backpack, hastily wrapped in magazine pages on my way out the door. Inside: my father's vintage beer coasters. I knew she'd like them. Colleen was a collector of cultural detritus, but a picky one.

"These are beautiful," she cooed. "Where are they from?"

"From my father's house. And before that, San Francisco, 1960."

"I'm such an idiot," she gasped. "I haven't even asked about the funeral."

I worked up a series of tragicomic encounters—my father's mattress, my aunt's fur coat, my cousin's tipsy confessions, the streets full of slush, my shoes full of slush, my head full of slush—beneath which I hoped Colleen could hear the truth: I wanted to put the entire trip behind me.

All of it, that is, except what I found in the attic.

"It's Pandora's box," she pronounced after I summed it up. "Be careful. Some of those ghosts are going to have fangs. What does Woody have to say?"

"He probably thinks its sort of cute, you know? *There goes Jamie, off on another tangent.*"

"We hardly saw Woody at all while you were gone." She looked away for a moment, her eyes moving toward the ubiquitous Ché Guevara poster. "We've got to rescue him from that place."

"He doesn't want to be rescued. He wants to get rich."

"On second thought, let's let him. He's the only person I know who might actually make money off this dot-com thing."

We finished our coffee and then wandered up 16th Street to the Castro, arms interlocked, pointing each other's attention toward cute boys.

"What about him, the bald in the camo?" she whispered.

The *bald* in question was sauntering towards us, a shiny shaved head, a thin sweater shrink-wrapped on a hard torso, baggy camouflage pants drooping invitingly from narrow hips. A perfect specimen of what it took to be sexy these days. "What's up?" he grumbled, his voice all bass.

"Woof," Colleen whispered as we passed.

I turned to look back and found him doing the same. I snapped my gaze away: I recognized him. "I had sex with that guy. Years ago, when I was going out with David."

"Who didn't you have sex with when you were going out with David?"

"Um, David."

I peered back again. He'd stopped in his tracks, idling in the middle of the sidewalk, daring me to come talk to him. I couldn't even remember his name, but I remembered our athletic sex, which had begun like this, with eye contact on the street.

"Stop it," Colleen admonished. "You know if you look again you have to talk to him, and that's not okay." She was right: One glance was curiosity, a second showed your interest, the third was a commitment.

Dish was central to my friendship with Colleen, which for all its longevity still had the soul of a sorority. And so when we parted company an hour later I was painfully aware that the only thing I hadn't told her about from my time on the East Coast was my tryst with Rick. In the past, I'd have gone right to her with this kind of thing. She and I used to bond as sluts, trading our explicitly dirty adventures, happy when we could outdo each other. But these days Colleen was a huge supporter of my relationship with Woody. "Monogamy is the new promiscuity," I had announced to her as things with him were growing serious. "Sexual exclusivity, in your thirties, gives you the buzz that sleeping around did in your twenties." Colleen liked that Woody had reined me in. His jealousy, which often frustrated me, was charming to her. She wanted a Wormy of her own.

On this afternoon, I didn't have the heart to tell her that the new promiscuity had started to feel a lot like the old.

I had a date to cook dinner for Woody that night. I overloaded my bike with expensive groceries and spent hours preparing. Pork loin, butternut squash ratatouille, wild rice pilaf. I had hoped to have the knives back from Anton, to present the gift that evening, but Anton had called to say that one of the handles was shot and he was waiting for a replacement to be sent from a dealer in Los Angeles. That was my first disappointment. My second came at seven o'clock—with the oven heated and the gas burners blazing—when Woody phoned to say he'd be late. He'd forgotten tonight was set aside to take the new guy at work, Roger, out for drinks. "I would skip it," he said, "except he's the only other gay guy we've hired. I feel like I should be there for solidarity." From behind him, I could hear a volley of male voices chanting "Wood-man!" He begged me for an hour's leeway.

I thought about what Colleen had said to me, wondering how I could possibly rescue Woody from Digitent when I couldn't even lure him to dinner on time. A year earlier Woody had been the assistant director of Learn Media, a nonprofit that trained underprivileged teens how to use computers. The small, embattled staff spent half its time fending off a landlord who wanted them out so he could triple the rent, and half acting as surrogate parents for the troubled kids—sorry, *at-risk youth*—who came into their keep. Woody was doing all that plus acting as Learn's self-taught webmaster. Two jobs for half the price of one: a recipe for burnout. I didn't question his decision to make the leap to the for-profit world—time to give Saint Woodrow a rest, time to climb out of debt—and when he got hired at Digitent at a salary more than twice what he'd been making, I gathered together our friends for a celebration. But those dot-com dollars were casting a dark shadow. The hours were longer and the stress more pronounced, and all of it without the warm-fuzzy of teaching some kid from the projects how to use a PC. A month ago, I'd gone with him to Learn's holiday party, where he was greeted with family-style hugs for the prodigal son and then forced to endure his former boss leading the crowd in the buoyant toast, "To all of us who haven't been lured away by the boom!" When the room erupted in cheers, she added, "Keep fighting the good fight!"

"That was awkward," I offered after we'd left.

"She knew exactly what she was doing," he grunted. "She's jealous of anyone who takes control of his life." He spent the rest of that night in an uncharacteristically glum mood. The next morning, a Saturday, he was called in to work and stayed for hours.

He made it to dinner, well past nine-thirty, carrying a spray of red flowers and a bottle of Merlot way more expensive than our usual $4.99 Trader Joe's special. It was his apology. I couldn't stay mad.

"How's the new guy?" I asked.

"Funny. Smart. Good style."

"Is he cute?"

"Not as cute as you." *Plup* went the cork.

I shook my head. "You don't have to say that. I can handle you working with a cute gay guy, Woody."

He poured me a glass and changed the subject. "I had to threaten one of the slackers today. He's *this close* to being fired. I swear, he's always stoned."

I thought about how many hours I'd spent stoned since I visited Anton, hours I'd kept hidden from Woody, who rarely joined me in my favorite vice. It was my turn to change the subject: "Sit and start eating. It's all getting cold."

He flattened a cloth napkin in his lap. "You're mad that I'm late."

"Not after tasting this wine I'm not." I sat down and held my glass aloft.

"Here's to being back together," he toasted. "And to true love."

"Sure, here's to." I felt my face flush even before the wine went down.

His eyes were fixed on me. "Even after a year, that makes you uncomfortable."

"No. Well, a little." I started cutting my food. "Come on, eat. Tell me how it tastes." He was staring, waiting. "I love you too, Woody. I'm just not so good with the words."

"You write words in your journal all the time."

"Speaking them is harder."

"How about this," he said. "Speak to me about your trip. Tell me something you haven't told me yet."

An image of Rick at the urinal flitted by like a sprite. I washed down the food with more wine. "Well . . . I found out that my high school fuckbuddy is married with children."

"Eric-something, right? Was that a surprise?"

"Considering everything we did together, plus the fact that he went into the Navy after high school, yes."

"It's a mystery to me how you managed to have sex with boys in high school."

"Sex wasn't the mystery for me. Friendship was, friendship with other guys." I paused. "This is what I was trying to explain to you, about why I got so interested in my father's friendship with Danny."

He wiped his mouth, then reached across the table, surprising me by taking my hand. "You know, I've been wanting to raise an issue with you."

"Uh-oh. The I-word."

He sighed. "Annie mentioned a friend of hers who lost a parent recently, and this person decided to see a therapist."

I slid my hand out of his, tried to joke this away. "I cried at the wake. In the bathroom. I told you that, right?"

"Annie thought this therapist might be a good candidate. If you were looking."

"Um, *I* haven't even talked to Annie about my father." In addition to being a good friend of Woody's, Annie was Brady's girlfriend. I cringed at the idea of them sharing a dinner like this one, trading theories about me and my *issues.*

Woody said, "Your friends care about you."

I gathered up a forkful of the ratatouille. "You haven't tried the squash yet." I leaned in close and brought it to his lips. He frowned, then blew on it, and I felt the tickle of his breath on my cheek. I watched his eyelids lower as he chewed. His lashes so lush for a guy. His concentrated brow so elegant.

"I wish I was as good as you in the kitchen," he said.

"Wormy, I know you're looking out for me. But the idea of therapy makes me feel like this ugly damaged thing."

"Baby," he said, a smile returning, "you're a *beautiful* damaged thing."

We spent the rest of the meal staying away from the I-word.

After dinner, walking backwards down the hall, he peeled off my clothes. My T-shirt, ripe from hours in the kitchen, went over my head. He planted his lips on my chest, his tongue on my nipple. My weakness. He pulled me by my belt loops and then slid my pants down. I nearly fell into him, eager for his kisses. We hadn't had sex since I'd returned from New Jersey. I'd been avoiding it. For months we'd been fucking unprotected. We'd been tested, we were both negative, we were monogamous; we didn't need condoms to have safe sex. But I'd crossed a line with Rick: My lips had been winter-chapped, he could have been HIV-positive, that tablespoon of cum in my mouth could have been the instance of transmission. Now I was going to give it to Woody.

He pushed me onto my bed, pulled my cock through the fly of my boxers, wrapped his warm hand around it. In a moment he was down on his knees in front of me. I hooked my fingers under his armpits, tried to raise him back up. I needed to be the bottom tonight. He wasn't having it. He was hungry, determined, inspired by half a bottle of wine. I watched his lips wrap around the head of my dick and slide down its length, his eyes closed, his eyelids like two gentle smiles, his blonde curls bobbing. I fell back on the pillow and stared up at the ugly light fixture over my bed.

Stop him. Tell him.

I can't tell him now, not right here in the middle of sex.

Tell him now, before you give him AIDS!

Rick didn't have AIDS.

You don't know that.

Woody won't get HIV from oral sex.

Are you certain? Really certain?

But that would mean I have AIDS, too—

The amazing sensation of being deep down Woody's throat, my thighs tickled by his hot breath, my body held in place by the weight of him. He was servicing me and dominating me all at once. I don't know that I'd ever felt so physically close to him and so mentally far away at the same time.

The physical won out. I didn't stop him to confess. I squashed the conversation inside my skull: It was based on guilt, not medical information. The odds were against this being dangerous: *I did not get HIV from a couple of seconds of aerated semen on my tongue. It's only unsafe for Woody if I have HIV, and I don't have HIV!* I repeated this like a mantra, not sure where rationality ended and wishful thinking began—a familiar, unwelcome confusion that I could trace back to the late eighties, when penetration was new to me and AIDS truly was capital-letter deadly. This panicky mind-chatter went back to every time I'd read reports of a study claiming the virus might in fact be transmitted by oral sex; to every article claiming a new, more virulent strain of HIV had been discovered; to every time someone I knew seroconverted. I shut out the studies; I focused on all the anecdotal evidence to the contrary. I slammed the lid down on the cauldron and just breathed the humid mist of the moment. I gave in to Woody's effort.

He lifted me farther back on the bed and then undressed. His long, lean torso—broad bony shoulders, broad flat chest, a slanting ridge of muscle highlighting his lower abdomen. Skin the color of parchment. His cock rigid without either of us touching it. I watched a crystal bead glistening at the tip drop to the floor, a filament stretching and vanishing. I would be on my hands and knees tomorrow, looking for the spot that sacred drop had blessed. He sucked me some more and I watched the elongated slope of his lower back, his ass raising up like a cat's hoping to be scratched, more of that golden skin, gleaming exquisitely. And when he planted a knee on either side of my ribs and lifted himself up, and dropped back down onto my lap, and guided me up inside of him, I let it happen. I fucked him, as he clearly wanted it, the way we always did this. *Bareback.* I looked up and met his eyes and I told myself, *It's going to be okay,* and then thrust up until he groaned and we found the rhythm.

I said to him out loud, "I'm yours."

He matched the intensity of my gaze and held it and nodded his head, telling me: *Yes*.

He called the next day from work. I was sitting at my desk in my underwear, checking my e-mail, a mug of coffee cooling at my side, two dead cigarettes already in the ashtray. A tiny thump of a hangover persisted through the caffeine, less from the Merlot than from the lingering feeling that I'd not only fucked Woody the night before, I'd *screwed* him.

"I had an idea," he said.

"As long as it's not about therapy," I said, "I'm game."

"Have you done an Internet search for Danny Ficchino?"

That I hadn't wasn't surprising. I'd been a slow starter in the wired world, the last of all my friends to get an e-mail account. I was trekking to the library to do research when everyone else was swearing by search engines. This wasn't the smartest attitude for a radio producer to take. True, I often found sources on library databases that didn't quickly appear when using the 'net. But when I finally got screamed at by an executive producer for taking too long to put together a list of possible interviewees for a deadline-driven project, I learned that I needed to pick up the pace.

At home, I was still using a modem to connect. Woody had a T1 line at work, which was about a zillion times faster. "I'll do it for you," he was saying. "I'll try PeopleSearch."

"Search, people! Search!" I commanded, listening to his keyboard clacking.

In an instant, he had results: nothing under *Dan* or *Daniel* or *Danny Ficchino*, but almost thirty variations of *Dean Foster*. He forwarded the page to me, and when we got off the phone I looked it over.

Some of the names were clearly wrong—*Roderick Dean Foster, Dean Smith-Foster*—and I eliminated those immediately. Any listing with a middle name or initial—*Dean Thomas Foster, Dean M. Foster*—I cut as well; I figured since *Dean Foster* was an alias, it was unlikely that Danny would have made up a middle name. That left about eighteen to consider. Of those, five were in California, including three in Los Angeles and a couple in towns not far from San Francisco. I stared at the screen, at all the possible Deans. I debated whether or not to make phone calls first or send each one an e-mail. Both choices seemed presumptuous, invasive—somewhere between junk mail and stalking. I could mention my professional credentials, the possibility of a public-radio story, but how would I back that up? I couldn't even convince Brady that this was anything but personal.

All but two of the entries had street addresses. That seemed best: I'd send a letter, a good old-fashioned winds-up-in-your-mailbox letter. Time wasn't pressing; in the interest of not scaring him off, I could wait.

I jammed some of Anton's pot into my pipe and spent the afternoon composing letters:

> Dear Mr. Foster:
>
> Forgive me for intruding, but I tracked your address down through the Internet and was hoping you might be the same Dean Foster who grew up on the West Side of Manhattan under the name "Danny Ficchino," departed for California in 1960, and was once a friend of my father, Edward "Rusty" Garner. If you are not, please disregard

this request. If you are the person I think you might be, I would like to speak with you.

Sadly, my father recently passed away after a long illness, and I uncovered your name and photo in his belongings. I understand that, owing to circumstances which I know next to nothing about, you have become estranged from the family, including your sister-in-law, who is my aunt, Katie Ficchino. I am writing to you not only to share the news of my father's passing but to see about reestablishing contact. I have only the best intentions at heart. If you are interested, please contact me.

Very truly yours,
Jamie Garner

. . . which decomposed as the morning progressed and I got more and more stoned . . .

Dear Dean:

I have a hunch that you might be someone I'm trying to track down—Danny Ficchino. You were once my father's friend, and your brother was married to my aunt, but for some reason, which no one will tell me, you dropped out of everyone's life. This past month, my father, Teddy Garner, died, and I've taken it upon myself to piece together some of the missing links of his past. That seems to include you, Dean. Are you interested? I sure hope so, because even though all of this stuff took place forty years ago, it's never too late to mend a fence. Don't you agree?

Your sort-of nephew,
Jamie Garner

. . . until at last I was typing out the true, fucked-up heart of the matter:

Hey Danny Ficchino:

Yeah, you read that right. I know who you are, and I know you've been hiding from your relatives for a long, long time. I don't know why, but I plan on finding out, so why not go right to the horse's mouth? Who am I? I'm Teddy Garner's son, all grown up and homosexual, which is a detail that's only important because what I really want to know is if you and my father had some kind of teenage jack-off buddy thing going on way back when. And the reason I want to know is because he turned out to be a homophobic prick, and drove me away from him, which I find kind of interesting given the bisexual porn hidden in his bedroom. Maybe I'm a pervert, but that's just the way my mind works.

By the way, Teddy is dead. So I'm the closest you can get to him now. They say I kind of look like him, though that's debatable.

One more thing: you were white-hot when you were young. I'd have sucked your dick, for sure.

Cheers,
Jamie

I didn't print any of these out. I didn't send anything. I couldn't. Not yet.

Anton was sliding the knife set across the glass counter, the blades gleaming, the handles buffed and creamy, the velvet brushed clean. "A thing of beauty," he marveled, as if he had no idea how these shining objects had wound up in his shop.

I liked witnessing this side of Anton, the proud tradesman emerging from beneath the pot-addled painter and the paranoid drug dealer. I plopped down sixty bucks, more than I'd ever given him at once—for knives, that is—and said, "Better than new."

As I turned to leave, Anton said, "Hold on." He disappeared into the back room, returning with a newspaper clipping in hand. "The lady painter. Ray Gladwell. I knew the name was familiar." He handed me the clipping, a review from a gallery show, dated about a year previous. There she was: a short, curvy woman with cropped, salt-and-pepper hair, wearing a dark turtleneck sweater and an ornate, metal necklace. Her smile told you she'd be the easiest person in the world to talk to.

"We were both in a show at the Berkeley Gallery, in '68 or '69," Anton said.

The article reviewed a show of abstract landscapes at a gallery near Union Square. *A transformer of reality into dream, Ray Gladwell is a tireless career artist, one of the last of the California-landscape generation receiving much deserved recognition.* Sixty-five and finally getting her due—no wonder she was smiling (though she could just as easily have bitterness scarred across her face). The text said she lived on the Peninsula, south of the city. Assuming she hadn't died in the past year, she was still alive, this woman who'd been my father's—what? Lover? Girlfriend? *Old lady*? What would they have called it in 1960?

"Do you remember her at all?" I asked Anton.

"I remember thinking she painted like a man."

I pulled from my father's San Francisco box the break-up letter Ray had written to him, the one I'd first skimmed in New Jersey. I hadn't noticed before how fragile the paper felt. The creases where it had been folded were splitting and frayed.

> Dear Teddy,
>
> This smothering fog is terrible for one's state of mind. Outside it presses down, and inside I sit wishing I wasn't so poor with words so that I might explain myself, your "magic girl" with too many tricks up her sleeve.
>
> I believe in the freedom of the individual, whether that means I paint the way I wish, or I take a spin out of Mountain View without telling my husband (who sits in the next room, wielding his influence even though you never see him), or I spend the party with Kelsey without worrying that you've shown up. And again I remind you, you weren't supposed to be there. Can't you understand how that makes a difference? I am not as cold as you'd have me be.
>
> Above all, this is about my life as the "second sex." For a woman, love and dependence are the same thing, and so I don't let myself get too far in love. You say you understand, but if you did, you would not have threatened me.
>
> When you ran out, I called after you, but I'm glad you didn't come back. <u>Don't</u> come back, Teddy. I can't change my situation, and you have a lot of living to do. You'd do

> well to forget my troubles, and cherish our good memories and tender nights, and years later you'll look back on this and I won't seem so monstrous.
>
> If you see me at a party, smile and walk by. Smile for the past, and walk away for your future.
>
> You are a fine young man.

She had signed it "Ray Gladwell," as if there could be any other Ray in his life. Her handwriting was curvaceous, penmanship-perfect; she was a lady of the 1950s, schooled to handwrite notes with soothing legibility. How, then, did she wind up as a self-reliant adulteress, running around without explanation, sneaking past her husband, all in the name of freedom?

I wondered, too, about the threat she'd referred to. Here, at last, was a hint of Teddy as I knew him—bark worse than bite, but what a bark! That baritone voice, hard and resonant as steel as it conjured the fear of punishment, the force gathered up under his skin just barely held in check. He'd never raised a hand to me, but he scared me many a time. Ray had felt this, too, forty years ago, though she must have been a match for him: alluring, always in motion, calling the shots. *You are a fine young man.* Such a withering, patronizing thing to say to a lover! She'd broken his heart because it was good for him.

In a desk drawer crammed with unsorted photographs, I found a picture of my father that I'd snapped at the barbecue celebrating AJ's birth. Dad stands in the backyard in his silly apron, wielding spatula and tongs, smiling toward me. The last good moment between us. Not a hint of the fateful argument to follow.

I placed the gallery clipping on the desk, next to this photo. Teddy and Ray. His aged face next to hers. Long before my mother, my father had crossed paths with this woman, had followed that winning smile into an illicit affair. Somehow, they'd found places where they could be alone—his apartment, a motel room, perhaps a locked bedroom at a party. They'd seen each other naked. They'd whispered into each other's ears. They'd ignited something tender, and then, soon enough, it ceased.

I didn't know of any woman who'd been with my father except my mother and a lady he dated after she died, who, like my mother, was named Shirley. She'd been at that barbecue, too. This second Shirley had broken things off after a few months. (Later, Deirdre read in the paper that she'd been killed in a car accident—*so surreal,* Dee said. She took Dad to the funeral, but he, already slipping, was mostly just confused by it.) That's all I knew about my father's romantic life. Ray Gladwell might be the last person alive who'd had sex with my father, who'd held his body next to hers, who'd felt him inside of her. The possessor of secret knowledge—if she even remembered that far back.

I knew I had to talk to her. But when I called the gallery and left a voice mail message saying that I needed to get in touch with one of their painters "for an interview," my words emerged in stammers. Cold calls are my downfall; I find it difficult to be precise. One on one, in person, I'm fine. I interview people for a living. I can gauge the temperature of a conversation by facial expressions and body language. But on the phone I'm fumbling in the dark. And here again, I found myself unsure of why I was calling. Was this business or personal?

I was at my computer, transcribing the shampoo-conditioner testimony and, fortuitously, not stoned, when she called back. As soon as I heard the words coming from my mouth—"I'm the son of someone you once knew, Teddy Garner"—I had no doubt that this was personal.

"Yes!" she said. "Yes, I remember Teddy Garner! My God!" She was so enthusiastic, I could hear the exclamation points.

"I didn't know if you would. It's been forty years."

"Forty years! Oh, jeez, I'm a *fossil.*" Her laugh was gleeful, but tinged with nervous energy. "How is he? Where is he?"

So then I had to break the news, and that seemed to upset her, and it left me feeling cruel. Here I'd just brought back a youthful memory, and then smack, down came the guillotine. I apologized, and told her a little bit about the circumstances: the "Alzheimer's," my grandmother taking care of him, his death in early January. I heard shame undulate beneath my words, and I wondered if Ray Gladwell could figure out from my description that I'd stayed away during his illness.

"So you found me through the gallery," she said.

"I had your name."

"Oh, you are sweet. He mentioned me?"

I made a sound of agreement. She asked me where he'd lived, what had happened to my mother, were there other children? She asked me if I was married, and I answered, "Well, I'm gay, but I'm seriously involved," and she actually said, "Oh, wonderful!" which just about melted my heart.

"So you're on the Peninsula?" I asked.

"Yes, in Mountain View." Just like in the letter. Was she still married to the same man, all these years later?

"That's a lovely place," I said, not having any idea if it was. "Aren't some of the older buildings rather charming?"

"The town center is quite nice. They're fixing it up. But you still can't find parking!" She had returned to finishing off her sentences with that lively burst of laughter.

"You know, I'm heading down there this week," I said, the lie forming easily. "For work. Maybe I could visit you."

"Well, sure! Great!"

I said I'd be taking the train, she offered to pick me up, and easy as that, we had a date. Her voice hung around long after the conversation, attaching itself to the newspaper photo of her, coalescing into a presence, a hologram. I felt elated, impatient to meet this artistic old lady with the checkered history who laughed so easily and thought my gay relationship was *wonderful.* I sent an e-mail to Woody that said, "I think she's going to turn out to be my fairy godmother."

"Jamie? It's Deirdre."

"Oh, hi. What's going on?" My voice casual, as if we'd been in regular contact lately, though this was the first attempt either of us had made since I got back. I'd thought about calling her many times. The idea would strike, and I'd immediately determine why the timing was bad: I'm too tired, I'm too frazzled, I'm too stoned, she's probably not home, she's probably making dinner, I'm sure she's already in bed, I'm just not in the mood, I just can't deal with her this very second.

"I need to talk to you about some stuff—" Behind her I heard AJ whining for her attention. "Okay, honey just a minute," she said to him.

"I've been meaning to call you, too," I said.

"Okay, AJ, that's it! This is a time-out. Mommy's having a grown-up call." She must have cupped the phone because the sounds grew muted. Then she was back, or rather AJ was back, saying hello and asking when I was coming for a visit and did I know his half-birthday was coming up, which meant he was six months from being six years old? I heard myself telling him maybe I'd come to his sixth-birthday party, and he asked me if I'd bring him a special present from California.

"Now you've got his hopes up," Deirdre said, then took a deep breath. "Nana fell. She was cleaning out Dad's closet and slipped off the chair. She has a fractured ankle. Practically a break."

"Oh, no. Is she in the hospital?"

"She's here, at my place, on the couch." She lowered her voice to a conspiratorial hush. "We told her about the senior housing, and she got really pissed off at us."

"Meaning what?" I thought about Nana's brand of *pissed off,* the frosty silence, the locked posture, the averted eyes.

"She keeps saying she wants to go back to Ireland."

"Where families take care of each other."

"Plus, the home we wanted to put her in won't take her because she's not perambulatory."

"That's no way to talk about your grandmother."

I regretted the lame joke as soon as she spoke again. Her voice, so tense throughout the conversation, seemed to crack open, raw and throaty. "I swear, Jamie, it's like Dad all over again. Having this older person dependent on me. I need a break."

I'd never heard her complain like this, and it threw me into silence. She told me how the past ten days had been all struggle. Carly Fazio's company had offered her a job right before Nana's accident; now Dee was worried that they wouldn't hold it for her. AJ had been getting picked on by some older kids in school and was *acting out* at home. On top of that there had been some legal trouble brewing with one of Dad's neighbors. A year before, a tree from Dad's property, that old oak I'd noticed missing, had fallen into the street. This woman swerved to miss it and wrecked her car. Andy had written her a check to cover the repair bill, but now she'd brought a lawsuit for further medical expenses plus emotional damages.

"Who is this woman? Do I know her?"

"No, someone new. Andy calls her the Angry White Lady."

We chuckled together about that (who knew Average Andy had a sense of humor?), and before the conversation ended she apologized for *dumping on me*. I told her I didn't mind. I had considered bringing up the money I was owed, but at the moment, it seemed crass to do anything besides listen. She'd given me the benefit of her confidence, which was rare enough not to risk spoiling.

The afternoon mail delivery brought a Visa statement: an eight-hundred-dollar plane ticket, a seventy-dollar car-service to Newark, a two-hundred-fifty-dollar cash advance (pot, groceries, knives), plus a thirty-nine-dollar *overlimit fee*. My noble silence on the phone suddenly seemed foolish.

6

The day I went to visit Ray was drenched in rain—fat, wet drops smacking my skin like pellets. I rode along a new streetcar line to the train station. The last time I was in this part of the city, this was a warehouse district; I would ride my bike to the No Nothing Cinema, a little collective on Berry Street where you could eat grilled sausages for free in the concrete yard and watch strange short films with people who'd been living this scene for thirty years. Now a gargantuan baseball stadium, ringed by sleek streetlights, had replaced the demolished warehouses. Between the rail tracks and a new six-lane boulevard, Berry Street had been obliterated. I felt like I was visiting another city.

The train station was mostly empty. Everyone who didn't look homeless seemed to be a tourist, a student, or a retiree—the rare folks without jobs in boomtime San Francisco. With my dry-cleaned overcoat, wool trousers ironed just for the occasion and a to-go cup of coffee clutched in my fist, I might have been heading for a job interview. In my shoulder bag I'd stowed my tape recorder, something I hadn't prepared Ray for.

I read the *New York Times* on the train—ten years away from the East Coast and I still relied on it for news—distracting myself with the day's headlines: the latest polls predicting the outcome of the Super Tuesday primaries; the escalating body count from ethnic warfare raging through a half-dozen central African nations; the stock prices that kept rising, rising, rising. My eyes looked up to catch images blurring grayly out the window: ashy men with their hoods up and heads down, lumbering along the sidewalk. Cargo trucks disrupting the traffic flow with wide left turns. Parking lots and squat houses bordering the tracks. I tried to imagine all of it gone or, rather, not yet here.

Instead of endless sprawl south to San Jose, the view filled up with green orchards, two-lane state roads, intermittent small-town junctions. Ray Gladwell must have traveled this route, her foot on the gas, racing from her husband to the world of parties and multiple lovers she'd found in San Francisco.

I picked her out of the crowd on the platform. Her face brightened when I waved—open smile, plump cheekbones, laugh lines around her eyes. A young old face. She wore a black jacket with bright scarlet piping, a vaguely Chinese design; chunky jewelry hung from her neck as in the news photo. She extended a rough-textured hand toward me, a painter's hand. She was laughing and talking at once as she led me to an SUV where a man her age sat waiting behind the wheel. She introduced him as David Stroh, "like the beer," he said.

"Stroh's beer. Been a long time since I thought about that." I spoke heartily, man-to-man. "My dad used to drink it."

"No relation," he said. "I mean to the beer, not your dad." All three of us laughed a bit too hard. He was about her age. He might have been her husband, or lover, or maybe just a friend with wheels. Was mentioning my father a faux pas? This man might be uncomfortable meeting with the son of one of Ray's old beaus. He started the engine and off we went through the streets, small-talking about the rain and the traffic. I thanked Ray for agreeing to meet me, at which point she sputtered, "How could I refuse? I mean, gee, Teddy Garner's son."

She turned and stared, her eyes just inches from mine. I held still, letting her search my face for traces of him, an offering I felt I owed her. When at last she turned away—I was blushing self-consciously—her gaze drifted out through the rain-slaked windshield, as if she was waiting for the past to come into view amidst the wet, silvery air. I half expected us to blur out of focus and reemerge in this same landscape forty years earlier—a corny movie transition, after which actors playing the young Ray and the young Teddy would materialize in our places.

David drove carefully through the slick streets, guiding us from the downtown shops and restaurants into rolling foothills. The rooftops of two-story houses poked out from thick, heavy greenery. After fifteen minutes of chitchat, Ray pointed out the window, newly animated. "Oh, there—that place!" A small cottage, set back from the street by a radiant, well-tended lawn, caught my eye, then slid quickly from view. "They were the only other folks here in the fifties. It was them and us.

The daughter still lives there. Her mother was Diana—she used to watch the kids for me. Oh, man, it was the boonies then!"

David let us out at the end of a cul-de-sac, announcing, "Your castle, my lady." Ray and I dashed through the steady downpour toward a high wooden fence with a simple latch on the gate. The front yard was dense with vegetation: tall bushes, blossoming trees, flower beds quivering under the rainfall. I counted three buildings—a house, a garage and a side cottage that would turn out to be Ray's studio. Having lived in apartment buildings for so many years, I quickly felt the difference of entering an enclosed yard, the place where privacy began and the nosy world was held at bay.

Ray directed me toward the studio, a newish, thirty-foot-square building with a high ceiling and a skylight. I stood on a pale linoleum floor and peeled off my damp coat, taking in the artwork resting everywhere. To the left, small paintings were stored sideways, like garments on a rack. To the right, large canvases, some taller than me, leaned at angles, as if buttressing the wall. Throughout the room, easels displayed either abstract landscapes—pleasing swirls of color coalescing into sky, water, land—or moody portraits of women.

One large canvas dominated. On it, a woman with short, graying hair like Ray's, but eyes much more frightened, stared out from behind a cup of coffee. Her blouse hung open, revealing drooping breasts. The effect was unsettling, the kind of sight you're trained to look away from. I had a quick memory of my mother in her hospital bed the afternoon when I slid my arms under her back, turning her onto her side, and her gown fell open, revealing her flesh to me. The side of a breast, a plane of ass, a swatch of pubic hair—parts of her I'd gazed upon only at the beginning of my life and at the end of hers. I looked away from the painting, half expecting to see my mother herself approaching. But no, just Ray, crossing the room after turning up the thermostat, and I saw that she looked nothing like my mother. Her face was round where Mom's had been angular; fleshy rather than sharp-boned.

"My entire apartment could fit in here," I said. "I'm jealous."

"Oh, ho, ho," she said. "Don't be. You don't know the sheer hell I went through to get it." She might have been hinting at real misfortune, but her sentence still ended with a disarmingly light chuckle.

A very wet David emerged through a back door carrying a teapot and three mugs on a tray. I prepared a cup for myself and was taking a seat when Ray turned around and flapped her hand at him. "Okay, shoo. This isn't for you."

He had paused midway between standing and sitting, and was now looking at me earnestly. "I was around back then. I could tell you stories."

"No, no, David. You didn't know Teddy," Ray insisted, her expression resolute, and David quickly left as he'd entered. I averted my eyes from his glumly retreating figure.

Ray was all brightness. "Look at you! I see him in you. It's not quite exact, but it's there. The lightness of your eyes. Something in your jaw."

"I'm not so Irish as he is—was," I said. "I mean, I have a lot of my mother. She was German."

"I'm German, too. German-Jewish. My parents got out before the Nazis."

"Is Ray your given name?"

"Rachel. But for a woman painting in the sixties, you needed a man's name. One time I won an award and they were all set to present it to Mr. Ray Gladwell. When I walked up there, oh, boy. Surprise!"

"And Gladwell?"

"That was my first husband. The monster." Her smile left for a moment; as she paused tentatively above the brim of her mug, I watched something grave pass over her. "I had a brief second marriage, too. David and I aren't. We're common-law, I suppose. Is thirteen years enough for common-law?"

"It's longer than most marriages these days."

"After two husbands I said, why bother? Just live together, don't worry about the legal bs. Marriage isn't for women anyway. It's a man's institution."

"Too bad we aren't better at it," I said, punctuating with a nervous titter of my own. The fast familiarity between us was unsettling. I felt a touch of altitude sickness at how quickly I'd been lifted into the flow of her biography. "Ray, I'm not sure if it's okay, but I brought a tape recorder. I work in radio, so I tend to tape everything. You never know when something might—" I didn't finish the sentence because a look of surprise, even consternation, had settled upon her face.

"I just hate the sound of my voice. It's like a little girl's. They did some videotaping at a museum once, and oh, I can't watch it at all."

"This would mostly be for me. You know, family history."

She gave me a go-ahead wave. I fished the machine out of my bag and fussed with loading the tape. I double-checked the batteries; they sprung out of their narrow chamber and tumbled onto the table. When I looked up at Ray, I saw a blind-date smile, the kind you adopt when you realize your suave suitor is counting his cash, ready to announce he can't cover the bill.

Perhaps I'm exaggerating. When I listened to the tape later, she didn't sound dubious at all. She didn't sound like a little girl, either, for all her worries. I liked her voice; it had an unguarded quality; the romance of youth was still able to work its magic on her.

"What do you want to know?" she asked.

"Do you remember when you met my father? Can you start there?"

"Well, let me think. Sure I remember. Not exactly everything. It was a long time ago. But I remember seeing him across the room at a party—"

> —across the room at a party. I would come up to the city and go to parties with the artists I was meeting. They'd have wine and grass—grass was the new thing back then. The painters would get it from the musicians. And, oh, the music would be so exciting. Bebop and blues, which you never heard on the radio. The radio was all Top Forty, which was what the teenagers liked. And I remember your father because he looked like a teenager.
>
> *He was only twenty. That's practically a teenager.*
>
> So young! We were all so young, but Teddy seemed younger. He had the hairstyle with the greasy kid stuff in it.
>
> *I can picture it. I found a photo of him like that. But it's hard to picture the rest of it—pot smoking, parties, all that. He spent his whole life at a desk job.*
>
> I can still see my first impression of him, with that hair and a red jacket, like James Dean. So out of place! The men all wore beards, and the women—oh, back then it would have been black stockings and skirts above the knee, not yet miniskirts but shorter than the regular girls. I made a point

of saying hello to Teddy. I always said, make people feel comfortable. Because the artists didn't always. Once they knew you, everyone was so wonderful. When you first showed up, there was more of a "Who is that guy? Is he hip? Does he *get it?*"

Do you mind me asking how old you were at the time?

Gosh, I must have been twenty-five. Well, yes, because I had the two children already, a girl and a boy. I started young. I was here in this house, with my husband, who was a bastard. Really just a mean, mean SOB. And I would go to the city to get away from him and be with the artists. Here, I can show you—

She led me to the wall and pointed to a couple of framed, black-and-white photographs. The first was a posed portrait, taken outdoors. A very young Ray in a cinch-waist dress and pumps. Sculpted waves of hair bubbled softly around her face—the kind of frozen, bounce-free 'do only achieved under a hot-air dryer at a beauty parlor. She explained that it was taken in New York, where she and *the SOB* met and were married. I guess she couldn't have been more than twenty, but as I often find when looking at old photographs, in which the formal styles of the times seem to age their subjects, I felt like I was looking at someone older than me. The second photo, which she dated from the mid-sixties, was more casual. She stood indoors against a bare wall wearing hip-hugging pants and a poncho. Her hair had grown to below her shoulders, frizzy. The light-hearted look in her eyes indicated a younger spirit.

I can't believe you have two kids here. You're one hip-lookin' mama.

It was the city, it just fed my soul. I was hanging out with the group on Fillmore—the building full of artists? It's sort of legendary now. What was the number? 22-something. Or 23- . . . It'll come to me.

Do you remember the cross street?

There was a café there, where we used to get Irish coffee. They had the most wonderful stuff hanging everywhere—old watering cans and teapots and foreign film posters. Nothing you'd expect. Everything was creative. There was a curtain of spoons across the doorway. People were making their own jewelry. And some of the gay men were the most wonderful. I became known as someone you could dress up. A lot of my clothes were very boring, like in that picture, because he was so strict about what I wore, right down to the hat on my head. My evil ex. But the queens—they would say, "Miss Ray, we're going to make you into an Egyptian Princess." They did me as Nefertiti once.

So, the people you became friends with—did they know your situation at home?

Oh, yes. It was common knowledge. Jane would say, "Come on, Ray, leave him," but you know the expression, "Don't jump unless you have a place to land." I didn't even have a checking account. He was so controlling.

Would that be Jane Chase?

Yes, a very well-known painter. She was one of the main women on the scene at the time. She had parties—you'd wonder whether or not you could drink from the glasses for fear of hepatitis. We hated the stereotype of the dirty beatnik, but there we were, drinking from dirty glasses.

I imagine it was so different from your life at home, where you had to do everything just so.

I got a car, and every chance I got I drove into the city. I would drive on no gas, just to go, driving on fumes. The first few times it was pure desperation. I remember thinking I could drive my car into an abutment and end it all. Not to be melodramatic, because I survived—but that's why I say the city literally saved my life. It was Oz to me. By '65 it was really rolling. Everybody wanted to be a painter.

So by '65 you weren't with your husband?

I was with him all through the sixties. He was the breadwinner, and he was an attorney, so I knew he'd take the children away. There were days, when—oh, I'll spare you the sob story. He didn't want me to paint, even though I was a painter when he met me. Well, an art student. In New York.

But—I don't understand—how did you manage to get away to the city?

Remember the house I pointed to? Diana would watch the kids—though I don't think she approved of me. She was another lawyer's wife. One of those women, they concentrate on controlling their family, and their big thing is food. They win their kids over by stuffing them. Always something in the oven.

Wow. I never thought of it like that.

It's true. Today they don't use baked goods, but they stuff their kids with candy and junk. Oh, don't get me started. What was I saying?

Diana—

I'd just make up stories—a doctor's appointment—and I'd take off for the day. I'd go to museums. I'd walk into a gallery and talk to strangers. That's how I started to meet people. There's a saying, "Better to smother an infant in its crib than to stifle artistic desires." Something like that. It's very true.

So, I guess what I'm wondering, was my dad like an escape from your husband?

At this point the phone rang, and Ray sprang up, saying, "Hold that thought." I stopped the tape while she spoke to her gallery, which was calling with news that the Santa Cruz Museum of Art wanted one of her landscapes—"my bread and butter paintings," she said, when she got off the phone. With a gesture to the woman drinking coffee, she added, "No one wants the meaningful ones." She called these her *quasi-self-portraits*, pointing out a few that she did after her divorce from *the dictator,* which had a liberated feeling to them—one showed a woman boarding a ship, having abandoned a large steamer trunk on the dock. Next was a round of paintings done after marriage number two came apart (she'd married *someone from the scene* on the heels of the first divorce). Moody, middle-aged women in the garish palette of a 1970s kitchen—avocado, goldenrod, sienna—parked on bar stools or surrounded by dressing-room mirrors, squeezing their fleshy figures into once-sexy outfits. These portraits struck me as didactic, but Ray said she wanted her viewers "to get every sentence of the message."

I thought about Mom and Dad in the seventies, far away from singles bars and party outfits, driving my sister to dance class, driving me along my newspaper delivery route. This life of quiet routine had seemed to me, growing up, a given. Fated. But now I saw a glimmer of how my father might have taken a different course, not safely and smoothly into the nuclear family but deeper into risk.

Ray caught me staring off into space, and suddenly we were both apologizing, she for *the boring lecture*, and I for *zoning out*. She ushered me back to the table, the tape machine, the RECORD button.

—In the city, I was the new girl. The men liked to flirt with me, and the women took me under their wing and let me paint in their studios. When Teddy came along and wanted to be a painter—to him I was already a painter. He looked up to me. Though he had very different ideas about painting! See, back then you only painted in a studio. And he wanted to set up in the park. This just wasn't the way you did it. The main thing for us was the brushstroke, the action of it, that was what mattered. Not painting pretty park scenes.

And then someone called him a "Sunday Painter."

Oh, my gosh! I remember that.

I read about it, in one of his letters. Here, let me show you.

I retrieved the "Dear Teddy" letter from my bag. Ray looked it over, at first with excitement—"That's my handwriting!"—and then, as she read, with obvious melancholy, morphing into one of her quasi-self-portraits. This was the aspect of reporting I liked least, the way an interview often pushed into emotional territory the interviewee didn't expect. Just the same, I let the tape roll, wondering what I'd do if she got angry, or cried, or if she just stopped talking altogether.

At last, she let out a heavy sigh and began fiddling with the teapot, trying to resuscitate the sodden teabags.

Golly, that brings me back.

I'm sorry—I hope I didn't upset you.

It's not you. It's just—the thing I remember is, I fell for Teddy, but more in a protective way, a sisterly way.

But you were lovers, right?

I don't think we made love more than a couple of times. I mostly remember afternoons in the park, him with his easel and me giving him tips. We'd hold hands and walk together. He didn't talk a lot around other people, but with me he had so much to say. He'd send me letters, care of Jane.

Did you save them? Because I'd love to see them, if you were okay with it.

Well, sure, but don't get your hopes up. That was so long ago, I'd really have to dig. You know, it wasn't a big, passionate thing for me, more like, oh, a heated friendship? Does that make sense?

I've had plenty of heated friendships myself.

Teddy was someone who needed to be taken care of. And how could I do that? With two kids?

That letter makes it sound like he was very jealous.

Yes, and that was not where I was at. If I was having an affair with X, then Y also knew about it, and so did Y's other lover, too. But feelings did get hurt.

I didn't mean to upset you. I've showed up out of the blue, and this is all so long ago. It's just that with my dad dying—see, he and I didn't get along.

I know all about it. I fought with my mother, and my kids fight with me. It's the universal cycle.

But we had the gay thing on top of that. He had so much trouble—

He did? Because I thought—well, I wondered about it.

You wondered about what?

Teddy had gay friends and went to the mixed bars.

He did?

Everyone went to the mixed bars, the queens and the artists and the blacks. What was the famous one? The Black Cat. But Teddy had that friend—they were always together. A gay fellow, though not a queen. More rugged.

Danny? Danny Ficchino?

No, not an Italian.

He might have been called Dean Foster? A friend from New York—

No, not someone from New York. Older than we were. With the hamburger stand. Such a sweetheart, that one.

Don Drebinski?

Yes! Oh, you really are bringing me back! It was Don who introduced us. Don wasn't an artist, but he'd feed the artists for free at his grill. I adored him! We'd tease Teddy, we'd tell him, "Come on, just dig the city." Everything about it—the smells, the colors, the people—it was like going to the Casbah. But Teddy could be kind of tight about things. He was curious, but also kind of stuck.

Did you ever think—

—that my father and Don were sleeping together? was the rest of the question, though it didn't wind up on the tape because the machine malfunctioned. The tape just stopped, though the mic was still picking up sound, sending the needle bobbing. Later, this would leave me devastated, not only for missing the rest of Ray's interview, but because I'd been using this recorder for ten years. This was the day it decided to die.

Ray's answer to my question about my father and Don, as I remember it, was yes, it had crossed her mind, they had been so close. But she also dredged up a memory of my father's fling with another woman, who'd also been older than him, had also been an artist—a poet, perhaps. She said *the times were different, the artists tried everything once, the spirit of the sixties was already in the air*—and so on. In her break-up letter to Teddy, Ray had written *love and dependence are the same thing.* But the San Francisco she spoke of to me was radiating with goodness, innocence, freedom from jealousy. And art, especially art. I wish I had on tape her exact words as she talked about color, about her husband yelling at her while she disappeared into thoughts about peach or cream or yellow, the next vibrant strokes she'd make on a canvas waiting for her in an artist's studio in San Francisco. The city lived in her memory as Oz, where wishes were granted and everything reached out from a glowing horizon, beckoning her forth.

Riding home on the train, I sat across the aisle from a hip-looking guy, younger than me, who never turned off his phone, chain-dialing calls, broadcasting his personal life for all to hear. Cell phones were turning up everywhere lately, not just in the hands of businesspeople on the run, and were for me the most public sign of the new gold rush—a venture-capital-funded mania that had lured a hundred thousand newcomers to the city to get rich quick. Young people these days didn't seem to be creating the next wave of the counterculture. Ray's words still echoing, I wondered, What would the city look like to me, to my friends, four decades from now? Would we talk about love and creation, or money and technology? Even those of us for whom San Francisco had been a haven, a place for art and experimentation, a release from the great big burden of conservative America, even we struggled in the shadow of the city's mythic decades. The Beat Generation, the Flower Children, the Gay Liberationists, they hovered about like older brothers and sisters back from college, reminding you how tame, how lame, your high school parties were.

And then there was another path, the one my father took: looking back in anger. Had his rejection of bohemia happened all at once, a big, loud "No sir, not for me!" followed by a dramatic exit? Or did a series of smaller choices slowly accrete until he was simply on his way home, putting behind him the abandon embraced by Ray? Somewhere in this grid of possibilities lay what I needed to know: why he fled Oz, and why he denounced it. Why he never looked back.

QUEST FOR FATHER

7

Woody insisted that he take me out to dinner that night. "I want to reward you."

"For what?"

"You took a chance, and it paid off." I was still feeling guilty about letting him do anything for me—cheater's guilt, stirring somewhere behind my eyes, weeks after my transgression—but I wanted to see him. To share Ray with him, the conversation, the new questions.

As usual, he worked late—later even than the late he'd anticipated—and I spent the evening in my apartment reading *On the Road*. I was surprised how fast time flew by while I got sucked into Kerouac's never-sitting-still characters and their exuberant proclamations. They all seemed younger than I'd been at that age, and freer than I'd ever been, period. The men, anyway. After my day with Ray I was newly aware of the lot of women amidst the men's club that was mid-century bohemia. Nearly every woman in Kerouac's book is determined to be an obstacle to male friendship, male mobility, and is, sooner or later, denounced as a whore. In this context, Ray's escapes from the boonies to the city seemed to me as risky as a trek across America.

My phone rang after nine. It was Woody, shouting to be heard above a crowd.

"Where are you?"

"Impala." This was the restaurant around the corner, the one with valet parking. Woody said they'd have a table ready for us in ten minutes.

"Let's go somewhere else, please."

"Come on, Jamie. I'm standing at the hostess station. I'm handing her a twenty so we can get seated as soon as you show up."

"You're not."

"I am. But—" His voice fritzed out. The poor connection had a particularly clipped quality to it.

"Are you on a cell phone?" I asked in disbelief.

"Shit! Busted."

"Whose? Yours?"

"Mine. Well, Digitent's, actually. They're paying for it."

"You better put that thing away before I get there. I am not going to be seen at Impala with you on a cell phone."

"No one will see you. We'll hide you in the crowd. Don't argue—come now."

He hung up without saying good-bye. I guess that's one of the perks of having a cell phone. You snap it shut dramatically, no need for formalities when you're saving every minute in your *plan*.

I had scorned Impala from the outside, but I'll admit I was curious. I showed up smoking a cigarette, exhaling a gray streak through the crowd on the sidewalk (cologne, khakis, phone chatter). Inside, the art on the walls was painted to look like a pixilated computer screen: colorful, pleasing and absorbed as quickly as a glossy magazine layout. The hostess wore fashionably slender heels, defiantly inappropriate for a night spent on her feet. I spied Woody at the bar, lording over two enormous pink cocktails and holding his phone—a little silver *Star Trek*-y thing—to his ear. He broke into a smile when I wagged a finger at him. "Please explain to me," I huffed, "why you can talk on that thing in here, but I can't smoke."

"Some public nuisances are more okay than others," he said. "Kiss, please."

The hostess led us three paces to a cramped two-top in the middle of a long row of cramped two-tops. The menu revealed itself to be the latest rage: *comfort food*. Big portions of meatloaf and mashed potatoes, chicken cutlet and roasted carrots, pasta, pasta and more pasta—all stuff you could easily whip up in your own kitchen but probably wouldn't because you were in your twenties and busy spending your new money at a new restaurant. In the eighties, a place catering to urban trendies would have featured a menu full of snobbishly exotic cuisine—foie gras on brioche toast, squab with chanterelle reduction, gnocchi in squid ink. This was the antithesis of that type of fussiness; you were secure in your hipness even though you hadn't strayed very far from the kitchen staples of your formative years. It cost too much, though not too-too much.

"I can't believe we're here," I said. "Aren't we, like, against this place on principle?"

"Order another Cosmopolitan," Woody told me. "You'll feel better. Or should we split a bottle of wine? Or both? I'm paying. Get whatever you want."

"I think what I want is to get out of here," I said.

"Have you ever heard of the phrase *guilty pleasure*?"

Our appetizer was the chef's specialty, something like sliced bread soaked in Minestrone soup, then pan-fried. The waitress had gushed over it—"*It's really popular*"—but basically it was a snack you'd make for yourself as a kid, home alone from school on a sick day.

"Do you think the chef's specialty is whatever's left over from last night?" I asked Woody.

"I like it," he said with his mouth full. "I feel popular just eating it."

"It's way too salty."

"Jamie, if you don't start enjoying yourself, I'm getting on my phone and calling everyone I know."

"Why don't you call everyone *I* know, so one of them can save me from this place?"

He shook his head. "Think of all the self-righteous mileage you'll get out of this later."

"True." I sipped the Cosmo, which was strong and tasty. "Look, I'm sorry. My mind is full of 1960. I'm experiencing culture shock."

I launched into my day, what Ray had revealed to me about my father, about their short-lived affair, and how she'd once thought he could have turned out gay because he had all these gay friends and went to gay bars. I told him how there was no mention of Danny and about the omnipresence of Don Drebinski, who seemed to be my father's link to both the gay world and the Beat scene.

"So now you think he was a fledgling faggot?"

"I don't know. The sex he was having with Ray seemed pretty underwhelming."

"God, this is just like *American Beauty*. The homophobic guy is the secret homosexual. No—how about *The Lost Language of Cranes*? Next you'll find out your dad's been secretly visiting gay porno houses on his lunch break."

My mind flashed quickly on a certain East Village porn palace I'd frequented back in the day—a pattern of shadowy hallways, the air bitter from poppers, the floor sticky. I imagined my father in the blue light of a dirty-video projector. "Yuck. I'm not sure I can go there. It's weird to think about him being sexual, period."

"I got it!" Woody exclaimed in the middle of a gulp of wine. "Maybe Ray's actually a transsexual. She was this guy named Raymond and—"

"There's the small detail of the two children she gave birth to."

"Or maybe he was peddling his ass for money, getting passed around in some sordid beatnik orgy—"

Woody went on, having a tipsy good time "solving" this mystery. But I got caught up in a memory triggered by the word he'd just uttered: *sordid.* In one of the arguments I'd had with my father when I first came out to him, he'd used that word: *I know all about the sordid stuff that goes on in gay bars*. At the time it had sounded like the raving of a sheltered man who got his news from the tabloids.

I related this to Woody, who leaned closer and whispered in a slightly slurry voice, "I'd like to further examine these sordid concepts with you. After this dinner, as a matter of fact."

"You're drunk, cell-phone boy."

"Yes, drunk and sordid."

He was cute when he'd had too much—boyish, corruptible. And indeed, all this what-if speculation, the supposing-this-happened, the sending-myself-back-in-time-as-a-twenty-year-old-on-the-verge-of-sexual-awakening, was starting to fire me up. It was indeed peculiar to be trying to recreate my father's erotic life, but, in truth, I *could* go there—my imagination was stirred. "Teddy" had become a kind of character for me, not my middle-aged father, but someone out of Kerouac, an erotically charged young man from San Francisco past.

Back at my place, Woody oohed and ahhed over the knives but claimed he'd be best served by leaving them with me. "We both know who's the cook in this couple," he said.

Later, after some quick sex in which I managed to keep any of my possibly tainted fluids out of his body, I sat awake in bed with my notebook in my lap. He whimpered in his sleep next to me. In the half-light I watched his eyes flutter under their creamy lids, a vein pulsing rhythmically in his long neck. Blood flowing through him, part of me in there, too. I wrote:

It's strange that my father never met Woody. Woody's probably upstanding enough to have impressed even Teddy. Strange also to take notes about him as he lays next to me unknowing. But I want to remember the details, because it all seems so precious and fleeting, impossible. Why is that? . . . His eyes open. "Are you writing about me?" he asks/ I write. "Yes." "Will you show me one day?" I can't answer.

Woody's phone jolted us awake, its chimey space-age ring like a call from the mothership. Indeed it was the mothership, Digitent, tracking him down because he was late for the mandatory morning meeting. He sat at the foot of the bed pulling up his pants, his back to me before I'd fully come to consciousness. His long, beautiful back in the orange morning light returned me to the night before, the haze of kneeling in front of him, licking between his legs—a reverie curtailed by Woody jumping to his feet, barking, "Why didn't you set your fucking alarm?"

"Why didn't you remind me?"

He was out the door without even a perfunctory kiss.

I e-mailed a few producers I knew around the country, pitching the idea of a story about Ray Gladwell. I used the language of the news clipping Anton had given me: *the last of her generation, deserving some much-delayed recognition,* and so on. *A dynamic woman,* I wrote. *A survivor.*

No one bit, not even Brady, who wrote back: *Maybe you should be thinking TV for this one. Visual art on the radio? Not such a good fit.* Thanks, Brady. Not that I have any TV connections, but thanks. He ended with an invitation to dinner. *Me and Annie want to have you over, find out how you're doing.*

Before I could reply, the phone rang.

I answered it gruffly, as I sometimes do: "I hope this is good news."

"The time is now."

This was, in fact, excellent news. "Hooray! Come rescue me!"

"Name the place."

"I don't know. Pick me up and we'll go somewhere?"

"It's going up to eighty degrees today," he said. "San Francisco's yearly February heat wave."

"Should we go to the beach?"

"Excellent choice."

That was the entire conversation. That was Ian. *The time is now* was our secret code for *Stop everything, come out and play*. Years ago Ian had announced that being his friend meant being available for spontaneous getting-together. At the time I was involved in a semi-steady thing with a guy named Stu (squeezed into my failed relationships between Nathan and David), and Ian felt neglected. Ian took action. One afternoon I heard a persistent, alarming tapping on my front door. Ian had gotten into my building and was nailing a homemade sign into the wood:

A MANIFESTO REGARDING THE RIGHTS &
EXPECTATIONS OF FRIENDSHIP
Whereas it is acknowledged that friendships are The Relationships We Choose for Ourselves & are in fact the very things That Make Life Worth Living, & Whereas it has been noticed that friendships often Suffer Ignominy & Neglect when a "lover/boyfriend/some guy you're seeing" comes into the picture, & Whereas it is true that Frequent Booty is a splendid thing, especially if you can make an argument that "love" has entered into the equation,
It is nonetheless noted that Friendships will always be Superior because they A) last longer, B) are marked by greater honesty, & C) are not exclusive. It is hereby Proclaimed that you, Jamie Garner, A) Will Make Time for me, Ian Gillespie, when I request it, & B) that such time Will Not Be Subjected To a Long, Drawn Out Process of "Finding an Opening in Your Schedule." The intention of this proclamation is to demand & encourage the very thing that lovers take away from friends, which is Spontaneity. Both parties will work to not abuse the terms of this proclamation (for example, No interrupting an act of Booty already underway & No interfering in the Making of One's Living), & both will enter into it freely and willingly, with as many Other Friends as possible, the ultimate goal being to
MAKE ADULTHOOD SAFE FOR FRIENDSHIP AGAIN.
NOTE: Ditching friends for lovers is unacceptable behavior according to this Manifesto & will be prosecuted by full-on social shunning.

We both signed it, and it cemented us. Our cue had developed over the years. One of us would place a call beginning "The time is now," and the other one would be required to drop everything and name the meeting place. "The time is now" had led to some of the best times we'd ever had—helmetless motorcycle rides along the coast, all-night problem solving over greasy diner food, life-altering hallucinogenic episodes—and also some of the worst. We hit a rough spot when I first started seeing Woody, leading to an episode of *full-on social shunning* that made me believe, for about two weeks, that Ian might never talk to me again. But Woody solved the problem by marching over to Ian's apartment and hand delivering a proclamation of his own, "The Noncompetitive Clause Between Boyfriends and Best Friends," which declared that the role of friendship was to *subvert the pressures of being a grown-up,* therefore making someone feel shitty about his new boyfriend was *counterrevolutionary*. Ian was so impressed by Woody's act—Ian and Woody share this in common, a love of the grand gesture—that the air was immediately cleared, and we'd all been living happily ever after since. Well, sort of. Ian's still kind of jealous, which is what it all comes down to, but even he understands that frequent booty has its privileges.

I hadn't spent any time with Ian since the funeral. For all the grandeur of the Manifesto we had the kind of relationship in which a month could go by without even a phone call. Then we'd get in touch and be inseparable for days on end. Ian had a lot of time on his hands these days. Eight months earlier, his motorcycle, parked downtown, was knocked over by a Porsche backing out of the adjacent spot. Ian witnessed the hit and ran to the corner, where the Porsche was stopped at a light; he leaned into the driver's open window to confront him. When the light turned green, the driver hit the gas and took off, and Ian, his elbow crooked inside the car, was dragged a block and a half. He wound up with a concussion and a broken leg—and, a few months later, a big, fat settlement from the driver, who turned out to be a newly wealthy software engineer. Ian immediately quit his bartending job and began teaching himself, from scratch, all there was to know about web design.

Since then he'd been obsessed with creating a webzine, which was just him and the people he knew uploading whatever they were interested in—highly opinionated essays about idiosyncratic topics and surreal cartoons that made you laugh even if you didn't get the humor.

The site, called *Better Example*, was guided by the foundation myth Ian put forth: One day, he was Windexing dead bugs from his motorcycle headlight when the face of Kurt Cobain appeared in the glass and commanded, "Set a better example than I did." Ian, after some reflection, decided this meant A) don't get addicted to heroin, B) don't commit suicide, C) don't get mental if people like your art. (Everything in life was indicated by *A, B, and C* for Ian.) For years, he'd been the epitome of a frustrated artist; he made stuff all the time but never showed it to anyone and often destroyed it. His new productivity had inspired the rest of us. Colleen had created a paper-doll project that let visitors to the site dress naked celebrities in costumes she'd designed. I'd recorded a batch of sound effects, and Brady had digitized them for downloading. Ian himself had written a long, nonsensical play populated by Tolkien-esque fantasy creatures and the ghosts of dead gay porn stars. I think it was nonsensical; it might have been a brilliant satire. That was Ian.

He plowed into my apartment like a bull, heavy footsteps, downward gaze, dark head of hair leading him forward. Ian was Black Irish, his family from the north. He had what he called a peasant's body: short and thick, with wide, rounded shoulders and a strong chest. He wore a black motorcycle jacket and black boots and jeans, and carried his helmet in one hand. "They're tearing down the building across the street," he said.

"I cheated on Woody," I replied, handing him an already-packed bowl.

A corollary of the Spontaneity Principle: small talk was not required. Pot usually was.

He stopped in his tracks. "Wow. Okay, you first."

"That's so hot," he kept saying as I related the story. I wasn't surprised that he found Rick enticing. For all of Ian's adamant individuality his lust was often triggered by the blandest signifiers: baseball caps, hiking shoes, neutral-toned cotton clothing. For weeks I'd borne my infidelity like a personal cross, so it was a relief, and surprisingly uplifting, to relive it through Ian's giddy reaction. Out of context, without morality attached, it was, simply, a quick orgasm with a stranger in a men's room. It was *hot*.

We'd moved into the living room and sat ourselves down on the floor, passing the pipe back and forth. "You didn't tell Woody, did you?" Ian asked.

"I've been torturing myself about it. What if this guy was positive?"

"If cock-sucking was a risk factor we'd all have died a long time ago."

"That's sort of where I wound up."

"You're queer. Screwing around is your birthright."

"*Honesty is the best policy,*" I countered.

"There's far too much honesty these days. This damn culture of confession we live in. It's just a lot of behavior control."

I threw on a shanty Irish accent. "You don't understand the healing power of confession, Mr. Gillespie. You're a bloody atheist."

"Just deal with your fucking Catholic guilt and leave Woody out of it. Why would you tell him something that hurt his feelings? It's a no-brainer."

The matter was settled as far as he was concerned—*no-brainer* being Ian's sign that he's about to dismiss the topic at hand—but I wasn't quite done. "Woody told me he helped you with a computer crash while I was gone. Now you're encouraging me to cheat on him."

"I'm not encouraging—oh, enough already." He shook his head, and leaned in closer. "Listen—last night I picked up this kid on my motorcycle, brought him back to my garage, bent him over the seat and ate his ass for an hour."

Taking advice from Ian about relationships was dangerous—ludicrous, even—because he'd never been in one that lasted. Temperamentally, he was a member of an older generation, the Stonewall radical. Liberation *was* his birthright, and nothing was a more concrete example of this than multiple sex partners. He'd found most of his friends through sex. Including me.

We met the first year I was in San Francisco. I sometimes forgot that it had started as a fumbly sexual pickup at the Detour, a dark bar with a chain-link fence running down the middle, once a reliable place to find sex with interesting guys. We had gabbed about music, both of us way into *grunge* back then, and I'd found him sexy. When he asked me to go home with him I said, "Oh, yeah, absolutely." Ian remembers that, the "absolutely." I don't remember the sex too well—it was mostly jacking off and wrestling—but I remember listening to *Nevermind* afterwards and trying to figure out if the lyrics to "Lounge Act" were actually the coded story of Kurt Cobain's crush on a straight boy: *I've got this friend you see who makes me feel and I wanted more than I could steal.* We commiserated about how hard it was to find friends among *the gays* in San Francisco if you didn't have a gym membership or weren't into house music at certain big Saturday night clubs. In the days that followed I felt a little stab of something mushy and romantic when I thought of him. The next time we saw each other was for a movie, *Poison,* playing in rep at the Red Vic, and we talked about it for hours afterwards. Parts of the film are deliriously erotic—prisoners comparing their scars, reform school boys getting "married" to each other—but our conversation was without sexual tension. Flirtation had given way to intellect.

Sex with Ian still crossed my mind, usually during spontaneous hangout days—both of us stoned, our improvised brotherhood like a private, secret clubhouse—though it wasn't kissing and cocksucking that I wanted. What I wanted didn't exist: a way for two intensely adoring friends to snap into one another, like Lego blocks, and stay there, conjoined. For us, that's what language did. Fastened us together.

We walked out into the glaring afternoon, instantly aware of the rising mercury—one of those unexpected mid-winter heat waves San Francisco did so well. Loading up Ian's motorcycle, I watched glumly as a bulldozer flattened the single-family house that had stood across the street just this morning. The red-shingled bungalow, with its sign under the cornice reading BUILT IN 1897, had survived the big earthquake and fire of 1906 and the quake in '89, just before I moved here, but could not outlast the current economy. That sweet red home would go down in half a day, leveled unceremoniously, a hundred years of history reduced to splinters and dust.

Anton the Straight Blade stood watching, too. Along with the Jordanian guy who ran the corner market and Eleanor, the elderly woman in the apartment across the hall from me (her yappy dog was my alarm clock most mornings), we were the only witnesses to mark the passing. The couple who'd rented the red house for twenty years—a guy who built boats right in the garage and his wife, a tough-talking acupuncturist, an ex-New Yorker, whose clients came and went through the side alley—had departed a few days earlier, relocating farther north, to somewhere rural. I'd given them my condolences before they drove away, but she shushed my sentimentality: "We don't like it here anymore. Too many cars double-parked in our driveway." I didn't know them well—first names only—but I liked them. The *concept* of them. Once a year he opened up his garage to anyone who wanted a look, proudly displaying the beautiful wooden sailing vessels he'd crafted with his own hands.

"What are they gonna build here now?" I asked Anton.

"What do you think?" He pointed to a recently erected four-story building—the tallest on the block, four-room flats starting at a half million dollars. For as long as I'd lived here, that lot had been undeveloped, a fragrant riot of wild fennel, spearmint and night-blooming jasmine.

"He had on a clean Gap sweatshirt," Ian whispered to me. "But underneath he was a dirty little piggy." Back to last night's rimjob. I turned away from the bulldozer, slid Ian's extra helmet over my ears and got on the bike. As we were pulling away it occurred to me through the haze of my high that I'd neglected to tell Anton I'd tracked down Ray Gladwell. Remember to tell him, I told myself, and then forgot again.

We rode out to the Golden Gate Bridge, me hanging on to Ian's waist, *riding bitch* he called it, like he was some sinister Hell's Angel on a Harley.

I pointed to a Chevron station on the corner. "Two twenty-five per gallon!"

"A culturally significant moment," Ian yelled back, something almost gleeful in his voice. "The highest gas prices in U.S. history are in San Francisco. Today! And you're here for it!"

"How are we supposed to revive bohemia when we're living in the most expensive place in the country?" He didn't answer. My Kerouacian fantasies were mocked by everything I saw. The city blurred in swaths at the periphery of my vision, flashes of storefronts, billboards, street signs. Everything appeared impermanent, here today and gone soon enough, like that little red house, like that flower-filled lot, like most of what had stood in 1960, when my father looked upon it.

Like my promise to Woody that I wouldn't cheat on him.

We got to the edge of the city, just below the Golden Gate Bridge, and trudged down steep cliffs lined with untamed vegetation—ice plant, orange poppies, tiny wild irises—following a path worn into the rocks by countless homosexuals seeking this secluded cove. On the beach we sat on a bedsheet, surrounding ourselves with rocks and driftwood, sealing ourselves into a little fortress, a piece of beachfront real estate on a prime cruising day. We sat in our underwear while guys paraded back and forth showing off their classically sculpted gym bodies and, if they were naked, their stylishly trimmed pubic hair. Back and forth they went, shoulders high, abs taut, cocks bobbing, in search of an afternoon dose of happiness. I rubbed in sunscreen, complaining about my softening midsection, my love handles. Ian patted his furry belly and laughed, saying, "I've decided the only way for me to go is to become a bear."

I told him about meeting Ray and about my frustration that I couldn't seem to work a radio program out of it. He wanted to know if I thought Ray's paintings were any good.

"Yeah. You could see the skill even from far away." I told him about the two different styles. "I didn't like the portraits as much, until she referred to the abstract landscapes as her bread-and-butter, which made me feel bourgeois for liking them better. They're probably popular with rich people who buy art to match the furniture."

"Painting is dead," Ian said, exhaling. "It *should* match the furniture. I can't relate to feminist art, that whole message thing."

"She was part of this age of discovery, when people were looking to figure out something new and then share every bit of it with the world."

"I want art to be new, and smart."

"But smart for you means already-got-it-figured-out. The way she described it, they used to sit around talking about their canvases while the paint was still wet, drinking jug wine and passing around joints, staying up all night arguing the meaning of things."

"I don't like you in a beatnik phase," he said forcefully, dragging on a cigarette, dark eyes following a lanky naked prince at the water's edge. "You have to resist this kind of cliché. It's no longer relevant."

"Look, I know Levi's sells khakis using Kerouac's picture in their ads. But still, when you read his actual words—" I pulled *On the Road* out of my backpack.

He grabbed the paperback from me and flipped randomly to a page. "Ugh," he groaned, and then speed-read aloud through the offending passage: Dean and Sal at "a little Frisco nightclub," listening to a jazz musician named Slim playing piano while the crowd chants "Go!" and "Yes!" When Ian got to where Slim busts out the bongos and "goes mad," Ian slapped down the book, saying, "This is completely without irony. You're going to waste a lot of time romanticizing a bunch of drunk, sexually repressed straight guys who thought it was a big deal to write in run-on sentences."

"Well, back then no one was deconstructing their pleasure. They were just—" I grasped for the right phrase. "The life they were living was directly related to what they believed in."

"Listen, Jamie: A, you don't believe in anything."

I laughed; he was going to be such a prick about this that I had no choice.

He gestured with his cigarette like a professor repeating yesterday's lesson to a dim student. "And B, you can't take instruction from people who didn't even have televisions and phones in their houses. It's a new world. You have to keep up." He paused; his eyes had locked in on a piece of jailbait—bare chested, his shirt hanging from the back pocket of his baggy jeans—ambling along the tide line. "Oh my God, look at this kid."

"I'm sorry officer, he told me he was eighteen."

"See how he kind of walks on his toes? God that gets me hard." The boy was nervously checking us out behind our rock-and-driftwood wall. When Ian called out to him, he sped away without another glance. Ian was newly inspired. "Jamie, you should be on newsgroups, in chatrooms. That's where the kids today are creating interesting space. Learning from the past is overrated."

"I'm just trying to learn from my own past." I squashed what was left of my cigarette in the sand. "I think I miss my ideals."

"Ideals? Jesus. You know there are plenty of people living according to their ideals. In Berkeley. In Santa Cruz. In Eugene, Oregon." He paused for effect. "They dress in hempwear and they're self-righteous about recycling and they talk in paranoid generalizations—and you don't even like them, Jamie! If Jack Kerouac were alive today you'd think he was an asshole."

"Okay, you win!" I threw up my hands and cheered, "Fuck Kerouac!"

Ian went walking in one direction, hoping to catch up with the skinny jailbait boy, and I went in the other. My stoned brain fixated on the ocean, waves breaking foamy white upon jutting rocks. The rumbling majesty of the Pacific, the colorful dots of wildflowers on the cliffs above, the craggy saddles running down from the ridge to the waves. I got caught up in the wonderment of living in a city that, for all my complaints, still contained this breathtaking vista within its borders. Then I snapped back to that other vista: the naked and the half naked, all stares and no smiles. Men on the prowl take their burning desire so seriously.

In my bare feet I hiked until the high tide, meeting the cliff side, blocked my passage. I climbed up to a ledge, mostly shielded from view on either side, and shut my eyes, listening to the crashing water and reveling in the salty mist settling on my skin. When I opened them again, a guy in red surf trunks was climbing up the rocks to take his place on the ledge.

He looked at me and then looked away. I did the same: toward him and away. My cock started to get hard, knowing what he was there for, knowing I was being desired. He had broad shoulders and a soft belly—the same early-thirties body as mine, but tanner and hairier. He rubbed his crotch, then moved his hand away to reveal the outline of his dickhead straining against the damp red cloth.

I stood paralyzed, heartbeat quickening, unsure of what to do. I told myself, *Think of Woody,* and flashed back to sucking him off the night before, which had the wrong effect: it amplified the sex-buzz in the air. Red Shorts moved closer, nodded confidently, kept his eyes locked on mine. Oh, how I wanted to pull out my cock, to have this guy show me his, to jack off together in the sun and the spray, let it feel natural. That's what this beach was for, that's why guys went wandering into the cracks and crevices, as I'd done.

Red Shorts is waiting. It's my move. I haven't stepped closer, but I haven't turned away. A vague image of a confession—of me confessing to Woody—forms and dissolves, replaced by an image of me lying to Woody, telling him about my day and leaving out the part about this guy on the rocks, furthering a pattern of deceit that I'd propagated so many times before, with Nathan, Stu, David, others who didn't last long, men I'd always put second to myself. I'm losing my hard-on. There's my salvation: mind over matter. I've been tricked into not doing this by my own better half. I press my lips together, a message of regret for my would-be fuckbuddy, and then I lower my head and walk past him without further eye contact. It's hell not to look back; I want to see him still looking at me, want to be sure I *could have*, even though I didn't. I had probably seemed like a sure bet to him. Now I am just another perplexing homo, transmitting mixed signals. I make a secret wish that he'll find someone else to get him off with a screaming blast, someone without a boyfriend, without *guilt issues*—and I shuffle back to my little fortress, slowly feeling relief wash over me, glad to have outsmarted my own messy desires.

* * *

Actually, that's not what happened.

I didn't lose my hard-on, and I didn't walk away. I moved closer to Red Shorts and grabbed a fistful of his package and nodded. I muttered, "Yeah," and he repeated "Yeah," both of us in pornspeak, and we got into it right there on the rocks, bathing suits tugged down, cocks exposed, faces together, tongues finding each other. The kissing was magnetic, not something you could count on with a stranger. Our breathing grew short and heavy; our hands crawled all over and then we spit into our palms and grabbed each other down below. The intensity built, fast and easy, and then we were coming, one after the other, shooting onto the rocks, watching it blend into the sea spray. *That's* what happened. It didn't take long.

I wish I could say I listened to my better judgment, that after the torment I'd been putting myself through I'd learned a lesson. But I didn't. Maybe it was the pot. Maybe it was all the sex talk with Ian, and Ian's vibe in general, his do-what-you-want attitude. Maybe it was the force of history, my history, all the times over the years I didn't resist, didn't walk away, didn't even consider it. What I'm saying is, maybe I didn't know how to be monogamous, not in the long term. A yearning inside of me, a need to escape, a kind of wanderlust that didn't require a cross-country highway. Sizzling inside my skull like a fuse.

8

I finally found the courage to contact my list of Dean Fosters. For weeks I'd stared at the names, pinned to a corkboard above my desk, putting off the task, fearful that sending my letters would yield nothing more than silence, a deafening nonresponse. What if, having shuffled through the box, talked to Anton, tracked down Ray, what if after all this contemplation, what if there was nothing more? In the end, sending the letters was less a matter of courage than of disgust: I looked at the list one morning and saw a fine film of dust gathered along the black pushpin holding it to the wall, and in that dust I saw time passing, and in that passage the general state of neglect into which my life itself seemed to be settling.

I fired off e-mails or printed my request on paper, whichever was quickest; I sent the formal version of my original letter, not the casual or obnoxious ones. Several replies came back right away: *You've got the wrong guy. Not me, but good luck. Sorry to read of your father's death.*

One man I sent a letter to in North Hollywood actually phoned, leaving a cantankerous voice mail: "I never authorized the Internet to give out my information! I will sue you for invasion of privacy! I suggest you take this very seriously!" A dog was barking ferociously in the background, as if at that very moment the caller was provoking it with a stick, the better to stir fear in me. The paranoia evident in his response was so absurd I transcribed the entire message word for word, bark for bark, and stowed it in a file I had created, growing thicker all the time. I typed a label for the file: QUEST FOR FATHER.

Mostly, I lost track of time. My datebook from those days is mostly empty. I even blew off my volunteer shift for the radio station's pledge drive. Listeners hate pledge drives, though for us behind the scenes, it's like summer camp, with everyone pitching in for the cause. But I couldn't face my old co-workers asking me what I had done lately, what I was working on.

Since my beach tryst, I'd been dissolving. I wanted to understand what I had done, and how I'd let myself do it again, but found no answer that didn't lead back to some essential weakness in my character. *Get motivated!* I wrote in my journal one Tuesday in February, when, most likely, I had stayed on the couch all day flipping channels. Afternoons disappeared in a haze of pot smoke and television, where Jerry and Ricki and Sally Jesse grilled ordinary citizens about their monstrous defects. Talk shows, once topical and serious, had become screaming matches, and I watched them religiously, feeling a spiritual kinship with anyone booed by a studio audience.

Out of this pit erupted an argument. Late on a Thursday night, waiting for Woody's phone call. I had no food in the fridge, hadn't actually prepared to cook, but I felt put on hold, unable to proceed until I'd heard from him about dinner. He finally called from a noisy South of Market club, shouting above the din, "Come hang out, I think you'll be into this." I protested; he insisted; I got on my bike.

The place turned out to be a so-called lounge with the baffling name N Is a Number. A burly guy in a black jacket and a knit cap pulled below his eyebrows demanded eight dollars from me at the door. I found Woody inside under a whir of kaleidoscopic lighting, nestled deep in a plush purple booth, wearing a tight, shiny shirt I'd never seen on him before. He was surrounded by people I didn't know, all of them shouting to be heard. It took him a moment to notice me, but finally he waved and pushed his way out of the booth to plant a kiss on my lips.

"You didn't say there'd be a cover," I said.

"Shit—there wasn't one before ten. I'll buy you a drink. They're very potent."

"What kind of bar charges eight bucks to get in?"

"It's for the DJ. He's good. A total performer." He made a motion with his hands, *scratching*, and a glint of silver flashed between his fingers. His phone.

"It sounds like someone hiccuping on speed."

"Could be, in this place."

"What? Speed?"

"Roger has some. He's looking for someone to do it with."

"Who's Roger? Have you been—?"

"No, no, of course not. Roger's the new gay at work." He nodded to the guy he'd been sitting beside: thick lips suckling a martini glass, a protrusion of cheekbones beneath a glossy broom of dark bangs. "I told you about him, remember? He's only been at Digitent a few weeks and he's already *reading* everyone within an inch of their life. He's a little heartbreaker."

He stared toward Roger with obvious admiration, which alarmed me. Woody never expressed his attraction for anyone but me. "He looks like a whiny British pop star," I growled.

He cocked his head. "Okay, what's wrong?"

"Nothing." Pause. "You didn't call."

"Sorry." Pause. "You didn't call me either."

"I was going to make us dinner. I left you messages."

"You did?" With one swift motion he raised his palm, flipped open his phone and squinted at the display, like a mechanic checking under the hood of a toy car.

"On your work phone," I said.

"Oh, I never check that anymore. It gets so backed up. You should have called the mobile unit."

"I'm not encouraging the mobile unit."

"It's the best way to get in touch with me right now."

"It's obnoxious. It's a social ill."

"I think they used to say that about the telegraph. Like, a hundred years ago."

Even in this pulsating room, the tension between us roared like an engine. I looked away from his eyes, down to his snugly draped torso.

"Where'd you get that shirt?" I asked. "You look sexy."

"Some underwear store in the Castro." He smiled, disarmed by the compliment. "Look, I'm sorry. I should have called. But we can have fun, right?"

"Yeah, sure."

"So let's get you a drink. "

"Okay, but you're buying."

As promised, the drinks were strong, the DJ was talented and the crowd was into it. But I hardly had fun. Squeezed into the booth next to Woody, I listened to him and Roger and their acolytes magnify the absurdities of their workplace. The girl to my left, a glittery, dew-droppy wisp in a child's ski jacket, was already wasted, and she kept bobbling my drink with the back of her hand, which Roger, similarly inebriated, found hilarious. The two of them got up to do a bump in the bathroom, then returned to pull Woody onto the dance floor. As he started to rise, I announced I was leaving. Woody chased me outside, and we were instantly hurling our frustration back and forth—one of those fights that ends with someone shouting "Be that way! Fine! " when nothing's fine at all. I went home without waiting for him.

The fight shook me out of my comfy-couch numbness into an angrier state. Sure, I'd cheated on him—twice—but wasn't he working long hours all the time? Wasn't I always at the mercy of his schedule? Wasn't his job the only thing he could talk about anymore? And since when did he trade in his thrift-store flannels for formfitting clubwear and start hanging out with twenty-five-year-old tweakers?

Woody called in the morning from the sidewalk outside his office. "I don't want to hold onto bad emotions," he said, hollering to be heard above the whooshing commuter traffic on Bryant Street. I imagined the Digitent kids striding past him on their way into the building—them eavesdropping, him exposed—and I felt protectiveness well up. I invited him over for dinner.

I dragged Colleen out of Café Frida that day and had her take me grocery shopping. Off we went to Whole Foods in her late-seventies Plymouth, a splashy boat of a car that she looked perfect driving. Shopping for food usually elevates my spirits, but as I loaded up on organic greens, free-range chicken, Yukon Gold potatoes and fancy cheese, my glum mood alerted Colleen that something was wrong.

"I just need to get some work," I told her, "so I can justify spending all this money on groceries."

"I heard you didn't show up for your pledge-drive shift," she said.

This stopped me in my tracks, mid-aisle. "Brady told you?"

"He said it would have been a good chance to network, get yourself back out there." A gentle but unmistakable reprimand.

"Brady hasn't made any effort to help me lately," I complained. "Now he knows what's best?"

"He said he invited you to dinner and you never responded."

Oh, yeah, that.

I was running out of defensive postures. When she probed a bit more, I crumbled. "Colleen," I told her. "I've been fucking up." Standing in front of the meat counter, across a shopping cart full of pricey, fancy food meant to impress my boyfriend, I confessed about Rick and Red Shorts. In a torrent of detail.

Colleen did what friends are supposed to do in situations like this, she loyally made excuses for me: "You're under a lot of stress. Your father just died. You haven't been able to find work." When I offered a "Yeah, but," she trotted out the catch-all, the umbrella under which every other rationalization takes shelter: "Don't be so hard on yourself." (Ian had offered his own metaphor: "There's no use crying over spilled seed.")

"Just don't do it again," were Colleen's final words, delivered with a theatrical slap on my wrist that couldn't hide the disapproval in her eyes.

I prepped for dinner with the newly sharpened knives. The afternoon flew by as vegetable peels and plastic wrap and chicken fat took over my counter and the oven steamed up my windows. This meal had to be as perfect as the last one I cooked for Woody—it had to be *more perfect*. Poached pears and toasted walnuts for the salad! Fresh-cut flowers for the table! A cheese course! I moved in a frenzy, once again the Red Tornado. And then, at a critical juncture—the potato casserole needed to come out, the chicken needed to go in, the salad was behind schedule—my heedless pace split open: I slipped with the chef's knife while slicing an onion. I watched the blade's sleek silver edge—*Ow*—slide slow and deep—*Holy shit*—into the pad of my—*Fucking hell*— thumb. I watched the skin bubble crimson.

The blood or the food or the stove or the pain—which to deal with first? I roared self-accusations—*Goddamn klutz, why can't you ever learn?*—that morphed into the voice of Ray Gladwell disparaging women who control their loved ones with food. I wrapped a dish towel around my finger and turned off everything, and after I got the wound dressed, wondering if I might need stitches, wondering if there'd be nerve damage, I went out to the sidewalk and stood smoking in front of my building. Across the street a construction crew poured concrete for a new foundation. Far down the block I could see the familiar silhouette of Anton, seated in front of his easel, his arm moving languidly. Though I knew I was too far away to be heard, I called out, waving my bloody bandage. "Excellent work, Anton! Sharper than ever!"

Woody finished cooking for me, salvaging most of the meal while I sat at the table high on wine and painkillers (he'd brought the remnants of a bottle of Vicodin from his medicine cabinet). He had on a wide-collared, button-up shirt that I'd once talked him into buying at a vintage store, a shirt he rarely wore because he'd decided its slim cut and vertical stripes made him look *freakishly tall.* (No matter how dashingly he dressed, how handsome I told him he was, he always saw himself as a beanpole, the guy they called Scarecrow in middle school.) As he worked at the counter, he said, "I think we need a relationship session. We haven't been looking at our process lately, and it's starting to show."

"We had one fight," I said. I didn't want a relationship session, whatever that was. I wanted to put my cheating behind me, not work it through.

"We're not relating," he said. "Don't you feel it? I'm not saying it's all you; it's me, too. There's something going on under the surface."

"Right now, it's the Vicodin."

"That's funny, Jamie."

I waved my bloodied, bandaged thumb in surrender. "Let's go to a hot spring in the country. We can loll about with the naked middle-aged hippies, away from work, away from the city." *Away from faggot temptation.*

"A long weekend will be hard to swing," he said. "Everyone's super tense at work since the fourth-quarter reports. We are totally hemorrhaging money."

"Everything gets planned around your job."

He shook his head, frustrated. "I'm just saying a weekend is more than I can do. But we can still make time to work on our stuff."

He carried the salad to the table. I grabbed him by the wrist, pulled him down to my lap, turned his face to mine and kissed him. I concentrated all my effort into my lips, and finally he melted.

"The food's ready," he said.

"Fuck it," I responded. "Actually, fuck me."

I maneuvered him to my bed, and that's just what we did: He fucked me, tentatively at first, tenderly, and then, at my urging, harder, with as much force as he could muster. I took it like punishment I knew I had coming, and afterwards I think we both felt better.

But I wasn't cured. Yielding to desire had given it the upper hand, and everywhere I went it flaunted its authority. *I want you,* I'd think, the words a growl caught in my throat, as some oblivious guy went about his life in my general vicinity. In one afternoon alone: an hour spent trying to catch a gaze across a row of café tables, imagining this hunk's big hands gripping the sides of my head as I serviced his equally large need; then a stroll along several out-of-the-way blocks, following a boy who'd been in front of me at the post office, watching the sway of his ass inside cargo pants; then an extended chat about the Giants' spring training, all bullshit on my part, with a delivery guy wheeling a dolly into my corner market—beer belly, furry forearms, wedding ring—all the while trying to seduce him telepathically: *Hey man, letting a guy suck your dick doesn't make you gay.*

A few days after dinner with Woody, I was awakened by my apartment's prehistoric door buzzer, an amplified rattle like a lawn mower revving and dying and revving again. The voice on the intercom announced, "FedEx package for Jamie." In the hallway stood a fresh-faced black guy in his formfitting indigo uniform. Maybe I was just disheveled enough that my bed-head looked sexy, or maybe my grubby threads—cutoff sweat shorts and a torn T-shirt—presented some kind of come-on, because it was not my imagination that he was holding his stare a bit too long, his eyes flirtatious. Before I could even compute the particulars—such as, who sent this package? what's in it? and how is it possible that the FedEx guy has already determined, within two seconds of contact, that this is a flirt-friendly environment?—I was nodding back at him, my lips parting, my drowsy voice murmuring, "Sorry, I just got out of bed." It was not my imagination that he was brazenly looking me up and down as he replied, "No problem for me." This is the remarkable fact of being a gay guy in San Francisco: Your next sexual liaison might literally be waiting outside your door.

That morning, I managed not to succumb. I averted my eyes, signed my name with the little electronic pen on his portable data box, and muttered a curt thank-you. He sneaked in a final pass—"This isn't my usual route, hope I see you again"—and I offered a "Yeah, definitely," as I withdrew into my apartment, my pulse thumping.

The return address on the package was Mountain View. I peeled open the flap and unleashed the smell of old paper. Inside was a stack of envelopes marked by my father's unmistakable handwriting. They were addressed to Ray Gladwell, care of a San Francisco post office box. Clipped to the top was a four-color postcard showing one of Ray's landscapes, announcing an upcoming exhibition. I flipped it over.

> Dear Jamey,
>
> Your visit stirred up so many memories. David and I spent an afternoon at my storage space. I was pretty sure we'd dredge up something for you, and sure enough! I started

reading these letters from Teddy, but to be honest it was a bit too painful to travel down memory lane. They're of more use to you than me probably.

Fondly, Ray

PS: Please come to my next gallery show in Frisco!

Ray had organized Teddy's letters for me in chronological order. The earlier ones were handwritten, the latter pounded out on a typewriter.

I'll read them slowly, I thought. I'll savor them, one at a time.

An hour later I'd read them all, without even a cigarette break, sitting on the kitchen floor. I got up and paced through the apartment, letting motion do the work of absorption. I'd slipped into a dangerous dream in which the noise of the everyday world had dropped to a hush as a roaring train sped toward me, building in urgency. The train was my father's voice, on the page, now inside my head—or rather, it was the voice of a young man who would, impossibly, mutate into the man I knew as my father. A voice rising up from history, from secrecy, from the dead.

I brought the stack to my bed and read everything again.

October 24, 1960

Dear Ray,

I woke up this morning and the first thought of the day was lonely because without you. Our hours yesterday came back like a fresh vision for me. Oh how I wish I could have woken up and seen your hair on my pillow. Forgive me for starting with heart on sleeve, but I tell you only because you'll appreciate how this moment passed very quick, and I took your sagely advice of "do not stay sad long because life is short." Because my eyes (my "painter's eyes," as you told me to cultivate) spied something very nice at the edge of my new orange window curtains, which was the brilliant blue of the sky. It's a Pacific blue purer than the hazy factorysmoke blue over the Hudson.

When Don brought me those orange curtains I told him he'd make my bedroom look like a whore's room. Mrs. Casey would look up from her backyard sweeping and wonder what kind of a tenant brings such a color to a respectable Irish house. And would I tell her what Don told me that day? "Bring some contrast into your life, that way you'll see everything different." I understand that I never saw the blue sky quite the same until it was up against the orange.

I think Ray maybe you put a spell on me and now the sights are all changed. Come back soon, if you can stand me gushing.

Teddy

October 26, 1960

Dear Ray,

All my thoughts are about you this fine day, hotter in October than it was in the foggy summer. But before you think, Here he goes again, Teddy Garner the Sadsack, you'll be happy to know that I'm not sitting still, longfaced with empty pockets. I'm doing something important.

Yesterday morning, first thing I heard was Mrs. Casey in the alley with her infernal broom, yelling about overdue rent and wanting to know who was it I had coming down the stairs after midnight? How could I tell her it's been a week since the tool and die job and if it wasn't for your groceries I'd be hungry and miserable instead of just miserable?

I walked toward the ocean hoping for an inspiring idea though I never made it to the dunes, because there's Don outside the Hideaway with some big news—"I fired The Cyclops." Remember him? The big Neanderthal with eyes too close together, who flipped burgers like he was playing scales on the piano but also siphoned off beer from the tap. Don finally had enough of his drunktempered antics. So I'm the Hideaway's new shortorder cook! I work ten through two, then four thirty until close. I can kiss factory work goodbye.

With my new job and my new curtains and my new you, I'm full of inspiration. I woke up today and guess what, I started painting. I set up for the first time the easel which we purchased together, got a shirt cardboard and painted a landscape of the curtains, the window frame, the sky behind them, and rooftops. A whole hour passed right by before I took any notice, just like you said happens. It's probably no good, and the blue's not right, but it's a good first try I think.

Ray, you have blown in like an angel and kept me from harm during a time of aimless worry. Please write and say you're coming back up here soon, my magic girl! Even a postcard is great.

Teddy

November 10, 1960

Dear Ray,

High spirits at the Hideaway these days. We had a crowd on election night sitting around a television set which Don brought in for the occasion, all of us cheering on Kennedy. The lunch regulars are friendly and like to pick on me for my New York accent, but it's all oldtimers so I can handle them. At nights the beat crowd spills out onto the sidewalk, one hamburger split for every two of them, and always the jugwine in a juice glass. I get the feeling they think I'm deaf or speak only a foreign tongue and can't understand their intellectualism. Excuse me Mr. Bearded Artist while I wipe up your spill but I happen to be a painter too and for your information I have so read "The Stranger" by Albert Camus. One of them left behind a copy of "Tristessa" which I'm reading but it's full of junktalk and nowhere as good as "Subterraneans." The word from Don is that Kerouac is a drunkard and past his prime and the writing of this book might prove it.

I am sad your visit was delayed again, I guess it never sinks in for me the life you're leading down there in the mysterious wilds. Here's the phone number of the Hideaway where you can leave me a message, please: Judah 5-1124.

With you on my mind—Teddy

November 15, 1960

Ray,

Today I am lonesome remembering the shouts between us at the end of the night and worst of all the shove I gave you. I may be a meantempered jealous Irish fool but you know I'm crazy about you, so forgive me for that reason, which I swear is true.

After you left Don said to raise my spirits he'd take me out to a "mixed bar" which I figured meant white and Negro but when I got there it was full of fairies and Don knew them all. The name of the bar was "The Who Cares?" with a sign that says "Leave your Cares at the Door." Don introduced me to the fruits, each of them giving me eyes up and down like cops with flashlights. One even had the nerve to call me handsome, so I said "Watch it!," then Don said, "He gave you a compliment, say thank-you." That'll be the day!

My mind was full of confusing thoughts such as the $64,000 Question, "Is Don one, too?" And should I be his friend knowing now what I think I know? Do you pick your friends because they are the familiar type, someone regular like you? Or on the otherhand when something is new and different do you take a chance because that's what makes life a kick? By which I'm trying to say, I figured I'd stick around instead of heading out the door. For the kicks. Plus where did I have to go anyway?

No secret I am shy with strangers (boy, were these strangers!) but Don got me soused enough to stop feeling so funny among a crowd of that kind. It was very peculiar knowing that some fellow regular enough in conversation is actually an invert who might be looking at you with unholy thoughts. In particular a brawny one a few barstools away staring at me with a severe look in his eye. He's got his own flock of queens surrounding him because he's the matinee idol of the bunch, a ringer for Rock Hudson, with possibly the largest chest muscles outside of Jack LaLanne, I kid you not. On the way out, I passed directly alongside this big guy and I hear him call me "trade" which was explained to me by Don and is unsavory. I was furious and demanded of Don, "What's the big idea bringing me there?" and him saying, "It's a fun place you never know what type of crowd you'll find," and me saying, "It was a fag crowd," and him saying, "The beer's the same as any other place." He had a furiating answer for everything.

I didn't want to even take the ride back from him, but we were in a fringe neighborhood full of spades, somewhere on Haight Street. And in the car I asked him "Are you one of them?" and he just dragged on his Camel and kept his eyes on the road and said very sagely "I supposed I've just learned to live my life." To which I asked, "Don't you worry about a black mark on your soul?" (him being from the seminary and so forth) and he said, "I worry about the cops arresting me. I worry about the newspaper printing my name the next day. I worry about the drunken sailor out looking for a fistfight because he didn't find a whore who might relieve him of his suppressed tension" and so forth with concerns that are not about God but about Man. When he finished I said, "Well, Don I guess you're all right by me." Though I wonder if I can look at him the same.

That's why to sort all this out I have come to the typewriter to you Ray because you are the one person who has been very straight with me and also you knew Don before I did. Even though I was a foulmouthed roughneck with you, I know you have a way of never holding a bad opinion about anyone. Sorry for the lengthy and lurid atmosphere of this letter, I hope it didn't upset you.

From Frisco, Soaked in Ale, Teddy

This next note was on a postcard with an image of the Sutro Baths. It was undated but seemed to fall into sequence here.

Your probably still laughing at that last letter of mine. Boy I sure do run at the mouth after a couple too many. Just forget about all that. Don and me are pals, and we have an understanding, he's that way and I'm not, so what's the worry? Today he drove me up the Highway past Playland to show me Sutro Museum. What a nuthouse! More wild junk than you've ever seen before, including every stitch of clothes ever worn by Tom Thumb the famous circus freak. Plus actual mummies and other curiosities. Ray, phone me up I miss your voice. Maybe you've tried but I don't always get the message. T.

November 28

Dear Ray,

It's been so long since I've heard from you, you must still be mad. Well I know your busy with family kids & the mean ogre husband but gosh Ray just a phone call is all I'm asking.

I thought of you on Thanksgiving, which Don used as a chance to close the Hideaway and cook a turkey for me and some other "orphans" as he called us, all a fine bunch. (Except for one clownish queen name of Benjamin but known to all as Betty. The worst of That Kind. A fineseeming fellow until he opens his mouth and then just a showering of womanly fussing and flirtation.) Best of the lot was Don's old pal Chick, who like Don fled from the seminary, and talks now of Buddha. (He says, "Read Dharma Bums. It's all in there, man.") Chick's lady is Mary, they're a couple of beat poets moving out of the city for a cabin in the mountains to the south. Mary seems sad and remote but she lights up after some wine with a face that's almost beautiful—don't get jealous Ray she's nothing compared to you! Chick and Mary told grand stories of San Francisco before Urban Renewal and they got a kick out of me listening to every word. Mary was at The Six Gallery the night of Ginsberg reading "Howl," and she claims to have conversed with Kerouac, Cassady, McClure, everyone! Mary and Chick say the best of San Francisco is past, but I think of you and how you see everything as hopeful.

Mr. and Mrs. Casey are leaving to visit "the relations" so I will have the place to myself for two days, maybe you can sneak up to visit and I'll show you my "masterpiece" which needs your advice as I've gotten stuck. Honestly Ray I can't bear too many more nights with nothing but booze for company. Please call!

Teddy

December 25, 1960, 3 o'clock in the morning

Dear Ray,

You stopping by was the best Christmas present anyone gave me, I'd given up hope I'd ever hold you tight and kiss you like that. I'm glad you still think of me and want me to write out the full flood of my thoughts.

Don cooked up a Christmas dinner of lamb stew tonight for the two of us plus Chick and his dark lady Mary, after which he made a presentation to me of a proper raincoat for this watery Frisco winter, and then surprised me by saying he's going to midnight mass and why don't I come along? He took me up Nob Hill to Grace Cathedral which is unfinished but an eyeful just the same. These Protestants build them tall just to make you feel small. You look up into those pointy arches and then you think about your own puny life down here, and you just got to hope there's someone up there keeping watch. I sat next to Don and prayed, "Dear God, I'm not in very good standing with you these days so I won't ask you for anything, just please watch over these people," mentioning you first and foremost, and then my family and my friend Danny, wherever he is these days hope he's OK and hasn't forgot about me. And thanks for Don taking good care of me and for Chick and Mary who gave me a bottle of Irish Whiskey for Christmas. Amen.

Don had his head bowed, on a prayer streak of his own. I wondered if he was asking God to put him normal. And it made me wonder truly why should Don, who is a decent fellow, be sitting here with his eyes squeezed tight enough to give himself a headache, asking God for anything? How about if God said to Don instead, "Sorry for making you a queer, Don, giving you all kinds of torment and then making it impossible for you to change." The whole thing got me thinking and afterwards I sat on the steps outside and had a smoke and felt the big bafflement of it all.

So I'm here now dipping into my bottle of Christmas Cheer typing my fingers so hard they're sore. Will I see you in the New Year? I don't know what I'd do in Frisco if it wasn't for you showing up now and then.

Yours, Teddy

I was deeply sympathetic with the writer of these letters—his romantic longing, his solo drinking, his empty pockets—but my sympathy confused me. Here was young Teddy, angry with God for making his friend gay, up against the memory of my father as I knew him, angry with me for thrusting my gayness in his face. Telling Don, *You're all right by me.* Telling me, *Keep your private life private.* Why had his mind, slowly opening up to new ideas under the influence of all that San Francisco had to offer, clamped shut again, so that by the time I came queerly along he could only avert his eyes, plug his ears and scold?

I found myself tumbling into my own past, the year of my life, 1988 to '89, when, fresh out of college, I lived through similarly wide-eyed days in New York City. I fell in with a group of people I'd met while busing tables at a restaurant near NYU. Like Chick and Mary, these folks claimed to already have seen the best of it, making me jealous with stories of the early eighties, before the East Village art scene had been co-opted by money, when St. Mark's Place was dotted with FOR RENT signs, Nan Goldin was exhibiting her frankly sexual slide show in church basements, and you might, at any time, stumble across a public surface tagged by the hand of Basquiat or Haring. I'd sat through a Christmas dinner much like the one Teddy described, where I was presented with gifts both practical and decadent by older friends all too happy to mold the mind of the new kid. Where were they all now? At least two of the gay guys and one of the women I knew had died of AIDS, another woman had last been seen checking into rehab and one guy I'd had a weekend affair with had reportedly moved to Berlin, where he was raising children with his lesbian best friend. The only person I still knew from that first year in New York was Colleen, the other impressionable newcomer to the crowd.

When I lived in New York I used to take the bus to Greenlawn—piercings in both my ears, hair slashed asymmetrically, doing my best to swagger in a black leather jacket—and when I got there, I'd inevitably argue with my father, sometimes because, jobless, I would ask him for money, sometimes because I reported holding jobs he didn't approve of, like a brief stint as a receptionist at a gay and lesbian legal aid group. There was never any glint of recognition in the stories I'd tell him of my East Village antics, no "I know what you're going through, son, because I've been there myself." Why hadn't he and I ever reached an *understanding* of our own? Yeah, Dad, I feel it too: *the big bafflement of it all.*

9

That night, and for several nights after, Woody and I spent hours picking over these letters, filling in the gaps of Teddy and Ray's affair as we imagined it. He was as excited as I was, fashioning us as Special Agent James Garner ("Rockford" once again) and Master Sleuth Woodrow Nelson, crouched together over a newfound pile of clues. I would read something aloud and pause to ask a question: "I wonder what Ray said to him after he apologized for shoving her?"

"Write it down, and we can ask her about it," Woody would instruct, and I would, studiously logging my question in the QUEST FOR FATHER file.

My sleuthing partner would call me up in the middle of the day to report some finding of his own, like the fact that the building that once housed Don's grill was now a café called Java Beach. Our conversations glistened with our favorite Teddy-speak. Me: "Why, you've got possibly the largest chest muscles outside of Jack LaLanne!" Woody: "Stop showering me with your womanly fussing and flirtation." We spent consecutive nights cross-legged on my bed, in boxers and T-shirts, sharing foil-wrapped burritos or pad Thai from take-out containers, throwing around hepcat lingo—*Frisco* this, *Frisco* that. Miraculously, we were back in tandem, as if once again in the light-headed bubble of new love, that time when whatever one of you most cares about is top of the other's list, too.

The first time I saw Woody I thought he was straight. I was at the Stud with Colleen for Trannyshack, the best night for fun in San Francisco, with drag artists of every gender pulling out all the stops on a dollar-bin budget. The theme that night had been "The Edge of

Aquarius," and the show had ended with the entire lineup of performers drinking "poisoned" Kool-Aid and dying on stage while a Jim Jones look-alike lip-synched to a David Bowie song—the kind of twisted genius that made me proud to be a San Franciscan.

After the performance, Colleen dragged me to the dance floor for "Ray of Light," the first decent Madonna song in years, and I soon noticed a head of blonde curly hair bouncing erratically, high above the crowd. This tall guy was dancing with a girl, or rather, was shaking his shoulders and arms and especially his head—though not his feet, which were glued in place—in the vicinity of a female of the species. I soaked up his gawky ease with his dancing partner, his frequent smiles as she shouted above the music to him, all the lovely ways his skin revealed itself to my spying eyes, in particular the palm-size patch of gold fur on his belly as he stretched his arms high. They looked like one of the many hip straight couples who show up every week at Trannyshack, the girl just wanting to have some trashy fun in a place where she wouldn't get pawed on the way to the ladies' room, the guy being a good sport despite the fact that he might get pawed on the way to the men's. But then it occurred to me that someone might conceivably make a similar misjudgment about Colleen and me—I'm not much of a dancer myself—so I asked Colleen to appraise the situation. Together we spun a new story: This guy wasn't sure where he fell on the Kinsey Scale of human sexuality, and though he was curious enough to venture out to a gay club, he was still so inexperienced and/or freaked by his attraction to men that he'd brought along the protective beard of a female companion. We dubbed him "Triple B": Bi-curious Blonde Boy.

Thereafter I spotted Triple B everywhere, sightings that were dutifully reported back to Colleen, and I quickly installed him high on my List of Favorites. They are always out there, the Favorites, desirable guys floating along the periphery of your world. Though you never actually meet them, your paths continue to cross—on a crowded sidewalk or a city bus, in theater lobbies or at your favorite record store scouring the CD bins. Each passing glimpse inflates the mystique. (Is this just an urban phenomenon? I imagine in small towns you'd soon discover this person was the cousin of your co-worker's husband.) To actually meet and be introduced to a Favorite wasn't the goal. Only the rarest fantasy survived its expectations.

Flash-forward a year and a couple of months, to a sunny Sunday in

Dolores Park. In a place where people go to get away from work, I was halfheartedly attempting to get some done, shuffling through the pages of a transcript I was editing, gnawing on the cap of a red pen. I was also, no doubt, peering above my papers at the male bodies laid out on display—the boys in Speedos and designer underwear, their shaved pecs and legs gleaming, as Ian once described it, like sealskin. This part of the park, unofficially known as Dolores Beach, crested high above a playground surrounded by palm trees and picnic tables. Down below, families gathered around coolers, dogs chased chew toys and *cholos* clustered tightly together, staring outward as a unit. The view up here took in all of downtown, and on clear days you could see far across the Bay, past Oakland to the peak of Mount Diablo. I lived two blocks from the park, so I often wound up there, though rarely with my shirt off. I had a love-hate reaction to the scene. Who were they, these seals, and how was it they had the time to sculpt all that muscle to classical perfection? They hid their eyes behind dark glasses and under the brims of baseball caps, asking to be looked at, giving nothing back.

That Sunday, I was hit by the smell of dog before I noticed a shiny, black, floppy-eared canine traipsing across my towel, sniffing its way toward my backpack, using my paperwork as a paw path, leaving muddy prints and puncture holes in the transcript. I'm not much of a dog person. I don't like the wet-fur smell or the drool or, least of all, the fecal matter that gets left behind in park grass where humans are meant to stretch out on towels. Now this dog had sent me bumbling between the islands of muscle in order to collect my mangled, scattered papers. When I looked up, the pup was being collared by a very tall guy: Triple B.

He was wearing a faded black T-shirt that hung casually off his broomstick shoulders and blue pants that looked like they'd once been part of a deliveryman's uniform. He was chastising the dog and apologizing to me at the same time. My speculation went into overdrive: *He's at Dolores Beach—he's gay . . . He's fully clothed and walking a dog—he's straight . . . He's controlling the dog with a strong hand—he's no sissy . . . He's looking me in the eyes, telling me he's soooooo sorry—he's gay.* Alongside this ran another current, an attempt to call up a single, perfect sentence, the one pithy line that would keep Triple B from slipping away—

I said, "I thought you'd never get here."

He made no response *(he's not responding—he's straight)* as he leashed up his charge, delivering it the kind of reprimand meant for the benefit of the humans around him, and then he was moving away.

I called out, "Hey!"

"Yes?"

He locked eyes with me, and based on the spark of interest I thought I saw there, I summoned the nerve to ask, "Got a name?"

"Woody."

I laughed, thinking he'd given me the dog's name. "No, your name."

"Woody," he repeated, and then flashed me one of those big grins that I'd first seen from across the dance floor. He pointed to my papers. "Sorry about—"

"No biggie."

"It's not even my dog," he said. "I'm just trying to keep him out of trouble while his mommy's reading on her blankie." He nuzzled its neck, his long fingers kneading its coat. "Aren't you a bad dog?"

"I suppose I am," I said.

Woody smiled again, blinked flirtatiously and replied, "I'm not surprised."

I watched him walk away, toward the far end of the slope, where he parked himself down on a blanket with the woman I'd seen him with at the Stud. They turned together to look toward me. I imagined calling Colleen, the scolding she'd give me for letting Triple B slip through my hands, so when I packed up my papers a short while later, I walked out of my way in order to pass by his blanket.

"Woody?"

"Oh. Hello again."

"You know, you never asked for *my* name."

His mouth opened in surprise, but no words came forth.

The girl spoke up at his side, shielding her brow with her hand. "Now why do you think that is?" I couldn't tell if she was being seriously bitchy—as she would have the right to be, were she his girlfriend—or if she was just toying with me, forcing me to work for my pickup.

"I don't know," I said to her, playing along. "Maybe he's not interested."

"You never know 'til you try."

So she wasn't his girlfriend. "I guess that's what I'm doing. Trying."

Woody spoke up, at last. "I'm sorry. It's just that I'm kinda seeing someone."

"Is it *kinda* enough to keep you from taking my number?"

"It's just that—"

The girl let out an exasperated sigh. "Woody, just take his number." She stretched forward to hand me a pad and pen.

Below my number I wrote: *Jamie. Dolores Park. Bad dog*. I handed the message back to her. "I can leave a résumé too, if you want."

She tore the page from her pad and passed it to Woody. "Here. Now say, 'Nice to meet you, Jamie.' "

He stuck out his hand. "Nice to meet you, Jamie."

I held his hand, and his stare, for as long as I could bear. We were both blushing. As I backed away, I mouthed, "Call me." I turned around and saw the two of them doubled over in a fit of giggles.

"He sleeps with men, but he's shy," Colleen proclaimed the next Friday at Café Frida. "That's why his friend stepped in. He's the kind of guy who complains about never meeting anyone, and here he was screwing up a perfect opportunity."

Brady, when I told him, was more forceful. "You should be at that park all the time, dude. If he was there once, he'll be there again, right? You've got to make it happen." Brady had recently told me about his new girlfriend, Annie, a visual artist whom he'd pursued with a diligence that negated any outcome other than her saying yes to a date. He'd *made it happen.* I hadn't met Annie yet—Brady had been keeping her away from his friends, sure that the exposure would jinx it—but right around this time he was turning thirty and throwing himself a party, which would also be their public debut as a couple. The party would be held at the warehouse he shared with three other guys near the freeway, a place crammed full of electronic equipment, computers, unidentifiable large metal objects, panels of sheet metal and recycled furniture. Colleen and I showed up early to help Brady decorate. His roommates were handling the audiovisual wiring of the party, but he was counting on us for decorative input. This was meant to impress Annie, who'd reportedly commented that Brady's loft looked like the inner chamber of a video game and smelled like a men's room.

We transformed a curtained-off corner into a comfy, candlelit chill space, then moved up to the roof to add some touches there, too. We hauled strings of Christmas lights up a harrowing steel ladder attached to the outside of the building, and we outlined the edge of the roof to keep carefree partiers from tumbling to the concrete below. In the midst of this work I heard Brady call my name.

"This is Annie," he was saying as I turned around, and my eyes landed on the woman from the blanket in Dolores Park. Not two feet behind her stood Triple B himself.

A gasp of intrigue ricocheted between all of us, except Brady, who had no idea what was going on. Lit from below by Christmas light, Woody's surprised expression bore a schoolboy's guilt; having failed to use my number, he'd have some explaining to do. Annie finally broke the ice, extending her hand to me, beaming at this collision of worlds. "So it looks like you didn't get away after all," she said.

Looking back, I realize what an astonishing moment it was. There I stood with two of my best friends, one of whom was newly dating this woman who was best friends with the guy I'd soon wind up seeing. (San Francisco is, in the end, just a small town.) When Brady was finally brought up to speed on the tangled web of relationships, he just shook his head and marveled, "Serious synchronicity." Colleen and Annie hit it off right away, conferring for a solid hour, like matchmaking aunties, about whether or not Woody and I would *make a love connection.*

Meanwhile, we had parked ourselves on the roof among the twisted vines of pinpoint lights, refilling our glasses from the makeshift bar we'd constructed to save ourselves trips up and down the precarious ladder. Music thumped up through our feet, but we stayed away from the dance floor. "I'm not much of a dancer," he told me, and it took all my restraint not to say, "I know." I got an earful about Mark, the *someone* Woody had been seeing, a *great guy* who nonetheless suffered from a long list of *intimacy issues,* and how things between them were over, though not officially. "It's a tricky situation," he kept saying. But as is usually the case, other people's breakups never seem particularly complicated from the outside. I figured that I'd get to sleep with Woody that night, or soon after, and then leave him alone to work out his relationship woes. But when I tried to propose this plan of action—we were huddled together under a blanket, insulating ourselves from a sudden onslaught of night fog and engaging in an adorable, tentative round of footsie—he told me that to sleep with anyone now, before giving Mark the heave-ho, would only create *bad karma*. Karma wasn't something that particularly swayed me, but I could tell that he would stick to his principles, so in the end I planted a kiss on him and said, "Call me when the dust settles." Then I went off to share a birthday joint with Brady.

Disentangling from Mark took Woody another month—at least, it was that long before he called me with an invitation to dinner. At a romantically lit restaurant we shared laughter and easy conversation and a bit of anticipatory knee knocking under the table, but again this dovetailed into a list of reasons why he wasn't yet ready to get involved with me. He delivered a speech, clearly prepared ahead of time, about how he was hurt because Mark had cheated on him, and needed to take things slowly, etc., etc., etc., at which point I blurted out, "Look, I've been clocking you for a year, I don't know how much more slowly I can go." I told him how I'd first noticed him at Trannyshack. I listed the various locations where I'd spotted him in the months since. I told him he was Favorite Number One. He kept saying, "That's amazing," a dazed cast to his eyes.

He kissed me quickly outside the restaurant, and then off into a cab he went, leaving me absolutely certain that, having exposed myself as a stalker, I'd not likely see Triple B again. He didn't call in the next few days, and so, convinced that I'd destroyed my chances, I did something I'd never done before—I answered a *party-and-play* phone sex ad. I lost a day and a half smoking crystal in this guy's apartment, while he continued to lure others over, a revolving door of sex hobbyists, a binge of lower brain-stem activity. The whole thing went zero to sixty in no time, then from sixty to a hundred. I guess that's why they call it *speed*. I needed a week to recover, not just from the amphetamine in my system but from the emotional tremors of having thrown myself in so recklessly with this particularly avid crowd. All these years I'd been jokingly calling myself a slut. But I didn't know the half of what was out there, or what I was capable of.

Woody did eventually call, after he returned from a family vacation, something he had told me about, something I'd stupidly failed to remember, and he wanted to see me again. Turns out that my dinner confession had tapped into his superstitious nature; Woody was very much a believer in *meant to be,* and learning that I'd nurtured a faraway crush only convinced him that we were destined to get involved. I was devastated. Thrilled and devastated. I could barely recall the details of my crystal binge—though a memory of asking for a condom while I was already getting fucked was clear enough. I needed a good couple weeks before I could get accurate results from the battery of tests offered at the city STD clinic. So I stalled Woody for time: a few chaste dates, a lot of making out, tension building within me as tenderness bloomed between us.

When we finally did hook up—our schedules cleared, my health in the clear—we locked ourselves away for the better part of a weekend. Our sex was probably the most highly anticipated of my entire life, and definitely the least disappointing.

From there, *this guy I've been seeing* transitioned into *my boyfriend,* and within weeks, talk of *falling for each other* started slipping into conversation. He was direct about what he wanted and what he didn't. "Cheating is a deal breaker," he told me early on, and without hesitation I said, "Cheating's always been an exit strategy for me. And I don't want out of this." We were spending every night together, not just at home (I was busting out all my best recipes) but wherever we could find something new to do in the city. One weekend we biked to the Presidio and sneaked behind a NO TRESPASSING sign to have sex among the eucalyptus trees, the fear of being discovered heightening every sensation. One night he insisted we go dancing at the Stud, demanding, once there, that I reenact the first sighting, complete with an imitation of his cement-shoes technique. He could laugh at himself, and made it possible for me to do the same. That was new to me. I was learning how to be happy in my own skin.

There was a catch, though: I had career plans. This is back when my freelance pieces for *All Things Considered* had gotten me noticed, and I'd hatched a plan to move to Washington, DC. I hoped that putting myself in proximity to NPR's headquarters would help me nab a coveted staff position. Despite the fact that our nation's capital, with its theme-park federalism, has always sort of given me the creeps—Welcome to Governmentland!—I was ready to pick up and move. Résumés had been rendered, personal contacts had been contacted.

"I can't believe I found someone so great just as I'm ready to leave San Francisco," I told Ian one night on the patio of the Eagle.

"It's no coincidence," he said, chugging beer, surveying the crowd over my shoulder. This was back when Ian was most jealous of Woody—the days leading up to Woody's "Noncompetitive Clause"—when Ian was digging into me at all times. "You only picked him because you know it can't last," he said. "Just like always." I told him to fuck off.

But I suspected he was right. Woody never asked me to reconsider my plans, though he was unambiguous in his belief that San Francisco was the future—the future being the Internet, which was starting to turn our arty, sleepy city into a Mecca. Jobs were popping up like weeds after a rainfall. Dilapidated neighborhoods were blossoming with new enterprise: *Look, honey, they're calling that decrepit warehouse district Multimedia Gulch.* People were arriving from all over the world to live and work in San Francisco.

I took my dilemma to Brady one afternoon, laying out the pros and cons. "Woody's right, dude," he said. "You have a rent-controlled apartment and a boyfriend. If you want to advance your career, figure out a way to do it here." That very night Brady and I hatched the idea that became *City Snapshot.* Pretty soon I had a job I'd created for myself and a steady boyfriend I'd picked out of a crowd, pursued and won.

Flash-forward to June, last year: The program director at the station tells me, "We're not going to renew your contract."

Woody tells me, "This promotion means that I'll be working longer hours."

Deirdre tells me, "He's going to die, Jamie. You need to figure out what you're going to do." Just like that, all of it at once.

And so here we were, now: Woody calling from his cell phone, saying, "Put on a coat. Meet me out front."

"Right this minute? I'm working." This was a lie. In truth I was stoned, and I didn't want him to know.

"Just do it," he said. "It's a surprise."

I looked up and down Manfred Alley. It took a minute to realize that the car horn honking from across the street was for me. Sitting behind the wheel of a silver SUV, double-parked, engine running, was my boyfriend.

"Hey, buddy, wanna take a ride?" He leaned out the window on one elbow, sugar in his voice, as if seducing a hitchhiker.

"Please tell me this is a rental."

"Baby, it's ours."

I stepped closer. "You *bought* this environmentally hazardous status symbol?"

"Check it out. It's got so much room in the back—"

"You could fit an entire car inside of it. One that gets better mileage."

"Hello, I'm six-foot-four. Plus this one's got all-wheel drive. We can take it up a mountain through a snowstorm. Do you like the color?"

"It matches your phone."

He threw open the door. "Come on, before you start complaining. You need to take a ride. You need to feel the power."

"Who are you? And what have you done with my boyfriend?" I climbed in—or, rather, up—and he aimed us into rush-hour traffic. The seats were slidey on the turns. I held on tight, paranoid that an accident was imminent, a baby stroller sucked under our enormous tires. SUVehicular Homicide.

"Drive carefully," I panted. "And watch out for bicyclists!"

Watching the roofs of smaller cars pass beneath my window, I did in fact *feel the power*: the immediate allure of looking down from a perch onto traffic, onto police cars, even. As he drove, Woody explained that he'd gotten a tip from Roger about a website with a one-day sale on *pre-owned vehicles* and had convinced Digitent to front him the money. It was a steal, he said, in mint condition but half the price of a new model—far cheaper than the fuel-efficient car he knew I'd rather he bought. He'd bought it for *us*, he repeated.

We were on the road for a half hour before I realized with a shudder where he was taking us. He drove toward the Golden Gate Bridge to watch the sunset, but pulled off early, into the parking lot on the bluff above the very beach where I'd last betrayed him. I half expected Red Shorts to parade on by and flash me a too-familiar smile. Woody hopped out, and through tinted windows I watched him step closer to the ledge. In that moment, separated by glass and steel, I felt the opposite of power. The awareness of power drained away. A slow leak of some vital fluid.

"Getting those letters has been so satisfying," Woody said, in bed, a few days after we'd first stayed up late reading Teddy's words to Ray. For Woody, Ray's package was a small treat, like a newly released video to watch before bed. A distraction after another exhausting day at Digitent.

But for me, the letters were a tease. A leap ahead on a path still coming into focus. "There's probably more," I replied. "There has to be." My hunger had increased as it had been fed.

I started traveling on my bike through the city, solo, unplanned, exploring. I rode all the way out to the ocean, where the N-Judah streetcar line met the beach. There, on the site of the Hideaway, I found Java Beach, as Woody had tipped me off. I bought a coffee and scoped the crowd. The younger folks sported all of today's *alternative* signifiers: nerdy glasses hovering over paperbacks, multicolored hair held back by barrettes, secondhand clothes. A small contingent of drawling, lion-haired surfers leaned back into their chairs, leathery legs stretched long. Some version of them had likely been here for many, many years, drinking beer at noon. There were no Irish old-timers except for one dingy-skinned fellow who looked like he hadn't left the premises since the day the locals cheered JFK's election. I hoped, in fact, that he hadn't, that he was the line of continuity between then and now—*here's my story, the angle I've been looking for*—and I was considering pulling up a chair to talk to him when he began talking to himself, his gestures indicating the workings of a short-circuited mind. Though it was difficult to imagine this place forty years earlier, with Teddy flipping burgers where now stood an espresso machine and glass refrigerator filled with bottled water and *energy drinks*, I was amazed to find even these traces. In a city full of disappearing history, this spot offered up the possibility of longevity, even permanence.

I fixated on the boy making coffee, who looked less hip than the patrons—gelled hair, teenage fashion (a huge Tommy Hilfiger logo on his sweatshirt)—and whose behavior defied an easily read sexuality. He gripped the steamer arm with a rag and slid it downward, wiping away milky foam, revealing a cartoon cat tattooed on his wrist. He giggled over his shoulder at the girl behind the register and spoke something that sounded like, but might not have been, "Do you think I'm too small for capoeira?" I wanted to know his life story, why he came to San Francisco, what he hoped for. It was so easy to project Teddy onto him. He caught me staring and did a double take, and soon after I drained my mug and fled, strangely unsettled.

I pedaled through the neighboring blocks, imagining I might find the place where my father had lived. I didn't have an address, but I fantasized that some telltale sign would point me to an upstairs tenant's apartment carved from a single-family home, with an exterior staircase for visitors like Ray Gladwell to tiptoe down after midnight, beneath which Mrs. Casey would be whisking her *infernal broom*. Though of course today, in this neighborhood, Mrs. Casey would be Mrs. Trahn or Mrs. Nguyen, and she probably had a job. I thought of that worker-boy at Java Beach. Did he live in this neighborhood, upstairs from a

Vietnamese family who didn't understand him, or he them, and didn't approve of the comings and goings of his late-night visitors? Or did he live even further out, in Daly City, say, in one of the boxy developments stretched like millipedes along the coastal hills? Was it even possible, financially, to live in San Francisco today on a café salary?

I spent an afternoon at City Lights bookstore, the city's best-known link to its bohemian past, huddling over history books and beatnik memoirs. Not beatnik—*beat.* By now I'd learned the distinction between the term used inside the subculture and the one that had been cast upon it by a derisive press. I started to piece together a better understanding of what San Francisco had been like in 1960 and '61. It was a hinge time, a pivot between two countercultural waves, the beats and the hippies. Tour buses were already creeping through North Beach, allowing passengers to snap photos of bongo-playing, beret-clad poets. The artists themselves had begun migrating to what my father's letter had called *fringe neighborhoods*, like the Haight.

But for every individual landmark still standing, there was an entire neighborhood demolished. Third Street below Market had been a skid row once known to all as Three Street. It was here that Jack Kerouac shacked up in filthy rooms, downed a sickly sweet booze called Tokay with the local winos and immortalized the experience in his pocket notebook. I bought a used copy of *San Francisco Blues,* the collection of poems that grew out of that notebook, and read them on a bench in Yerba Buena Gardens, the two-block landscaped park built up from bulldozed Three Street, surrounded now by a museum, a convention center and a mall. Kerouac's San Francisco was "bluer than misery." Maybe my father felt that, too. Maybe there was no great secret as to why he left San Francisco; maybe he just got lonely, felt the gnawing insanity of being alone and far from home. Sitting on that park bench, suspended between the prettified San Francisco of today and Kerouac's long-ago cry from the heart, I could imagine those blues sending me packing, too.

I did what I could to lure Woody along on my excursions. "Take a day off, just one day," I pleaded.

"Then who would bankroll your research and development?" he replied, the lilt in his voice masking a sharper accusation: I had begun borrowing money from him—first to make my February rent, then to cover bills, then for other expenses, like a new pair of sneakers, which he insisted on because the New Balance cross-trainers I'd been wearing since we'd started seeing each other had holes in them. My bank account was at rock bottom; my last paycheck from New World Transcripts had been spent before I earned it. But! I had ten thousand dollars coming my way; I would pay him back.

Research and development: Every important project begins this way. And this project would certainly be important—once I figured out where it was headed. I believed this. I had to.

Lying in bed, listening to Woody sleep.

I am awake. I tread softly to the living room, I get stoned, I go online. I type DON DREBINSKI into a search engine. Nothing. I find a queer-history newsgroup and throw out a posting with his name in the subject line. I send an e-mail to San Francisco's gay and lesbian archives. I find a site called Obits.com, but again, no Don—which is a relief. Don only just came alive for me; I'm not yet ready to bury him.

I spend hours in the glow of the monitor, working with a weak modem and an old computer. A night spent waiting for sites to load under these conditions is a night of anxiety: the blank page (the dread that it might stay blank forever); the random bits of graphics (popping up erratically, like a message being decoded); the frequent, maddening freezes. I hear the arguments I have made as to why the world should move slower, and I hear words like *upgrade* and *high-speed* blow right through these fixed thoughts. My skepticism about technology has been a dissent against greed, acquisition, a culture of convenience. But skepticism has slowed me down, almost, it seems, to a standstill.

I search the Web for Dean Foster, who has yet to surface. There's a Dean Foster in southern Illinois whose home page shows a 10K running team: fit, pale-skinned adults, their racing numbers pinned to brightly colored tank tops. Not a swarthy Ficchino among them. I find the published medical papers of Dr. Dean Foster, hematologist, and briefly entertain the notion that Danny gave up his dreams of stardom and enrolled in med school, the better to theorize about autoimmune diseases crossing the blood-brain barrier. I scroll through fostercreations.com, homespun greeting cards out of Flagstaff: slow-loading images of watercolor cacti, desert flowers, coyote bones "in the style of Georgia O'Keefe, painted by the artist Ms. Dean-Marie Foster herself."

And then. A movie database with a page on Dean Foster, actor. "No photo available." His films begin in 1962 with *Surf's Up in San Diego*.

This has to be him.

Seven titles are listed in all, six more than my conversation with Nana has led me to expect. Three are in Italian. All are obscure. Beach movies, foreign films, exploitation flicks. A kitsch-film buff would cream.

The last film listed is *The Criminal Kick,* made in 1974. I click on the title, which takes me to Bellwether Pictures, the "Premier Distributor of 1960s Youth Explosion Films," and its description of this movie:

> Out for money to buy LSD, teenagers Jack and Laura embark on a giddy crime spree from mugging little old ladies to kidnapping the young daughter of a drug kingpin. With Frankie Avalon as a cop on the trail, Mackenzie Phillips as the obnoxious ten-year-old kidnap victim, and spaghetti Western regular Dean Foster as a desperate gigolo.

I order a copy of *The Criminal Kick*, and a copy of *Surf's Up in San Diego*, also distributed by Bellwether. I include a note asking if they have information on Dean Foster's whereabouts. Their site is not equipped for online ordering, so I have to do this by fax, sending them my credit card number. If it was not five o'clock in the morning, if I was not, finally, bone tired, I would find this old technology charming.

The predawn sky is shading the windows pearl gray as I tread softly back to bed. Curled again next to Woody, I still cannot fall asleep.

The chronology, the database, the notion of a career spanning years: Dean Foster, actor—as opposed to Danny Ficchino, lost uncle—is coming into three dimensions for me. Not just a photograph, but real.

Maybe even alive.

SURVIVORS

10

I heard from Bellwether Pictures a couple days later, but not about Dean Foster's whereabouts. They sent a form letter telling me my credit card had been declined. In a bulging stack of mail on my desk, I found a notice from Visa informing me I was over my limit and past due. *All account activity has been suspended*.

I put in a call to my sister.

I found her in a subdued state. AJ was sleeping, Andy was online, and Nana had been moved to a clinic where she was undergoing physical therapy for her ankle. Deirdre was watching TV. "It's me and Regis," she said. "*Who Wants to Be a Millionaire?*"

"Who doesn't?" I said, warming up.

"I thought Woody was gonna become an Internet millionaire and support you."

"He's working on it." I paused, then forged ahead. "But meanwhile—"

"I know, your money. I'm sorry. Andy's just figuring out how to move some stocks around. Plus, the Angry White Lady had all these medical bills. I wanted to fight her on it, but Andy said let's settle and get it over with. We kinda went head-to-head."

"Why don't you let me talk to him?"

"I'll handle it. It's not a big deal."

"It's a big deal to me."

"I hear you. Let's not fight, Jamie. I swear. You'll get it. Any day now."

I exhaled, willing myself to give her the benefit of the doubt. She'd heard me. She'd apologized. I guess I'd called her at the right moment—she was bundled up on the couch, the house quiet, the TV on low—a moment where her defenses were down. Or perhaps something was wrong?

Without much prompting she opened up: "It's *so weird* not having Dad around. I got used to the whole routine. And now with Nana gone. It's just . . . weird." The job with Carly Fazio hadn't come through. She was thinking about looking around for something else, but couldn't get excited about it. "I don't want to do anything, you know? It's weird."

"You sound depressed," I offered.

"No, it's not that. I just don't have the energy or motivation or desire to do anything but sit around and watch TV."

"Like I said . . ."

She sighed. Behind her I heard televised claps and cheers. I was about to suggest all the ways she might spend her newfound free time—learn a language, start a garden, go back to school—but just as quickly I stifled it. What stopped me were the twin images of me on my couch, numbly watching the world flash by in pace with my remote control, and of my sister, on hers, three thousand miles away, suspended in the same uninspired vortex. And then—I hadn't planned on even talking about this, but suddenly it made sense—I mentioned the one thing that I had been motivated about lately: "Remember that box of stuff I took from the attic?"

I told her about finding Dean Foster on the movie database, about locating Ray Gladwell and going to meet her, about Dad's letters. Deirdre listened as I read a section from the first one, full of lovey-dovey prose: *How I wish I could have woken up and seen your hair on my pillow.*

"You're shittin' me," she exclaimed. "That doesn't sound like Dad at all."

"In this other one he talks about going to a gay bar."

"No way."

I read the description of his night at the Who Cares? and the part about going to Christmas mass and getting mad at God for *making Don a queer*. "It's so weird," I said, using her favorite adjective. "He talks about homosexuality as something that was impossible to change. That's more than I ever got from him."

"He knew you couldn't change, Jamie."

"I'm not so sure."

"Remember when you had that radio story on—about that famous performer guy, the one who fell in love with a guy from, like, Holland or somewhere, and they couldn't get married, and immigration deported the boyfriend? And you interviewed the guy's mother, who was crying?"

"Yeah, yeah. I know the one."

"We listened to it together. Me and Dad."

"You told me *you* listened to it," I said. "Not him."

"I told you him, too."

"I think I'd remember that."

"Look, my point is, it was such a good report. Really sad, you know? I totally cried. And Dad was really quiet, and afterwards I said, you know, Jamie's talented, don't you think?"

"Let me guess. He said, 'Talented, but queer!' "

She groaned. "Jamie—"

"I'm sorry, 'Talented but *homosexual*.' "

"If you're gonna be like that."

"I can't help it. It just gives me the creeps, my own father despising me."

"He was proud of that radio show."

Oh, please, I almost said, but I bit my tongue.

"He said it was very professional and well written. And then we started reminiscing about when you were little and walked around all the time with your tape recorder and asked us questions. Do you remember when you interviewed everyone in the neighborhood about their opinions of *Xanadu?*"

"I forgot about that."

"We were laughing about it. And I said, 'Dad, you should call Jamie and tell him you liked the report.' And that's when he said he knew you were never going to change, but he just wished it was different."

My ability to absorb this information was lagging behind the speed at which she was talking. "He never called me. He never said anything about it."

"I think he probably just forgot. If he hadn't been losing it, I think he would have come around eventually." She swallowed hard.

The sound of that gulp, *a lump in her throat,* threatened to trigger my own sentimental response, and this silenced me. I would not permit death to absolve him.

"Are you still there?" she asked.

"I'm gonna go."

"Okay. I'll keep an eye out for any more old stuff in the attic." She added quickly, "Unless you're still planning on coming back?"

"Maybe." Another visit to New Jersey was suddenly the last thing in the world I wanted. Why was I letting myself wade into these troubled waters, where I was likely to flail, to sink, to drown? What the fuck was I doing, churning up my father's past, my father who couldn't bring himself to make a simple phone call to tell me he liked my radio show?

"One more thing," she said. "Send Nana some flowers. Saturday is her eighty-fifth birthday." Dee gave me the phone number and address of the clinic. Then she signed off with a plaintive "Love you" that left me dumbstruck and ashamed.

Floral delivery cost money. I considered borrowing from Woody—what's another sixty dollars on a tab that had climbed past a thousand?—but I hesitated and then put it out of my mind. Saturday found me sitting at my desk, staring at the phone. Literally staring, as if the power of obligation would send it leaping from the cradle to my hand, the clinic's number magically dialed. And then staring anywhere *but*: out the window, where a jasmine-covered metal fence was rattling in the wind, scattering white delicacies into the weeds; at last weekend's *New York Times Magazine,* which featured an article about how young millionaires were spending their Internet riches (funding independent films and starting their own foundations and sponsoring eco-tourism to Third World countries—I thought of Rick and his Lonely Planet guides); at the list of Dean Fosters pushpinned to the corkboard, almost all of the entries now crossed out or marked up: *Disconnected. Wrong guy. Crazy guy with dog. Disconnected.*

The phone number Deirdre provided went to the floor nurse at the clinic, who cooed in an Indian accent, "Oh, you want the birthday girl. We'll get her on the phone there." *On duh phun dair.* I heard in the background a sea of murmuring elderly voices out of which rumbled the intermittent wave of a single old man protesting. I readied myself for Nana. I was met instead by a brash staccato.

"Who is it? Tommy? We found your gloves."

I swallowed, trying to moisten my suddenly arid tongue. "Aunt Katie. It's Jamie."

"Oh. She said a grandson. I thought for sure Tommy. He just left. Without his calfskin gloves."

"I'm sorry I missed him."

"Tommy, Mikey, Billy, Joanne. Deirdre. All the grandkids were here. Right, Mother?" *All of them except you!*

Cordless phone in hand, I began to pace, desk to kitchen to couch to bedroom. "Did Nana have a nice party?"

"It was very special. Except for the shooting pain."

"What happened?"

"The pain in her ankle, shooting up her leg. Half her body hurts." Her voice veered away from the phone. "No, Ma, don't do that. I'll get it for you." Back to me: "She's not supposed to drink so much, but you know she loves her coffee. I'll get it, Ma. No, it's not Tommy. It's Jimmy. From California. Hold on."

A clumsy handoff, hard plastic clunking onto a tabletop, and then Nana's strained "Hello?"

"Hi, Nana, it's Jamie. Calling to wish you a happy birthday."

"Well, thank you, Jimmy. Thank you for remembering." Her voice was so dim the *shush* of my socks on the carpet nearly swallowed it up. I stopped pacing, slid down to the floor and crossed my legs.

"So how's it going there?"

"As good as can be expected." She told me who'd stopped by that day, repeating Aunt Katie's list of names minus the underlying rancor. She told me about her gifts: the *lovely sweater,* the *beautiful scarf,* the *big bouquet of flowers.*

"Did you get the flowers I sent?"

"No, these were from Tommy and Amy."

"They were supposed to come today."

I am a terrible person.

"They're gonna give me the painkillers now," she said, finishing off with another thank-you and a call-me-again. I let the conversation end without asking any of my stored-up questions about my father as a teenager, what he'd told her about his time in SF, why he returned to New York so quickly.

Aunt Katie was back in my ear. "She said you sent flowers? We didn't get flowers."

"A few days ago. Maybe they don't deliver on weekends."

"Because I don't trust the nurses. There's a couple of colored girls who would take them home for themselves. In a heartbeat."

"Don't get anyone fired until I check with the florist," I pleaded, pacing again. Living room, kitchen, bathroom. A pause in front of the mirror to mouth "Help me."

A change in subject was necessary. "Aunt Katie, there's something I've been wanting to ask you. When I was in New Jersey, I found some old stuff of Dad's."

"He never threw anything away."

"I found some photographs from when he was a kid, and it turns out there were pictures of Uncle Angelo's brother, Danny."

No response. The crazy old man in the background let out a howl.

"Aunt Katie? Are you there?"

"Mmm-hmm."

"I was wondering what happened to him. Danny."

"Ugh, *that* one," she sighed. More silence, and then, at last, an outburst so drenched in anger I swear I heard spittle strike the phone. "I'll tell you what *didn't* happen. He never came to our wedding. His own brother's wedding, and he didn't show. No respect."

"Nana said that you all went to the movie premiere in Times Square."

"Yes, we did, and we all paid for our tickets, too! But later, when it's time for him to do the right thing and stand up for his brother, where is he?"

"He was in Los Angeles, right?"

"Broke his mother's heart, I'll tell you that. Angelo's, too. His own brother's wedding. That was the last straw." Her voice narrowed and drilled into me. "You know, Jimmy, you remind me of him."

"I do?"

"Same thing. Off to California and not a word to anyone else. And then he changed his name. Well, changing your name doesn't mean you don't have a family."

"Wait a minute—I've been in touch. With Deirdre. We talk on the phone."

"But not with your father." She sucked in her breath, as if momentarily startled by her own directness, and then gathered herself, grave, resolute: "Not. With. Your. Father."

So here it was, festering since our drive-by confrontation at the wake, splayed open at last.

"I stayed away because Dad and I had a falling out. Years ago. You know that, and you know why," I said, my voice faltering in a throat now dry as hard cement.

"It's always about you, isn't it? About *your* problems. I'll tell you what I told Danny Ficchino a long time ago, from my own lips to his ears: Certain things are unforgivable." A pause. "What is it, Ma? No, don't pay any attention. Yeah, it's still Jimmy." I listened, fuming, as she inserted herself into a transaction between Nana and a nurse, some necessary rearrangement of a wheelchair or a meal tray. Accents collided—Irish, Indian, New Jersey.

"Aunt Katie, let me finish."

"Look, I don't have time for this. Your grandmother wet herself."

"What?"

"Plus we're ringing up a bill. We pay for every call here, even incoming."

She said good-bye and hung up.

The phone sat at rest for just a moment, then rang again.

"Yes?" I snarled, ready for round two.

But it was a different voice that greeted me, an entirely different voice: "The time is now."

"Here, I found it," Ian was saying. Our bodies were laid out in T formation on a densely peopled spread of park grass, his head on my stomach, his thick black hair like dog fur against the pale blue cotton of my T-shirt. Ian had surprised me by biking us to Washington Park, the heart of once-bohemian, now-touristy North Beach—an appropriate site, he said, for something he wanted to share with me about Jack Kerouac, something he'd stumbled upon in the pages of another book, Gore Vidal's memoir, *Palimpsest,* which was propped up at that moment on Ian's belly. My copy of *The Subterraneans*, which Ian had insisted I bring along, lay next to him.

"What's this about?" I asked.

"The King of the Beats on his hands and knees."

Ian recited from Vidal's book, playing to the back row, a tad aggressive for Saturday in the park. In August 1953, in New York City, Kerouac, not yet famous, and Vidal, already notorious for his explicitly gay novel *The City and the Pillar,* finished off a night of heavy drinking by checking into a room at the Chelsea Hotel. They showered together. They "rubbed bellies for a while." Then Kerouac gave Vidal a "pro forma" blow job. Finally, Vidal flipped him onto his stomach and took him from behind:

> Jack raised his head from the pillow to look at me over his left shoulder . . . He stared at me a moment—I see this

> part very clearly now, forehead half covered with sweaty dark curls—then he sighed as his head dropped back onto the pillow.

Ian glanced up for a reaction. "He says Kerouac wrote about that night in *The Subterraneans*. Without the hot man-on-man action."

"Yeah, I know the part he means." I'd recently finished *The Subterraneans*, and I remembered the passage: Kerouac's narrator, Leo Percepied, chronicles the night when he ditched his female lover for a "glamorous" author, "a perfectly obvious homosexual." Kerouac gets them to the hotel room—and then cuts quickly to waking up on the couch. The fevered rush of events abruptly skids to a stop. The shower, the blow job, the sweaty locks on the pillow detailed by Vidal are reduced to a long dash on the page. Here comes the sex—there it went. A couple pages later Leo offers a hazy *mea culpa* for his "ludicrous fag behavior." Even the freest voice of his generation apparently had his limits.

I wondered if my father, reading the novel while working shifts at the Hideaway, could read between Jack's strategic dashes, could picture the debauchery underway inside the dimly lit hotel room of an *obvious homosexual.* Had that been part of his attraction to Kerouac? Or was it what killed the mystique for him?

When I voiced these questions to Ian, who was thumbing through *The Subterraneans*, he said, "I think it's pretty obvious that two guys had sex here."

"If you know to look for it," I said. "Most of the book is about an affair between a man and a woman. This is just a tangent. Like spending the night with Gore Vidal was for Jack Kerouac, probably." I let out a sigh so weary it made Ian laugh.

"Why so bummed out, my friend?" he grinned. "This is fun stuff."

"My father once told me that he ran into Kerouac at a bar. But I have no idea if it happened. And even if it did, even if I could pull all these pieces of the puzzle together, I'll never really know what any of this meant to him. I'll never get inside of him."

Ian said, "You've got to find this guy."

"Danny Ficchino?"

"Yeah, him. But the other one, from the letters. The gay one."

"Don. I've been trying. No luck." I ripped up a chunk of grass, let the blades fall. "Am I wasting my time? If I can't turn it into work, what's the point?"

Ian lit a couple of cigarettes and passed one to me. Through the expanding gray plume I watched his eyes widen. "Why don't you do something for *Better Example*? You could write an essay, or a script like you'd do for radio, about Kerouac, your father, whatever. We'll make it work for the site." He jumped to his feet, shaking them one at a time, hopping around in newfound excitement. "You could include sketches from your father's notebook, and we could scan in some of the letters—"

"And I could edit the interview with Ray, and maybe other people who'd lived back then, and get their stories online."

"Who needs public-fuckin'-radio? Do it yourself, man."

Well, I still needed public-fuckin'-radio, but his glee was contagious. We left the park on a roll, ideas flowing. I got so excited that I had Ian take me to an electronics store, where I found a digital minidisc recorder that I absolutely had to have. Had to, for the interviews I would conduct. Had to so badly that I wrote a check I knew would bounce. Gave them my driver's license number and everything.

We worked into the evening at Ian's apartment. Starting took forever: deciding what to include, conceptualizing the pages. Ian had been reading a book on information architecture and was determined to forge a master plan before he scanned a single image or wrote a line of code. We decided to start with the photos from the attic box, the mystery of Dean Foster, and Ian went to work. A perfectionist side of him, unexpectedly patient, emerged as the mouse skated and the graphics blinked. I sat in an old armchair, the stuffing protruding through cat-clawed holes, writing text to accompany the images. The cat itself, a skinny black thing, circled around, demanding attention and disappearing after she got it. We smoked so many cigarettes that Ian's roommate, Glen, complained that smoke was clouding the entire apartment. Ian promised we'd stop, but we didn't.

It was after nine when an impulse told me I needed to check in with my boyfriend. I called the mobile unit.

Agitation colored his voice. "Where are you? Everyone's already here."

"Everyone?" Clearly there was some event underway that I was supposed to know about. I tried to access a memory of a plan. Blank.

"Brady, Annie, Colleen, Roger—"

"Roger from work?" Roger from N Is a Number? Roger from a bump in the bathroom?

"Jamie, we're already eating. Where are you?" Ah, yes, there it was: Woody had accepted Annie's invitation for dinner after I'd failed to respond to Brady's. I was supposed to be there two hours ago.

"I'm at Ian's. We're having a creative explosion over here."

He paused. I could hear the gears of contemplation. "So you're totally stoned and don't want to leave, right?"

"Kinda."

A vacuum of silence. I asked him to put Brady on the phone. I told Brady I needed to keep the momentum going over here, did my best to get him interested in helping me edit Ray's interview so we could use it for the site. Laid on the charm as best I could, knowing Woody would be less pissed off if I got Brady's blessing.

I only got half of one. "Sounds awesome, Jamie. But you're missing Annie's pot roast. She never gets to cook meat for me, so she's going all out."

I said we'd already eaten. I said I'd call again later.

Throughout the conversation Ian had been at my side, signaling that I should go, but it had been so long since I'd felt this particular buzz, the one that comes only from making something, that I didn't want to leave. I felt the promise that this work would focus me, get me out of the research mindset, help me find that illusive angle, not just for the website, but for something larger. "Was that a bad-boyfriend move?" I asked Ian.

"He's your boyfriend. You tell me." On his monitor, he had added a sepia tint to the picture of Teddy and Danny by the Chevy.

"That looks fake," I said. "Trying too hard to be a documentary image."

"It's supposed to give it gravity," he said, but after a moment of concentration he removed the tint and tried a different effect, a pale blue saturation.

"I've been thinking lately about how Woody and I met," I said. "About that long anticipation, wanting him before I even knew him."

"Wanting him because you couldn't have him."

"I remember feeling so—" What was the word for it, that barely contained sensation, nearly explosive though not destructive, an eruption into a new life? "So fucking *ripe*."

"Well, you picked the fruit off that branch," he said, talking through the mouse clicks. "Once you have something, you no longer have to want it. So you start looking around to see what else is out there."

"I'm beyond looking."

"Because you're a slut," he said, finally turning to face me. "A reformed slut for a couple of years now, but you'll never be satisfied sucking only one cock. It's a no-brainer."

"It's not a no-brainer. It's a conundrum."

"Change the rules. Open up your relationship."

"Um, this is Woody we're talking about here."

"Shit!" A long ash had toppled off his cigarette into his keyboard. I lost his attention as he turned the board upside down, shaking out the dust. On screen, Teddy and Danny smiled from their blue world.

I left Ian's after midnight. I didn't call Woody. I was too wasted from a day of smoking and drinking to navigate my way through whatever scolding awaited me. I walked for a half hour, telling myself I needed air, needed motion, but where I took myself was to a South of Market bar called the Playpen, where the patrons were coated in a dim, scarlet light and the walls thrummed with music that sounded like dance-club repetition and hard rock all at once.

Men stood in clusters near the bar and the square support pillars, or sat alone on the benches that ringed a dingy green pool table. A television screen blinked images of hairless muscle mass, bulky body parts, the blurred thrusts of greased penetration. A short flight of steps led to a second bar, the air up there muskier, heavier with potential. A leather curtain in the back marked a doorway through which patrons passed all night long.

I thought about the danger of a room like that. Every man for himself, none to be trusted. STDs unleashed in swapped fluids, unfair payback for consensual sex. Or not. Because a room like that could just as easily be pure magic. Strangers communicating with hardly a word and still finding what they came for. I thought about my mouth finding flesh. The heat of contact.

I pushed my way in.

My eyes struggled to outline the crowd in the darkness. I saw someone bent in half, slurping. Someone else groped from behind. Silhouettes of bodies watching, waiting. I followed a fat ember, the flame-hot bowl of a pot pipe, to a set of lips. I moved closer, asked for a hit. He turned and blew herby smoke on me. I inhaled it, squinted at his face, saw a familiarity, even in the shadows. I took a hit, felt his eyes on me. Before I exhaled he was on me, mouth to mouth, trading spit for smoke. I hadn't even been here five minutes.

As I pulled away, he said, "How's it going, Jamie?"

What the fuck? "Do I know you?"

"Yeah, it's Abe." *Right, Abe.* One of those guys I ran into everywhere and knew hardly anything about. An ex–New Yorker with whom I'd bitched at parties about California. A grad student in something health-related at Berkeley. A good friend of a guy who was a good friend of Woody's. That Abe.

Abe was a reminder: You can't court temptation in a South of Market back room and expect it to be a covert act. At least I couldn't, after ten years in San Francisco.

"I'm supposed to meet a friend up front," I said, moving away.

"Too bad." Even in the dark, I knew what his face was telling me.

I got the hell out of there, already composing the e-mail I would send when I got home.

> *Hey Wormy,*
> *Don't be mad about tonight, I just couldn't deal with a crowd for dinner. Things are going great on the website, Ian and I went out for a drink, stayed up late. Call me when you wake up?*
>
> *Kisses, Germy*

After I sent this e-mail I found a message waiting for me. Not from Woody; from an official-looking address I didn't recognize.

> *Thanks for getting in touch with the Gay, Lesbian, Bisexual and Transgender Historical Society. We don't have any records from the estate of Don Drebinski, but since you said he was a business owner I searched through our obituary files, which we pull from local gay newspapers. Here's what I found:*
>
> Donald Peter Drebinski, an early member of the Tavern Guild and the owner of several gay bars, including Don's Place, a popular North Beach hangout, passed away at his

> home in the Upper Haight on July 9, 1992. He was 72. He follows his partner of 24 years, Ron Chester, who passed away a year ago.
>
> Drebinski was born in Denver and served as a chaplain in the U.S. Army during World War II. He left the church when he moved to San Francisco in the early 1950s, working in the restaurant business and becoming part of a group of gay bar owners and bartenders that grew into the Tavern Guild, San Francisco's first incorporated gay business organization. The Guild held auctions and benefits to raise money for various community causes, including legal aid for men arrested in police raids on gay bars and cruising spots. Drebinski briefly left San Francisco for Los Angeles, returning in 1964. He ran Don's Place, a neighborhood bar, for ten years, and also owned Lois Lane, a cafeteria in the Tenderloin, and briefly, the Coliseum, a South of Market leather bar. He retired in 1980, and spent his last decade volunteering for AIDS charities, traveling, and tending his garden.
>
> He has no survivors.

I released the breath I'd been holding and let myself feel the thrill of discovery, of watching this man's existence crystallize with each new fact (as Dean Foster's had when I stumbled upon that database). Don had lived into old age, found a long-term lover, played a role in his community. I felt, too, the adrenaline tingle of pushing deeper into my inquiry—understanding that Don's years in Los Angeles perhaps overlapped with Danny Ficchino's. And yet all of this crashed up against something darker: disappointment, even loss, at the knowledge of his death. His seventy-two years no more than a paltry collection of facts. *No records in the archives. No survivors.*

He was alive the first two years I lived here. I let myself trace a parallel history in which my father had never disowned his time in San Francisco and never lost touch with Don, so that when I moved here, I looked Don up, visited him and his partner in the Upper Haight, brought out my tape recorder. Sitting in their garden, listening to their histories, I took on the role of archivist. Of survivor.

11

Flat, shadowless light washed my bedroom. It was Sunday morning and I was alone. My father's letters sat on my nightstand, disorderly and curled at the edges from so much handling. In the dark hours before I fell asleep, I'd skimmed them again, reminding myself what else I knew about Don Drebinski, the facts not part of his obituary. Now I phoned Woody, left a froggy-voiced message on his home machine: "I'm awake. Call me." He didn't, and soon I was restless, sucking down mugs of coffee and repeatedly checking e-mail. No word from him. I paced for an hour. I tried his cell phone, left another message. I was paying the price for blowing off dinner.

A breeze brushed tree branches against my kitchen window, and a giddy play of sunshine and shadow tickled the cabinets. The world outside my claustrophobic apartment was calling. If Woody wasn't going to phone me, I wasn't going to stick around. I quickly layered clothes over my unwashed skin, left my apartment and unlocked my bike, which I stored in the covered walkway alongside my building. I had a new plan: motion as the cure.

A bicycle has been a reliable salvation all my life, going back to the first shiny three-speed that helped me escape endless, torturous middle-school days, my books in a wire basket, the thin, speedy wheels propelling me onto the side streets of Greenlawn, looking for other troublemakers on their own slick three-speeds. A wheeled army of misfit teens, lighting up cigarettes in the town park. I have always turned to a bicycle to lift me from bad moods, from brain jumbles needing to be undone and simmering, ugly emotions. Even during my years in New York, I would pedal along East River Park and revel in the high-rise atmosphere, or across Fourth Street to the West Side, to the still-undeveloped piers, where I cruised guys sitting shirtless in their cars. I felt like a kid when I got on my bike. A leg thrown over the crossbar, a foot finding the metal grip of the pedal, weight surging downward to start this small miracle of propulsion, of balance. The smell of rubber tires triggering a primal urge: escape.

I liked to say, in the boastful way of the urban cyclist, that bicycling was the fastest way around San Francisco—faster than the unreliable Muni system and the always-gridlocked traffic; faster, and easier on the shins, than trudging up and down hills on foot—though it was also one of the most dangerous. So now, unlike in Greenlawn, I mounted my bike with a helmet on my head and gloves to protect my hands should I wind up skidding along the pavement, and I cuffed my pants to keep them out of the chain. All this precaution left me feeling dorky, like I was my own mother bundling me up for the elements, but in ten years in San Francisco I'd fallen half a dozen times because of my own clumsiness or the obliviousness of others; I'd been doored, I'd been sideswiped, I'd been knocked down by that U-turning SUV on Valencia. I secretly yearned to be a bare-headed bike stud zipping confidently in and out of slow-moving traffic, a carefree messenger with tattoos on my overdeveloped calves, but I had an ingrained fear of injury that went all the way back to some lesson passed on by my father: *Protect yourself. Avoid trauma to the head.*

I rode through the warm Mission to the Castro, where the sidewalks hummed with relaxed-fit gays moving toward brunch, into the Lower Haight, where the pierced-and-tattooed subculture mixed with homeboys yelling to each other from opposite corners. Onward I pedaled, making my way to the Panhandle, a length of park where winding, paved paths were thronged with cyclists, rollerbladers, couples guiding strollers, the homeless pushing shopping carts, old-timers toddling between benches. On the grass, tai chi, Frisbee, guitar playing and gossip unfolded. I watched a shirts versus skins basketball game, marveling at taut, unselfconscious flesh. I grumbled at a teetering drunk veering sideways into my oncoming treads. The air carried conga drumming and pot smoke my way; I thought eagerly of the joint I'd stuffed in my pocket before leaving home.

On Sundays the city banned cars from the Golden Gate Park's main thoroughfare, so when I crossed Stanyan, I flowed into a wide boulevard crammed with even more of the Sunday masses. I slowed down to watch a line of rollerskaters dancing with ritualized precision, a lesbian couple teaching their son to bike without training wheels, a group of pretty, teenaged Latinas flirting with boys whose jeans drooped below their butts. Late-winter wildflowers crowned the hillsides. Eucalyptus infused the air. Up ahead I saw a face that pulled me toward it: a long-haired Asian guy in cool eyeglasses and a ratty thermal shirt. He could have been Brady's gay brother. Our eyes met in a moment of mutual check-you-out that I felt under my ribs. I held my breath, and his stare, until he turned away. I looked back, but he was gone.

I steered into a thicket of chilly, forested trails, out of sight of the regular folk, where I knew I'd find men standing at intervals, gaping with that familiar hunger, more attenuated here because it was Sunday, the weekend's possibilities nearly over. I pedaled slowly and took in some very bold, locked gazes, and others, more timid, eyes shifting away, wallflowers at the prom. I wasn't just looking, I was cruising, and I was surprised at how little guilt was attached to this knowledge. I felt anonymous, separate from my life and its demands. Not an individual bound by rules, but a piece of the larger, interlocking jigsaw, a necessary element of the city, doing my part to keep San Francisco the kind of place where guys got on their bikes on Sunday afternoons in pursuit of sex. But this wasn't really my scene. Middle-of-the-road fashion was the rule: patterned sweaters over pale blue jeans, imitation motorcycle jackets with khakis and white sneakers. Ian and I liked to joke that these trails were the best place in San Francisco to pick up a high school teacher.

I blasted out of the bramble, back onto the main drive. Around a bend, the Pacific came into view, blue-gray under silver-gray clouds, the air suddenly stinging with salt. I crossed the Great Highway and navigated the parking lot—cars jockeying for spaces, surfers peeling off wetsuits, dogs sniffing among the trash cans—and found a post to which I could lock my bike. At the top of a grassy dune I sat down and sparked up. Gulls arced overhead, their throaty squawks like little sirens. The edge of the ocean rippled and flattened on the sand, then slid back again into the vastness, perpetuating the cycle.

I pictured Teddy—out of work, late on his rent, pining for Ray—walking to the beach to clear his head. Forty years ago, contemplating this same infinite horizon. Did this view make him feel connected to everything around him, or apart from it? Strong enough to master this new city, or insignificant and far from home? I remembered us together—an actual picture from the past, not an imagined one—down the Jersey Shore. His arm sweeping through the air to explain the path of the Gulf Stream, how it traveled up from the Caribbean to give us warm water to swim in, how different this was from the ocean in California. *At this latitude, you can't swim in the Pacific. The water travels down from Alaska. When you're used to the Atlantic, the Pacific will make you feel all turned around.*

I could still redeem myself with Woody if I made the effort to hook up with him for the remainder of the afternoon. I looked around for a pay phone, but there was none along the beach. *Maybe I can borrow a cell phone from a stranger.* That's a call Woody would love to get. His annoyance would melt away knowing I had given in to the convenience of this reviled technology. For the sake of forgiveness, I would offer him the chance to say "I told you so." My relationship for a cell phone!

Oh, but look at me, heading not toward a crowd of strangers bearing Nokias, but onto the park road, back toward the lust-filled woods. I found another set of trails, different from the stretch I'd traveled earlier but equally notorious. Into my view came an older guy—older as in sixties or seventies, his face long and deeply lined, set off by a powerful jaw and a full crown of white hair with peaks like coconut frosting. He stood tall, six-foot-two, I guessed, with a trim body and slightly stooped shoulders, and stared back unabashedly from large, deep-set eyes bravely telegraphing desire. Grandpa was cruising me.

I rode past, then thought, Why not? and turned to look back over my shoulder. His gaze held tight. I'd give him something to brag about to the old-timers slugging Irish coffee at Twin Peaks—*This youngster flirted with me today*—a little boost, a charitable return. His eyes were focused, plain in their intent. He could easily be seventy. He could be Don Drebinski himself—could have been. The fact of Don's death returned in a gust, and I shook my head as if to clear a bad dream.

Next thing I knew I was pedaling toward him. This old guy in the park. This not-Don. He stood stock-still, waiting, his face impossible to read. "Hello," I said.

"Nice day for a ride." His voice had a sardonic creak, a William Burroughs archness. Come to think of it, he was a bit like Burroughs in his stance and looks, though not so pallid or strung out. Heartier.

"I love riding out to the ocean," I said.

He raised an eyebrow, offered a knowing smirk. "And cruising the park?"

I smiled. This guy was nothing if not confident. He's no closeted schoolteacher, he's Grandpa Stud, still working the trails decades beyond his heyday.

"Did you bike far? You're very fit," he said approvingly, daring to eye me up and down. I liked this attention. I might feel out of shape alongside the hardbodies at Dolores Beach, but to Grandpa I was still a hottie.

"From the Mission." I felt like showing off, turning him on. "It's great for my legs. Keeps me solid."

Silence lingered; him grinning, me wondering what to say or do. Up until now, this had hewn to the shape and substance of any other sexual transaction: the genesis of eye contact, the butterflies of excitement, the upswing of momentum. And now, the pause at the crossroads: Pursue? Retreat? The moment where you commit or pass. I wasn't actually planning to have sex with this geezer, right? Must find another option. Like conversation.

I introduced myself by name.

"Walt," he said, offering a handshake, bony but strong.

I small-talked about the weather. I mentioned the fact that the trails in this part of the park were being widened. "I guess the powers-that-be know what goes on back here."

"Every few years they try to clear out the cocksuckers. But we're like weeds, we always grow back."

I laughed again. "So you've been coming here for a long time?"

"I'd venture a lot longer than you."

"I've been in San Francisco for ten years. Among my friends I'm considered a lifer."

"Among my friends you're fresh as a farm boy."

I might have blushed then, as though he'd just announced his plan to deflower me on a hay bale, and felt a twinge of stiffness under my pants. I remembered something Ian once told me about dancing on stage in his early twenties, when he was a go-go boy at a nightclub: "I get hard because they want me." The undeniable connection between self-esteem and arousal. Feel yourself elevated, objectified, and feel your nerves respond.

Walt drew me back with a question: "Shall I show you something?"

He waved me along the path. I dismounted, curious, and pushed the bike, adjusting to his slower pace, noting the crunch of gravel and pine needles under our feet. He led me toward an old windmill tucked amid the tall trees. This was one of two windmills in the park; the other stood back by the road, renovated and landscaped, skirted by flowers, backdrop for a million snapshots. This one was ringed with bike tracks and boot prints. Garbage clung to its base—beer bottles, tissues, wrappers. I didn't actually see a used condom, but it was that kind of place.

"This," Walt said, tracing a crooked finger along an invisible circumference, "was the site of the biggest orgy I've ever seen. Dozens and dozens of fellows going at it."

I widened my eyes. "Here? When?"

My response had amused him. His mischievous smile pushed life into his sunken cheeks. "There was a time when they hardly patrolled at all."

"Was this in the sixties?"

"Young man, I'm speaking of the *forties.* After the war. This plot of land was notorious." He pivoted on his heels, sweeping his arm, inviting me to redraw the landscape with my own imagination. Dense vegetation swelled at each side of the muddy trail. The natural architecture of the bushes yielded caverns and crannies, dark grottoes canopied by twisty branches. I resurrected horny men from bygone decades, watched as they met at the windmill and ventured off, coupling, tripling, quadrupling, entire fleets of hunky sailors making the filthy best of shore leave. A Paul Cadmus painting come to life.

"With all due respect, Walt, I think you might be embellishing. I mean, the forties? Being queer was against the law."

He puffed a bit of air, a dismissive *pffft.* "Us enlisted men, we didn't care so much. We'd just risked life and limb for this country. We'd seen young men fall. To have survived, well, you felt like you were invincible. It gave you a very big appetite for life." He slapped his palms, brushed them together. "There were arrests, always. If you were a soldier, they'd put you in the stockades on Treasure Island. For the rest of us, the worst was later. The fifties. That's when the bars were raided all the time. Your name could wind up published in the newspaper." I redrew the porn tableaux, colored this time in anxious shades: your brain teetering between the explosion of desire and the fear of arrest, while a hot piece of sailor ass backed up onto your cock, the ocean roaring just beyond the fragrant, flowering bushes.

I felt the pressure of Walt's hand on the seat of my pants. "For a few years after the war," he was saying, "oh, times were good."

I couldn't help but grin. "You know, Walt, I have a boyfriend."

"Good for you. I myself have a husband."

"And he's okay with you—with this?"

"We've been married for most of my life. You don't last that long without having a little something extra on the side." His eyes were positively twinkling. "I live on the other side of the park, just off the Panhandle. Come with me."

I shook my head. "Walt, me and my boyfriend—we just don't—I mean, with other people."

"Yes, but you were pedaling through the glen, weren't you? Looking. Surely not for the likes of me, but nevertheless."

No, not looking. Cruising.

He took his hand off my ass. "I'll make you a cup of tea. I'll tell you more stories like this. You seem interested." With a tilt of his head he added, "Or I could blow you."

His smile told me that I would go with him, that my resistance was silly, that he knew better. And yes, I was charmed. He had so much spunk in him. Ian would have classified Walt as a forefather by sheer virtue of longevity, history, freedom of spirit. Getting a blow job from this guy wouldn't be simply sex. It would be an offering. A tribute. A concept Woody might even understand, I foolishly told myself.

I followed that confident smile back to the main drive. We lifted my bike into the trunk of his car, a big, twenty-year-old gas guzzler. He drove along the ocean, up past the Cliff House. The wind was whipping up the hair of tourists, who leaned against the concrete cliff-top wall, taking photos of each other, preserving for the future their postcard San Francisco.

He owned a three-story Victorian in the Western Addition, a neighborhood that at one time marked the city's western edge but was now smack in its center. The light in his house was dim, the walls adorned like a nineteenth-century salon, with a grid of oil paintings, old lithographs, outdated maps, framed newspaper headlines from yesteryear. He led me into a parlor, where a burgundy couch on carved wooden legs faced a charred fireplace. The mantle held brass candelabras, a couple of clocks, china bowls laden with chocolates; the mirror was dappled with irregularities and streaks of wax. I stole a glance at our reflection: Walt, a gleam in his eye, watching me take it all in; me, looking awed but unsure, like Alice down the rabbit hole.

He disappeared into the kitchen and returned with two cans of Budweiser, and we sat on the couch, which looked plush but felt stiff and lumpy. He told me he'd owned this place since 1954, when he and his lover bought it with a one-thousand-dollar down payment.

"Is he here now? Your lover?"

"No, no. Carter is staying in Monterey for the weekend. He has a fellow he visits from time to time. They were hot and heavy once, twenty years ago, but now they mostly just reminisce."

I downed a mouthful of beer. "I don't think I've ever met anyone like you."

"This neighborhood is full of us. We bought up the Victorians back in the fifties, when they were considered worthless eyesores. You'll find plenty of old queens living behind these doors."

He led me upstairs, pointing out the gaslight lamps, still in working order, at the top and bottom of the banister. On the second floor stood a wooden mannequin draped in an ornate bridal gown—"Worn by Joan Sutherland in *Il Trovatore,*" Walt boasted, and I acted impressed, though I was ignorant on this subject. Walt had worked for years in the props department of the San Francisco Opera, where much of this campy décor originated. Carter had been a travel agent, and they'd visited "every continent except the South Pole." He looked up at the mounted head of a wild boar brought back from Africa, when shooting game on safari was still commonplace. "You killed that?" I asked. "Carter," he replied with a sigh that could have indicated deference or disapproval. He slid up the lid of a rolltop desk crammed with playbills from local gay theater productions. On the wall above was a 1967 newspaper photo of Walt and a gang of friends the night they showed up in full flapper drag for the premiere of *Thoroughly Modern Millie* at the Alhambra Theater.

"I think the Alhambra just closed," I said.

He nodded. "They're turning it into a fitness club."

"That's terrible," I moaned.

He merely shrugged. "We enjoyed it while we had it."

He led me down a hallway past several closed doors to a small, sunlit bedroom, its walls covered in framed black-and-white snapshots. He pointed to one. "Here you go. This would have been before we moved in to this place. Carter's on the right."

Young Walt was lanky in a white T-shirt tucked into blue jeans.

Carter was broader, with a lantern jaw and an athletic neck. Their arms circled each other's waists. "What a couple of studs you were," I said.

"Up here," he said, tapping a finger against his temple, "I'm still a looker. Same dirty mind, same lusts. It's only the package that's failed me."

I asked his full name and got a bit of biography. Walter van der Neuen. Born Dutch, moved to the States as a kid in the mid-1930s. He fought in World War Two for the US Navy and afterwards came to San Francisco, where he discovered gay bars, stumbled upon orgies in Golden Gate Park and, at a house party, met his beau, John Carter—known as Carter to everyone because there were several Johns among their friends. As a couple, they became the center of a social circle, an elderly version of which survived today. "Best thing I ever did was buy this house," Walt told me, then corrected himself. "Second best. The first was marrying down with Carter."

I scanned the pictures of him and Carter and their friends, young guys at picnics, in restaurants, around a dinner table with glasses raised, preserved in silver, forever young. Bright eyes, thick, slicked-back hair, skin flushed with activity and inexperience—I could have fallen for any one of them. My gaze landed on a raven-haired, pale-skinned boy who carried himself with a Montgomery Clift unease, brooding to the point of smoldering. "Okay, I found him," I announced. "This one would have broken my heart."

Walt nodded knowingly. "Yup. Norman Berry. Norman suffered very romantically. Always a drama with that one. He lived here for a while."

"With you and Carter?"

"For about four or five years. A three-way affair at first, and later just friends. Very entangled friends. You had to take care of Norman. He was no good on his own. He drank a lot, and wrecked my car once, and got beaten up by the cops and roughed up by a trick. Carter never quite got over him." He guided me to a particularly ravishing image of Norman and Carter, in swimsuits on a sandy riverbank, nuzzling their heads together. Norman offered a rare smile in this one. "You were sandwiched between these two?" I marveled.

"On a regular basis. Norman slept right in there." He pointed through the connecting doorway to a room with a double bed, an antique wardrobe, its own washbasin. This room led to another, much the same in appearance—a corridor of hidden chambers. Walt said,

"I've lost count of how many strays we took in over the years. If these walls could talk, they'd sing Puccini."

I thought of my new recorder, cursed myself for not having it with me. But how could I have known where this day would lead me?

"Did you happen to know someone named Don Drebinski?" I asked.

He pressed his lips flat, furrowed his brows. "Rings a bell."

"I've been trying to get information about him. He was a bar owner. Don's Place?"

"Oh, that Don. The big Polack."

A spike of hope-fueled adrenaline—"Can you tell me about him?"

"Bit of a tippler, as I recall. He was the type to buy you a round on the house just so he could have another himself. But he kept his regulars happy."

"You wouldn't happen to have a picture of him, would you?"

Walt scanned the wall, shaking his head. "We can ask Carter. He's got stacks of albums in the basement. Carter might have known Don. Hell, he might have *had* Don."

"This is my lucky day," I gushed.

"You don't say." His eyes stroked me with approval, my enthusiasm clearly bringing him pleasure. I remembered his hand on my ass in the park, wondered whether, after this history lesson, I owed him something in return. Walt seemed heroic to me, brave; he'd created a dignified life at a time when it couldn't have been easy. And if he wasn't quite sexy to me now, he certainly would have been back then. Norman Berry may have been my instant favorite, but in picture after picture I found myself drawn to the tall guy with the confident smile at the edge of the frame. Walt had been the ringleader with the rooming house, the guy who watched over everyone, keeping track of personalities and affairs and the alliances that formed and dissolved—much like he was watching me now, so keenly that it seemed he could monitor my thoughts. I felt almost transparent, a filament, a sliver.

"This way," Walt said, his hand on my lower back, guiding me into Norman Berry's room. "There's your boyfriend." On the wall was a huge image of a naked Norman, an enlarged photograph, easily three feet tall and a foot wide, hand-tinted and glued to a knotty pine board. The wood was nicked and whittled along its edges and coated with varnish. What was the word for this particular kind of handicraft? Ah, yes: *decoupage*. It sounded French, but it was the tackiest Americana ever.

My eyes were wide with awe at the sight of Norman stepping out of a pair of trousers, one leg stuck among the folds of the material, the other bent at the knee and suspended above the floor. He was leaning forward, emphasizing his wiry frame. He had enough hair on his body at this young age to indicate he'd have much more of it later—his shoulders would flower like his forearms; the T pattern of curls on his chest and rigid abdomen would thicken, dense as his pubic bush. His cock was a short, plump sausage, raised up from hairy nuts, on its way to an erection.

As was mine.

Walt moved in front of me and began busying himself at my fly. I looked down at his hands, wrinkled and age spotted but still dexterous, ably getting my belt undone, my zipper lowered. As my pants slid over my butt and down my thighs, I thought, Well, here we go. My cock popped out and bobbed in front of him. "Good job," Walt said, a paternal approval in his voice, as if I'd brought home something I'd built in wood shop.

With one hand he freed his own cock, which was uncut and surprisingly large; the foreskin dangled loosely, battered from age, the skin weathered. With some exertion, he lowered himself to one knee, and plunged my cock into his mouth. It felt good. A mouth on your dick always feels good. I closed my eyes, lost in the sensation, but opened them again quickly. This was worth watching. The oddness of looking down on the top of his head, where his ruddy scalp was visible through a thinning snow-white patch; at his old man's face, his thin lips concealing, then revealing my cock. He kept his shirt on, but I could see a crescent of his abdomen droop over his wiry, gray pubic hair. He tugged on his own slowly stiffening cock, the foreskin drawing back to reveal the sensitive cap. I could smell him for the first time, not unclean, just aged. For some reason what came to mind was the backseat of a car, when you're a kid and you've fallen asleep on a long ride home and your nose is right up against the vinyl; a memory of driving home from Nana and Papa's apartment. Weird. All of it weird. *He's seventy and he's giving me head.*

On the wall, Norman, undressing for the ages, stared with his seductive, Monty Clift eyes.

Walt was sucking with gusto, his face reddening. Was he overexerting himself, heading toward cardiac arrest, the blow job to end all blow jobs? I was ready to suggest that he stop, that we take a break, a *breather*, as it were (his breath was truly sounding strained), when I noticed that all around me—on the dresser and the end table and the wall to either side—were more pictures of Norman Berry. Norman in a dozen sexy poses: shirtless, in a swimsuit, in a sweat-stained T-shirt. The room was a fucking tribute to Norman Berry's beauty and intensity, his damaged, needy, boyish soul. He'd been gone for years, but Walt and Carter, who'd been his lovers and caretakers and the prime recipients of his troublemaking appeal, had enshrined him here. Walt had brought me to this room, out of all the rooms in this big house, to participate in a lineage of desire extending back half a century.

I was fixating on one photo, Norman in a bar, Carter next to him on a stool, behind them, dimly lit, a slightly older, stocky bartender who, I decided, was Don Drebinski. *The big Polack. Carter might have had him.* Carter and Don and Norman and Walt—everywhere I looked were men preserved in silver, in amber, all of them somehow connected to me, to me through Teddy Garner, and somewhere in the midst of this was Walt slipping a spit-soaked finger up inside me, finding my prostate, pressing. *Tap, tap, tap* was all it took. I pulled back and tilted sideways, letting loose onto the carpet. He wrapped his hand where his mouth had been and extended my agitation, the endorphin rush stretching past its time-bound limits. Eyes closed, I might have been suspended in the air, floating in varnish like Norman Berry.

Walt was looking up in admiration, coughing a little and licking his lips. "Sorry about the rug," I said. He shook his head, looking pretty winded. "Are you okay?" I asked, which might have been a youthful faux pas, a blow to his vanity. Still, he didn't seem to mind when I helped him to his feet. His joints cracked as I sat him on the bed. He put his hand on my forehead and very tenderly wiped sweat from my brow.

"What about you?" I asked.

He flapped his hand. "I don't think you have that much time."

"I want to," I said.

He scrutinized me, for sincerity, I suppose, then reached into a drawer from which he pulled a cylinder of lube. He slathered my hand with the stuff, and then guided my hand to his cock, establishing a particular rhythm. He closed his eyes, and his face took on a contentment that made it almost childlike. The lines around his eyes smoothed out, his wet lips loosened and quivered, his breath deepened. I watched him relax into a different state, one that allowed him to take instead of give. It was the most remarkable face I'd ever watched on its way to an orgasm. I talked dirty and praised him—"That felt so good, Walt, you're the best cocksucker ever, you're a fucking master, I hope one day I'm as good as you"—caressing his ego along with his skin. From somewhere in the house a clock chimed, reminding me of the minutes passing as I stood above him, methodical, incantatory, studious. At last his body stiffened and moaned, until he was nearly keening from the depths of his throat, erupting with a vulnerable cry.

Now it was his turn to be disoriented, to quiver and blink with confusion and gratitude. I felt remarkably liberated, as if I'd busted through a membrane into a purer atmosphere. He pulled a towel from under the bed, wiping up this mess we'd made, and we giggled wordlessly, like guilty lovers in a secret hideout, at once proud and shy of the pleasure we'd discovered.

He offered to fix me something from the *icebox*, though the fridge was in fact modern, as was much of the kitchen. The stove was an enormous, restaurant-size six-burner, with a separate grill and two ovens. Walt explained that another housemate, a chef, had lived here for over ten years, and the equipment was left over from his tenure. The chef had died in the late eighties. I asked him if it was AIDS. "No, no. Very few of us died from AIDS. We watched the youngsters who came out in the seventies and eighties drop like flies. By then, we were already past our prime."

"But you're still sexually active."

"Not like that, not with so many partners and so much fucking. I certainly wasn't going to bathhouses."

Walt assembled a couple of ham sandwiches on white bread with mustard. Pretty bland stuff, but I devoured it. I told him then what I was up to, the details of my search. He said I had to meet Carter, whose recollections were crisper than Walt's. "All I remember are the boys," Walt said with a smirk. Would he tell Carter about what we did? "Course I'll tell him about a catch like you." We parted with a tight hug and an agreement to talk again. He stood at the door and waved as I biked away.

Out on the street, an afternoon fog, that San Francisco specialty, had settled thickly, the air crystalline with moisture. Pedaling uphill, I quickly dampened from weather soaking in and sweat leaking out. Back at my apartment, my body chilled, my head throbbing, I picked up a voice mail from Woody, steeped in annoyance and closing with, "We have to talk." I turned off my phone's ringer and fell asleep.

I went to his apartment the following night to confess, after a day spent trying to figure out how. I'd consulted no one; I'd gotten no advice. I'd simply brooded: alone, sober, inert in my bed for hours. After Rick, I had felt confused; after Red Shorts, depressed. But those encounters had been anonymous, or nearly so—trees that fell in the forest with no one around to hear but me. Walt would reverberate. I wanted to interview him, to meet his lover, perhaps with Woody in tow. There was no way to do that and expect the secret to keep. More than that, Walt was strike three, the threat, even the proof, of a pattern. Telling Woody about Walt was a way to make myself stop.

Woody sat in his state-of-the-art adjustable ergonomic chair, his back to his desk. Behind him, his laptop's screensaver was looping through repetitions, a DNA helix turning inside a coal-black void, collapsing, disappearing, rebuilding itself.

"I had an adventure," I began, and I told him everything about Walt, chronologically, so that he might be seduced into Walt's charms as I had been. I watched his interest deepening as I piled on the details, and when I got to Walt's sailor orgy, Woody's eyes blinked wide in amazement, and this gesture alone calmed my nerves. But as I continued on, he seemed to realize where the story was headed: his legs began bouncing, his arms crossed, his back arched away. By the time I got to the bedroom, with Norman on the wall and Walt on his knees in front of me, Woody had been shaking his head for half a minute. "Why would you do that?"

"That's what I've been telling you."

"Yeah, *how*. Not the same as *why*." The twisting colored light of the computer lit one side of his face like a mask, a sloppy blot of rouge, a bruise.

"I was in a weird mood," I said. "The thing about Don dying, I mean, being dead. Finding out."

Through clenched teeth, he said, "You're saying you had sex with him because you read an obituary?"

"He was really old!" Exclaiming these words at full volume didn't make them more convincing. Walt's advanced age, my loophole, wasn't working. "All I'm saying is that it's not the same thing as if, like, I'd gone to Blow Buddies or picked up someone on the street—"

"Yeah, okay, Jamie. Those things would have been worse. But they don't change the fact that you did *something*. You could at least admit that."

"I am admitting it."

He stood and walked out of the room, stirring the air as he passed. From the kitchen I heard him crack a tray of ice and fill a glass with liquid—a gurgle, a fizz, the little snaps of the unthawed cubes, each particular sound extending his absence.

He carried back a tumbler full of dark liquid, speaking as he entered. "It's not like I don't understand the lure of sex with someone else. It's not like I haven't been attracted—" He paused, lips curving downward. "But I haven't let anything go this far."

"What are you drinking?" I asked.

He dropped heavily into his chair, elbows on knees, forehead toppling into the weave of his long fingers. "Remember that night you came downtown to meet me? At that lounge where we had that fight in the street? You left early, and I was so mad."

I nodded. That was right after Red Shorts.

"I made out with Roger," he said.

"Roger the tweaker?"

"He's not a *tweaker*."

"He did a little bit in the bathroom, right?"

"That was a joke. It's a routine he does: *I'm going to the men's room to smoke some gay crack!*"

I didn't smile.

"We were drunk," he said. "We made out for a little while in the bathroom. Nothing happened. Nothing *else*. I was tempted, but I held back."

He sat up and gulped his drink down to the ice, then clattered the glass on his desk, the impact jolting his computer. The DNA ladder disappeared into a uniform gray glow that revealed an open e-mail window, an e-mail that I decided must be from, or to, Roger.

"Well, this is unexpected," I said.

"We were drunk," he repeated. "See, this is why I wanted you to come to dinner at Annie's."

"But wasn't Roger there?"

"I wanted him to see us together, to get the picture of you and I as a couple, because I'm pretty sure he has a crush on me, and I probably gave him the wrong impression by kissing him that night."

"That little bitch," I muttered.

"He's not a bitch. You don't even know him."

No, I didn't. He'd been a joke to me: a gossipy little technofag with a baggie of speed in the pocket of his designer jeans. Now all of a sudden he was my rival—my younger, cuter, less depressed rival.

"Must self-medicate," I said.

On the kitchen counter I found a bottle of bourbon, a liter of ginger ale, and the tray of ice, already puddling. All the makings of something sweet and watery, when what I craved in that moment was a lick of salt—dry, abrasive, cauterizing. I wanted to be sanded-down raw, not rubbed in sugar. "Do you have any tequila?" I shouted, opening a cupboard.

"You have no right to be mad," Woody said, startling me from the doorway.

"I'm not mad." *I'm sure he has tequila somewhere.* "I just never imagined that you—" I couldn't finish the sentence. I turned to look at him. "Ian thinks we should have an open relationship."

"Ian's not your boyfriend."

"This guy Walt and his *husband*, they've been together forever and they've always had guys on the side."

"Is that what you want?" he asked. A challenge.

I gave up on the tequila, grabbed the bourbon by its neck, dumped some into a glass. "I want things to be like they were a week ago, when we were playing detective."

He began shaking his head again. "I want you to think about whatever it is you're going through because ever since your father died—"

"Oh, Woody, not that again. I'm dealing with it. I am, in my own way."

"You still haven't owned it."

"But I'm sure paying for it."

"Actually, I'm paying for it, Jamie. Literally and figuratively."

Ugh, look at us. Me, wisecracking through a shot of liquor. Him, standing tall, arms akimbo, mouth a wounded crease, wronged. I saw us on TV as talk-show guests, a caption beneath him reading TOO MUCH PSYCHOBABBLE and another beneath me saying CAN'T BE TRUSTED.

The bourbon was hot in my throat as I muttered my way from the room, announcing that I was leaving. When he started to follow, I grabbed my coat and scurried away like a startled yard cat. He called out, "Don't be that way." But I was that way, so I kept going.

12

Do not sleep-in late. Do not reach for the remote control first thing. Do not wake and bake. Caffeinate, but not too much. Shower and report for duty in the living room. Clear that mess on the desk. Throw out dried-up pens. File those dusty folders! Make work-related calls. Apologize for how out of touch you've been. Let your alleged busy-ness impress them. Let it exhaust you. (People who contribute to society are tired at the end of the day.) Stay alert and productive. Avoid outdoors, where sex waits in ambush—particularly the Castro, South of Market, Polk Street, the beach, the park and stores that sell "gay underwear." This is how you will get your shit together.

A strategy recorded on a fresh page in my notebook. Enacted, too, for several remarkably sober days. A strategy not only for jump-starting my career but for keeping my boyfriend.

Except my boyfriend didn't want updates on my productivity. He didn't even want conversation. He wanted ten days of no contact. "It's not a breakup," he explained, the night after we argued in his apartment. "It's a time-out."

Like what Deirdre decrees when AJ is shouting, scampering and splattering food all at once.

I opened my mouth to ask why, but what I heard myself saying instead was, "Sure, whatever you need." And, "Sounds like a smart idea." For all my flaws I'm not clueless. I know when I'm being put on notice.

Get the blood circulating. Push-ups and crunches. The pot paraphernalia stays in the drawer.

Two boring days later, I left him a voice mail. "Hey-ey, Wormy. Just thinking about you. Hoping everything's okay. Nothing much to report. Just—everything's fine. A little lonely. But I'm making good use of the time, so that's good. Misssss yooooou." Sighs and sweet nothings. A thirteen-year-old girl daydreaming of her boy-crush, feeling sorry for herself and thinking he should know that.

I didn't really expect a call back, so it wasn't a problem when he didn't.

Four days in. "Hey, sorry to bother you. Quick question: I talked to Gold's Gym today about joining up, and I'm not sure, but it seems expensive to me. There's this sale, but then there's this enrollment fee, so the per-month cost seems . . . What do you pay at 24 Hour Fitness? What's the max you would pay? Can you leave me a quick message, because the sale ends tomorrow." A concrete request. Time-sensitive. A reply wouldn't have violated the time-out, right? A little flexibility, please. I wouldn't have called if it wasn't important.

No doubt he'd gleaned an unsurprising subtext: *I wouldn't have called if it wasn't about money. If it didn't seem like I might need to probably borrow a bit of money for this.*

Well, fine, there would be another sale, and in the meantime I could take advantage of a one-week trial membership. A gym in the Castro screamed *Warning! Danger! Sluts-in-Recovery Keep Out!,* but I was six days into my separation, newly resolute, and let's face it, Roger was easily twenty pounds slimmer than me (maybe thirty, the fucking waif), a reality that must be battled head-on.

During my intake session, a very buff young Asian guy asked me personal questions. I did not answer them all truthfully.

"Have you worked out before?"

"Oh, sure, but it's been a few years."

When he asked my age, I lied, too, but I lied up, said I was five years older. "You look great for thirty-eight," he said, which was what I'd been aiming for.

Set loose inside the gym, I was overwhelmed by the clutter of metal structures, each machine engineered to allow a single muscle group to harden into classical prominence. Where to begin? I lingered near two strongmen in conversation: "What are you working on today?" "Back and bi." "I'm on chest and tri." "Tomorrow I do legs." "I hate legs." "Yeah, legs kick my ass."

I headed for the treadmills and stepping machines. Yes, this is what I needed: *cardio.* I climbed up on an empty one, pressing a button labeled FAT BURN. The display remained blank. I pressed START. Nothing started. I pressed CLEAR, though there was nothing on the display to clear. Ruby-red LED digits burst into life. I keyed in my weight, my (actual) age, FAT BURN, ENTER. ENJOY YOUR WORKOUT, the display commanded. My feet settled into the flat, black plastic flippers, which glided smoothly through sweat-producing revolutions without taking me anywhere, a treadmill without the tread, a StairMaster without stairs. I was doing it, just like I belonged. The display kept track of how many calories I was shedding and how far a "distance" I was traveling. I could stay in this spot for miles. I would watch as five hundred calories were stripped away, one step at a time. The residue of an entire meal, eradicated in forty minutes. (Was that right? I'd have to start reading the calorie charts on my groceries.)

All day I had dreaded that I would stand out, undeveloped and uncoordinated, but it soon became evident that my lack of perfect pecs and washboard abs rendered me invisible among the muscled beauties. From my fat-burning perch I stared at the hunks; I noticed others watching, too. All eyes were on the white tank top, who might have stepped out of a Bruce Weber photo: trim, bronzed, his smooth surfaces unblemished, his smooth angles polished like ice. And that one over there, proportioned as though by an edict from Mount Olympus: shoulders a meter wide, waist trim and tight, his sculpted arm tugging a cable that turned a pulley that moved a stack of weights as tall as a hydrant.

As I laid on a floor mat, stretching after my workout, I listened to the white noise of all those rotating, sliding, slamming devices and the pulsing dance music over the speakers, and I noted the concentration on the many glistening faces, and I wondered how all this exertion might be tapped and made into something useful. Five hundred calories times five hundred people times five hundred gyms times five hundred days—together we could solve the world's energy problems! No more oil, no more coal, shut down the nuclear reactors! People Make the Power!

In the communal shower, a brightly lit, blue-tiled area where eight chrome fixtures pointed inward, a guy stood facing the door, running soap suds across his chest. Like me, he was not among the hottest of the hotties, not a Dolores Park Speedo stud, just a thirtysomething guy soft around the middle. I smiled, Mr. Friendly, as if I didn't know why he looked my way, and I turned my back to him. When I spun around to rinse, I saw that his soapy ministrations had stiffened him up below. In his eyes was so much confidence that I got hard, too. *Goddamn it*. I looked away. My eyes found a sign on the wall proclaiming SEXUAL ACTIVITY IS STRICTLY FORBIDDEN AND WILL RESULT IN LOSS OF MEMBERSHIP. Someone had blacked out the SHIP. Loss of member: the ultimate punishment. Still, he was undeterred. He tilted his head toward the steam room, just off the showers.

It occurred to me right then, feeling the chafe of temptation, that Woody wanted me to fail. That ten days, he knew, was plenty of time for me to stumble into trouble. This wasn't about *space*. This was a test. With a violent jerk, I spun the temperature dial from red to blue. I let the frigid water punish me until I shriveled.

As I exited, another guy walked in, and my shower pal turned his attention toward the newcomer. I dressed and packed quickly. On my way out of the locker room I glanced back and saw the second guy following the first through the steam-room door, their bare asses disappearing into a cloud of vapor.

I smoked a lot of pot that night. The next morning, I did not go back to the gym. Nor did I at any point for the rest of my free-trial week. But that final image of *strictly forbidden* activity stayed with me, and I used it, alone in bed every night.

Day Eight. I left him another voice mail, this one a giddy performance: "We interrupt this time-out to issue a bulletin from Special Agent Garner to Master Sleuth Nelson. Come in Nelson. I have been forced to breach the no-contact zone to issue this urgent update to our investigation. This evening, Saturday, from six to nine p.m., at a gallery in downtown San Francisco, a certain lady painter from the days of Frisco past will be exhibiting her artwork. This is a rare chance to meet one of our investigation's key informants in person. Your presence is highly encouraged."

I did not receive a reply.

"He's smarter than I realized," Colleen said of Woody.

"Because he's with Roger all day, every day, while I'm here alone, imagining him with Roger?"

"No." She paused to apply lipstick, blood-dark to complement her new black hair. The furrow of her brow indicated either concentration on her task or annoyance with me. Or both. We stood side by side in her bathroom, readying ourselves for Ray's opening. The hour I'd been here had been spent updating her on boyfriend drama. She'd been attentive, prettying herself up as the story grew uglier. "Because he's realized the only way to get you to look at your shit is to stop babying you."

"Why, that's brilliant!" I slapped my forehead in astonishment.

She capped the lipstick. "I told you, give the guy credit."

"I'm being sarcastic, in case you didn't notice. Don't you see? He imposes this silence, which is so patronizing, so controlling, and now he's convincing my friends that it's good for me. He's showing his true colors. Underneath the friendly surface he's very manipulative." As the separation had gestated, I'd stretched about as far as I thought I could, and I now felt a tinge of mania. "How can he resist this? I know for sure that he wants to meet Ray."

"There are two more days to the time-out," Colleen said, marching into the hall to fill a vertical mirror with the evening's outfit. I watched as she modeled: silver leather boots climbing to the top of her calves, a snug dark dress dropping to the knee. She'd found the dress in a vintage store and bedazzled the hell out of it. Tendrils of rhinestones roped from shoulders to hips, catching lamplight and throwing back sparks.

"You look like a million bucks."

"Or at least fifty," she replied, though I could tell she was pleased. Colleen had always been tough, outspoken, opinionated—but strangely, not always confident. In her thirties she bore a visible polish; she'd sloughed off the remnants of an extended, sometimes awkward girlhood, and now a sexy, self-assured woman stood in her place.

I stepped next to her at the mirror. My hair had grown out, and tonight I'd stopped trying to tamp down the flyaways and was letting it go its own rakish way. I wore a secondhand, gray wool suit originally purchased a couple of years earlier, on the big side at the time, but a perfect fit now. I had the perfect pale blue shirt to wear with it. I'd left the neck untied, and now I opened an extra button, freeing a few sprouts of reddish chest fur. Cool suit, wild hair, hot babe at my side: Who needs a gym body when you've got fifty-dollar style?

"I'm glad you're my date tonight," I said to Colleen. "No more talk about Woody."

"Woody?" she feigned breezily.

"Ha! That's my girl."

Arms linked, we strolled early evening Market Street, downtown's glass doors still discharging working folks, nine-to-fivers who'd been stretched to seven, eight p.m. I watched one desk-weary businessman after another eyeball Colleen, and instead of slipping into the usual sister act with her—*Oh, girl, that one just checked you out!*—I made a game of glaring at them: *Back off! She's mine.* While she talked, I held myself on alert, walking taller, coiling her into me securely, pretending for a few blocks that we were a couple, that I wasn't a philandering fag out with his gal pal, but actually straight, on a date, *the man*—an approximation that on the surface took almost no effort at all, and beneath warranted just a small shift in consciousness: to see men not as possible conquests but as competitors. Desire transformed into rivalry. The appeal of that shift—a dram of power, swallowed quickly—was immediately intoxicating, and I daydreamed the possibility that this other life existed for me, a straight guy's life, if I could just slip into its inverse flow and ride it standing.

Early evening in San Francisco, when the city feels most like a jewel of the Wild West: The blue-black sky hangs wide, hugging the clutter of tall buildings. Honky-tonk illumination—neon, tungsten, halogen—bounces from a hundred sources: wrought iron street lamps floodlighting the pavement, red warning hands blinking at the far end of crosswalks, static crackling on the guide wires of electric buses. In your cool suit, in your cool city, you can forget the problems that plagued you that day, because the night is coming, bringing with it, maybe, another chance.

The gallery was clogged by the time we strolled in. The crowd seemed at first glance of a uniform age and height—sixty-five at the youngest, five-foot-eight at the tallest. Elderly and stooped, gray haired or bald pated. Woody would have towered here. Professorial blazers mixed with outdoorsy fleece and silk-screened Indonesian prints. Colleen and I handed over our coats to a young woman guarding a rack of hangers, and then I guided Colleen through the room, once again noting the eyes drinking her in, and once again deeming this my victory, too: her public appeal also elevating me, the guy whose hand, pressing with assurance on the small of her back, swept her forward.

The walls beamed with the robust colors of Ray's landscape paintings, but there was no immediate sign of Ray. So I scanned for the evening's number-two priority, the food table. "Cross your fingers," I whispered to Colleen. "I think I see dinner." I let myself imagine sushi rolls and Middle Eastern sandwiches, maybe even something warmed over a blue flame, requiring a fork. Up close, the buffet revealed only cubes of cheese, seeded crackers, humus and pita, baby carrots. *Party starters,* we called this spread, we who had depended upon many an opening over the years to fill our bellies.

"We'll get some real grub later," Colleen said under her breath. "My treat."

"No biggie," I muttered, snapping a carrot with my teeth. *Can't play the man if you don't have the cash.* I turned to the adjacent table, decked with plastic cups of wine. "Can I get you one?" I asked her.

The gallery, L shaped, turned a corner, and in this second wing, filled with Ray's quasi-self-portraits, I spied her. Surrounded by well wishers, she was animated, fluttering, her inviting smile a contrast to the many pained, sober versions of her face that hung from the walls. I started to move across the room to say hello, pulling Colleen with me.

"Are you nervous?" she asked. "Because you haven't let go of me for the past hour."

"That's just because you're extra hot tonight."

"Yes, I am. So don't scare off potential dates."

I dropped my arm. A trickle of sweat slid along the seam of my uncrooked elbow. "After you."

"Lead the way," she insisted. "And girl, just relax."

Sisters again.

I waved to Ray, catching her attention at last. Recognition took a moment—I watched her eyes uncloud—but as I got closer she called my name. We leaned toward each other for a loose, friendly hug. "Did you bring your special friend with you?" she asked. Over her shoulder, I saw David Stroh, her own *special friend*, who reached out for a handshake before Ray had even let go. I was being gripped by him, still tangled up in her, and was trying to formulate an explanation for Woody's absence, when in my other hand I sensed the pliable plastic wineglass slipping from my grasp: a bobble, a splash, a gasp, the cup skittering on the floor, my ankles doused in Merlot.

"That's what I call making an entrance," said an older man to my side, as several others chuckled. One tall woman, ten years younger than Ray but with the same postmenopausal hairdo, patted a cocktail napkin against her pant leg.

I apologized repeatedly, while Ray turned to David, saying, "Hurry and find a wipe-up," and the crowd stepped back, emphasizing my culpability with a clearly drawn ring-around-the-klutz. Before any of us had recovered, Colleen was stepping forward with a bar rag. She sopped up the spill, her silver boot arcing terry cloth across hardwood, while I stood by, exhaling helplessly.

"Hi," I said, addressing the enclave with a feeble wave of my hand. "I'm Jamie."

"He's the son of a fellow I knew when I was just starting out as a painter, one of my original bad boys!" Ray announced, punctuating with her familiar burst of laughter. "Jamie's doing research on the sixties."

"The early sixties," I clarified, not sure whose eyes to meet, still very much aware of the spectacle I'd made. Colleen was gliding away, soaked towel dangling. The surrounding silence seemed to beg more from me. This is the point where Woody, arm over my shoulder, would usually interject a remark appropriate enough—just enough humor, just enough apology—to put the entire sloppy moment behind me.

"He interviewed me about the old days," Ray said.

"It's a history project I'm going to put online," I said.

"I'm next," David said. "I'll give him the real story."

"And then I'll give him the truth!" Another man's voice, from behind.

A wave of insider laughter rose up: *Oh, the stories we could tell!* I chuckled along, making a mental note to extract myself before I was bombarded with unsolicited testimony.

"Are you in computers?" the cropped-hair woman asked, her penetrating voice supplanting the niceties.

"Not really. Radio, by profession."

"Audio streaming will probably make radio obsolete," she pronounced.

"Not everyone has Internet access or even a computer," I said. "But anyone with a cheap transistor—"

"Sure, the *digital divide*. Give it time. That will change."

I withheld comment. I had found myself in this argument repeatedly over the past few years, but radio wasn't going anywhere. *The fucking spectrum wasn't going away.*

"I've got a website in development," the cropped-hair woman was saying. She began telling me about it; my force field went up and I heard nothing.

The man at her side, the one who'd commented upon my entrance—her husband, her lover, whomever he was—murmured agreement as she spoke. "It's a big idea," he said. "Guaranteed to attract venture capital."

"If you can't make money off the Internet," said David, "you're doing something wrong."

"Guilty as charged." I laughed at myself, *hahaha.*

Returning to the huddle was Colleen, bringing me, bless her, a much-needed fresh drink. "Let me introduce you to Ray," I said, steering us from the boomtown buzz.

I couldn't eat enough cheese cubes to keep pace with the wine I imbibed. Two hours later, food was crucial. Colleen and I wrangled Ray and David for a meal. I'm not sure who suggested we go to Al's, though I know it was me who said, "Let's just eat at a greasy spoon, one that serves beer," and that when I said this what I had in mind was the kind of diner I'd haunted in my youth in Greenlawn: red vinyl booths, white stone exterior, middle-aged waitresses, French fries in gravy. Of course, with one or two exceptions, this is not what diners look like in San Francisco today, or rather, this is what diners look like, but this is not what diners are. Diners today *suggest* the diners of my youth. They've got the red vinyl, but without the cigarette burns; the milkshakes, but with chunks of name-brand candy *blasted* into them; the waitresses in white skirts and gingham, though few of them are past college age. Even the name Al's is a retro reference: the name of the diner on *Happy Days,* a TV show about the 1950s that aired in the 1970s. A copy of a copy.

Colleen and I slid into a booth, across from Ray and David. "I want to say again how much I liked your work," Colleen said to Ray. "And how elegant you looked in the midst of it all."

Ray beamed. "Coming from you, dear, that's a compliment." Colleen's cheeks flushed. "The two of you," Ray said, flagging both of us. "Perfectly dashing."

"Isn't she great?" I said, squeezing Colleen's shoulder.

David asked, "How long have you two been together?"

"We go way back, to New York," I said.

"But we're not together," Colleen quickly added, the words seemingly directed at me. "Jamie has a boyfriend. A very nice guy named Woody."

I reeled my arm back in, letting the ridiculous fantasy of *passing* crumble again.

"I was so looking forward to meeting him," Ray said. "Where is he tonight?"

"We had a fight," I blurted, then gulped down the rest of my wine.

I'd hoped blunt truth would halt further questions, but Ray followed up with, "Oh, dear. Was it your fault?"

"Takes two to tango," David interjected.

"Though someone has to lead," Ray said.

An image reared up: me on my bike, cruising along the park trails. "I guess it's my fault," I said. "If Woody was to blame, he'd be here now, making nice." I could feel a burn in my cheeks, from alcohol, emotion, social ineptitude; my tongue suddenly swollen and uncontrolled. "Ray, you understand. It's hard to be monogamous—."

"You don't have to get into it, Jamie," Colleen said, clearly hoping I wouldn't.

"I'm just saying, Ray, when you were my age, you felt the need to wander—."

"True," Ray said, "But you're not dealing with abuse. I believe I told you?"

"About your controlling ex-husband?" I said.

"Ja-mie," Colleen cautioned.

"Beyond controlling." Ray said, adding, after the slightest hesitation, "It was physical."

"Oh." *Did I know that?* "I'm not sure I knew that."

"He was a D.A., so what could I do? Show my bruises to the police?"

"So that's why you had an affair with my father," I slurred.

"Jamie, maybe you shouldn't—." Colleen put her hand on mine as if to impart sangfroid.

"I had to end it with Teddy for the same reason," Ray continued. "Because he hit me, too."

Teddy hit Ray. Yes, right, it was in the letter. "He shoved you that time."

"I wouldn't call it shoving." I watched her eyes dart away and return before she spoke again. "There were a couple of incidents. The second one left a mark. I didn't wait for strike three."

"But he was crazy about you."

"He was a little crazy, period," Ray said. "Crazy with jealousy, and also something else. Something angry inside. Teddy didn't like things that seemed bigger than him."

"Did he just, like, slug you?" I asked, trying to understand.

Colleen moved her hand across the table to rest on Ray's. "I'm truly sorry you went through this."

I nodded vigorously. "I am, too."

"Good thing she finally found the right guy," David said too brightly, raising his beer in a kind of toast. Ray smiled back at him distractedly.

Colleen to Ray, again: "You don't have to talk about this if you don't want to."

Ray: "The truth will set you free."

David: "This food will set us free."

Our waitress had materialized with platters on her outstretched arms, all four entrées at once. David gazed upon her with enormous gratitude, not just for the food but for her timing. Colleen sent a resolute scowl my way, bidding me to cease and desist. Ray, in the midst of all of this, bore a vague expression, not unlike what I'd seen in her studio when I first confronted her with the breakup letter she wrote to Teddy. Not unlike the face she put in her paintings.

My need to clarify what I'd been trying to say, or ask, or—well, I couldn't catch hold of the thoughts weaving through my boozy brain. *A couple of incidents. The second one left a mark. Something angry inside.* My father had absolutely never hit my mother, nor had he delivered more than the most basic spanking to me as a kid. Was Ray misremembering? No, no, of course not: He'd hit her, she'd left him, he'd learned a life lesson from it. He took that crazy anger and buried it so deep it only came out in his cold, deprecating voice and not with his fists.

I ordered another glass of wine.

"Eat something," Colleen told me.

I stood next to her on a concrete island in the center of Market Street, clutching myself in the damp night air, waiting for the streetcar. Lined up against the railing with us were a couple of down-and-out black men who looked far older than they probably were, one talking through drool and the other nodding along, and two younger, geeky guys, one white, one Asian, with nearly identical eyeglass frames, the small, dark rectangles that were everywhere these days. "That was awkward," Colleen said.

"At the diner?"

"Why were you pushing like that?"

"I wasn't pushing her." The accusation confused me. Ray trusted me; if she didn't, she would not have spoken of difficult things. I could handle the tension; I grew up in a house where conversation sometimes flared hot; I interviewed people who occasionally got upset. I made a stab at explaining this to Colleen, but intoxication got in the way. I asked her if she was ready to go home, but got no reply. I tried again: "Let's get a drink somewhere. It's not that late."

"I'm done buying you drinks," she said.

"I can buy for myself," I said. "For that matter, I can buy for you, too." I pulled out my wallet and found a ten-dollar bill. "A beer, anyway."

"Don't bother."

A suited-up, goateed white guy about my age, carrying a rolled playbill in his fist, stepped onto the island. He gave me the once-over as he approached. I met his eyes out of habit, then looked away quickly.

"He checked you out," Colleen noted, also out of habit.

"So?"

"So, he's cute." She stepped back and scrutinized me. "What the fuck is up with you tonight?"

"What's up with *you*?" The edge of anger in her voice had brought the same out in mine. "First you're taking Woody's side, then you're acting like I'm, like, *inappropriate* with Ray—."

"And in between I was cleaning up your spill and paying for your dinner."

I knew from the set of her jaw that if I pitched a battle I would not win. I shuffled toward her pitifully, nuzzling her shoulder. "I'm sorry. I can't help myself."

So this is when she consoles me with a pat on the head; she accepts my apology; she makes sure I get home safely, with aspirin and water before bed. I wake the next day, hungover but relieved that I wasn't an excessively drunken fool, that I knew when to reel it in. Colleen is my oldest friend. We had our share of arguments back in the day—when we were both twenty-one and we enacted our troubles in plain view, the unspoken but agreed-upon way to traverse the blind tunnels into adulthood. We forgave each other's every excess and in this way, over time, we made fewer mistakes. I wake the next day happy that I didn't mess things up with Colleen, the way I'd done with Woody. Drunken mood swings, erratic behavior, public tantrums: I wake happy that I have outgrown all this.

If only.

What actually happened: Colleen pushed me off her, probably more roughly than she intended, but rough enough to send me stumbling heavily and ungracefully into the guy who'd cruised me. He muttered a startled, "Be careful!" which inflamed me.

"Don't push me!" I hissed at Colleen. Our eyes locked. Her hands tightened into fists at her sides. I took an angry stride forward, wanting to charge at her, knock her off balance, watch her fall to the ground—a desire that drew force through my legs, up my spine, down my arms into my own clenched fists. It would be so easy to let this raging impulse carry me without hesitation toward an impact. It was in my blood. I had learned that tonight.

Colleen jabbed a rigid finger at me, a warning, and she spoke loudly, with steel in her voice: "You don't even see what you're doing, do you?"

"Why are you being such a bitch?" I was yelling now, nearly doubled over with the power of it.

From behind me the goateed guy spoke. "Do you need help, miss?"

I snarled at him, "Butt out, faggot."

A bright beam of light washed across us, accompanied by the metallic grind of brakes and a tinny bell announcing the streetcar's arrival: a yellow-and-green model, one of the decades-old cars brought in from faraway cities to jazz up Market Street. Usually I liked these trains, but this one appeared to me as an outdated toy, a gimmicky, cloying distraction.

"I'm getting on," Colleen said, rushing past me, "and you're going to wait for the next one. Do you hear me? The night is over for us." She ran alongside the car as it pulled up.

The goateed guy inserted himself between Colleen and me. "You should leave her alone," he commanded. I'd pegged him for a theater queen, a sissy, but here he was, gathered up like a linebacker. My protest strangled in my throat.

I watched him back away, climb aboard and find Colleen—her black hair, night-tossed, visible through the window. He leaned in, touched the back of her seat, sat down across the aisle. She didn't look back to find me.

I didn't stick around for the next streetcar because I didn't have exact change for the fare, and the trendy-eyeglass guys, waiting to ride a different line, were watching me like I was dangerous and pathetic all at once. So I wandered down Market to a skeevy late-night bodega, where I used my ten dollars to buy a pint of Wild Turkey and told some thug blocking the aisle to "get the fuck out of the way"—then had to cross the street in the middle of traffic while he threatened, "I kill you, bitch." Suit disheveled, face colored with fear and fury, I slugged from a paper bag and staggered toward the Mission. My dress shoes pinched, and when I got home I uncovered new, broken blisters.

I sparked a bowl—the last thing I needed; it just flattened whatever shred of reason I had left—and turned on the computer, looking for I don't know what.

When I woke—mouth begging for moisture, eyeballs aching—I did believe for a moment that Colleen had tucked me into bed, that there had been no shouting, that I had not embarrassed myself. Then a slice of daylight through my window blinds brought back the streetcar's beam, and I saw myself lumbering through that final hour, a derelict zombie in a wine-stained suit.

First question: Did I want to eat something or make myself vomit?

What I really wanted was the comfort of Woody. But it was only Day Nine.

I left Colleen a groggy, apologetic message; I called Ray and left one for her, too. That afternoon Colleen sent back a voice mail saying I had *freaked her out,* that I should figure out *what this hostility and internalized homophobia was all about.* I called again, got voice mail again—she must have been screening her calls—so I ate more humble pie, telling her: *You are better than I deserve, your forgiveness means everything, let's talk Friday at the café. PS: My homophobia is externalized. I don't hate myself, just all other gay men. Hahaha.*

I didn't hear from her again, and when Friday came, she didn't show at the café. *Work is getting busy,* she said later, in another sent message, though she didn't propose another time to meet, and weeks went by before we spoke again.

IN THE WOODS

13

Colleen's wasn't the only message I got that day. This, from Deirdre: "Good news and bad news. I sent you a check; you'll probably get it tomorrow. It's not the full ten thousand. It's only one thousand. Better than nothing, right? Oh—I put the check in a package with some pictures and writing I found in the attic, which I thought you'd want to see. They were Dad's."

Right before she called I'd been staring at the minidisc recorder, wondering if I needed to return it to the store, which earlier that week had discovered my check was worthless and left me a threatening message. Deirdre's check would cover the cost. I could worry about my other bills later.

I owned a contraption that allowed me to record phone calls (I'd used it with my previous recorder to tape interviews for radio shows). I dug this out of a drawer and connected it between my new recorder and the phone. I told myself I wanted to test the quality of the machine, but I also knew that Andy was behind the delay in my getting the money, and if I got him on the phone I wanted to hear him explain.

I still have the transcript:

Hey, Deirdre. Got your message.

Hi. How's it going?

Not that good. I mean, I'm broke here, and you're telling me that you're still holding nine thousand dollars I was supposed to get a month ago.

I told you it was going to take a while. I thought you'd be happy—.

I'm not happy. Let me talk to Andy.

[Silence.]
Dee?
He's not here.
[Silence.]
Tell him to call me. I want him to tell me why.
He's hoping he's going to make you more money. By investing your share.
I need money now, Deirdre.
[Silence.]
Is something else wrong?
Jamie, he lost his job.
He's out of work?
He's working for himself now. Day-trading. He was doing it on the job so much, he was, like, why don't I just do it for myself?
They fired him for buying stocks online?
It's better this way, because he could make a lot of money. I mean, a lot.
And you're okay with this?
He's a little obsessive, but he seems good at it. I mean, that's how it sounds to me, but what do I know, right?
Jesus Christ. This is like being a full-time gambler, Dee.
Do you think? Because I'm kind of worried—.

She choked on her words, so I turned off the recorder. Andy was picking stocks according to tips he was getting in Internet chatrooms and from newsgroups, Deirdre said. He was buying and selling every waking hour, using Dad's money. On most days he was up very high, but he was reluctant to sell off too much because everything was still going up, up, up. On other days he followed leads that didn't pay off, which sent him scurrying to regain lost ground. He said he would slow down as soon as he met his goal: a new house for them. He wanted to liquidate a million dollars and pay the mortgage in cash.

My hangover squeezed my skull like a hat two sizes too small, and I wasn't sure if I was furious about the risks he was taking or thrilled to see more money flowing into the family, some of it, perhaps, into my hands. "There has to be a middle ground," I told her. "Tell him not to overdo it," I ordered, and through her sniffles she said she would. I parroted words of warning I'd been hearing about the stock market lately: *"There's no such thing as an elevator that only goes up."*

Day Ten. From the moment I woke, only one thing on my mind: Would I hear from Woody today? Was he watching the calendar as closely as I was? Or had he been swept into an affair with Roger, these ten days for him a blur of infatuation—sweet nothings e-mailed across the office, furtive midday make-out sessions in Digitent's empty conference rooms, weekend-long fuckathons sprinkled in crystal meth?

I fled my silent apartment at noon and biked to the bank, depositing a one-thousand-dollar check with the signature of my day-trade-addicted brother-in-law on the bottom line. And then to the electronics store, paying them, with a money order, the price of the recorder, plus a penalty fee, punishment for my deceit. I lied through my smile at the crew-cutted ex-Marine store manager, spinning a story of money I'd been screwed out of by an unscrupulous client, which then had fouled up my payments this month, and how relieved I was to finally set things right with them. I pretended he believed me.

Next stop, Anton. Time to replenish the stash.

"How are those knives doing?" he asked.

"Sharp as can be," I said, showing him the bandage on my still-healing thumb.

"Some people think it's bad luck to give knives as a gift," he said.

"Bad luck for the giver or the getter?" I pictured the velvet interior of the knife box, splayed open on my kitchen counter.

"Good question," he said with a chuckle. "I try not to believe in superstition."

"Everyone should be a little superstitious, Anton." Superstition had once convinced Woody that fate pushed us together.

Anton led me into the back. As he filled a baggie for me, I told him about my encounters with Ray. For a moment I wasn't even sure he grasped who I was talking about. My father's voice intruded—*Marijuana is scientifically proven to kill brain cells*—and instantly I was hit with a vision of myself at Anton's age: alone, wrinkled and burned out, living in the same small apartment, walls dingy from thirty years of smoke, piles of journals gathering dust, my handwriting increasingly illegible, even to me.

But Anton wasn't just foggy, he was anxious: His building was being sold. The same family had owned it for years, rarely raising the rent. Now the parents were retiring and the kids were selling. New owners in a four-unit building would certainly mean a rent hike—for Anton nearly as catastrophic as a drug bust. In the *Chronicle* that morning I'd skimmed a story about the increasing number of San Francisco arts groups facing evictions for the very same reason; a week earlier the *Bay Guardian* had written of a downtown building that housed rehearsal spaces for five hundred bands also up for sale to owners likely to convert the space to lucrative offices. It was a time of changing hands.

Walking back to my building, staring at the foundation being poured where the old red house had stood, the vision I'd just had of my future worsened: Now I was homeless, the detritus of my life contained by a shopping cart, and I cycled through a psychotic rant about evil landlords, corrupt real estate developers, *you people who let this happen to me.*

And then, back home, a message from Woody.

The shock of his voice in my ear, expanding into the air like scent, as if I could turn my shoulder and there he'd stand, near enough to touch.

His words: "Hi, Jamie, it's Woody. It's time to talk. And we definitely need to. Not just about the old guy in the park, but about anything else you might want to tell me. Think about it. Call me when you're ready."

No *Germy.* No *Wormy.* No *I missed you.* The menacing sound of *anything else you might want to tell me.* As if he knew something. This was not a message of reconciliation.

I hovered above the phone, trembling. My eyes went to the shelf where photos of my friends were lined up, among them several of Woody. In my favorite, he's removed his shirt, and daylight reflects from his skin, nearly gold under a brush of fawn-colored chest hair. Behind him, greenery blurs into a generic outdoor background. It could be any sunny day. He could be any healthy, pale-skinned guy. But I remembered this specific afternoon, and him inside it: a Saturday picnic in Golden Gate Park, where we played a sweaty round of Frisbee and drank bottles of Mexican beer with lime squeezed in. Ian was there, Brady and Annie, Colleen with a date. The smile on Woody's face in this picture seems to say, *Hurry up, so I can get back to the game.* But he doesn't really mind stopping to pose; for a moment he'll offer himself, self-consciously shirtless (*My chest is practically concave,* he protests when I praise his body), because that's what you do for your boyfriend: You stop everything and indulge his desire for you. Later that day I rested my head on his belly, under a tree, and now I touched the photo as if I might bring to life the pliant warmth of his skin. It had been so long since I'd felt the real thing. *And whose fault is that?* I pulled my finger away, leaving behind a glassy stripe: The photo had been sitting undisturbed for months, and had long ago surrendered to dust.

I looked away, sickened by the idea he might be ready to break up with me, that he knew there were other infidelities. Maybe he'd heard about the stoned lip-lock I'd shared with Abe in the back room of the Playpen, Abe who was the friend-of-a-friend-of-Woody's. Or maybe Colleen told Woody something about Newark Airport or the guy at the beach. But Colleen wouldn't. Would she? I could easily be reading too much into his message. I saw, at last, why he'd instigated this separation: Time apart is time to think. Only now, out of time, did I get it. I'd squandered the last ten days spinning fantasies about his affair with Roger and feeling terrible about almost everything I'd done, but I had no insight, no clarity, no conclusion, beyond this: I was still in love with the smiling guy in the photo who had inspired in me the desire to capture an enviable golden moment. But were either of us the same as we were on that day?

Flailing, I didn't call Woody back. And then something else caught my attention and distracted me. For days.

On the kitchen counter rested a spiral-bound sketch pad, the *pictures* Deirdre had included when she mailed me the check. I had yet to open it. A single word, CALIFORNIA, had been scrawled on its cover in what I immediately recognized as Teddy's handwriting. Inside I found sketches of ketchup bottles, filled ashtrays, people conversing in three-quarter profile. Life inside the Hideaway, captured by the burger flipper on his break. A portrait of a woman's face and bare shoulders: I knew right away these eyes were Ray's. Other faces followed, one ghost after another. And then, a series of attempts, each from a different angle, of a guy whose high forehead and receding hairline contrasted with a certain youthful brightness in his eyes. A close-up brought out the shadow of beard on his jaw; another, from farther back, showed a cook's apron over his plaid flannel shirt. None of them was complete, as if the sitter had eluded the sketcher.

I wanted an epiphany here, some revelation of who this older gay man, if this was indeed Don, had been to my father—the way I could see who Woody was to me in that park photograph. But the renderings in my father's sketchbook were not only unfinished, but unskilled, beginner's strokes that failed to convey meaning. My father's eye had seen; my father's hand had drawn. My father's heart was not on display.

I remembered Deidre's message that she was sending Dad's writing as well. I flipped through the sketches and found, tucked between the last sheet of woven bond and the cardboard back cover, a folder stuffed with paper, thirty or forty lightweight, yellowing pages festooned in the choppy annotation of a manual typewriter.

In the Woods
by
Teddy Garner

March 21-March 30, 1961

I.

Don brought me to this place because he needed to getaway and I needed to see something of California beyond the sordid Frisco city limits. When they came up with the phrase Gods green earth I bet they were standing here looking down on the endless greengreen hillsides and the brickred road going miles down to the blue Pacific. Through the cabin's window I spy the purplepink end of the day knockout pastel floods of color and I want to be out there wrapped up in the spunsugar sky.

This typewriter roars louder than anything except Chick and Mary whose voices burst with whiskey laughter. I see them standing down at the end of the hall of this narrow cabin down by the living room laughing over the couch where laying prone is the lifeless body of one Don Drebinski. He has upchucked and the stench of it smells up the cabin like a bar bathroom. I expected Don to lay off the drink while he was here since getaway meant so I thought "Get away from the sauce my friend." But our drive here made him moan and groan with twisty road-sickness made worse when I took the wheel. "Slow down,

James Dean" Don said. Teddy Garner Reckless Drag Racer thats me. We got here and he went straight for a cold compress and a nip from the bottle and then Mary who is happy any time of the day to pour a stiff one announced drinks are on the house. So that was the beginning.

Don knows Chick from the seminary days. Don went gay and Chick got married and now Chick's a Buddhaist with his own patch of mountainside and pretty tipsy Mary at his side. Its a peaceful way to live and you dont need quantities of booze to pass time though lately I too have poured plenty of embarrassment down my throat and spit it back up later. Still it repulses me to see Don drunken and buried under a soaking blanket. Chick put on a Mingus recording which seems like a cruel thing as the music is like knife to the eardrum with all the quick slices and puncturing trumpeteers and the bass going thisway and that like the music of a wild party exploding open with all posts abandoned no one on lookout. How Don can pass out during this is a mystery but also it occurs to me its just as well since now the double guestbed will be all mine no tossing and turning from nervousness of the two of us under one wool blanket. Night time comes early out here in the dark back beyond.

II.

I slept dead to everything last night and woke up and went with a rucksack into the woods and it was a big beautiful trembling place and I came back in a happy mood but the cabin is full of old sad people. Don drinking five eight ten cups o' Joe staring out the window at the bright fog in the same rumpled shirt as yesterday speckled with upchucked discoloration. He looked off into the zerowhite sky while I sat across the room from him studying his mumbling silent lips his eerie expression telegraphing some kind of mental trouble that is more than a hangover that must be about his tainted homosexual life is my deduction. I'm Teddy Garner Psychological Spy and I'll peer into your neurotic brain with transcendental powers of analysis.

Now I have carried the precious Royal like an easel to a more remote corner of the cabin to continue on with my filthy words. Thats how Don said it "Can you bang out your filthy words somewhere else?" Because all the coffee did not save Don from the pain in his head and suddenly he needed to get into bed. Clackclackclacketyclack like a hammer against the bent skull of Don Drebinski.

All Dons words since we arrived in the woods have been meanspirited. Maybe its the booze or its my drag racing or maybe the quarrel we had before leaving Frisco wherein he wouldnt let me pack my paints and easel because of the mess I would make of his car and ontop of it he said "your not really painting anymore are you?" So now I am certainly not painting out in the plain air which was one of my reasons to take this trip as I can't paint in the city full of distraction. But in this cabin I found the Royal like a gift from above as if to say "Maybe a painter is not your destiny but to put down these true words is" as if these greenwoods are a place of deliverance and I have been Brought Here to make this discovery. I can feel a powerful force in the clacketyclack of the metal which is more welcome than the torture of waiting for a proper color to come through to the canvas. I can paint with ink. Teddy Garner Kill the Painter Long Live the Poet! I am quite pleased with my chronicle thus far and cannot wait to tell all I know about this beat life I am living.

I have an inspiration now which is to stay here then truly go out on the road. I can pitch a tent on Chicks land and help him with chores like picking apples for money and driving down to the crossroads store to buy their liquor. And eventually save up money to visit Mexico. San Francisco is not Where Its At no matter what Ray says. Frisco is dead but I Teddy Garner am running doublespeed and all of it on a broken heart. I will send Don back to the city with his sordid soul dipped in badluck so I can grow wise without him. I will march into your room Donnie Sadsack and tell you Ive got a limited amount of hamburg sandwhiches left in me. We must break our ties and balance our books and cross our eyes and dot our tees and no more Hekyll and Jekyll come hell or high water.

I better calm down. Ive raised such a typeracket he has just reappeared to present the Evil Eye. Forgive me Donnie Sadsack. Forgive me my noisy clacketyclack and big ideas of poetry. Forgive me Jack Kerouac forgive me Ernest Hemingway forgive me Albert Camus I am not as smart as you.

I hadn't thought about this for a long time: a conversation with my father during college after I'd come home with Camus's *The Stranger*. I must have left the book sitting out; I remember finding him in the kitchen looking it over. "This isn't *The Stranger* I remember," he said and went to his bookshelf to pull down the yellowed copy he'd read years earlier, which turned out to be an older translation, British English instead of American, as my newer edition was. We compared the opening sentences, the gunshot scene, the argument with the priest. We joked that we should learn to read the original French to come up with our own definitive Garner edition. Two hours, maybe more, sitting side by side, peering into each other's hands, discussing the motivation of each translator, considering how words strung together made meaning. I remember he said *The Stranger* was one of the few books he'd saved from his "younger days." He told me it taught him something about how the world works. I wish I could remember the lesson.

III.

A night and a day and another night has been lost to liquor in the blood my blood included this time. They poured this poison upon me and now I am angry with the memory of being such a laughing then cursing drunkard. Cursing Chick and Mary for seeing me as the housejester to be goofy for them and take their insults and cursing Don for his control over me like a warlock. And then comes morning with its splitting headaches with neither me or Don able to lift heads from pillows. Which is when I made my attempt to tell Don the new plan to bum down to Mexico and be pure of heart in the outdoors only to have him insist he must come too or else I shouldnt go because even the hobos travel in twos and then his talk of the brotherly love between us such as saying only he understands me though nobody has understood me not ever not now. I will not speak of what followed except to say that his physical persuasion was a kind of animal sorcery and I fear there exists a realm of my subconscious that does what it wants with me even as my conscious mind repels and is repulsed. This will pass. One more reason I must not return to Frisco with him.

A hot day even the clouds are no relief as I sweated climbing high into the blue dome. Walking past large black canine bowel movements and Lo there across the grassy slope is one Mr. Coyote. I didnt know what to do should I run like a deer or set a trap like a mountainman? Instead I did what I failed to do with Don which is look into its eyes with the truth. When I stared into the eyes of Mr. Coyote he spoke to me a warning because he saw something in me to which he did not approve. I stood frozen and deeply thinking upon that warning and the mistakes I have mistakenly made and how to set Teddy Garner right again.

IV.

I think I should make it with Mary although I suspect that those parts of her are empty and dry. She is a smart broad a oncepretty lady who becomes ugly when sad. Mary in her oldlady dresses and complaints of bellyaches Mary of the Bottle Mary with her Used-to-Be History. Last night Don and Chick left us alone and I joked I would seduce Mary while I had my chance. Mary said "Your probably a virgin" and I said in fact I was the lover of a married woman so watch out! Mary smiled for me I am a clown in her eyes. Teddy Garner Dumb Schlumb Clown.

Mary wrote poems years ago in North Beach. Now she lives here with Chick weary with life and she doesnt write poems. She walks around holding her belly with some unknown pain. She doesnt have art she doesnt have North Beach and she hardly even has Chick who prepares himself for a higher incarnation and ignores his wife. I spied him in

> a meditation position behind the cabin looking like a piece of cheese grilling on a rock in the sun.
>
> Don walks past me now at the Royal and his hand rests on my head heavy as in the night. I know now I am right to hatch my new plan. I must escape. Either that or suffocate in this cabin where there is too much booze and sorcery.

I interrupted my reading and called Ian. "I think I've found the smoking gun," I said, and read aloud to him: *his physical persuasion was a kind of animal sorcery, his hand rests heavy as in the night.*

"This is amazing," he said. "Your father and this guy Don—."

"That's what it sounds like, right?"

"Why else would he be referring to being *repulsed* and making *mistakes*?"

I took a deep breath, aware of my heightened, jittery state. "But how can I know what's true in here, what's not?"

"Anything he brags about, he's embellishing. Anything he's evasive about, it really happened." He paused, and I could almost hear him smile. "Like Kerouac."

I promised to call him after I finished.

V.

> I awakened early to shut my dreams up and smelled the cabinair thick with coffee and bacon and standing over the misty stove was the lady of the house in a bath of sunlight and steam. Out the clear window was more visible ocean than in the past five days of this foggy purgatory. "Mary we must walk together through this sunshine" I exclaimed but she whimpered of a bumleg to match her other illfeelings. I swear it is no easy job to break through the depressive neurosis of the aging Beat.
>
> I told her we would only climb high enough to get a widerview and if your too tired to walk back down or if your trick leg starts walking away on its own I'll carry you triumphantly back. I was of course using one of my jokervoices and so made her smile and at last her Resistance was worn down by my Persistence. Teddy Garner you don't need to be a poet you need to be a salesman selling ideas

to an unknowing public. If you were a square you would make a great ad man.

Then up and up we went with Mary holding my hand for steadiness until the day became like a great Arthurian play with Our Hero and His Queen isolated on mountain-top.

Queen Mary: This morning over bitter coffee I stared at this hill thinking it was forever out of reach and here I stand now at the great risingup and all the pain in my leg and belly are sweetened by the sun.

Our Hero: Plus for an older lady you also got a sweet piece of ass.

Queen Mary: My husband finds it too much for his shrunken appetite. Methinks his sweettooth runs more toward fruit.

Our Hero: Then to the fruithouse with him! With all the other fruits and their fruit flyes flittering forth. Let those of us who wish to stand on the mountaintop and ball like coyotes not linger in the valley of the rotting fruit.

Queen Mary: You are a foulmouthed knave!

And so Our Hero slipped his hands inside of His Queen's royal robe and shuffled down bloomers to the familiar weeps and sighs he has come to know from the female of the species. Our Hero layed her down first checking for rocks or coyote bowel movements or any other pea that would disturb this princess. And what followed was a lustful act that grew into great noises of man and woman loud enough to rattle birds from trees but hopefully not alert the Queen's husband down in the valley below. For surely if he is in earshot the shrunken husband will recognize the completion of Queen Mary's conquest.

Down drops the curtain as Hero and Queen begin the descent, not so friendly now that they're spent.

Here I became confused. There had been a time—a phone conversation from one coast to another—when I asked my father to tell me what he remembered about San Francisco, and he said only, "I could write a book." Is that what he had attempted to do here? Write a book modeled on Kerouac, where the "truth" of autobiography guides each word choice, but the names get changed, rendering everything "fiction"? And once labeled as such, were these pages free to move away from the confessions of a diary and toward the boundlessness of wish fulfillment? This inserted script—was it the story of a conquest any twenty-year-old would brag about? Or the fantasy of that conquest? Or, more menacing, a whitewashing of forced sex? I winced, remembering what Ray said about his roughness, confronting, once again, my tangled, contradictory reactions to Teddy.

VI.

> I must catch up on my adventurous sudden turn of events. Three nights have passed since I sat at this Royal. That was when in a foulmouthed exit from the cabin I raised a fist at Don and Chick and Mary and shouted that they were doomed and everything was <u>shit</u> and "I shall <u>not</u> return!" Marching away I swung a heavy rucksack over one shoulder and hoofed it from their Transylvanian shack where Don with his warlock charm and Mary with her accusations and Chick the Most Furious Budhist in the Western World watched with dumbfounded faces. (But your Hero is a Fool, as has well been documented in these pages—I add this now back at the Royal where I look upon the handscrawled notes I kept and now type into the chronicle so that I may report that these three days have taught me all I need to know about being a man and facing down nature and death with hunting and gathering and solitude.)
>
> In the woods I was quickly lost on my journey to Mexico. Water was rushing atop the soil somewhere whistling like my Irish mothers fervent prayers and I directed myself to this creekflow. I traveled hours downstream to a fragrant flowery place and was as an old lady at the New York Botanical Gardens stooping to smell flora

along the way. I decided this place would be a welcome womb for the night. Or perhaps it is the pungent trap of a hidden she lion. One must always be prepared for traps from She. Eventually darkness came and cold air and with it my first solo night in the woods or ever.

VII.

I awoke next to a creek on damp silty shore with biting-bugs upon me. Light shone only in top branches of trees but it looked heavenly which may be a good omen. Then I searched upstream to see where I had last fumbled in the dark and was stopped cold by the sight of pawprints in the mud. Paws without claws which means cat and the prints big as DiMaggios mitt.

The hills go on for miles green on green on green all the way from here to the ocean. At first I just looked and saw hills and trees. Now different versions of tree are defined as I study roots and trunks and the spinal chaos that is the branches. I see how trees grow twisted with age and influence. And how birds fly in twos. I could hear the flutter of their very wings against the air. They call to each other speaking their private language amid all the other languages. Do birds speak to each other across species? Is the maker of that warble over there understood by the producer of that foul cry over thataway?

All my thoughts were loud like conversation in my ear. I heard the voice of my father talk to me a thick brogue announcing that summer camp will be an experience to put hair on my chest. But years later here was the prophecy come to pass not summer camp but the real thing.

I became determined to make a mark to Plant a Flag. And so when I got to the hilltop where the pine trees replaced the twisty ones below and where the water spills forth like the very eternal juices of Mother Earth herself I did the thing which is known to men as taking care of the Need. That was my way to claim this hilltop for all the bums like me past and present with my own seed mixed into nature as who knows how many have done before.

VIII.

They call her Mother Earth but I think she is a cruel Father who punishes us as we conquer him. That hilltop was no more mine than the air I breathed or this water that ran down the creek through my clumsy fingers in my vain attempt to grab a fish. It was a time of going a little cuckoo from being alone. Visions of Mexico meant to soothe me through this loneliness turn into just more foolhardy thoughts.

Darkness was coming again and I wondered if I might find others in the woods for directions or to share some precious food and water. Was it only two nights ago Mary fed me pie baked from her own profane hands? My belly questions if it ever knew food. In a desperate act I ripped a piece of leather from the inside of my rotten broken muddy shoe and sucked on it so as to cheat the sense of eating.

IX.

A victory! I killed a perching bird with a stick. Snuck up like the Irish Warrior King that runs in my veins and brained the piteous creature. But as I stared at the cold body deadeye wetblood feathers never to fly again I shivered for the murder. I cooked the bird over a fire only useful enough for cooking not heat. Happily I had matches and in a rare instance of not being a dumb schlumb with no sense I kept them dry those two and a half days. My head was heavy with confusion and my stomach gurgling as it transformed the dead thing into achy gas.

I pushed on and found shelter in a railroad car abandoned here from a rancher who has let his herd roam on this hillside. I am so relieved for the shelter that I see it must have been left here for me for the drifters before me and the mad ones to follow the long linking of wandering warriors.

X.

I have had thoughts and questions of death such as how long a man lasts like this stupidly lost and without food and unfit for killing. I wondered what was happening back there in the regular world. What was falling apart and coming undone and dying. I thought especially of Danny and how once he would have been my bosom buddy adventurer partner but he has been silent for months and maybe dead too for all I know.

But in my lowest low I spotted a tree on a far hill that looked like one I remembered from being with Mary on the mountain. So thats where I decided to head. I found a dirtroad and after some traveling I met a stoic suspicious rancher who refused me a ride but directed my unshaven madman self toward the road which it turned out was not so far from the cabin though it seemed a hundred miles had passed.

Thus I went back to from where I fled.

XI.

The prodigal son returned repentant stumbling up cabin stairs falling to the cabinfloor in a state of exhaustion and stomach pain. Don carried me and ministered to me and fed healing soup and now delays his return to the city so as to watch me in my sickbed. I do not understand all that stirs in him but truly he is a true friend.

I made a general apology to every one of them but Mary will not forgive me either for my angry walking away or for coming back I do not know and Chick with liquor on breath stares like an enemy. Don whispers to me her claims that I took advantage of her though she was a seducer as much as me. This seems like a lifetime ago. Today for my sanity I am back at the Royal clacketyclacking.

I took a walk out into the drygrass this morning and smoked a cigarette daydreaming of brushfires started by flyaway embers. Hearing in the wind the sound of traveling flames. A vision of this poisoned paradise burned away.

XII.

Now I am back in San Francisco and still nursing gutpain and everywhere I look I find a city steamy with usedup legend. Rising from the pavement are the rank vapors of artistic excrement all those poets and painters stumbling around unwashed. I am queasy from breathing in the rotting of yesterdays genius. The same rot Mary carries with her the reason she must clutch at her aching insides the reason she lives with an unsmiling drunken monk.

Yesterday I turned a corner into an alley where among cement walls stands a bearded fellow teetering on his denim legs. He upchucks on cue as I watch wrapped in attention. Two weeks ago I might have called this downtrodden fellow a beat king imagining myself with him five years earlier arms over shoulders we stumble forth from the Six Gallery stoned on booze and the glory of poets remaking the world wetbrushstrokes on canvas newjazz cracking open the veil of the commonplace. But now I see he is just a guy retching gruesome in an alley in North Beach not a poet not a hero not a saint. Not a warrior of the mountains who has had to kill to eat to survive the dark.

I no longer want the world to split open. The sun on this alley blanches out all my past visions and I find myself made angry at Frisco which is a City of Lies and I am no more understood here than I was in Hell's Kitchen.

Thus I did something to prove myself more than just a dumb schlumb and the courtjester to the oldtime sadsacks. I strided up to that beat bum and I pointed to where he had spewed forth his boozey innards and I shouted at him "Look at that mess you made you good for nothing oaf." I shook him until with fear in his bleary eyes he begged "Leave me alone!" Then I let him go because I thought, my feelings exactly.

THE END

There was one more page. A map.

Scrawled in pencil, the soft gray lines had been smudged blurry over time. At the top he had drawn a clump of buildings and bridges marked FRISCO from which dangled a route marked 101. From 101 a squiggle went leftward: LION'S GATE ROAD, 6.5 MILES TURNOFF TO CABIN. Here the map bloomed into detail, out of scale: an illustration of the cabin and a couple of outbuildings (SHED, ROTTING BARN), an inverted V inscribed MARY ON THE MOUNTAIN, another marked PLANTED MY FLAG. A zigzagging string of arrows was bordered by the words SOLO TRAVELING. I traced this route to its end point, a CATTLE GATE leading to a RAILROAD CAR. Beneath all of this, spaced out horizontally, was M-E-X-I-C-O, Teddy's never-reached destination. And beneath that—written not in ancient smudged pencil but in ballpoint-blue ink—was appended one extra word, followed by a question mark and circled: JIMMY?

This blue ink revealed my father's adult hand—the font on the outside of attic boxes, on legal pads in his malpractice-suit files, on Christmas and birthday cards before they stopped coming. It was evidence that he had revisited his youthful chronicle at some later date. I imagined this revisitation: Rooting through the attic, looking for who-knows-what, he uncovers, by chance, this old sketch pad with these typewritten pages in the back. He pauses to sit and read. He studies the map he once doodled with his sketch pencil, and maybe somewhere in this process of reading and recalling, his mind lands on me, his son, in *Frisco.* He writes my name, but as a question, the unanswerable question that is Jimmy. Maybe here he allows himself to think about Don, about whatever intimacy passed between them; maybe this is when he circles my name. Maybe, maybe, maybe. Only one thing is sure: He returned the map and the typewritten pages to the back of the sketchbook, sent the sketchbook to its pile in a corner of the attic, banished his youth to its locked chamber.

My eyes were burning, wanting to spill tears. I gritted my teeth and held back, knowing the flood that would rage if I let it. I was instantly inside another moment: the aftermath of the HIV test I took following my crystal-sex weekend. The results came back negative, but on my walk home from the clinic I broke down in the middle of Market Street, the bawling thundering out of me. Some quality of astonishment unified that moment and this one. The way feeling lucky, getting what you wished for, can leave you feeling vulnerable as well, frighteningly aware of the random distribution of life's offerings. The tremulous wake of the close call. What had it meant all those years ago to be spared infection, when it might just as easily have gone the other way? What did it mean now to uncover this testimony from my father, which seemed to verify my suspicions of his California past, when I might have been left unfulfilled, never knowing? Two years ago, those test results moved me forward, to Woody. These pages would lead me somewhere, too.

I found Lion's Gate Road on a California state map, forty miles down the Peninsula in San Mateo County. A connecting road joined it to 101. Along its length, Lion's Gate bordered a huge swatch of undeveloped public land, a land trust, tinted green on the foldout paper. Perhaps, amidst these thousands of acres, Chick's cabin was standing. A ruin, ready to be reclaimed.

A map tells you where to go. A map with your name on it begs to be followed.

I would make a pilgrimage. I would find this hallowed ground. I'd drive the six and a half miles to the turnoff, follow my father's path along the stream, maybe even spend a night in the woods as he did. I'd climb the mountains he had climbed and *plant my flag.* I'd do it because I could. Because he had circled my name like a destination.

14

I told no one, not even Ian. I did not return Woody's message. *Call me when you're ready,* he had said, but I wasn't ready, not for the talk that we needed to have. I had just enough in the bank to make a hundred-dollar transfer payment to a credit card. The yellow pages yielded 1-800-CHEP-CAR, from which I rented, with this newly available sliver of credit, a cut-rate two-door. It was just a couple of notches up from a bumper car, with tiny wheels, a tape deck and power nothing. But so what? Driving out of the city, blasting an old Elton John cassette through the whooshy speakers (everything else I owned was on CD), I inhaled this new momentum. A man with a plan! Elton sang of sweet freedom.

I took 101 South, guided by my father's pencil-sketched map. Fifty minutes later I was deep in Silicon Valley, with signs appearing for San Jose, realizing there would be no exit for Lion's Gate Road. All around me, billboards flaunted the esoteric spoils of the New Economy—B2B, DSL, SQL; more bandwidth, extra storage, stronger networks. *Save time. Make your world wireless. Grow your business faster. Do it faster.* Visions of Andy sequestered with his laptop, minting virtual money; of Woody in his cubicle, counting his stock options before they hatched; of all those faceless Dean Fosters I'd tracked down online, none of whom turned out to be my man. All of us trying to grab a piece of the better world promised by *connecting*.

One hand on the wheel, I struggled to locate myself on a real map. The gorgon's blare of a truck horn snapped me back to attention, and I swerved to prevent a multivehicle pileup across multiple lanes of traffic. In the contorted rage on the face of the truck driver, I glimpsed the ghost of every near miss I'd been at the root of, the accumulated mistakes and missteps of my life, all the people I'd pissed off, and my skin went clammy. The afternoon sun was falling and I was already off track.

It took another fifty minutes and directions from a gas station to get me back on course. I found my way to the connecting route, then to Skyline Drive, and finally to Lion's Gate. Like a tourist entering a church whispering, I lowered the volume on the tape deck. All my life I've feared the woods: the darkness at the base of trees, the squish of moss underfoot, the unidentifiable rustling that circles the periphery no matter where you stand. On my side of the road, an overgrown grade fell steeply away. I was certain I could spy wreckage down among the redwood trunks—contorted metal settling into the pine needles, rubbery baby ferns arcing out of demolished windshields. I navigated perilous turns carefully, all too aware of driving a subcompact in a world of monster cars. The opposite side of the road sloped upward and was lined with fences and residential gates—old-fashioned gates with chains and locks, and newfangled ones with imposing vertical bars and driver-side boxes into which you punch access codes. As I reached the 6.5-mile marker and no *turnoff to cabin,* no land trust, made itself apparent, I felt the last of my initial optimism deflating into foolishness. Forty years had erased Teddy's landmarks and replaced them with gated driveways. There was no access code to 1961.

But then—one more twist of the road and the view opened up, the trees thinned out, the windshield shone with the colors of a late-day sky. Below me, billowy green hills, capped by the bristly silhouettes of conifers, arced for miles, abutting at the wide wall of the ocean, which looked flat as a ribbon, a two-dimensional soundstage backdrop. The water was pale blue, nearly silver, dissolving into the blue-orange sky. Behind a faraway rim of clouds, the setting sun was shooting out tendrils of pink fire. An art department's idea of sunset.

The road was wide enough for me to pull over and park. Near as I could calculate, somewhere in all that nature before me sat the very land I was seeking. Teddy's *endless greengreen hillsides.* I exhaled, felt my muscles relax.

When I stepped outside, the wind, stronger than I expected, blew off the bucket hat I'd been wearing and sent it tumbling over the roadside ledge. I peered down and saw it resting on a belligerent patch of thistles. I started toward it, stepping sideways, one foot, then the other. Then I felt the earth release, my ankle pivot. Down onto my hip

I toppled, doubling over in a sideways somersault, sliding the length of my body, nothing to grab at except wild grass, which uprooted from the damp ground as I rolled by. A flapping of bird wings followed, a startled exodus. As my weight slowed me down, I sensed that I'd cried out; the air was reverberating with an alien echo.

The hat rested above me, within reach. I plucked it off the thistles, plopped it on my head, and was answered with a piercing sting across my brow.

I crawled back up the slope on my knees, achy, hat in hand.

In the fumey air around the car, I pored over the contents of my backpack (cigarettes, pot, lip balm, my father's journal and my own), marveling at everything I had failed to pack (sunscreen, flashlight, pocketknife, water bottle, quarters for phone calls, address book with necessary phone numbers and, most important in this moment, a first-aid kit.) I tried to extract thistle ends from the raw patch on my forehead. I gave up and lit a cigarette.

Dusk was pressing down. The idea of trying to find my way into these woods tonight had been a whim; the idea I would actually find something there was starting to seem ridiculous. I could turn back and be in San Francisco in under an hour's drive. Cut my losses; call Woody; have that talk. Maybe even, if all went miraculously well, spend a warm night in bed with him. (If he was in my position now, what would Woody do?)

The force that had impelled me here would not loosen its grip: Teddy's dharma-bum-warrior prose, the tears I'd suppressed in the kitchen, that JIMMY beckoning from the bottom of the map. Above all, the simple fact of those yellowed pages in my hands, the way they spoke to the yearning that had been building in me for months. Why had I come this far, if only to retreat from a thistle's sting?

I stubbed out my cigarette. There had to be a general store somewhere along the coast. I started up the car and continued forward toward the blackening sea.

In my ten years in San Francisco I almost never left the city. No car equals no day trips; thus no clue that Route 1 along this stretch of the coast is undeveloped, beautiful to behold in the setting sun but not conducive to shopping. I had to drive north to Half Moon Bay before I found a strip mall with a convenience store. Next door was Casa Adios, a Mexican restaurant whose sign announced NO MSG, NO LARD, NO PROBLEM. Through the windows, instead of the all-Latina service crew I'd find in the Mission, I saw a handful of youthful workers of various skin tones, each emitting a nonverbal, suburban ennui. Among them was a sexy white guy in a white work shirt, ambling between tables, soiled washcloth in hand. He was boyishly towheaded and freckle-faced, but his ears sported thick silver hoops and his right forearm was obliterated by a riot of inky scrollwork and scarlet flames.

I went inside and ordered. Up close, the tattooed busboy was compact and firm, with a ledge of ass filling out his gray Dickies. From my corner booth, I watched that ass move from table to table as its operator cleared away abandoned burrito heels and salsa-flecked chip trays. I couldn't quite read his style. Grungy snowboarder? Small-town post-punk rebel? Except for whatever gel he'd used to spike his hair, he read as straight, and he was definitely much younger than me. Twenty or twenty-one, tops. He was being trailed by a manager, a middle-aged Latino in a button-up shirt with a loud, patronizing voice. I got this manager's attention to ask him for help, but he had never heard of the land trust and wasn't sure about camping. He suggested a room at the Sea Fort, a motel down the highway. Done with me, he barked at the sexy busboy, "Jed, you stuffed too many napkins in this dispenser."

I looked over, caught Jed's eye and smirked at his bossy boss, an offering of solidarity that was rewarded with a smile. Jed's lips parted to reveal a gap between his front teeth, wider than the edge of a butter knife, just goofy enough to humanize his too-cute face.

At the pay phone in the rear of the parking lot, I attempted, unsuccessfully, to call the Sea Fort Motel. I fumbled for a cigarette, and then turned to follow the sound of a lighter being summoned into flame. Standing at the back door of the building was Jed, silhouetted in kitchen fluorescence, sparking up one of his own, looking my way. I wandered toward him, into the shadow zone behind the taqueria, alongside a Dumpster wafting out currents of charred meat and cilantro. "Got one for me?"

He had torn the childproof guard off his lighter, which he flicked for me. I did the thing I like to do when a guy lights my cigarette and I'm feeling daring: touch the hand that holds the lighter in order to steady the flame. A natural-enough gesture that's also just at the edge of unnerving. A test.

In the peach-hued glow, his face seemed fleshier, the kind of softness that guys don't entirely shed until their mid-twenties (which is different from the softness we take on in our mid-thirties).

"You know what the problem is?" he asked as he lowered the flame.

"The problem?"

"He told you Sea Fort? Dude, it's Sea *Foam*." He nodded and narrowed his eyes, as if daring me to disagree.

"You're sure about that?" I asked.

"Fully. I've stayed there. It's down the coast, more toward Santa Cruz." His voice surprised me. It was pitched higher than I'd expected; something whiny, a touch panicked, about it.

"Do you know anything about the land trust in the hills? I was planning on camping there."

"That's private land. Day use only. There's always the beach, though you might get busted by the sheriff."

I was disappointed. Check into a motel after I'd worked myself halfway into warrior mode? "I don't suppose there's anything to do around here for fun?"

"Drinking." He narrowed his gaze. "I mean, if you're of age."

I fought back a smile. "Uh, yeah, I'm over twenty-one. By a few years."

"Figured; just didn't want to assume. So, dude, listen—you're not a cop?" I shook my head. "Sorry. Just gotta get that taken care of. Because, see, if you're interested—" he glanced furtively over his shoulder toward the kitchen door "—I can get you acid, E, speed, coke, K and this new shit, kinda like GHB, but without the zonk factor. I don't have any on me, but I could definitely hook you up later tonight."

I laughed, short and sharp.

He deflated. "What?"

"Nothing, nothing. It's cool." I wiped off the smile, not wanting to explain how improbable this seemed: a guy like me and a guy like him having this conversation in the parking lot of Casa Adios.

He stamped out his cigarette and tried again. "I figured a dude traveling usually needs a little something. A bump, a chill, whatever. Right?"

"Right. But I'm mostly just a pothead."

He looked at me intently for the first time, surveying me from my mud-caked sneakers to the thistle blotches on my forehead. "Dude, this E is the bomb. I did some, and *then* smoked a blunt. Yo, I melted *down*. That shit made me *crazy*." His delivery was half sales pitch, half report from Wonderland. His trusting eyes stayed fixed on mine.

"How much for the E?" I asked.

"Twenty-five a hit."

"You're charging city prices. Capsules or tablets?"

"Capsules." He bounced on his toes, jittery. "I could maybe do it for twenty. It's seriously bad shit."

Jed, *crazy* on *some seriously bad shit*—I wondered what that might look like.

"Dude, you do this E with your girlfriend, she'll fucking love you forever." He must have seen something in my eyes then, because he quickly added, "I mean, if you have one."

"Yeah, I have one," I heard myself saying, "but things aren't going so well lately."

"The Sea Foam's kind of a fuck-your-secretary place."

"Shit! I didn't bring my secretary with me."

We both laughed, the same laugh. It was effortless.

"Jed! Salsa spill at table two." This from the boss, poking his glossy head out the back door.

"I get off at eleven," Jed whispered, raising his eyebrows at me expectantly and rubbing fingertips together, signaling *cash.*

I didn't need the ecstasy and didn't have the money to spare; it was also likely that Jed operated so low on the retail-drug food chain that what he was selling wasn't *seriously bad shit*, but just bad. But I heard myself saying, "Eleven's good."

As he turned to leave, he said, "I'm Jed."

"Teddy," I replied, the name like a blue spark shooting out from crossed wires.

"Later, Teddy," he said.

I opened my mouth as if to correct this error, but he had turned away. I watched him retreat into the cone of kitchen light. A genie sucked back into the bottle.

I drove south to the Sea Foam and checked into a room that smelled heavily of cleanser and faintly of whatever rotten odor the cleanser was meant to eliminate. I stripped off my clothes and studied my body in the mirror. I was lucky to have naturally broad shoulders; even without a gym membership they looked strong, balancing out the softness that had settled at my waist. My upper torso had some of my father's thickness, but without his mat of rust-colored hair; my own chest hair whorled unevenly, and my pink nipples poked out, their innocence long ago sacrificed to sex play. The tattoo on my left bicep—a trinity of snakes, each swallowing the other's tail—had begun to fade to greenish gray. My life experience was written on my body, a man's body, when inside I still felt like a boy who could put off the big decisions indefinitely. No wonder I was planning to go back and meet Jed—with him I could rewrite the script, recast myself as younger and straighter, change my name. I dropped to the floor in my underwear, alternating between push-ups and sit-ups, driving myself to a satisfying exhaustion. In the shower I lingered over my cock—which, unlike the rest of me, was still as unruly and eager as its adolescent version—and I focused on the smiling apparition of Jed's little package, the fat-free body and half-moon ass, the dark rings of worker's sweat under his arms.

I showered, then put on the same clothes I'd taken off. I tried to nap but kept checking the clock. Time was teasing me through an agonizingly slow dance. I rolled a couple of fatties, puffing away until I slipped into a twinkly high that turned truly surreal in front of the strobing cable TV wasteland. At ten thirty I shuffled back to the car.

He was standing in the parking lot, checking his pager and punching numbers into the pay phone. A heap of clutter surrounded his ankles—a filled backpack busting against its zippers, a blanket, a pile of compact discs, and a dark, sculptural object revealed by my headlights to be a two-foot tall replica of Darth Vader's head.

I stepped out of the car and leaned against the door, and the blistering tirade Jed was delivering into the phone rumbled over in agitated waves: "That's bullshit, dude . . . That's totally a lie . . . I am definitely not *dealing*, dude." I was halfway through a fresh cigarette by the time he took note of me. Still his ranting went on, climaxing at last in a "Fuck you" and the chunky slam of the receiver.

He approached me with an arm extended and was immediately guiding my fingers through a ritualized three-part handshake. "Dude, I am seriously stoked to see you, 'cause they just fired my ass."

The sudden nearness of him put me off balance; my brain was trapped somewhere between the idling pot high and the adrenaline rush of finding myself back in this alien world. He shuffled on his feet, relaying an argument between him and Miguel, his boss, that had culminated in Jed clearing out his locker.

"You kept all that junk here?" I asked, walking toward the Darth Vader bust.

"This isn't junk, dude. This is my *shit.*" The rant started back up: His parents had kicked him out of their *fifty-room mansion* when he dropped out of college; his stepfather, George, was a *cheap asshole millionaire,* his mother *a two-faced cunt*—that was her on the phone, the "dude" he'd just told to fuck off—and they wouldn't let him back until he agreed to take *some bullshit computer job*. " 'George has a friend with a promising new Internet start-up,' " he mimicked. "I'm like, dude, go to my website, it's called Suck My Cock Dot-Com."

I hadn't figured him for a spoiled rich kid, though this was possible, with Silicon Valley so close. Still, it occurred to me that he was making the whole thing up—that he was broke by circumstance, not by choice, just some liar drug dealing his way through California—but that hardly mattered to me, because I was lying, too.

I kicked up a corner of his blanket with the toe of my boot. "So, are you, like, homeless?"

"Whatever. I just keep moving. Sometimes I sleep on the beach or crash at a friend's. I'm saving up—I got a fat stash locked away, and I'm about ready to take off to some rad Third World country like Costa Rica, where my parents can't hassle me and I can live hella cheap." He exhaled and added, almost as an afterthought, "And fuck hella pussy."

"Right on," I said, playing my part.

"You got a cigarette? Thanks, dude. No, let me light it." He turned around and flipped his middle finger at the restaurant. "Fuck you, Miguel! I should bring down some vengeance on his greasy ass. So, dude, you want that E? I'm using all the Force I can on you so you'll say yes, 'cause I could seriously use the Jackson."

Puffing on the cigarette and bouncing on his toes, he waited for my answer with alluring, con-man eyes. It was a relief to have him silent for the moment. I slowly pulled out another cigarette, pinched it between my thumb and middle finger and sparked it up in my best cool-eyed Johnny Depp imitation. Through an extended exhale, at last I spoke. "That's why I came back."

"Rad." He turned and started moving toward his bags. "We gotta do this somewhere besides this parking lot, 'cause they will fully call the cops on my ass."

He said his car was being fixed, and that I should drive us to the beach, so I helped him gather his things up, making a point of throwing most of it in the trunk, a half-assed security attempt in case he was planning on pulling a knife and robbing me. He climbed into the front seat and dropped his backpack between his legs.

"Say adios to Casa Adios," I announced. I spun the wheels toward Route 1 and slammed on the gas, burning rubber like a sixteen-year-old doing donuts behind the high school. Jed tumbled into his door and whooped.

"Adi-mother-fuckin-os!" he yelled at the restaurant. Its lights went off at this very moment, as if shouting good riddance back at him, leaving him to his own devices. Leaving him to me.

I'd heard about San Gregorio, a beach marked by driftwood deposits, from which structures were built by overnight campers. The parking lot was a slab of black, hedged by dunes, disappearing into a bigger slab of black, which was the dark Pacific. The night was featureless, thick enough to skim with a spoon, ready to swallow unsheltered travelers whole. In the newly quiet car, forty bucks and two capsules of Ecstasy changed hands. I mentioned to Jed that I was from San Francisco, and he immediately launched into a monologue about how the rave scene in San Francisco had *totally tanked*, how the police had been busting all the warehouse parties so that you had to *haul it to Oak-town for kicks*, but now *Oak-town was blowing up* and *the cops were coming down on that shit*, so now he was saving up for a big rave in Baja, though this friend of his said it might be *all hippies and older people*. "No offense," he added.

"You calling me a hippie?"

He laughed, muttering, "True, true," and reassured me that his whole life he'd *kicked it with an older crew*. At this point I brought out the joint I'd started back at the hotel and proceeded to get him high and me higher. I'd been bluffing my way through this conversation—my rave experience consisted of two parties, one on each side of the Bay, where I'd tripped away the hours transfixed by the body-painted flesh of the shirtless, skinny boys spiraling around me. I drifted in and out of Jed's stories, so crushed out on him aesthetically that any words he spoke were beside the point. Every now and then he'd look to me for encouragement, and I'd glimpse again that trust I'd spied back at the restaurant.

"Hey dude, you find the Sea Foam?"

"Yeah, thanks for helping me out."

"Dude, you gotta get your girlfriend down here and take advantage of the pay-per-view. Stay up all night watching some rug-munching porn, some total *Red Shoe Diaries* shit." He raised his palm, and I met it in a high five.

"I almost called her. Even though she's mad at me, I thought I could get her to talk dirty. You know, tell her I was horny and missed her and shit."

"Take matters into your own hands," he said.

"Almost did that, too," I said. I laughed too loud, too enthusiastically, entertaining thoughts of enacting one of those bi-curious porn scenarios: *Man, my girlfriend won't let me fuck her, and I'm so horny. Wanna help a buddy out?* A host of clichéd warnings was ringing loudly: *playing with fire, walking on thin ice.* Fire and ice was about right. My temples throbbed with hot blood and my legs were shivering. But for some reason the possibility that I'd wind up on the knife end of Jed's potential homosexual panic was not deterring me.

"Speaking of pulling my dick out," I said, "I gotta take a piss."

"Yeah, me too."

I stood with my back to the car hood, looking over the dunes to the ocean, and next thing, Jed was planting his feet alongside mine, unsnapping his fly and lowering his zipper. I heard the rustle of his underwear. It was torture not to look down there. Nerves, arousal and confusion conspired against me, and I couldn't piss. Jed hadn't started up yet either. The silence stretched awkwardly.

Then he spoke. "Faggot."

My breath stopped. I darted a glance at him. His head was lowered, his gaze on his cock, both hands at his crotch—but he was also smiling, and not maliciously.

I took a chance and fired back: "Cocksucker."

His smile widened. "Ass licker."

"Fudge packer."

He burst out laughing. "Butt muncher." I heard his piss slice the air and hit the sand.

His laugh was downright giddy, infectious. Whatever muscles had been damming up my piss finally let loose. I spit out, "Corn holer."

He had the giggles now, barely able to get out the words. "Ball biter."

"Finger fucker."

"Turd pirate."

And on like that until we ran out of insults and our dicks were back in our pants—but still we laughed. Uncontrollable, side splitting, the mother of all laughter birthing a litter of fresh laughter. One of us would run out of breath and the other would get quiet for a moment. Then the pregnant silence would burst open again.

From some other set of eyes I looked upon the whole scene with rapt astonishment.

We stumbled along the shoreline, smoking more pot and checking out the driftwood huts, empty of vagabonds but fascinating to look at—sculptural, inventive, spooky. The sky was pricked with stars, and we stared up at them together.

"When I was little," I told him, "I thought that constellations were actually signs from faraway civilizations."

"What, like intergalactic commercials?" he asked. "Alien Coke?"

"No. I thought they were directions. Telling us how to find them."

"Those stars are already burned out," he said. "So even if you followed the directions, like, where would they take you?"

"I didn't think that far ahead," I said, and fell quiet.

He turned to me. I could see in his stare that he'd registered my mood shift. He asked, "What are we gonna do now, Teddy?"

Hearing Jed call me by my father's name made it all wrong. Because if anyone here was cast in the role of Teddy, it was Jed, which made me a latter-day Don Drebinski, lusting over the shoulder of this wide-eyed kid, and probably winding up the worse for it.

He came back to the Sea Foam with me; there wasn't any doubt about it at a certain point. I had a room with two beds; he had nowhere else to go.

I lit the second joint as we drove. The coast road was narrow and twisty, but I was less concerned about driving stoned than I was about the unpredictability of him. His piss-and-insults game was a sure sign he had picked up a sexual vibe from me—or else a sure sign he hadn't. And if he had and was still here, what did that mean; and if he hadn't and still might, what would that bring? I was attuned to his every gesture and inflection, on alert for an unambiguous message.

His pager went off in the car—a *client* he needed to call back. "What's up with not having a cell phone?" he demanded.

"I don't believe in them."

"Dude, you're living in the past. Join the new millennium."

"You sound like someone I know in San Francisco," I said. "I'll introduce you. You guys can gang up on me." Woody meeting Jed: In a night of unlikely fantasies, this was the most cockeyed.

"I was thinking I need to check out SF again," he said eagerly. "Can't think of one fucking reason to stick around here."

"What would you do in the city?"

"I dunno. Maybe I could crash with you."

Sure, Jed, but first, let's say we do something about this tension, knock around a bit in that motel bed, see how that fits, and then, maybe, we'll drive to SF, one of my hands on the wheel, the other on the back of your neck, you trying out your newly acquired oral skills, while I try not to lose control, not take one last flying ride over the edge; if we get that far, then yeah, definitely, the city, welcome to my world, you'll fit right in, it's already a mess—.

"What's so funny?" he was asking.

"Did I laugh?"

"You got that fucking evil smile going on. With that red hair, you're, like, fully satanic."

I squinted at him. "Are you afraid of the devil?"

"Whatever," he said. A meaningless word, and no meaning on his face. Conversation over.

I didn't mind that I'd spooked him a little.

At the Sea Foam he dumped his stuff on the bed closest to the bathroom—the one that I'd wanted—and picked up the phone.

I went into the bathroom. Over the peal of urine on porcelain, I eavesdropped on Jed as he talked drugs, recounted his ejection from Casa Adios, replayed his argument with his mother. "I checked my ass into a motel," he said, with no mention of me. Then, floating the promise of *serious quality shit* and pay-per-view, he was inviting this client to the Sea Foam. Visions of white powder piled on the coffee table, submachine guns, a guy named Yuri in dark sunglasses. I nearly pissed on my leg.

"Hey, uh, Jed?" I called from the bathroom, doing my best to keep cool. "Look, dude, no strangers in the room. And easy on the phone; I'm paying for it."

Face to face, he flashed me his gap-toothed smile. "No worries. He'll never show. He doesn't even have a driver's license."

He'd already found the remote and was selecting PLAY on the pay-TV menu. The credits for *American Pie* began to roll, with Jed enthusing, "This is my favorite fucking movie." He laid himself out on his stomach, propped on his elbows, announcing lines before they were spoken.

"This is stupid," I said, averting my gaze from his ass. "You know how many movies like this have been made?"

"Tell me you've seen another movie where a guy bones a pie. It's a classic, dude."

"*Porky's* is a classic," I answered. "This is a rip-off."

"What's *Porky's?*"

"Before your time."

"How old are you, anyway?" He eyed me with mild suspicion, as if he'd just learned I was a personal friend of his father's.

"Sixty," I said, and threw a pillow, which he bunched under his chest, jamming the lumpy foam into his damp pits.

"I want that back later," I said, already anticipating the musk he'd leave behind.

When the famous pie-fucking scene appeared, Jed began humping the bed. I leaned back against the headboard and watched the communion of his hips and the mattress, the rhythmic clenching of his perfect gluteal spheres, the traction-curl of his toes in holey white socks. All the while giggling at the screen and calling back to me, "Dude, are you watching this?"

"I'm riveted."

This was either the luckiest day of my life or the hour of my death. GAY MAN SLAIN IN NO-TELL MOTEL. SUSPECT CLAIMS SELF-DEFENSE.

There was something exquisite about the prolonged, seesawing torture of this night, the not-knowing, the wanting-but-not-daring. Time was meaningless, stretching like elastic in the fullness of my fantasies, then snapping back as fear or decorum or a big, bright image of Woody's face exerted its oppositional pressure. I was sending mixed messages, even to myself: standing under the coldest shower I could bear, then strolling past the TV in just a towel.

Me: "Not sure if I packed clean underwear."

Jed: "Boxers or briefs? Dude, I'm betting you're a briefs man."

He knows I'm queer.

Jed: "If your girlfriend's been buying your underwear, its definitely briefs."

OK, so maybe not.

I dug a pair out of my backpack, held them aloft: "Boxer briefs."

Jed: "Sweet."

He's way too interested in my underwear.

Jed: "So why'd you guys break up?"

Or he's just being friendly.

I slid the underwear up my legs, like a surfer getting dressed under his towel, offering a flash of full frontal at the last pull. Jed's gaze landed right there, unabashed, but without the follow-up eye contact that would definitively tip this in my favor. So, I told him about my ex-girlfriend, a creature who probably sounded to Jed like the sexiest woman in San Francisco—tall, with blonde curly hair, great tits and great fashion sense, a motorcycle rider who worked at a dot-com—but who was, in fact, a grotesque stitching together of Woody, Ian, and Colleen. "Things are rocky," I said, "because I cheated."

"Girls hate that," he said.

"Guys, too." Woops; restate: "I mean, she did the same to me, with this guy Roger? But I guess that's my fault, too, because I've been such a loser for the past few months. Since my father died, which is a long story—."

And then I was telling him the long story, a version of it anyway, one that started in the attic with the puzzle of that missing year of Dad's life (glossing over dreamy Dean Foster), and went on to encompass Ray's letters and Deirdre's package with its paper trail of Teddy in the woods (glossing over Don Drebinski's *sorcery*), and ended with how I'd fled town without telling anyone (glossing over Woody).

"I'm probably kidding myself. The thing about following your impulses is that it never plays out according to plan—you can't make a plan out of an impulse; one is a rational process, the other is pure intuition—and now here I am in this motel, and no offense to you, but I have to wonder what the fuck I'm doing here—." I cut myself off. "Too much information?"

He shook his head. "Dude, I'm your guy."

"Meaning?"

"Yo, I grew up around here. My grandfather was one of the rich fuckers who put together that land trust. I'm a fucking encyclopedia of this place. Come on, ask me anything."

"Can you get me onto that land?"

"No problem."

"Do you think there's still a cabin there?"

"I don't know about that, but I'm pretty sure I can find that railroad car or, like, where I think it used to be. There's only three actual peaks, the rest are just hills, so we'll just climb them all."

"Really?"

"One hundred percent."

"You can hang with me tomorrow?"

"Nothing else to do." Then he slapped his hands together. "Dude! I'll show you the Goddess Twat."

"Huh?"

"This big rock with a fucking split. Looks like total vagina. Luckily doesn't smell like one. Right?" We bumped knuckles together as I added feminist solidarity to the list of all I was currently betraying.

The desire to have sex with Jed ebbed under the promise of tomorrow's adventure. Even after he stripped off his Rage Against the Machine T-shirt to reveal a wife beater tank top, a fluffy tangle of curls poking out above the scoop neck; after he peeled down to his own underwear (boxers, plaid, baggy) and I watched him poke his hand through the fly and linger over a thorough ball scratching; after he dropped to the floor and sweated his way through countless push-ups; even then I resisted. He'd been delivered here for a reason—not to lead me astray but to guide me—and I'd be a fool to tamper with this kind of fate. Jed would help me, and then I'd go home. To Woody.

I turned out the lights and curled up with my pillow, duly scented with Jed's perspiration. The last thing I remember hearing were his footfalls on the carpet, the phone cord dragging behind him, the click of the bathroom door.

I woke to the sight of Jed seated in front of the window, quiet and still. Behind him was the glare of the sky or the sea, one indistinguishable from the other. His neck and shoulders curved gracefully; his white-gold hair, flattened by sleep, framed him like an aura. He was spacing out, or deep in thought, sipping coffee from a take-out cup, his expression either sublime or blank.

He pivoted, sensing me awake. "I got you coffee." He nodded toward a second cup on the chest of drawers.

"From the front desk?"

"No. There's an ex-presso place down the road. I borrowed your car." He pulled a metallic knot of keys from his pants pocket and tossed it to the table. My keys, last located in my pants pocket. "What's up with the no-CD-player situation?"

I sat up, blinked, rubbed my scalp, all the while knocking around the situation, lifting it up by the heels and shaking it hard, hoping something definite would fall to my feet. The main thing seemed to be that he was here, that he'd come back; he hadn't stolen my car. So I could trust him; that was the lesson, right?

He was either completely guileless or so crafty it was scary.

I had half a boner from sleep, and I noted Jed noting it, bobbing in my boxer briefs as I made my way to the waiting cup of coffee, feeling like a beast, furry man on top, tumescent schlong below. I hovered and sipped. "No milk?"

"You seemed like a black kinda guy."

I rubbed a hand on my belly. "I'm about as white as they come." He looked away. The coffee was already cool enough to gulp. "Actually tastes pretty good."

"If I'd gotten the free coffee from the desk you'd be complaining it was burnt." I could see his need for approval side by side with his natural defiance. He knew he'd taken a chance by using the car. He wanted that to be okay with me.

I picked up the keys and clutched them tight. "Thanks for the coffee. But no one drives the car except me, okay?"

He mocked me with a little salute. "Okay, Dad."

"I'm not old enough to be your dad."

"I thought you were sixty."

I gave him the finger and went into the bathroom to restart the day.

I drove toward the hills I'd last seen at sunset, up and up to a thousand feet, everything around me bright and green in the slanting March sun. Jed sat in the passenger seat, his boots on the dashboard, complaining about the music selection. "I've got a fucking killer pile of CDs, and all you've got is a tape deck and Elton John."

"Consider it an education in pop history." I'd glanced at Jed's collection, made up of bands I'd seen photographed in magazines but had never actually heard, whose names were spelled strangely (Limp Bizkit, Linkin Park) or bore cryptic numbers (Blink-182, 311). He had a CD by Christina Aguilera—her single was inescapable right around then—though Jed claimed this one had been left behind by *someone I went out with*.

On Lion's Gate, he directed me to a turnoff I hadn't seen last night, not far from where I'd chased my hat. A small sign read MID-PENINSULA

LAND TRUST, DAY PERMITS REQUIRED. The trust, Jed explained, kept its acreage undeveloped and paid property owners along its borders to limit their own construction, creating a secondary ring of green around the core. On the other side of these peaks, stretching from SF to San Jose, was the sprawling fact of modern life—the freeways and passenger rails, the strip malls and office parks—but here, in front of us, was the local gentry's gift to the public.

I slowed down the car when we got to a clearing, and Jed pointed things out to me: a little valley down below belonging to a rock star; the parcel next to that owned by a famous scientist; a hill still being ranched for cattle. Jed claimed that at this time of year we could pull off the dirt road, jimmy the car behind some dense greenery and not worry about getting caught. Sounded like a plan to me.

He talked as we started our walk, telling me about his family, who had farmed in this area for generations (first hops, then apples) before donating their land to the trust, and how, as a kid, he'd explored these hills with his cousins. He threw his arms wide, animation taking over his face. "This is what I was talking about, dude. Tripping hella natural. You could get into that, right?" He spun around, head back, eyes on the sky, and I joined him, a couple of dervishes making ourselves dizzy, whistling as we collapsed.

"Teddy, we should take that E."

It took me a second to understand that he was serious.

Reasons this was a bad idea: We'd get lost or sidetracked, my mission abandoned to the vagaries of the high. I'd already paid him for it, now he was looking to take it for free. And most worrisome of all, ecstasy didn't get its reputation as the *love drug* for nothing. I have come to regret some of the overblown, intimate confessions I've made while listening to ecstasy's sweet nothings pulse in my ears. I had a rule: only with longtime friends, only with committed lovers. (Realizing suddenly, wistfully, that Woody and I had never shared anything stronger than cocktails together.)

"I just met you," I stammered, imagining the dangerous flood of feeling I'd no doubt have to share with Jed as the drug built toward its peak.

"Dude," he said to me, "you'd be an awesome person to trip with."

Reason I gave in to a bad idea: He put his hands on my shoulders and squeezed. I'd been frowning at the dirt, avoiding his eyes, but now I looked up and felt him wipe away all my caution with something like sincerity on his face. That was all it took.

15

We hadn't eaten breakfast, so there was little doubt that we'd feel the E soon enough. Empty stomach equals fast absorption. With a capsule pinched between his fingers, Jed traced a figure eight in the air, a magician readying for the trick.

"Wait!" I said. "We have to state our intentions first." Good intentions, I explained, make for good trips. Don't mess with your brain unless you know why you're doing it. Clarify your intention and the drug will work with you, not against you. I had confidence in this reliable ritual of past hallucinogenic intake. Under the current circumstances, I felt that I needed it.

Jed said, "I intend to have fun and get off on nature."

Before I'd met Jed (was it only last night?), before his presence changed the color of this adventure, my intentions were, if not clear, at least directed. "I'm looking for my father, so to speak, and I want to walk on the ground that he walked on and maybe even have the relationship to this place that he did. I intend for this ecstasy to make it a happy connection and not such a fucked-up one, which is what it's always been."

"It would take more than one hit to make me feel good about *my* father."

"You think I'm asking for too much?"

"I think you're being too heavy. You don't do this every time you smoke pot, do you?" he asked.

"Pot's not a drug," I answered. But he was right. "Okay. I intend to have fun and get off on nature, too."

Down went the magic bullets.

* * *

He led us along a deer path that paralleled a trickling creek. Overgrown manzanita bushes and twisty scrub oaks lined the way. Deeper in, redwoods stood in circles that marked the circumferences of long-gone center trees. The offspring grew, Jed said, not from dropped seeds, but up from the roots. He explained that the entire peninsula south of San Francisco had once been solid redwood forest, all of it logged to build the city, all of it obliterated soon after by earthquake and fire. So the gorgeous green fields and expansive views to the ocean that had awed me yesterday had come at a price: the old growth, twice destroyed.

The hike took us downhill and then back up, through a constant chorus of birdcalls. In his pages Teddy had wondered if birds *speak to each other across species;* I understood perfectly how he came to this question, and I listened closely to a volley of squawks and chirps with the idea that I might answer it. Jed was grabbing my attention, pointing in every direction with his strong, tattooed arm. He showed me different paw prints in the mud (coyote prints have claws extended, bobcats' don't, deer's look like quotation marks); and poison oak budding down low ("leaves of three, let it be," he instructed); and holes made by gophers that were now homes to snakes. "All of this wildlife should be freaking me out," I told him. "But it isn't." I filled up with wonder, at the light filtering down through the leafy canopy, at the rising smell of wet earth at creekside, at the song the wind was making of everything it touched. "Nature is so detailed," I whispered.

A big smile from Jed. "I can tell you're feeling it, Teddy."

"You can?"

The thrill of the onset: extended eye contact, grins of admiration, exuberance at whatever caught our attention. He was chattering away as usual but no longer seemed like he was trying to prove something. Instead of "dude" he was using my name—the name I'd given him. His almost clownish toughness had been replaced with a sweet enthusiasm. I felt the giddiness of witnessing his transformation. I felt the opposite, too: *Remember who you told him you are.* But it seemed now that my masquerade might simply dissolve, a clump of mud in moving water.

Sweat on my brow dampened my hat, sweat under my shirt tickled my chest, heat gathered in my feet. We stepped into a dusty clearing and sunshine struck like a searchlight, casting the trees at the periphery into velvety shadows. Jed thrust his chin skyward, his face pure contentment. Then he grabbed the bottom of his T-shirt and tugged it up over his head, scrunching it behind his neck.

His torso: flat, downy, glistening. Skin flush from exertion. An unexpected, tiny silver ring piercing his right nipple. His jeans sagged below the long runway of his abdomen, exposing the underwear I'd seen last night and a patch of darker hair, curling out like a hundred little antennae. He said, "You feel it. Right?"

"I feel so much."

"Didn't I tell you?"

Whatever he'd told me hadn't prepared me for this. Desire boiled up, groin to chest to brain, my skull a kettle already rattling as the steam built to the warning whistle.

"We need to find a secret meadow," I told him. "The secret meadow is the goal of all drug trips. A little womby place to sit in while you're peaking."

"We already have a goal, Teddy. The railway car!"

"Oh, yeah." I was bursting with appreciation. "It's so amazing how you're keeping me on track." Jed was beautiful on the outside, but now I saw it came from underneath his perfect surface—a core of solid gold. He was my trusty cub blazing the trail, my magic boy with his bag of potions, a studly version of my own younger, brazen self. I formed thoughts beginning with his name, sentences I needed to utter, needed him to hear—and then I sealed them off. *Think like Teddy.* Had Teddy known this awe that couldn't be voiced? This risk that felt like joy?

"Dude, let's look at each other's tattoos up close." Not sure how long we've been here, sitting side by side, stripped down to our underwear. Jed's sun-warmed skin is only inches from mine. Now he peers at the snakes wiggling around my upper arm. "Infinity," I say. "Change. The cycle of life." All I can muster for explanation.

His right arm is dense with symbols, flames and roses, crosses and ankhs and daggers from his wrist to the cuff of his shoulder, all of it bright and new, as if wet to the touch. "No one ever looks really close," he whispers. "You want people to, but they don't, they stay back." He lifts a fingertip to my snakes, traces the ink, goosebumps my skin, wave-crashes my brain. I clench a fist, making what I can of the muscle. "If you worked out you'd be gigantic," he says, gripping me.

"How long have you been working out?" I ask. "How long to get like this?" My hand goes to his chest. Soft surface, solid beneath.

"Since freshman year. I started before everyone." He leans back, closes his eyes, offers himself up for display. He says, "I did everything first."

A risk: my fingers on the nipple ring. A tug, a twist. "Oh, fuck, Teddy, don't do that." A half-hearted protest, a no-means-yes. Another tug, then I release, pull back. It's too much.

I tell him I need to lie down. I roll away from him. Grass under my head, along my skin, tickly, itchy. Exhale to relax. Examine the tiny yellow and purple wildflowers, like starbursts of pigment. The heady moist smell of growing things. My face in the blades. A caravan of bugs, so many of them, crawling along as always. A whole world down here where human feet trample without noticing, without care.

My eyes are closed when he douses me. A shock of wet from above. Jed laughing as he drains his water bottle onto my skin.

"No fair!"

"Yes. Fair. Now do me," he says.

I stand up. He arches back. I pour water onto his forehead, face, neck. His strong neck. I want those tendons between my teeth, against my tongue. Water flows where my hands want to roam, beads on his skin, saturates his underwear. The fabric clings. Then we're two wet dogs shaking off, flinging droplets at each other. Then we're squeegees, hands upon each other, slicking each other dry, mussing hair, giggling, falling into an almost-naked embrace.

Heartbeat deafening now. I have to say something. I try, "It's hard to be regular," but it comes out, "It's hard to be regal."

To which he smiles and says, "It's hard to be legal."

And I say, "It's hard to fly like an eagle."

And he, "It's hard to bark like a beagle."

And me, "And now I'm hard as a steeple."

Which is how we both wind up staring at my crotch. "Not quite," he says, reaching down, squeezing me there, hanging on too long, not long enough.

I whimper his name.

Which is when he sprints across the secret meadow in his boots and his socks and his soggy boxers, looking less like a nature boy than a punk go-go dancer at the Stud on a Saturday night. He jumps up to an oak branch. Climbs, turns, waves.

Is he running away or showing off? I remember our intention, to *have fun.* I run to join him. Bark sandpapers my skin as I follow him up. Wet skin now cold in the breeze. The sky through the branches is iridescent, a sheet of glimmering pearls, glowing atoms, precisely daubed paint. The two of us in the tree's leafy hold, pausing to find some breath.

"I gotta say it, dude." He stares at me across a branch, his pupils enormous and dark. "I fucking love you like a brother."

"Yeah, I feel it, too."

Except brothers don't lean toward each other and kiss. With their mouths open and ready.

Like this.

We hike further uphill, pants and shirts stuffed in my bag. It's a definite climb, tough work on smoker's lungs, and we've foolishly wasted most of our water. But my steps are strong; I could sprint with the vitality I took from locking onto Jed's lips. The unskilled hunger of the moment, the unsure tittering that ended it, the matter-of-fact words that followed: "Dude, I just had to do that." "No problem. I was feeling it." "Cool."

Now Jed takes the lead, a few paces ahead. Silent now. There's something troubling in this arrangement. Is it the cold shoulder, because things went too far? Or it may be that the trip has already peaked. You never know until you've passed it.

"Do you know where you're going?" I ask.

"That bunch of trees, there." He points higher up, licks sweat off his upper lip. His eyes are expectant.

An unseen critter darts through the weeds—a startling, dry rustle. A finger of fear traces my neck. A clench takes hold of my jaw and stays there. Teeth grinding.

We find the creek again—or else it's a different creek, I can't tell—and follow it up toward what must be its source, or near to it. The gurgle louder as the slope intensifies. The soft earth underfoot giving way to rocky terrain. This must be the highest hilltop around. Oaks give way to evergreens; pinecones crumble underfoot.

"Check it out," Jed says, indicating up ahead.

A convex wall of gray rock, a giant triangle, upside-down, with a thick vertical split bisecting it. Top to bottom the crease is nearly four feet long. Spring water erupts in a firehose flow from its center, where a nub of rock swells clitorally. At the base, nearly symmetrical boulders, giant solid tubes, project forth like thighs.

I know before he tells me. It's the promised Goddess Twat.

Those hills behind could be her swollen belly, her ripe green breasts.

"The owner of this vagina would have to be fifty feet tall," he says.

"What about the dick that could fill it up?"

"I'd like to see that," he says.

"Oh, would you now?" My tone is too arch, it shoves him back to silence.

"You still feel the E?" he asks finally.

"Sure, but not so strong."

"Time for the dope." He retrieves the pipe from my bag—remarkable how comfortable he is going through my stuff. Remarkable that I don't mind. He puts flame to the bowl. "This will kick it back in."

He's right. Suddenly it's all there again: the euphoria up on stilts, wobbly, the pot-heat gurgling down below like quicksand. And in between, filling up my vision, the giant vulva, blotched with parallelograms of light, purple shadows, rust-red lichen.

For some length of time, I watch the entire mass of it throb.

"Jed, it's like it's talking to me."

"What's it saying?"

I comprehend something I didn't just a moment before. It settles upon me like sunshine: This is it, the place he wrote about, where he *planted his flag*. It must be: the pine trees, the fountain, the highest peak. I say, "He was here."

"You're talking about your old man?"

I reach in the bag, retrieve my father's pages, read the passage: "*Where the water spills forth like the very eternal juices of Mother Earth herself.*" For a moment Jed, who has occupied my every thought for hours, is not what I'm thinking about. I'm thinking instead of what I came here for; I'm thinking it has found me, and I can't speak fast enough to pace my thoughts. "This is why I'm here, the place I was meant to find. Remember what I said, how I wanted to make a connection with my father?" He nods, trying to keep up. I read: "*And so I did the thing which is known to men as taking care of the Need. That was my way to claim this hilltop for all the bums like me past and present.* Jed, I have to pay tribute."

He says, "I'm with you, dude." But his eyes ask me what the fuck I'm talking about.

I spell out what it means to *take care of the Need*. He laughs. I tell him that's what I think I should do. Here. Now. His smile flattens. He grabs the lighter, brings the pipe to his mouth. Sucks in deeply.

I'm removing what's left of my clothes, boots kicked out, socks peeled off. I step out of my still-damp underwear, my feet scrunching pine needles, the breeze blowing on my already stiffening cock.

Jed is staring. At the rock formation, at me, at the rock. At me.

"I'll give you some space," he says, holding smoke, but he stays put.

I tell him, "You brought me here. You're part of the connection." These words rise up from instinct, too. Everything locking into focus.

Jed exhales. Nods. It could be the drugs, or desire. Could be he actually gets what I've said, though I could hardly explain it myself if asked. I can see him make a decision even before he whispers, in an almost solemn voice, "Just tell me what to do."

He sheds his clothes. I stare unabashedly at his cock, which like the rest of him is compact and charismatic, a glistening head poking out from a tight foreskin. He follows me and we approach the giant totem together. We stand side by side within spitting distance of it. The water rushes forth, the ground damp with spray. I close my eyes and try to see it: my father at twenty, standing here—planting his flag, spilling his seed, taking care of his need—like Jed and I are now, exposed, aroused. "Do you feel it, Jed? There's this chain of history, and we're part of it. All the guys who've been in these woods and found this place, not just my father but all these drifters and fur trappers and sailors who jumped ship and Indian scouts who went too far, men who left behind their homes to explore, looking for who-knows-what, probably some of them as fucked up as us, and they found this place and felt it talking to them, just like we did. Think about how many of them had to whip it out just like us, 'cause that's the way to pay tribute to this big motherfucking goddess. Go for it, Jed, get it rock hard for her, you're part of that chain, little brother. Offer it up, yeah, that's right, don't hold back, show me how you make your cock feel good." Hypnosis, pornography, scripture, at once unplanned and from deep within, I'm like a bell being struck. The notes could be on-pitch or off-key but all of them are already within me.

Slats of sunshine land on our sweaty skin, igniting the copper in my hair, the flames inked into his arms. His eyes stay closed, making some mental landscape from my words, but I stay alert, transfixed upon the spectacle of Jed adrift in sensation. He cups one palm beneath his furry balls, wraps the other around his shaft, the unsnipped hood sliding beneath his thumb's pressure. I restrain myself from laying a hand upon him, though it's all I want to do. I fear the delicacy of our equilibrium, the potential eruption of disaster, even as Jed merges more deeply into my fever-dream. And the more I urge him on the more his hands roam free across his skin, fingers tugging on the nipple ring, fingers between his lips, fingers disappearing between his thighs, slipping out of sight, probing.

Could be the drugs, could be desire, could be the collision of two fucked-up lives: When his eyes open and meet mine, I see in his expression—so concentrated, almost furious—a mirror of my own aggressive need. I see how this need is always there, how it makes me powerful and brings me low. This urgency boomerangs between us, our eyes unblinking. No more words. We are both shaking our heads in the universal sign for *no.* Why *no* when we are refusing nothing? I peer deep into that negative void, where I see desire like a primal ooze, sticky and inescapable as a tar pit. I feel the heat and the trap of it, and I hate that I can't refuse it, and I hate that Jed is deep in it too, another trapped man. I see that being part of this sexualized chain of men means carrying this desire, this conflict, all the time, feeding off it even as it outflanks you. Hating and desiring Jed because I hate and desire something deep in myself. A feeling close to desperation seizes hold and I drop to my knees on the clay in front of him, I reach out and place my hand where his has been stroking and in that gesture I am five years old in the shower with my father, we are on vacation, a camping trip, saving water showering together, and as he soaps his penis I reach out to touch it, I let the heft of it register in my palm in the split second before Teddy grabs my wrist and thrusts me away, his voice an angry panic, *What's wrong with you what are you thinking*, and when I open my eyes what I'm thinking is don't hate me don't hate me don't hate me, but it's Jed who has my wrist and is lifting me back to my feet asking, *What's wrong what's wrong why are you crying*?

I was a mess of tears. Jed kept asking, "What did I do?" and no matter how much I assured him it wasn't his fault he remained visibly distressed, helpless in a way that reminded me how young and inexperienced he was. After a minute I couldn't even be sure why I'd broken down; I had woken up still trembling from a nightmare whose matter was already forgotten.

He walked away and stayed out of sight long enough to leave me wondering if he'd come back at all. Our unfinished wank had been abandoned without comment—a relief. Jed no longer seemed like my soul brother, just a stranger with an unsettled sexuality. My crying jag had flushed clean my brain, and, newly sober, I couldn't locate that mythical connection that had seemed so clear a half hour before. My deranged monologue still resonated in the air, embarrassingly, the way a cheesy porn soundtrack loops in your head long after you've shut off the set and stowed away the video. The rock formation didn't even look like a vagina anymore. More like a giant walrus.

Jed returned, saying, "Getting emotional is the first sign of dehydration. You need water." But we had almost none left.

"I bet the stream is safe to drink," I said, though Jed was worried about giardia. Take your pick: an intestinal parasite or drug-induced dehydration? I gulped until I felt bloated.

Teeth chattering, queasy and colder now in the dropping sun, I wanted only to get home. My mission, to whatever degree it still mattered to me, had been concluded. But Jed insisted that it was a short hike to where we'd find the railroad car, and that he could get us back to where we started, even after dark. We got dressed and went on, together.

With the sky beginning to blaze the colors of sunset, we came out of the woods. Different terrain again: a rolling grassy plane. A pasture. We picked up what seemed to be a tractor trail curving around a gentle slope. "This was probably where the railroad tracks were," Jed said. "They had to have a way to get the cows to the ranch."

We hopped a fence. Around another bend, Jed stopped short.

"That's it," Jed said.

"Where?"

"Dude, it's right there. Do you need glasses?"

Toward the horizon was a smudge of darkness. "That's not a railroad car."

"Not anymore. Come on." He broke into a jog.

As I approached, it came into focus: a dilapidated structure, three rotting walls supporting the remains of a roof. A partially exposed rectangular box, deep and narrow. Forty years ago, it could very well have been a freight car.

I stepped up onto a springy floor. "So this is it. This is where he slept."

"He's not the only one."

My eyes adjusted to the dark interior: beer bottles, torn condom wrappers, a wad of dirty blankets.

Jed had my backpack opened and was groping around inside. "Where's the flashlight?"

"I saw it this morning." I stuck my hand in the bag. It wasn't in there.

"Dude, we can't get back without a flashlight."

"You said you could make it in the dark."

"Yeah—with a flashlight!" he yelled. "This is totally fucked!"

"Why am I not surprised," I said, running my hands through my hair. I cursed my name out loud.

Jed looked at me askance. "Dude."

"What?"

"Dude, what did you just say?"

"Enough with the *dude* already!" I protested, though I was pretty sure I knew what he was referring to.

"Who's 'Jamie'?"

That's what I was afraid of. I was too depleted to do anything but cave in. "Jamie is me. That's my name."

"Your name is Teddy."

"Teddy is my father's name."

"I don't get it. You said—."

"It's an alias." Trying to cover my tracks only made me irate. "We've got bigger problems. Don't be a freak about it."

"You were the one talking about our *connection* before. All that bullshit about the *chain of history*."

"Yeah, it was bullshit," I spat and turned away. The westward sky was all bruise-colored vapors stretched long and thin. "We have to get out of here," I said, "while there's still some light."

"I seriously think we missed our window of opportunity."

"You missed it," I hissed. "I wanted to go home before."

"Who lost the flashlight, huh? Look, if the moon comes out and it's bright enough, we can do it. But for now . . ." His voice trailed off.

My body chemistry moved to its next phase: pangs of hunger, clawing like a rat trapped under my ribs. Worse than that, the creeping in of depression. A haunted paranoia.

It was the sex: what I'd said, what he'd done, who we'd been together. The elephant in the room. We were most likely going to spend the night out here, and it was going to be an awkward stretch of hours before we could sleep, if we could sleep at all. The temperature had fallen with the sun, the air was damp with incoming valley fog, and nature's noise was constant and alive, conjuring images of slimy crawling things and prowling beasts with sharp teeth. Vibrant birdcalls had given way to an eerie chorus of frogs. Jed wouldn't sit near me, and he didn't want to hear about sleeping in the railway car, though it was moderately more sheltered. "It smells like cow butt in there."

Everything he said was tinged with menace. I feared that he might assault me in my sleep or, more likely, steal away with my bag and the car keys. So I summoned what strength I could to cheer him up. "Look, it's one night. We know we're capable of lasting out here one night. My father did it, right here."

"Who cares? It still sucks."

"It's just how you look at it. This is all supposed to be an adventure. That's what my father was writing about in his diary—."

"Dude, you ever think you're a little obsessed? I mean, you fucking gave his name as yours."

I scrambled for a comeback, but all I came up with was "Ouch." I spoke so meekly it seemed to embolden him.

"Let me spell it out, dude. You're a liar, and I don't trust you. You're probably just waiting for me to fall asleep so you can rape me."

"Jed, that's absurd."

"You try anything," he threatened, "and I'll fuck you up." I heard his footsteps moving away. When they stopped, all visual trace of him had disappeared.

Time passed, unmeasured.

Two coyotes howled. One, then the other. They didn't sound far.

"Jed, are you still out there?"

"Yeah." His voice was nearer than I expected. All at once he was back in the car with me. "It's a good sign," he insisted. "The coyotes would stay away if mountain lions were hanging out here."

"What if they come over here for a sniff? Check out the new meat?"

"They eat rabbits and gophers and shit," his voice mocked. "They don't eat full-grown men."

"Uh-oh," I joked, "what are *you* gonna do?"

"Fuck off."

"Why don't you just smoke more pot and quit tripping on me?"

He sat down, close enough that I could sense his mass alongside me. After a long pause, he said, "I don't know why I'm so tense. It's not like I have anything waiting for me."

"Where are you going after this?" I asked, digging a cigarette out of my bag; I'd been rationing, but now was the time to put one into action. In the lighter's flare I saw his face for the first time in hours. The paranoid harshness was gone. He appeared simply unhappy. Even before he answered my question, I sensed that I was at last going to get something real from Jed.

Jeffrey Edward Howland was nineteen years old. He was indeed a college dropout, but he'd lasted less than a semester and moved back home. He had sneaked out of the house—his mother and stepfather's, in San Jose—late at night two weeks ago. He'd only been working at Casa Adios for a handful of days before I'd turned up, before he'd been fired. That pay-phone call to his mother had been his first since leaving. Those calls he'd made at the Sea Foam had been to friends, not clients.

"So why'd you run away?"

"I'm not a fucking runaway, dude. I'm nineteen, I can do whatever I want."

"And that is?"

"I gotta fly free."

I suppressed a smile: In the short time I'd known him, he'd never seemed so tethered to the world.

"My mom claims if I go back to school, they'll buy me a car. It's fucking blackmail, but I could use the wheels."

"If you don't go home, what will you do?"

"Maybe what I've been doing." He shook his head, dragged deeply on the cigarette. "You know, hanging in motels. With guys like you."

"Guys who buy drugs from you?" I asked, pretty sure that wasn't what he meant.

"Actually, I kind of overstated the dealing aspect. Someone gave me that E." He sighed deeply, letting loose a confessional rush. "Most of them are older than you. Usually businessmen. Married, middle-aged guys who'll cough up fifty bucks to smoke my pole."

I suppose I wasn't surprised by this. Jed had a hustler's personality, whether or not he was actually getting paid for sex. But I felt bad just the same, and not only for him. I didn't like the idea of being the latest in a string of freeway johns. I didn't like the company.

"Look, I can drive you home. First thing tomorrow." I needed to do this, not just to clear my throbbing conscience but for his own good. Counsel him back to the nest, set him on course for a college degree, a new car, a stocked fridge, central heating. Get him away from *guys like me*.

"I don't know about going home," he replied. "I need some time to think."

"Time we've got a lot of."

"Teddy? Or Jamie—what am I supposed to call you?"

"How about Obi Wan Kenobi?"

"How about Jar Jar?"

"How about Ass Kicker?"

"How about Fudge Packer?"

At least we were trying to have fun again.

He asked, "Does your girlfriend know about you?"

Here goes. "There is no girlfriend, Jed. There's a boyfriend."

"Really?"

"Maybe an ex-boyfriend by now."

A long, absorbent pause. "You know something, dude? I can't figure you out."

"Neither can he," I said. "Neither can I."

The fog came in high, stripping the charcoal sky of stars and eventually dropping to claim our hilltop. Banks of moisture wrapped around us like cold smoke. This was the absolute absence of light. You couldn't see your own hand gesturing. We were out of cigarettes, desperately thirsty, and both complaining of headaches. My mouth was gummy and sour. I thought about trying to kiss him, less from desire than as a tactic to work up some spit.

We laid down on the floorboards and covered ourselves in the least vile of the blankets in the corner. There were long stretches of silence, both of us aware of the other not sleeping. Bouts of shuffling and erratic breathing. Failure to find comfort.

"Hey, Jamie?"

"What?"

"Do you feel your father's spirit here?"

I concentrated, as if to tune in the astral plane. "Not here. I felt something by the Goddess."

"That was the drugs."

"Yeah, for sure. But this whole experience—meeting you, and you knowing all the places I was looking for—there's something spooky about it. Something I should probably pay attention to."

"Yeah, totally." He fumbled for me with his fingers, found my hand, rested his on top of mine. "Just making sure you're nearby."

"You're not worried I'm going to rape you?"

He pulled himself closer to me. He whispered, his voice as tender as I'd ever heard it, "All those guys I've done stuff with?"

"Yeah?"

"I never wanted to kiss any of them. Except you."

He drew his weight along the length of my body, an arm clamping around me, his breath cuffing my neck. I couldn't see, but I knew exactly where I'd find his lips if I wanted them and what they'd taste like. I remembered something about our kiss earlier that day: in the midst of the exhilaration, I'd briefly, involuntarily, compared him to Woody. I hadn't known Jed's age, but there was no mistaking he had the stabbing tongue of a teenage boy. His unruliness had been part of the thrill. Now I thought about how much life you had to live to communicate with a kiss the way Woody could.

I held him close without making another move. I laid awake like that for hours, suspended over the precipice of tomorrow. I waited until his breathing regulated, his grip relaxed. Until he'd fallen asleep and let me pass this test.

The sun intruded bright and early and sent us hiking to the car groggy, cotton mouthed, stiff backed. We found the flashlight on the seat next to a half-full water bottle, which we quickly emptied. At a restaurant on Skyline I sprung for breakfast: eggs and bacon for me, pancakes slobbered in syrup for Jed. I got the full history of his vegetarianism, which wasn't any different from anyone else's—the early influence of beloved family pets, a full awakening after seeing documentary footage of chicken slaughter. *It's totally a moral issue, dude.* I mumbled something vaguely supportive in response, as if I'd never heard it put quite that way, and added a phrase about the Buddhist *respect for all sentient beings*, which I'd picked up from Kerouac. Newly caffeinated, Jed did most of the talking. He had a kind of prostitute's etiquette, not asking about his john's private life, and also a prostitute's delusion, in the way he announced big plans for the future, most of which, like venturing to Baja to buy *a phat boat*, seemed unlikely in the short term. This was a guy who ran away from home lugging a two-foot-high Darth Vader head.

He said he had a friend at Stanford and insisted that I drop him in Palo Alto, just over the hill. We pulled into a shopping plaza. Against my sense that I would need to quickly put all of this behind me, I watched myself hand him my business card, heard myself say, "If you're in the city, call me," then felt the immediate regret of my gesture when he replied, "Dude, just keep this in your trunk, and I'll get it from you later," as he pointed to Darth Vader. I tried to refuse, but he said he wouldn't be able to manage it on the train to San Jose, and besides it had been a gift from a *totally rad teacher,* and I should appreciate that it came with *intense emotional value*. In the end, I kept the black plastic hunk and gave him a hug good-bye.

I drove slowly out of the parking lot, one eye on Jed in the rearview mirror. I watched him approach a man in an overcoat emerging from the Safeway, watched the guy pat down his pockets and pull out a box of Marlboros, watched Jed take the pack from this stranger and put the begged-for cigarette into his mouth.

PLUNGE

16

My day had begun at dawn, and as I hit the outskirts of San Francisco, morning rush hour was still gumming up the freeway. Not having a car for so many years has withered my driving reflexes. I'm hesitant when I should be confident and too easily inflamed by the aggression most drivers live by. I was coming down from two days of being high around the clock. Moments after screaming "Use your fucking blinker!" at someone who obviously couldn't hear me, I caught sight in the mirror of my scarlet cheeks, my wild eyes, the strained tendons of my neck. The hideous face of road rage.

I peeled off at Cesar Chavez, a few exits early, which put me in Woody's part of the Mission. It wasn't yet nine-thirty, the time he usually grabbed the bus for his short commute downtown. I turned onto his block, imagining I might catch him coming out of his front door at precisely that moment and not knowing what I'd do if he did. I planted a seed: Whatever I saw when I approached his building would be my sign.

He lived in a tall, narrow apartment building with enough scrollwork around the windows and under the cornice to suggest the Edwardian era, a suggestion immediately undone by its grime-collecting stucco front and prison-bar entry gate. On either side stood a more attractive, more authentically Edwardian building; Woody had dubbed his *the middle child*. A middle child himself, fully aware of having been overlooked and underphotographed as a kid, Woody felt an affinity for his building. "We have to find some place equally ugly when we move in together," I would say to him, "so you'll feel at home." Moving in together hadn't been mentioned in a long while, not even as a joke.

Woody's bedroom light was on. The sky had gone gray in the past hour and seemed to strip everything else of color, too. Gray sky, gray street, gray stucco, and one yellow rectangle of light, a shining frame within which I could see the flurry of a shadow. Not a shadow, a figure. Woody.

An empty parking spot across the street: I had my sign. Before I could lose my nerve I pulled over, got out, walked to his building, pressed the bell. After a moment, the gate buzzed. I hopped the four concrete steps to the front door, which opened on a steep interior staircase up to Woody's flat.

He stood way at the top, wearing white boxer briefs and a white V-neck and gripping a toothbrush. Through a still-foamy mouth he said my name.

"Surprise," I said.

He blinked tightly, as if clearing his vision of gunk, then said, "I'm late for work," and walked out of view.

I climbed the stairs tentatively, watching mountain dirt crumble from my cuffs, inhaling my two-day body stink, hating that it had come to this: unsure of my status in Woody's apartment. I followed the sound of water running from the bathroom faucet and found him poised over the sink, spitting. So much of him was exposed to me—his stringy calves, an ass emphasized by the cotton stretched across it, a crescent of flesh and a nub of spine above his waistband where the T-shirt pulled up. He stood, wiped his face, reached into the medicine chest to grab deodorant and sprayed a scent that was so completely his, some natural citrus-pine stuff, that it doubled his presence in the room. If he'd been trying, he couldn't have seduced me any better. No mystery. No fantasy. Just the comfort of what I already knew. I felt myself getting hard—a woody for Woody—so quickly, so adolescent-eager, it made me grin.

It wasn't until he was facing me that I saw he'd gotten a haircut.

"Your curls are gone," I said. The sides had been buzzed short, the top trimmed to waves. It drew attention to his brow and jaw, the hard bones under his sunny face. It turned him older and butch-er. "You look like you should be coaching a team."

He was scrutinizing me, too. "What happened to your forehead?"

I peered into the mirror to look at the still-puffy welts. "Thistle," I said.

"This what?"

"This-*ull*. The plant. I've been off in the woods."

"You went camping?"

"Sort of. It's a long story that has to do with my father."

"Of course." His face conveyed a kind of willful neutrality, only partly masking something less agreeable beneath it. He slid past me into the hallway, his body torqued as though to avoid contact with mine.

"That's why I didn't return your message," I called after him.

"Messa*ges*. More than one."

"I've been away for two days. I just got back now."

From the hallway he called out a question, but I didn't hear it. My sights had locked on the orange plastic garbage pail wedged next to the toilet—on what I saw inside the garbage: a torn-open condom wrapper. Black foil resting atop a layer of crumpled white tissues. I didn't recognize the brand.

"Woody?" I called out, still staring into the pail, looking for the dead soldier itself. I stepped from the bathroom, peered down the hall.

He was pulling on a pair of pants. "I said, were you out of town when the market blew up?"

"Blew up?" I pictured an explosion downtown—the weekly farmers' market sent to smithereens, the millennium cataclysm striking at last.

"The stock market," he said. "I personally lost four hundred thousand dollars."

My mouth fell open and then filled with a nervous snicker. The idea that Woody had four hundred thousand dollars to lose was absurd. Until he'd bought that SUV there was little about his life to indicate excess—a powerful computer, a taste for expensive sneakers, the occasional bottle of forty-dollar Merlot—and much of that was on credit.

He grimaced, confounded by my laugh, and I felt myself shrink in front of him. "By the end of the day, Jamie, I'm not even sure I'll have a job."

"That sucks," I mumbled.

Someone fucked you here, I thought.

While Woody finished dressing, I looked at yesterday's 72-point headline:

PLUNGE!
STOCKS TAKE STEEPEST DROP IN 12 YEARS

I skimmed the cover story. After a couple years of up, up, and up, the market had precipitously slid down and down some more But some *market indicators* were almost immediately rising again, and by last night, though the second largest drop of all time had been recorded, the business-page pundits were declaring optimism. This was merely a *correction,* they instructed, painting the entire phenomenon as not only inevitable, but welcome.

For a start-up like Digitent, kept afloat on venture capital and not yet spinning any of its vague potential into profit, the drop was absolutely unwelcome, an acknowledgment of widespread anxiety that no one previously dared to voice. Woody was being paid in large part with stock options, meaning that his value on paper was hefty with shares that he could cash-in six months or a year after the company went public. This business model had always sounded fishy to me, even in name, as if fair compensation for labor was the optional part. But Woody had been a believer; I don't think I'd realized quite how deeply he believed until that morning.

"Have I told you about Magoo.net?" he asked me as we rode downtown. I'd offered to drive him to work, wanting more time before the Digitent vacuum sucked him back in. "They've been in talks to buy us out, but since we haven't proven our value the whole thing's on hold. Yesterday we instituted an immediate hiring freeze."

"But that doesn't affect you."

"It affects a lot of the people I work with. All the consultants."

Like Roger? I pictured the two of them huddled in a cubicle, weathering the bad news. Or tangled up on Woody's bed, Roger on his knees, erect, black foil, ready to be ripped, clenched between his teeth.

"So where the hell were you?" Woody asked. His tone conveyed no emotion, merely exhaustion.

"I went to this beautiful place down the Peninsula, full of redwoods and wildflowers, with these unbelievable sunsets. I saw bobcat prints, and I heard coyotes howling at night."

"You're gone two days and you turn into a nature boy?" The first lilt of warmth I'd heard in his voice so far.

"It was like the landscape wasn't just something to look at, but something you could actually get inside of. And there were birds singing like crazy. So many bird sounds! We'd sit still and they'd just start talking and singing all around us—"

"You went with someone?"

For the second time in two days I'd slipped, as fools with secrets always do. I felt my mouth go dry, as if Jed was suddenly there in the car with us, poking his face between the seats to complain about the music. "I went to this land trust, this place I found out about, where my father had been. Where it seems that my father had sex with Don Drebinski." I looked to him for a reaction. He was listening, so I went on quickly, "And I met this guy—this kid, really—Jed, who led me to this place I was trying to find, a railroad car that my father had slept in forty years ago."

"You were with this guy for two days in the woods?"

At least I didn't have sex with him, I thought. *I mean, I did, kind of, but not in the railroad car.* "Hey, maybe you can answer me this," I said, backtracking. "Do birds talk to each other across species?"

"Shit, did I forget my phone?" He was suddenly rifling through his bag.

I sensed him cooling off again, but I wasn't going to give up; we were only a couple of blocks from his office. "Like a robin and a red-wing blackbird—do they communicate? Because one of them's going *peep* and the other one's in the next tree going *ke-woop-ke-woop.* It sounds like they understand each other, but who knows? Then there's the loud one that sounds like *kee-ree-kee.* But she's a total bitch. No one wants to talk to her." Hoping for a hint of a laugh from him, I met his eyes.

"I can't believe I forgot my phone," he said.

Digitent's red-and-black light box hovered up ahead. I swerved into a handicapped spot and turned on the hazards. For a few interminable moments, their clicking was all I could hear. I took a gulp of air and said, "I'm sorry."

"What exactly are you apologizing for?"

"Disappearing. Showing up out of nowhere."

"Oh." His voice no more than a chuff of air. "Seems like a bit of a stunt."

"I missed you," I said. "I have a lot to tell you."

He stared through the windshield to where Digitent's brushed-steel door was swinging open, drawing in the workforce. At last he cleared his throat. "I've got so much on my plate right now. I don't know if I can save our relationship and save my job, too."

"Come here." I pulled him toward me, positioning for a kiss, but he maneuvered us into a disappointingly fraternal hug. *Pat, pat, pat.* I sent my hands down his back, pried up his sweater, reached under his T-shirt. My fingers grazed a familiar mole on his lower back, small and round like the flat bottom of a chocolate chip. A reference point on the map of his skin.

Woody's hands, resting upon my coat, remained inert.

"Don't," he said, breaking away, opening the door, filling the car with cold air.

The phone was ringing as I tottered into my apartment lugging the head of Darth Vader. I dropped my bundle—the *boing* of hard plastic on linoleum—hoping it was Woody calling with some nugget of love he'd failed to deliver in the car, an *I missed you, too,* a *Yes, we're still boyfriends*.

I was greeted with the deep, creaky voice of Walt van der Neuen. "Hello, son," he said. "Got a minute for an old-timer?"

"Of course, Walt. How are you?" Was this a *booty call* from Grandpa?

"Truthfully, I'm being very good today," he said. "Taking care of my responsibilities. Carter and I want to have you and your lover over for dinner next week. We could use a few twinks to liven up this house."

I forced some levity into my voice. "There aren't many places where I can still pass myself off as a twink."

"I'll take that as a yes."

He named the time and date, and was already saying good-bye when I felt compelled to say, "I can't promise Woody will come along."

"If he doesn't, you'll be fending off the dirty old men by yourself."

He said this with such good humor that I let the conversation end without further protest. It would have been ungracious, even unfair, to explain to Walt that sex with him had triggered Woody's separation from me. Why were Woody and I so traumatized by infidelity when he and Carter had managed to fool around for decades, had even exploited their wandering eyes to widen their circle of friends? I felt so contemporary, so conservative. Maybe I'd bring Ian along. He'd fit right in.

I shoved Darth Vader into the hall closet and went to check my voice mail. I was out of town for only two days, but the world had rushed on:

> *Jamie? Ian. I think we should put those pages from your father on* Better Example. *Just enter the whole thing into a Word document and I'll code it. Do it!*

> *Hi, Jamie. It's your sister. Have you seen the news? Andy's freaking . . . Stop it, AJ. I'm on the phone with*

Uncle Jamie. AJ wanted to tell you he's joining a soccer league. Listen, Andy's weirded out. I'll be on a playdate with some of AJ's friends, but I got a cell phone, so you can call me anytime. The number is —.

Hi. It's Deirdre again. I forgot to tell you, Nana's leaving the home and moving in with me. For a little while. Okay, call me.

This is a message for James. This is LaTonya at Dr. Lee's office. Listen, hon, your next dental visit is scheduled for Wednesday, but our records show that we never got paid for August. That's invoice number 099-256. Seventy-five dollars. Okay, hon? Give me a ring before Wednesday,

Jamie, hi. Bob Flick. Accounting thinks that they overpaid you for that job you did, the shampoo focus group? Probably their fuckup but take a look at your records. Also, I've got a pile of work for a quick turnaround. Call me ASAP.

Jamie? Ian. All my files for the site are gone. What the fuck? I was going to call Woody for help—but, can I? What is the protocol? Are you talking to him yet? Call me.

This is the Sallie Mae Servicing Center. It is important that we speak to you today about your student loan payments. Call 1-800-GO-SALLIE and speak to any of our Customer Care Representatives.

Hello? Hello? Um, Jamie, this is Ray. Ray Gladwell. Thanks for your sweet message. Don't worry about any of that. It was so thoughtful of you to come to the opening! And what was the name of your lovely friend? David and I just adored her. Please thank her for me.

Jamie, Bob Flick. Never mind about that job today. I got someone else to do it. But check out that double-payment thingy, okay?

Jamie? Ian. I'm calling Woody about my computer, which won't even boot up now. Also, Glen got laid off and he's leaving San Francisco. Will you help me find a roommate?

Hey, it's Woody. I was hoping I'd hear from you today. I guess it's your move. I'll hear from you when I hear from you.

Jamie, it's Brady. So, listen, I think I fucked up. See, Colleen told me some stuff about you kinda messing around, you know? And not that I have any moral judgment, you know? But I mentioned it to Annie, and that was stupid, because Annie talks to Woody three times a day, and—fuck. Not to be part of some chain of gossip, dude, but I think I fucked up. So call me. Peace.

Jamie, Ian. This is my fourth message. Should I be worried about you?

"What exactly are you apologizing for?" Woody had asked in the car. After hearing Brady's message, I guessed what Woody was fishing for: an admission of *messing around*, some version of which had reached him through the telephone-game of our friends.

I returned only one call: "Brady, this is Jamie. Yeah, it does sound like you fucked up. And it sounds like Colleen went behind my back, and Annie passed on third-hand information to Woody. So, yeah, everyone's talking about me, no one's talking to me. Thanks. I appreciate it." Click.

If I'd just gone to that fucking dinner party at Brady's, I would have spent that night with Woody and not set off to the park the next day, to Walt. If I hadn't upset Colleen after the gallery opening, she might not have dished my secrets to Brady. And maybe if I'd just returned Woody's call before I'd left town—if I'd just been able to have the conversation he wanted—maybe Roger's condom would not have wound up in Woody's garbage pail. Each move I'd made for weeks had been a tactical error, the cause of an unwanted effect.

And now I had Jed to add to the list. Jed.

* * *

The gray sky had finally opened up. A steady, snapping rain came down on me as I dashed a couple blocks to a café on Guerrero called the Roast. I waited in line at the counter behind a small-boned white woman dressed in black, with a crown of magenta dreadlocks, and her male companion, apparently a bike messenger—raggedy pants cut off mid-calf, a double-wide shoulder bag, a U-lock in his back pocket. "It's because of the government coming down on Microsoft," she was saying to him. "That judge ordering them to split up. So the market is, like, the party's over. Hit the brakes, the feds are getting involved."

"Fuck Microsoft," he snarled. "They eat up every original idea."

"I know, but they've brought the Internet to a lot of people. Which is ultimately a subversive thing, because the government can't control it."

"Good, so now we've got the Internet, and we don't need Microsoft." The counter guy handed the messenger a to-go cup of coffee, which he lifted high, proposing a toast to the entire café. "I hope the whole fucking system comes crashing down and all you yuppies will leave San Francisco. Rats from a sinking ship."

She smiled at his theatrics, but smugly. "Get a real ideology. When the ship sinks, the rats drown, too."

Were conversations like this going on all over the country on this day? In San Francisco, the news had hit like the death of a public figure. The topic on every tongue.

The caffeine had an inverse effect on me, calling up two days of exhaustion. Ready for sleep, I curled up on my mattress, but sleep didn't come. I was disoriented, nearly dizzy, a sensation that felt thrust upon me—a pounding by a heavy wave—and also internal, a sonic force vibrating through my bones involving all the voices of the day: the people leaving me messages and the pundits in the paper and Woody saying, quite distinctly, *I don't know if I can save our relationship.* Underneath this ran a constant hum, the ghost of Teddy Garner whispering from the wings, grabbing attention. *Leave me alone, Teddy. I've been to your mountaintop, I've planted my fucking flag. Now get out of my head.*

Zombie-eyed, I wrote in my journal, trying to work out, Ian-style, the a, b, and c of my near future: *(A) Figure out how to turn this "quest" into a paying gig. (B) Let Woody call the shots so you don't lose him.* I pulled out *Desolation Angels,* one of the Kerouac titles I hadn't yet opened, and I read for a couple hours about Kerouac and

Ginsberg slumming in Mexico City. Instantly my future filled up, not with practical dictates of job and boyfriend but with cinematic visions of trekking south of the border with Jed. Maybe that was the point of JIMMY on my father's map; maybe I was supposed to complete the journey for him. *(C) Forget Jed. You want your life back. What happened with Jed is not your life.* I tossed Kerouac aside with a groan, made my way to the kitchen, opened a cookbook. Something for Woody: a peace offering. A Red Velvet Cake. I wrote a list of ingredients, stuck it to the fridge. Having expended this great effort, I slumped on the couch, channel surfing.

I remembered spending days like this, whole weeks in fact, when I was twenty-three and working my first job in San Francisco, a couple days a week at a bed-and-breakfast. The winter of 1991. I had come West, leaving my boyfriend, Nathan, behind, based on a vague promise from a friend that there was a radio job waiting for me here (so vague it disappeared once I arrived). Nathan showed up at my door just a few weeks later. We rekindled in the Mission the lifestyle we'd created in Jersey City: lazing around in our underwear, reading novels to each other in bed, eating oatmeal for breakfast and stir-fry for dinner and skipping lunch. That was the good part. The rest was arguing and hurt feelings, and when it finally got to be too much—when Nathan rode his motorcycle south to Los Angeles and told me in no uncertain terms not to follow—I turned back to the idea of a career. I put myself on a schedule. I found myself a production position, figured out how to *network*. Still, the allure of inactivity had taken hold, and I never stopped seeing aimlessness as a higher state of being. In this way I'd always considered myself emblematic of my so-called generation, marked with an X as though we lacked identifiable traits.

I understood that bike messenger's battle cry: curtail the money-hungry frenzy, notch back the arrogance of the virtual millionaires, correct the madness! Maybe we'd get a moratorium on the overpriced condos glutting my block; maybe artists and musicians would stop losing their leases; maybe I'd find fewer SUV's on Valencia nipping at my back tire. Vindication for those of us who hadn't profited from the boom and never wanted it in the first place. This notable news day might be a bookend to any of those ten years ago, when the economic recession of the early nineties had been a welcome reminder that the greed-is-good eighties were finally over.

But try as I might to paint the stock market's fortunes as us versus them, the dividing line was blurry. My boyfriend could lose his job, my brother-in-law might have squandered my inheritance, new chances for freelance work would diminish. I was a rat on this ship.

I found a Vicodin in the bathroom and downed it with a mug of Sleepytime tea. And then I grabbed my backpack, still smelling of cow butt, and dug out a bud. Back in bed, wrapped in the sheets, seeking a cocoon—to be transformed by sleep into a more majestic creature!—I was struck with the certainty that I simply couldn't cope. Every adult life was a one-person show: written, directed and acted solo in front of a fickle audience. To keep from getting the hook, you had to perform. To perform, you had to have drive. There were large forces at work out there. You needed a plan, not just the ABCs of intention.

Tomorrow, I told myself, I'd have the energy to make a plan to take action. Tomorrow.

I slept for fourteen hours: through the ringing of the phone and the clamor of the garbage trucks on their weekly tank roll down Manfred Alley and the daybreak yapping of the mutt across the hall. Out the window the ground was still wet, but the sun ruled the sky and the only clouds were fluffy and harmless. After a hot shower, my head felt relatively clear. Even the welts on my forehead had subsided. I understood now what yesterday's disorientation had been: the chemical coda of the ecstasy, the dreaded *suicide Tuesday* that follows every weekend binge. What a difference a day makes.

I listened once more to that dismal record of disappointment and confrontations-in-the-making that was my voice mail, and I returned the necessary phone calls—the ones that had to do with money. This turned out to be less painful than imagined, as is often the case when you finally tackle the thing you've put off. Bob at New World Transcripts had an assignment for me after all, and he even agreed to pay me at a slightly higher rate so that I didn't get screwed for their previous overpayment. The student loan people talked me through a long-term deferment. The dentist's office agreed to another month's delay. Even Deirdre was agreeable, saying she would *force* Andy to forward the remaining nine thousand dollars. Andy was being extra-secretive about the specifics of his investments, telling Deirdre he was going to *normalize* their portfolio without worrying her about the details. "To hell with Andy and his cockamamie schemes," she said. "I'm taking some of the money, and I'm going on vacation. Don't be surprised if I show up on your doorstep." She made it sound like a joke, but I heard the tremor in her throat.

Woody, when I got hold of him at work, reported that he still had a job. The first round of cutbacks had been announced; severe, but less mercenary than expected.

He came over after work—after nine-thirty that night—and I presented him, with a hopeful flourish, the pink-frosted cake I'd baked that day. He took a bite, complimented me, took another. Put down his fork. Chewed. Swallowed. I was stuffing a forkful between my lips when he said, "I know that you've been sneaking around behind my back."

The wad in my mouth turned to cement. I could only mix it around; it would not dissolve. Woody sat waiting for a reply. Spitting cake into my napkin, I said, "I know that you had sex with someone in the last few days."

He nodded very slowly, revealing almost nothing.

I looked away. Breathed. Tried again. "Okay, yes, there were a couple of times."

"A couple?"

"Why, what did you hear?"

"Just, in general. That you'd said something to Colleen."

"I would have told you eventually," I said. "You gotta believe me."

"Why?" he asked. "You've broken my trust. You've been a poor communicator. You haven't been fully present for some time. And you're still holding secrets."

What about you? I wanted to shout but didn't, because the pull to tell all was strong: to purge myself of every lie and omission, to clear a path to redemption. But even stronger was the knowledge—knowledge that had guided me most of my life (since my mother's death, since my father first shunned me)—that mistakes cannot be undone. Why hurt Woody's feelings further by providing the gory details?

So instead I said, "Let me tell you about my trip," and a river of words rushed forth. I told him about *In the Woods,* about the map my father had sketched, about *the kid* who helped me find the land trust. I told Woody that as I laid awake in that fog-drenched railcar, all I could think about was getting home to him. He listened, but when my river stopped flowing, I could see he was waiting for more. My confession was without a therapeutic payoff. Instead of a thunderous epiphany there was an empty echo, no doubt because I'd all but removed Jed (and the motel and the ecstasy and using my father's name) from the story. "Look, I'm no good at this," I pleaded. "But I'm willing to try."

Woody's cell phone rang. "Fuck, I have to take this." It was someone from work. He stepped to the living room. The conversation went on for many minutes as they strategized for their next big meeting in this make-or-break week.

At the kitchen table, I lit up a cigarette. My reflection stared back from a night-black windowpane. Light from above highlighted the gray ribbon of rising smoke, sculpting my torso in shadows. A picture of cool, muted isolation—I might have been trapped in a film-noir interrogation. Gone was klutzy Jamie, nervous Jamie, needy Jamie. In his place was a solitary, brooding outlaw, the kind of image that I'd flirted with for years, a pose so comfortable that I hardly recognized it as a pose. On some level, this was the me that Woody fell for. "I like that you go your own way," he said on one of our first dates. A few weeks after we'd started having sex, he confessed that he was surprised we hadn't burned out yet. "It's that moody redhead thing you give off. I knew you'd come on strong, but I didn't think you had staying power."

When he returned, I pulled him close, determined to draw him into a kiss, one that would demonstrate my *staying power*. I pressed my hips into his. I held his face in my hands.

"You're humping my leg," he said.

"You should take that as a sign that I want to jump your bones."

A range of near-responses passed across his face.

"Please tell me you're still interested in having sex with me," I said.

"God, yeah." His cheeks flared with color. His voice was hushed, almost reverent, making a shrine to the nearly two years of intimacy we'd created together. "I always want to have sex with you, Jamie."

"But?"

"But there are still so many questions."

I tightened my hold on him. "We both have questions," I said. "Let's just do this."

Here's a question that's all mine: When at last I was naked with Woody, our bodies clamped together as if magnetized, my thoughts marked by astonishment at how good we could make each other feel; when at last we had consummated the slow, tense build and were lying leg folded over leg, arms tucked under necks, bodies wet with a number of substances; and I turned my face to his and saw the multi-colored stubble and the blonde eyebrows and the flush of his neck still pumped full of heat (and it almost made me weep, the way his beauty coalesced for me—impulsive, manipulative, doesn't-deserve-it me); why in this moment did I allow another impression, a howl of doubt, to push its way to the surface like nausea after a feast? *This is not love, it's sex! You are attracted to the surface and nothing deeper! Stop fooling each other!* A masculine bellow, so sure of its authority it seemed to have controlled me forever. Why didn't I just grab this demon by the throat and throttle it? Why, instead, did I think, *You might have a point,* and let it grow stronger?

Woody's phone rang again—the exact wrong thing. Worse, he moved to answer it.

"Don't," I said. "Stay here."

"It won't take long." With a shove he propelled himself from our entanglement. Instead of marveling at the grace of his form in motion, as I might have only moments before, I found fault: the way he answered by barking his last name, "Nelson," like a stockbroker; the fact that he put on his underwear, as if talking business required covering up. Even his preppie haircut was a betrayal, the curls cut to deny my fingers the chance to twirl through them romantically.

The call did indeed take long, and then he made another. When he came back, he took one look at whatever expression had affixed itself to my face and asked, "Where did you go?"

"I've been right here," I replied, mockery in my voice. "You left for work."

"It was important."

"And there'll be another *important* call in a minute."

"Hopefully not."

"I find it interesting that you spent the first part of this conversation outlining all of my defects but never once mentioned the fact that you've basically prioritized your job over me."

"It's my *job,* Jamie."

"Your job is bullshit. The stock market pretty much proved that this week."

"You don't know the first thing about what I do."

"I know how much it's changed you."

"I didn't come here to be judged," he snapped, retreating into the hall.

This reproach sent me into a rage. "Okay, go. Get away. That's smart. Leave while it's all really clear to you."

In the bathroom, he ran the water, gargled, ruffled a towel, all at a clip. He re-entered picking up his clothes, which trailed from the kitchen. I caught the whiff of his scent—his actual body tang, not that bottled citrus—which electrified the air even though he'd tried to wipe me off in the bathroom.

"Are you saying it's all about me?" I asked. "That none of our problems are yours?"

"You cheat on me, you disappear for two days with some kid—."

"While you were home fucking Roger."

"It wasn't Roger!"

His shout stilled the room. I sat on the bed, waiting for more.

"It was a guy I met online," he said at last. "I answered his ad. He came to my apartment. It was really fast and meaningless. I know I was acting out, and I'd be perfectly willing to talk this through if I had any indication that you were willing to do the same."

He looked to me for a response, but I was busy filling in the picture of this *meaningless* sex, coloring between the lines, wondering who did what to whom. My stomach churned acid. I crossed my arms protectively and said, "You're a hypocrite."

"You hadn't returned my calls. I didn't know what to think. I sure as hell didn't know what *you* were thinking." I stared, unable to speak.

Then he said, "I don't think you even like me, Jamie," and left the room.

I bolted from the bed, ran to the front of the apartment, blocked his path. "I do like you. I do. *I love you.* It's me I don't like. Me, myself, and I. In that order." Uncertainty flickered in his eyes. "I am not that far gone, Woody. You can still save me."

"Jamie, I won't *co* you."

That would be psychobabble for *codependent,* a jargony adjective tossed out as an abbreviated verb, and it made me wonder what I was doing with someone who would respond to my desperate request for salvation with self-help lingo. I stepped aside and pushed open the door. I put on my celebrity-lawyer voice and said, "If the boyfriend won't co, then you must let him go."

He didn't hesitate.

I stood naked in the doorway, our sex encrusted on my chest.

And then I did the honorable thing, the thing I never do, the spontaneous act of slate wiping. I stumbled into pants and ran out of my apartment without locking the door. I had to reach him on the street. This self-flagellation needed to be public. I spotted him, moving slowly, the forward lurch of his posture telegraphing dejection. He looked hurt, which was better than angry. Hurt was compassionate; hurt might allow forgiveness. Angry would not appreciate my gesture, my giving chase down Valencia, dodging baby strollers, shopping carts, dogs on springy leashes.

"Woody! Wait!"

He paused, turned, caught sight of me. Bless the forces of the universe, he waited.

I reached him and dropped to one knee, lifted my gaze, looked into his teary eyes, eyes that told me he would listen to what I had to say, he was *open* to it. And so I licked my lips, cleared my throat, and I said—.

I have no fucking idea what I would have said in that moment, if it had happened. I played the scene in my head as I crept back to bed, staring into the kitchen at the pink and red cake, two half-eaten slices cut from it, a mangled valentine. I could indeed make a run for it, a run toward Woody, toward the outside chance of fixing this mess, but no, no, there was not enough time, he was already too long gone. I didn't know which direction he was walking—or driving, in his monstrous automobile. And even if I did chase him down and supplicate myself, most contrite, most repentant, most well intended, what did I have to offer?

Three days with no contact. Then, in the mail, my keys. Woody's set. With a note:

> *I don't want access to your world anymore. And I don't think you want me that close.*

He didn't return my calls.

"What kind of person dumps you two months after your father dies?" Ian asked.

"What does that have to do with anything?" I countered.

"I always thought there was something calculating about Woody. All that therapy is so controlling."

"You're just mad because he won't help with your hard drive."

When Ian had called Woody, Woody told Ian he'd have to get computer advice from someone else, then told him it was over between us. Ian called me, annoyed that he'd heard this news secondhand. "I'm wallowing in pity," I deadpanned. "I don't need nobody but this bag of pot and this remote control."

He came over to my apartment right away. When he opened the hall closet to hang up his leather jacket, out tumbled Darth Vader.

"I suspect this has something to do with your breakup," he said, nudging it with his boot.

"If you want the details, let's go somewhere else," I insisted. I was finding it hard to stay in my apartment, which had begun to feel like a crime scene, complete with chalk outlines on the floor and bloodstains on the doorknobs.

Now we were at the Eagle, which still had a reputation as a biker bar even though it was mostly just a divey hangout for all kinds of unconventional types. The leathermen, with their harnesses and handlebar mustaches, had dwindled in number over the years, replaced by the bears, with their heavy bellies and beards and flannel shirts—a sort of lumberjack chic perfectly suited to Northern California. The Eagle even had a fire pit in the backyard. Ian and I stood at its edge, ashing our cigarettes into the blaze, while I caught him up on my road trip, on Jed—about whom no detail was too small for Ian—and on my failed attempt to pick things up with Woody.

"Woody's not calculating," I insisted. "I'm the one who played this wrong."

"Gore Vidal says that the secret to long-term relationships is to not have sex with your lover."

"Hard to call someone *lover* if you're not having sex."

"That's when you become *longtime companions.*"

I groaned. "A euphemism created by the *New York Times* obituary page."

"How about *significant other*? Do we like that one?"

"Calling someone significant automatically makes them seem insignificant," I said. "I always liked *boyfriend*."

"Not deep enough," he said. "A boyfriend is a crush who you wind up fucking for a while."

Maybe that was it: We never evolved beyond the first crush, beyond boyfriends. We were unprepared to venture into the territory of long term, where you can't rely on sex for fuel, where the labels don't suffice, where people who can't get married (or don't want to) figure out how to map a new path. "Stuck in the boyfriend rut. That was me and Woody," I told Ian. "Maybe we should have been fuck buddies and left it at that."

Ian lifted his gaze from the fire and looked at me with disbelief. "If you think your relationship with Woody was just about fucking a cute guy, you're clueless."

"That's because you never thought Woody was cute," I joked.

He didn't even crack a smile. "All I'm saying is, this wasn't unfixable."

"Well, I didn't know how to fix it, and Woody didn't want to."

"Or the other way around." He shot his cigarette into the fire.

Ah, fuck Ian. What does he know about relationships?

For three days I went to work, transcribing. The hours spent strapped into headphones, staring into a monitor, passed slowly and gave me a stiff neck, and I resented that half the money I'd earn would go to covering their incompetence. But I was relieved to be occupied. The job was done on-site, downtown, and the bike ride back and forth, a couple of miles each way, was invigorating, purposeful. Lunch breaks sitting on the Montgomery steps let me eavesdrop on the problems of strangers: bike messengers comparing near misses with taxicabs, clerical workers relaying office gossip over takeout containers, people on cell phones, more of them all the time, heedless of who was in earshot.

Evenings, I distracted myself with socializing, two nights at the movies with acquaintances I hadn't seen in months, the third night out for sushi with my temporary co-workers. One of the other transcribers, a toothy, flirty, twentysomething guy named Shane, dragged me along after dinner to a new bar in the Castro, where the air was so infused with cologne it made me light-headed. Shane introduced me to a crew of his cute friends, who sipped cocktails through straws and lip-synched to Jennifer Lopez and Britney Spears. These boys were primped and shellacked to a photogenic sheen, but even if any of them had been rougher around the edges—a little more mussed, the way I like 'em—I doubt I would have pursued anything. I was finally free to fuck around without guilt, but I felt myself pulled toward home, a newly unleashed dog staying put on the front porch.

That night, in my journal, I tossed around the idea that it was time to leave San Francisco.

> *I've had a good run here, and this stuff with my father makes me appreciate the history, but give me one good reason to stick around. Woody won't speak to me. My friends are all gossiping. There are better places to rebuild my career. I hear New York is happening again. I could try Los Angeles. Even better: I could disappear to somewhere far away and anonymous. No plans, no attachments. I could take this freedom and make something of it.*

THE CRIMINAL KICK

17

Walt's invitation was for six o'clock. I biked over with late-spring twilight to guide me. I'd arranged to interview them, and the recorder rested heavily in my backpack, solid in a way that few things seemed lately.

As I waited at the front door, I could see the dance of the gaslight flame through the stained-glass pane. The bell was answered by an elderly man whose features I immediately recognized as aged versions of those in the photos I'd seen: the distinguished jaw, now jowly; the high forehead exposed under fine, pewter-hued hair; the once-athletic shoulders curved by gravity.

"I'm Jamie," I said. "You must be Carter."

"Indeed I am. Enter." His voice was a thin rasp, as if from the aftermath of throat surgery. We shook hands.

I was led into the enormous parlor, still fascinating in its gothic opulence, but no longer the mysterious Wonderland it had seemed weeks ago. From the far end of the room, Walt emerged with a cocktail in hand, and at the sight of him an unexpected nervous flutter passed through my chest, a second-date skip of excitement.

"You're alone?" Walt asked.

"Woody's busy," I said.

"That's a shame."

I nodded. "Is it just the three of us?"

"Plus Her Highness."

"Always the last to arrive," said Carter, slipping to Walt's side, locking an arm around his waist. A stab of envy: Their ease with each other, and the longevity it grew out of, seemed wholly elusive to me, like a glamorous career path, architecture or couture, for which I had no training. I took a sip of what turned out to be a very strong vodka tonic. I asked about *Her Highness.*

"Queen Elizabeth," Carter said, "aka Betts, Betty, Bettina, Heavens to Betsy, La Liz. Am I forgetting anything?"

"Queen B," said Walt.

"Is she coming in drag?" I asked.

"If you mean women's clothes, no. But you won't miss the tiara."

Walt and I sat. Carter set up a TV table in front of each of us, then brought out toasted cheese sandwiches and bowls of tomato clam chowder. He apologized for the "lightness of the supper," saying that he had spent the day looking for a new car to replace their old boat, and hadn't had time to prepare. I thought about the sandwich Walt made me last time and wondered if they ever cooked, if their gourmet kitchen hid a snack-food lifestyle.

I brought out the recorder and placed it on the coffee table amid the candy bowls. I sketched out my research, my professional intentions, for Carter, who chuckled. "Radio? I better watch my French."

"Let it rip," I said. "Walt's already given me a taste of your stories."

"More than a taste, ahem," Carter said, and I felt myself blush even though his smile invited an alliance. "Did he tell you that park-orgy story? He's the only one in San Francisco who ever heard of it. The circle jerk that brought in half the Navy."

Walt said, "You're just jealous you weren't there."

"I might as well have been there, I've heard it so many times." They sat side by side on a sofa, sweetly playing out this well-worn routine for my benefit.

Carter said, "Walt mentioned that you were asking about Don Drebinski." I nodded. "I only knew him towards the end, when I was his travel agent. I knew Ron better. Don was busy with his nightclubs, and Ron was a lady of leisure."

"Old money, wasn't he?" Walt interjected.

"Gold Rush family. They inherited a lovely home in Pacific Heights."

"May I?" I asked, indicating the recorder, but before I could press PLAY the doorbell rang.

Carter shuffled through the parlor. I heard cooing and cackling from the foyer, and in flitted Her Highness, circling the furniture like a sparrow on a gust of air. "When will this city modernize its taxi fleet?

There are only twelve hundred cabs in a city of nearly a million people. It is absolutely unbearable." He was a man of about five-foot-five who seemed taller thanks to a fedora, dark glasses, a pashmina scarf wrapped several times around the neck and a royal-blue greatcoat that trailed like plumage.

"Dearest," Walt said, "may I introduce our guest of honor, Jamie Garner."

I nearly froze in the up-and-down scrutiny of his big brown eyes. "I thought I was the guest of honor," he said

"Be nice, you old showboater," Walt said.

Queen Betts gasped in mock horror, one hand on breastbone, the other dangling from the end of an arm extended to me.

"I'd never want to take the honor from someone as lovely as you," I said, pecking the back of Queen Betts's hand. "I'm just here for the cocktails."

"Charmed," he said. With a shooing motion to Walt, he added, "Speaking of which—the usual."

I said, "And how shall I address you?"

"Betts. As in all bets are off."

He was silly but alluring, and stripped of the costume and hauteur, rather handsome: olive skinned, brown eyed, thick lipped. His shaved head was buffed to a gloss. I could visualize a younger Betts, his substantial mouth serving equally well for boyish seduction and full female drag.

Carter said, "We've just begun our interview."

Betts's gaze landed on the recorder. "Where's the microphone?" He chose the seat closest to it, sitting upright, hands crossed in his lap like a finishing-school princess. Ready for my questions, though I had no idea what he had to offer.

"Shall we?" Walt said.

I began.

Have any of you ever heard of a gay bar called the Who Cares?

Walt: A social bar or a cruising bar?

A "mixed bar" was how my father referred to it.

Walt: Those were the social bars, where you would go to make friends.

Carter: As opposed to the kind of place you'd go to make-out. Remember the Ensign?

Betts: How could I forget?

A cruising bar?

Carter: It was on the waterfront, where the Embarcadero mall is now. They had a downstairs room where men could get very friendly with each other.

Betts: It's all landfill down there, and the basement walls would positively seep!

Carter: You'd be up to your ankles in water.

Betts: I swear that's why I have bad knees today. All those years kneeling on wet floors. Lord!

Walt: You'd walk in and the bar would be empty. Nothing but half-filled drinks lined up. You'd think, what a lousy bartender, but then you'd realize that everyone was down-stairs making out. When someone yelled "Police!" the men would scurry up and grab their cocktails.

I read something about the bars paying off the police.

Walt: If there was sex in a bar, it meant they paid the police. No sex meant they didn't pay off the cops. Didn't have to. If you had sex going on and you failed to fork a little money over, then you'd get raided. A pretty simple formula.

Did you ever hear of the Hideaway? It was at the end of Judah.

Betts: That was Donnie's place. It wasn't a gay bar.

You knew Don Drebinski?

Betts: Why do you think I was invited? I'm not just here for the double date, young man! Donnie and I were absolute sisters, but that was a long time ago! Before he moved to Los Angeles.

I looked at Walt, and he winked, a satisfied conspirator. I nodded back my thanks. The complete image of Walt-the-provider, the years he'd spent helming this circle of friends, came into focus in that moment. I was the latest beneficiary of the way he got things done. It wasn't until later that night, when I reread my father's letters to Ray, that I realized I'd already been introduced to Betts. Don's friend. He was right there on the page: *one clownish queen name of Benjamin but known to all as Betty . . . just a showering of womanly fussing and flirtation.*

Was this in 1961? The move to LA?

Betts: That sounds about right. I had a car, so I drove Donnie down there, with all his stuff. I was so butch, moving those heavy boxes. Chipped every last fingernail.

Do you remember if he had anyone with him? A young guy with red hair?

Betts: Now that you mention it. Oh, yes. How could I forget? Who worked at the Hideaway?

That was my father.

Betts: Don always fancied someone younger. That was his thing. Younger. Trade.

Carter: But Ron was older than him by several years.

Betts: That came later. It took Donnie a long time to not chase trade. A bit immature, if you ask me. Give me a real man, not a confused boy!

Walt: We're all a bit adolescent, aren't we? That's part of the thrill of being gay.

Carter: But my dear, you have to grow up eventually.

Walt: I'm still planning on it.

So you don't remember any of the details of Teddy in LA?

Betts: Teddy! Oh, that was the boy. A little hothead, wasn't he? They fought.

Teddy and Don?

Betts: Wait—I know what it was! On our drive south, we stopped at a roadside rest room and, well, I made the acquaintance of a stranger. Those poor truck drivers tend to overheat, don't they? Sitting behind the wheel for hours on end? I offered my, shall we say, services. Just call me Our Lady of the Highways.

Carter: Queen of the Lonely Road.

Betts: Well, that little hothead Teddy didn't like it one bit. It was none of his business, was it? I remained behind closed doors! But I'm sure we had words, and poor Donnie was stuck in the middle.

So when you got to LA, you parted ways?

Betts: We must have, because I certainly don't remember that boy accompanying me on my drive back to San Francisco. Come to think of it, that was sort of the end of my friendship with Donnie as well. I'm sure I positively scandalized him, flaunting myself in front of his little friend, but you know, I've always been a bit of a tearoom queen. It's a calling.

So I'm told.

Betts: You had to be careful because the police would try to catch you.

Carter: It was bad for a while in the late fifties. The newspapers suddenly woke up and realized there were gay bars and cruising spots.

Walt: It became an issue in the mayor's race. That's when the cops started cracking down.

Carter: I was arrested once at a public rest room. I had a job selling advertisements at the *Examiner*, and I quit the next day. I knew they'd run my name in the paper. I was *outed* before we had a word for it.

Betts: Getting caught either ruined your life or, if you were strong enough, it let you have a real life.

Walt: A real gay life.

Betts, Don moved back to San Francisco a few years later, right?

Betts: It was never quite the same between us. We didn't just pick up where we'd left off. You know how that goes, child. Your friend gets himself a rich boyfriend and forgets all about you. Tell me, where is the loyalty?

The conversation continued, as the three of them swapped stories of the old days and of Don, but for me, the interview ended with this journey to Los Angeles—Teddy's encounter with Betts's *sordid* behavior, his fight with Don, his disappearance in LA, the trail going cold again. As the clock pushed toward nine, Carter announced his bedtime. Walt ushered a still-chatty Betts into a cab for a ride home.

Saying good-bye to me, Walt insisted that I bring Woody along on my next visit. I'd had enough tongue-loosening vodka by now that I finally came clean to him about our breakup. "I'm not sure it was meant to be," I said.

"That sounds like Christian fatalism to me."

"I messed up."

"I always say, Don't let the good ones get away."

All along my bike ride home, Walt's words echoed, and when I got to my apartment, before I did anything else, before I'd even slipped the pack off my shoulders, I put in a call to Woody. No answer. For someone who had insisted the best way to reach him was on his cell phone, he never seemed to have it on when I called.

I'd been doing a lot of taping lately, but I hadn't listened to any of it, so that night, still buzzing from meeting another figure from Teddy's past, I got to work. I patched my old recorder into the new one, made a digital copy of the interview I'd done with Ray Gladwell, then transcribed it. Listening to the flow of our conversation, my fingers simultaneously tapping out our words, I understood how talking to Ray had shifted my questions away from Danny Ficchino and toward Don Drebinski. Danny had inspired my quest—just as his departure had inspired my father to come to California—but once in San Francisco, Don took over. Don opened up San Francisco to Teddy—gave him a job, took him to a gay bar, introduced him to everyone who became important to him. Perhaps Don started out as a mentor, a big brother, but his interest in Teddy obviously grew deep and messy. *In the Woods* contained one reference after another to Don's drunkenness. Was this a portrait of alcoholism, or did Don's crush on Teddy just leave him susceptible to overdoing it? They were both drunk at Chick's cabin when they had their shadowy sexual encounter, which culminated in Teddy alone in the woods, those hallucinatory woods I now knew firsthand. When he returned to San Francisco, Teddy saw the city differently, a *City of Lies*. End of story—or so I had thought. Now I knew that he'd gone with Don to Los Angeles, where I had to assume he reunited with Danny. (Dean Foster's headshot was signed LOS ANGELES, 1961.) This visit to LA was the unknown terrain on the map I'd been charting, the part ancient explorers would have marked HERE BE DRAGONS. I had come full circle, through Don and back to Danny. The snake eating its own tail.

That night, I picked up my search for Danny where I had left off: with his movie career. From my file, I dug out what information I had on Bellwether Pictures. My bank account was nearly at zero and my rent was past due, but I decided to use a bit of what I'd earned on that last transcribing job to send a money order to Bellwether, reordering videos for *The Criminal Kick* and *Surf's Up in San Diego*. Then I e-mailed them a query that began, *This is a long shot, but perhaps you can help. I'm trying to get information on an actor . . .*

I spent the evening labeling tapes and adding transcripts to my file, dusting off my desk, straightening up the apartment a bit. When I got off line, satisfied with my productivity, I found my voice mail indicator flashing. I sent out a wish: Woody.

What I heard instead was *Whassup, dude,* the voice at a familiar, runty pitch. *Check it out. I'm kicking it in San Fran. Palo Alto turned into a bad scene. You should page me. I'm on Haight Ashbury Street. I'm serious, dude. Page me.*

Riding my bike home from downtown a few days earlier, I'd spotted a blonde-haired punk with a stuffed backpack exiting the bus terminal on Mission Street. From the corner of my eye it could have been Jed, but when I glanced back he was gone, and I pedaled away ridiculing myself for the hopeful flare this nonsighting had ignited. Now I felt myself hesitating to write down his pager number, ready to erase his message, when his voice slipped back in, like a hidden track on a music disc. With a faint exhale, he spoke in a tone so vulnerable he could have been curled next to me in the railcar again, the blinding fog encroaching: *Jamie, it would mean a lot to me to see you.*

Maybe if Woody had called me back that night. Maybe if I had another paying gig to occupy me the next morning. Maybe if Jed's voice mail hadn't mentioned Haight Street, which under its sheen of upscale, Summer of Love nostalgia was a vortex of shopping-cart homelessness, gutter punks on speed, cops making arrests. Maybe if the next day hadn't brought another downpour, I wouldn't have returned Jed's call and insisted he come over.

He needed a shower and clean clothes, so while he went into the bathroom I carried his now-familiar threads—the gray Dickies, the Rage Against the Machine concert jersey, the wife beaters and boxers—to the Laundromat. When I got back to the apartment, he was shaving—not his face, but his arm, dragging my razor through the white foam he'd slathered on his multicolored tattoos. The bathroom door was open, steam wafting out; a towel hung from his trim hips, clinging to the curve of his ass. The physical fact of Jed: another reason I'd answered his page.

His clothes weren't dry yet, so he dressed in mine, a pair of button-fly Levi's I'd outgrown that fit him perfectly and a thrift-store T-shirt whose logo read STAGG PHYSICAL EDUCATION. "This stuff is too small for me," he complained.

"It shows off your muscles," I told him.

"Dude, I look seriously gay."

"Not seriously. *Ironically*." I added, "Welcome to San Francisco, where all the guys look gay."

He grumbled some more, but he didn't change clothes.

His story—the version of it he gave me, anyway—came forth over the next few rainy hours. His *friend at Stanford* turned out to be a divorced professor, an acquaintance of his stepfather's who'd been sucking Jed's dick on and off for three years. Jed had spent a couple of days on his couch, until the prof, who was hosting a faculty cocktail party at his home, sent him away with two hundred bucks. Jed blew the money on a hotel suite, inviting his high school friends for some *mad partying*—mad enough, apparently, for Jed to lose his room deposit, which he'd paid in cash. He then went back to San Jose for a day and got into a fight with his mother, during which he outed the Stanford professor. At first she didn't believe the story and wanted to tell his stepfather. When Jed convinced her, in explicit detail, that he was telling the truth, she demanded his stepfather never know.

In a rage, he fled to San Francisco. He checked into a South of Market hostel but was kicked out after getting caught smoking pot with a guy he'd sneaked past the front desk. He spent a sleepless night in a Travelodge with a couple of gay guys on crystal—he swore he didn't do any of the drug or have sex with them, which I found hard to believe. Then he went to the Haight, where he *hooked up with this rad chick named Bethany*, until Bethany's boyfriend showed up and found them rolling around on her futon. Jed slept that night in Golden Gate Park. With the prospect of another cold, damp, dirty night ahead, he called me.

I felt the urge to play big brother to him: make him quit this runaway life before he wound up arrested, beaten up, hooked on crystal, infected with an STD. But come on, *make him quit?* As if his life was a job he could simply give notice to, on his way to finding a better one? The truth is, I was more envious than alarmed. I'd been having my Kerouac fantasies, but Jed was living them: doing what he wanted and, despite his no-money-all-trouble existence, landing on his feet every time. I admired his knack for survival—one part charisma, one part manipulation, one part knowing when to cut and run.

"You should stay here," I heard myself saying. "I don't want you on the street, and I definitely don't want you having crystal-sex in motel rooms."

I expected him to rebel against my parental tone, even though I was playing the *cool parent*, but he surprised me with his effusive gratitude. It was a hint that he was more desperate, or scared, than I'd realized.

"What about your, like, boyfriend?" he asked. "After that scene with Bethany, I don't need anymore jealous fuckers on my ass."

"He's not around much right now," I said. Jed nodded slowly, parsing my deliberately vague words. "Besides," I added, "you're sleeping on the couch."

"Where else would I?"

Was I imagining that he sounded defensive?

I cleared some shelf space in the living room for his clothes and CDs, and I freed Darth Vader's head from the coat closet and set it up next to the TV, a sentinel to watch over his things. With the rain still coming down, we camped in all day, running through cigarettes and surfing the limited number of channels available through my basic cable package. When that got boring we put on Radiohead's *OK Computer,* got stoned and analyzed the lyrics. We ordered pizza; Jed insisted, "It's on me," but when the delivery came he was short two bucks.

I thought it would be a chore having him around, like trying to housebreak a pound puppy; instead, he brought out the dog in me. The room filled with smoke, the dishes stayed dirty and we wiped our pizza-greased hands on our—my—pants. We arm wrestled (he won). We played Spit (I won). He was all assertions and hormones: "You've got no microwave, no Play Station, no cell phone and only a dial-up modem? This place is barely in the nineties." I made a point of showing him my digital recorder just to prove I wasn't a technophobe. When it was time to piss we stood side by side at the bowl, like at San Gregorio, hurling homophobic slurs at each other.

While he took a nap, I went to the kitchen, Saran-wrapped the last of that damn pink cake and left it out on the street for a homeless person. I thought about throwing it away, but that seemed like such a melodramatic thing to do—to throw a cake you made for someone you love in the trash.

Jed was up and out before I woke the next day. His backpack full of clothes was gone, and there was no note. When I paged him he didn't respond. His CDs were still in the living room, so I had to assume he'd be back. But I wondered.

I hadn't given him a key to the apartment, so I was reluctant to leave until I heard from him. I had the idea that I'd cook for him that night—even caught myself itemizing a vegetarian shopping list—but the expectation that he'd be *home for dinner* was laughable. In the light of a new day, my plan to be his temporary shelter was exposed for all its flaws. I hadn't made him accountable in any way. We hadn't communicated about anything important.

The phone rang.

"James Garner?" A woman's voice, abrupt and forceful.

"Speaking." I sensed immediately this was not a call I wanted to take.

"James, this is Eagle Credit and Collection. The current amount you owe us is $3,652.44. How do you plan to get that money to us today?"

"Excuse me?"

"We're through with excusing you, James."

"Who are you?"

"Eagle Credit and Collection. This is regarding the money you failed to pay to Visa. We bought that loan, and we want our money."

Of course. I'd ignored the statements piling up. I'd failed to set up a payment plan. Now I had this antagonistic money collector in my ear. I tried to stall for time, telling her I'd need to check my files—"Why don't I call you back when I find the paperwork, we can work something out"—but she was unrelenting.

"We're not customer service, James. We don't work *with* you. You owe us. Understand?"

"What you might want to understand"—I was getting louder, trying to mask the jitters—"is that I don't have thirty-six hundred dollars."

"We'll need the name of an employer or family member."

"Oh, right." I almost smiled, picturing Deirdre giving this woman a piece of her mind. "This is dangerously close to harassment."

"We haven't even begun." I could hear the glee in her voice. "I suggest, James, that you take us very seriously."

"Take this seriously, bitch." I banged down the phone, a knockout punch that felt victorious for about three seconds, after which I was simply left shaking. I've lived my entire adult life in debt. Bills get paid late, a little at a time. *I'll die owing money to someone,* was my standard line. *How bad can it get?* Now I was afraid to answer the phone. I didn't even have caller ID.

On my bike I pedaled fast in low gear, moving toward no destination, but with great force. The city landscape softened on either side of me; for an hour, the hassles and heartaches that had claimed me blurred beneath sweat and muscle strain.

I ran out of pavement, and breath, when I hit the Embarcadero. I looked out at the slate blue water, the sailboats lazing under the mighty Bay Bridge. The year before I moved to SF, a section of the bridge collapsed during an earthquake. A length of its roadway dropped, a trapdoor on a hinge, and a car went soaring into the sudden void, the driver killed in the course of a route he'd likely traveled a thousand times. Unbelievable that the ground can lurch without warning, can remove even the most basic certainty. We act on faith that when we wake to the next day of our lives and swing our feet from the bed, we have somewhere solid to land.

Back on my block, I discovered Anton hoisting a cardboard box into a cargo van. I pulled over. "Moving something, Anton?"

"Moving everything. They've priced me out, brother."

"No!" I'd forgotten about this possibility.

"It's official."

"What can we do? Did you call the tenants' union? Can we get the Board of Supervisors involved?" Anton was so closely associated with political causes that it seemed he himself was one. But I could hear how wishful this *we* sounded, as if a phone tree could be activated to rally his customers.

"Got myself an office on Seventh Street, near Market," he said.

"That'll be colorful." It was hard to keep the gloom out of my voice as I pictured the street people thronging the subway escalator there, the scabby junkies nodding off at the skeevy McDonald's on the corner, the piss that ran in dark rivulets from the sides of buildings to the curb. Where would Anton set up his easel in the midst of all that?

"The revolution always starts among the down and out," he said. "That's why the CIA introduced crack into the ghetto. It's the control-the-poor-folk story."

"Right on," I said without vigor.

I spent some time helping him load the van, and when we were done he waved me into the store. "Big changes underway," he said. "I'm going legit."

"You're not selling pot?" I asked.

"I'm gonna work with the cannabis clubs. Medicinal, dig? No need to go it alone when there's a legalization movement happening."

"What's going to happen to all us poor stoners who rely on you?"

He handed me a bulging kitchen garbage bag, the size of a small pillowcase. I undid a twist-tie and peered in. It was crammed full of browned, crunchy marijuana leaves.

"You're giving me this?" I asked, astonished.

"I'm only taking the *kind bud* with me," he said. "Not this old shake."

"I could smoke this 'round the clock for five years."

"Heh, heh. I don't recommend that. It's very dry. Hell on the lungs, but good for cooking."

I protested, but he wouldn't hear it. "It's a gift," he said. "I've always dug you, brother."

The one-block walk to my front door had never taken as long as it did that morning, as I pushed my bike with one arm and with the other lugged that criminally large bundle, looking over my shoulder every step, expecting the cops to come whirring down the street, sirens blaring.

18

A reply from Bellwether Pictures was waiting when I got home. According to their outdated records, Dean Foster was represented by the William Morris Agency. I phoned Morris right away, announcing myself as an NPR producer doing a where-are-they-now story on *spaghetti Western legend Dean Foster*. The receptionist informed me that he hadn't been their client for years, though an old notation on his file said that he was represented by an agency called Schwartz and Fields. When I looked them up online, I was surprised to find that they were not a talent agency, but a literary one. I sent them a request for information.

I felt myself closing in on Danny Ficchino. But for what? I was hardly an NPR producer. I'd cut myself off from Brady, who was better situated in the field than I was these days, and even if I hadn't, I was no closer to that elusive *angle* Brady had prodded me for. I didn't even have Ian's website as an outlet, not until he figured out how to get his server up and running. Maybe nothing more would come of this search than a reunion, the rekindling of a fire long gone cold. Just another conversation with someone who knew my father. Danny Ficchino and Rusty Garner's son, talking about the years gone by. Maybe that wasn't so terrible.

It was dark outside the kitchen window, maybe eight o'clock, when Jed finally reappeared. I buzzed him in, stepping into the hallway at the same moment Eleanor, the old lady in the apartment across from me, opened her door. Her hyperactive mutt came sprinting past her and planted itself in the middle of the carpet, unleashing its machine gun yap: *rrr-rrr-rrr-rrr-rrr-rrr-rrr-rrr.* "Dinky, shet up!" Eleanor commanded in her Texas drawl, craning her neck to stare into my apartment, her fluffy hair like a lone cloud bobbing. The air was thick with the herbal aroma coming from my kitchen—a batch of pot brownies baking in my oven.

"Whoa, what's for dinner, stoner?" Jed said.

His appearance at the end of the hallway ignited another round of fire from Dinky, another "Shet up!" from Eleanor. I saw curiosity on her face as she asked, "Is somethin' burnin'?"

"New recipe. Middle Eastern. Very spicy." I waved Jed past the dog and into the apartment.

Rrr-rrr-rrr-rrr-rrr—slam!

I followed Jed into the kitchen. "You've been gone since I woke up."

"I had a crazy day." He was surveying the countertop, which was strewn with kitchen utensils, baking ingredients, and a butter-stained recipe printed out from the Internet. "Serious chemistry experiment going on here."

"Why didn't I hear from you?"

"About what?"

"About what you've been doing for ten hours."

"You want me to spell out my every move?"

I shook my head no—though maybe that's exactly what I wanted: a picture of what ten hours in Jed's life were like. "Look, I don't know if I made it clear, but you can't use this place as a revolving door between drug deals or whatever you're out there selling." I saw that he was suppressing a smile. "Do you think this is funny?"

"You might want to light some incense before that lady calls the cops on you." He was staring not at me but at something on the floor near my feet: the Hefty bag full of pot. "So who's the dealer around here?"

"Shit," I muttered, grabbing the bag and tying it shut. "This was a gift. I don't know where I'm going to hide this. It doesn't fit in any of the cabinets."

"I have an idea," Jed said. He walked to the living room and lifted up the Darth Vader head, revealing its open bottom, its hollow center. I handed him the bag, which he wedged snugly inside the molded plastic. My illegal stash disappeared behind those deep, black eye sockets, which looked both sinister and vacant at once.

Jed reached out and rubbed a reassuring hand on my shoulder. "Don't worry about me, dude. I got a job. At a Starbucks downtown."

"Starbucks? They're the Evil Empire destroying café culture."

"Whatever, dude. I used to work for them in San Jose, so I fully impressed them with my barista IQ."

"You did?"

He nodded, self-impressed but inviting reassurance. At any given moment his expression held the possibility of truth and lies in equal measure.

"I used you as a reference," he added quickly, "so if they call, you're my brother."

"Your brother who has a different last name?"

"Yeah, like, half-brother. And you hired me for this internship in radio. Isn't that what you do?"

"That's what's on my résumé."

"I told them all about how you showed me that recorder." His voice carried a note of pride, a little heat lamp melting down my annoyance.

The timer began chirping from the kitchen.

I pulled the tray from the oven. The brownies were nearly the same shade as Darth Vader, an inky, glossy darkness. They smelled potent and green. My stomach stirred, activating the memory of tripping with Jed on the mountain—more a generalized disturbance than a specific image. I glanced over my shoulder and there he stood in the flesh, beaming gap-toothed trouble. In his hand he held one of the German knives, the big chef's blade, prepared to dig in.

"They need to cool off," I said.

He stepped directly in front of me, so close his puffed-up chest made contact with mine, so close that when I exhaled, his eyelids fluttered with the force of my breath. He grabbed my arm and pinned it behind my back, growling, "Your brownies or your life." Trying to be funny, I guess, though in his other hand was the knife. The blade framed my eyes like a rearview mirror, the plummeting rearview mirror of a car soaring into the bay where the road has dropped away.

"You don't need anything this sharp," I said, taking hold of his wrist, easing away the blade. He dropped it on the counter. I held my grip; he still had my other arm in his. An equilibrium of restraint. Anything could have happened next, though I knew what I wanted, if he gave me the sign.

There was no safe place for his eyes to rest. When our eyes met, it was all but unbearable. I felt a jab of pressure against my hardening cock: his cock, pulsing. I telegraphed back my assent. He dropped his head, his forehead sinking into my chest. The sign.

I let go of his wrist and ran my palm up his spine and over the angles of his shoulder blades. My fingers clasped his neck. He let his head fall back. His eyes fluttered and shut. A small sound parted his lips, like a cry, but not so helpless. The sound of an ache about to be tended.

He had a beautiful ass and I wanted to fuck him, his ass so smooth, the skin so much firmer than my own, than Woody's. I wanted to fuck him but he was nineteen and I was thirty-three, and I didn't know who he'd been with and what he'd done, and I didn't ask because we didn't speak. I didn't know if he'd ever been fucked before. I didn't want to be his first, to be bound to him that way, though I wondered if maybe I should, because I would be kind to him, even as some part of me wanted to tear him in two, because he wasn't Woody. I let him lead. I watched for his cues. What he wanted was to bury his face in my crotch, and for me to do the same to him, at the same time. We attached ourselves that way, taking from each other at once, another equilibrium, or the posture of one. We did this until we came, him first, quite suddenly, and me after taking some time, pushing and holding back, making it last because perhaps this was it, the one and only time we'd be here, naked, silent and needy, with no one to answer to. When we were done, he curled into himself, and I draped around him, drawing a circle from curved flesh and crooked limbs. We stayed that way for a long time, a tiny, humid island. He fell asleep, but not deeply at first. The room turned slowly, as if on an axis. I remained alert, wondering where Woody might be at this very moment, and if in some way I was still cheating on him, and if this thought was disloyal to Jed. Wondering when my heart became unknown to me.

We started up again in the middle of the night, fumbling in the dark, clandestine, all tongues and hands and grinding hips, rushing like soldiers in a bunkhouse. Half blind from lack of light, I questioned if this was a dream inside a dream. Spent, we collapsed away from each other. No tender cuddling. Eyes shut like it had never happened.

He woke me to a room already bright, rock hard and humping as if he hadn't been laid in weeks, ignoring my squinting demand for more sleep. He sucked me until not just my cock but my entire body came alive, infused with adrenaline, fresh determination. I got him on his back, his legs forking into his chest. He secured his calves in the crook of his inky arm, offering me access to where I hadn't dared go the night before, waiting in that position as I fumbled through the bedside drawer for a condom, but there was none, because Woody and I didn't use them. "Don't worry about it," Jed said, so I didn't, which meant, I suppose, that I'd stopped caring, for myself or anyone else. I asked, "Are you sure?" even as I'd begun the slide in, halting at the inner ring while he drew breath to ease the effort. In the patience on his face I saw that he knew what to expect. Who had taught him what this would be like? The professor at Stanford? A stranger at the Sea Foam, paying double to do it without a rubber? A boy his own age, a version of my high school love, Eric? He lowered his legs over my hips, and I inched forward, amping up the current that went from him to me, greedy for as much heat as he'd allow. His eyes stayed closed. I couldn't take mine off him. The cotton-white light through the blinds swabbed us in a clinical hue. I measured him, counted blemishes on what had been flawless skin last night, compared the color of his chest hair to mine, the shape of his cock to Woody's, my beaten-up man's body to his carved physique. I took in as much as possible, a need for knowledge that pushed me toward dominance.

He stopped me suddenly. Discomfort had taken over his face. I tried different positions, but nothing worked, and I had to back away from what now felt like a failing experiment. When I pulled out we discovered that we needed to clean things up. In the shower, he asked if I was negative. "Probably," I said. "What about you?" He didn't know. He rubbed soap on my chest, looking up at me so tenderly it seemed that I'd done nothing wrong. I pulled him into a hug meant to be protective, so he would never know that all night long part of me wished to destroy him. Drying off, we traded awkward glances. If he'd been a trick, now would be the time to swap phone numbers and compliments on the way to the door. But he wasn't going any farther than the living room, if even there.

I went to the corner for coffee, needing air, needing contact with the outside world to abrade the sensation of him from my body. I imagined my thoughts were obvious to people who passed me on the street, that I could be read like a front-page headline blaring the developments of the night.

Walking back, a coffee in each hand, steam rising in tufts through oval holes in the plastic lids, I noticed two things at once: a FedEx truck parked in front of my building's garage, probably delivering the videos I'd ordered, and a pale-green boat of a car pulling in across the street, in front of the construction site, where parking was prohibited. It was Colleen's car, with Colleen stepping from it now, dressed up for work. I slowed down, collecting myself. We hadn't spoken since that night on the MINI platform.

When she saw me, she called out, by way of explanation, "It's Friday." Our standing date.

"It's not noon yet, is it?"

"I'm going in earlier these days." In rapid cadence she described a fashion show in Los Angeles to which her boutique had been invited and where they'd be putting their clothes onto recording artists recently signed to a major label. The event was coming up soon, and she had a lot to do.

"Sounds like the big time," I said. "Up and Down must be pretty excited."

"Could be huge for them. For me, it's extra work without credit. I'm getting to design some of my own stuff, but they're driving me crazy with the pressure." She was staring at the two cups in my hands.

"I have someone staying with me," I said.

"I should have called first."

"Probably would have been better that way. Everything considered."

She looked toward my building, wondering, I suppose, if I would invite her in. And I felt a deep, almost feverish need to do so—to be the friends we'd always been—but there was no way. Not with Jed up there, and the place ripe with the stink of baked pot. Not with *everything considered.*

She said, "Last time we saw each other, I was really mad at you. And now, from what I've heard, I think you're pretty pissed at me."

My mouth contorted, but I said nothing.

She leaned in closer. "I just talked to Woody. Last weekend. I ran into him at this club."

"What club?"

"I forget the name. House music, shirts off. That whole scene."

"Woody had his shirt off at a club?"

She shook her head. "Jamie, I'm sorry it didn't work out."

"It might have worked out if it wasn't for you."

"I never meant to . . . I didn't . . . Look, he's worried about you."

"He mailed me back my keys!"

"Everyone's worried about you," she said, taking a step backward as if to accommodate *everyone*. Before I had time to respond to this sudden expansion, an electronic version of what sounded like "Brickhouse" pierced the air, and she reached into her purse to pull out a cell phone. "It's Up and Down," she said, scanning the display but not answering. "I'm supposed to be there to pack up this delivery."

"You got a phone."

"Mostly for this trip to LA." She wrote her number on a scrap of paper. "Will you call me, so we can talk stuff out?"

I nodded, convincing neither of us.

As she stood at her car door, I yelled across the alley, "Did Woody tell you how he answered his phone in the middle of having sex with me?" She waved as though she hadn't heard and slipped into the car.

My apartment door was unlocked. I nudged it open with my shoulder. Jed and the FedEx guy—the same sexy guy who'd cruised me the last time—stood face-to-face, too near to be simply talking, as if they'd just pulled out of a grope. Jed wore a stealthy grin that vanished when he caught sight of me. FedEx, too, made a transformation from slinky to upright. "There you are," he said, almost breathless.

Jed said, "I didn't know if I could sign."

"Right." I took the pen, scratched out a signature, said with finality, "Thanks."

FedEx sent me a wink on his way out, as if I'd been in on whatever they'd been up to. I suppose I could have been, that that was the plan.

I thrust a coffee at Jed. I saw that the brownies had been cut into; a chunk the size of an airmail stamp was missing.

"I'm supposed to go into work later," he said, "so I took a seriously small piece."

He strutted to the bedroom, his hands weaving through some kind of hip-hop improv. He looked nothing like the physically concentrated guy I'd spent the night with.

Colleen's visitation throbbed like an untended puncture wound. I could imagine the scene she'd hinted at: she and Woody bent over bar drinks, their serious faces dotted with disco light, their voices raised above a thumping bass line. I could hear him describing that last evening in my apartment, complete with my most embarrassing lines (the crack I made about codependency surely made the cut), his tone a mix of compassion and condescension as he concluded, "I'm worried about him." I could see Colleen nodding in agreement, relating her own recent run-in with my boorish behavior. I could imagine

Woody excusing himself to go flirt with a set of pecs that had caught his eye, trying out the dance floor, a free man. I'd rather he called me an asshole, said I was difficult, claimed he'd never speak to me again. I wanted fighting words, not his distant, useless worry.

What does it mean to be the one that everyone else is *worried about?* I thought of Steven Millsack, a college acquaintance who'd arrived in San Francisco a few years after I did, an eager, friendly newcomer charming everyone I hung out with. He had a brief fling with Ian; he became roommates with a friend of Stu, the guy I was dating. He volunteered for an AIDS-services group during the day and at night got work deejaying at different bars. A crowd of us used to hang around while he spun, commenting how adorable he looked bopping behind his turntables, living out his urban-nightlife dream. But over time, you'd never see him unless you went to the places where he deejayed, and when you did he was increasingly less charming, either hyped up and catty in a way he'd never been or distracted to the point of lethargic, his conversation full of alarming repetitions. He was bingeing on crystal and popping antidepressants to recover; in months, he'd aged a decade. "I'm worried about Steven," was our communal mantra, though none of us did anything to combat this. Our worry was a kind of gossip, the currency separating us from his declining state. A year after arriving, he checked into rehab. Last I heard, he was living with his parents in New Hampshire.

Everyone in San Francisco has a Steven in their orbit. But drugs weren't my *issue.* Sure, I needed to get a grip on my finances, which probably meant smoking a little less pot, and I'd been a bit erratic lately, sometimes when drunk, but I was sure this was some kind of phase, a valley in my biorhythms, a funk I'd been stuck in since—well, since I got back from New Jersey. My family had that effect on me. I just needed time to put the necessary distance between me and the funeral, and I would. Every valley led to a peak, eventually.

I hadn't been thinking concretely about Woody in the world, post-me; my thoughts of him had been longings without form. Now I typed his name into a search engine, which brought up three pages, most of them job-related. I found the text of a paper he'd delivered at a conference entitled "Setting Up a Continuing Education Program in the Digital Workplace," about motivating tech workers to take advantage of employer-paid learning. I remembered when he wrote this; he had read passages to me, trying to calm the jitters brought on by the prospect of addressing experienced people in his field. I remembered that he'd done well, that people in the audience came up afterwards to compliment his sincerity and humor; one man had argued a few points, but ultimately came around to Woody's ideas. Another conference had signed him up to sit on one of its panels, too. I'd gone out to celebrate with him, but as was often the case, surrounded by his co-workers and their shoptalk, I was the nineteenth-wheel on the Digitent big rig.

I visited Woody's home page, which he'd shown to me a year earlier. On it were his résumé, some photos and a half-sincere, half-cheeky chart called WELCOME TO MY WORLD. Under THINGS I LIKE he'd entered, JAMIE COOKING DINNER FOR ME. Under STATUS it read, IN A RELATIONSHIP. For all the world to see, I was still part of the official record of his life. Maybe he was leaving the door open.

"Woody is a pretty *rough* name, dude. You know what a woody is, right?" Jed had crept up from behind and was pointing at a JPEG of Woody in business drag: a button-down shirt, khakis, brown shoes.

"Here's a better picture." I reached to the shelf over my desk and pulled down the photo taken in the park. I could still see where I'd smeared away a streak of dust, though the streak was dusty now, too.

"I saw that picture," he said. "I thought that might be your brother."

"We don't look alike," I said, surprised.

He studied the picture for half a minute. "I take it back," he said. "There's something in common. But not enough to be related."

Surf's Up in San Diego was a bargain-basement Frankie and Annette movie, full of unfamiliar faces put through the usual machinations. Pretty-but-bookish blonde falls for swaggering surfer. She joins a *fast crowd,* but when she almost drowns after drinking jug wine at a luau, she understands that she must get back on track. The surfer is so impressed by her resolve he decides to return to high school in time for final exams, which he passes, with her help, of course. Then they all go back to the beach for the summer. Dean Foster's role was small, a dark head of hair amid the blonde beach bums, his arm always secure around a girl. But even if you weren't looking, you'd notice him. His beauty was almost unreasonable: long-lashed doe eyes and ripe lips; nose, cheekbones and jaw at the ideal structural angles. His torso, lean and sturdy, stretched from a boxy swimsuit like a sapling from a planter. He played the kid brother of a more important character, and in fact that's what everyone called him, the Kid. He only had a couple of lines. When he opened his mouth, the lingering grip of puberty was obvious, his voice catching in the top of his throat—not unlike Jed's. On top of that was his New York street accent. When he yelled, "Hey, scram! It's the fuzz!" the sound could have stopped traffic.

"That's the guy I'm looking for," I told Jed, who sat next to me on the couch, all elastic limbs and gluey eyes. I hadn't touched the brownies and had no idea how concentrated they were. Jed was the test case.

I rewound and paused on Dean Foster in close-up: *scram* stretching his mouth wide, telegraphing enthusiasm when the script called for alarm.

"You know him?" Jed asked. His vacant gaze was less animated than Dean's, frozen on the screen.

"My father knew him."

"Is he famous?"

"Not famous, just hot." He didn't respond. "Don't you think so?"

"I don't know."

"You don't think about whether guys are hot?" He shook his head no. "What about the guys you have sex with?"

"Usually they think I'm hot."

"Are you saying that you're not attracted to the guys you have sex with?" He looked bewildered. Given how high he was, this was probably the wrong time for analysis. But his guard was down, so I tried again. "Were you attracted to the FedEx guy?"

"That guy? We were just talking."

"What about me?" I wasn't fishing for a compliment, though it sounded that way to my own ears, so I added, "We had sex three times last night."

He nodded vigorously. "Yeah, totally. That was probably, like, a world record."

I might have blushed. "I'm just trying to understand where you're coming from, Jed."

"I'm . . . attracted . . . to . . . you"—each word balanced with the effort of a steep walk downhill—"because you were into . . . tripping in nature. Most people won't go there. But you tripped out for real."

It was nearly noon by now. He wasn't going to make it to work unless I pushed him. And I didn't want to push him. I wanted to be on the same foggy slope, moving at his tempo. I called his Starbucks and posed as the radio producer I was supposed to be: "Jed wasn't aware of some professional commitments I'd made for him today, so if he could start his shift tomorrow, it would greatly benefit his internship." While I was at it, I gave him a good reference. They thanked me for taking the time to call. Jed thanked me, too. So everyone was happy. The brownie I cut myself was so small Jed deemed it *pussy size* and broke me off another chunk, which he pushed to my lips with his fingers. I smelled the cooked grass in my nose before the chocolate hit my tongue. It balled up against the roof of my mouth as I chewed, and went down my throat in a gooey lump. Back in the living room, I pushed PLAY. Dean Foster jumped to life, said what he was supposed to, and faded back into the crowd.

Jed, studying a shot of waves crashing on the sand, put his hand on my thigh and said, "We're totally gonna hit Baja together, right?"

I nodded and smiled. This plan seemed as likely as any other.

The Criminal Kick was better than *Surf's Up*. Not better in quality. Worse, in fact: a stagnant camera that occasionally raced in for an extreme, obvious close-up, as if the operator had just jerked awake from a nap and reflexively hit the zoom button; a self-consciously jumpy editing style (someone had been studying the French New Wave); sloppy lighting that sent details into shadowed obscurity. But the story showed a willingness to go anywhere. The script, layered in pulp-fiction dialogue, stayed mercilessly unaccountable to all of its characters, humiliating and bumping them off creatively, so that by the end there was literally only one man standing, covered in blood, a suitcase of money in his clutches.

Dean Foster played Robbie the Greek, a flashy hustler in open-necked polyester shirts and tight, high-waisted pants. Robbie the Greek is hired for sex by a society widow, whom he quickly chokes to death and stuffs into a trunk; then he moves into her mansion. When the film's stars—an acid-freak Bonnie and Clyde who have kidnapped a ten-year-old girl—happen upon Robbie, he gives them refuge. He plies Bonnie and the child with pills, and when they're zonked out he puts the moves on handsome Clyde. The scene where Dean walks his fingers down the bare chest and lanky belly of the lead actor—a gesture completed with the gleeful unfastening of the stud's American-flag belt buckle—was for me a moment of electricity. A quick cut to Robbie's cigarette being lit makes it clear in the most rudimentary way that he'd successfully conquered his prey.

More than a decade after his debut as a surf stud, Dean Foster wasn't aging well. He was still handsome—there was no way to ruin those eyes—but his physique had a drawn quality to it, as if he'd shed his muscles on an amphetamine diet. The teen scratchiness of his voice had been outgrown, the New York edges planed away; he spoke every line at an intimidating volume. Maybe it was simply an actor's choice for a smarmy character, but Dean sounded like an angry god, calling down vengeance and relishing every moment. Of course, in keeping with the norms of the day, Dean's character is promptly and brutally knifed by the girlfriend after she wakes from her barbiturate stupor. The boyfriend, shedding any notion of sexual ambiguity, kicks Dean's writhing corpse with his cowboy boots and decrees him to be *one far-out sicko.*

At this moment of seduction-transformed-into-violence, Ian arrived. I'd put in a call to him earlier, alerting him to Jed's presence, inviting him for a brownie. He entered without saying hello, watched the on-screen assault, and announced, "Talk about a buzz kill." Jed shot me an amused look, which Ian took as encouragement: "Jamie's famous for picking exactly the wrong pop-cultural reference for a drug trip," he said.

Jed: "Last time he played Elton John."

Ian: "Be glad you're not on acid watching a political documentary."

Jed: "True, true."

"Ganging up on a mutual friend is a major violation," I said. But as I watched Jed keep pace, and watched Ian sail through Jed's three-part handshake, I was happy for their instant groove.

Within moments Jed was scampering back from the kitchen with the tray of brownies, holding it out to Ian. "Dive in, dude."

Ian declined. "Someone's got to play Party Nurse."

Party Nurse was a concept we'd come up with together after the death of one of our most beloved sensitive-boy actors, River Phoenix, who had spent his final night ingesting a vast pharmacopoeia washed down with booze before collapsing outside a Hollywood club. "He'd be alive today if someone had just kept a few of those substances out of his system," Ian had intoned. We decided then that serious drug trips needed a designated monitor to keep everyone from going off the deep end. This explanation didn't do much for Jed, who made the point that we weren't combining our brownies with anything, and anyway, hadn't I claimed *pot's not a drug*?

"Eating it is different than smoking it," I said.

"For such a big druggie you sure have a lot of judgments about what other people do," Jed said, cutting himself a brownie about three times the size of the first and swallowing it in a couple of bites.

I grabbed another square for myself. No need for restraint if Ian was staying clean. Jed was excited to realize that Ian didn't know about my windfall from Anton, even tried to persuade him to scavenge for it. (Another decline.) When the bag was revealed, Ian's eyes went wide. "I'm taking half of this with me," he declared. "For your own good."

The contrast of Ian's heavy-booted manliness with our increasingly floaty vibe accelerated the trip for me. I became aware of the vapors that Jed and I were drifting into, while Ian remained tightly tethered to the world—telling us about his ongoing computer problems and his need for a new roommate. I felt nowhere near the intensity or euphoria of the E we'd taken in the woods, but there was something familiar about this: the glazed enthusiasm on Jed's face, the way my focus rarely strayed from him, the fact that sexual attraction pulled like an undertow, one that had already knocked me over.

Ian announced we were going for a walk, and Jed pounced on this by stripping off his shirt and rummaging through a big pile of clothes I'd left out for him, mostly old T-shirts that I no longer wore. Jed wasn't Ian's *type*—too self-consciously tough, too much a peacock—but then again, it wasn't every day a buff nineteen-year-old stood shirtless in front of him. I watched Ian be carried through a range of reactions: stunned, amused, lustful. But as the display went on—Jed pulling off a different shirt every minute, flashing his skin while he dug through the pile, then sliding on another one, puffing out his chest, saying, "Check this out"—Ian seemed to sour to the display. When Jed rejected a ribbed tank top with the same complaint he'd delivered to me the day before—"too gay"—I could tell Ian had hit a limit. There were plenty of things that Ian and I thought were *too gay,* but he wasn't about to let Jed decide what they were.

"Enough with the fashion show," Ian grumbled. "You ain't all that."

Jed, caught off guard, put on the same shirt he'd been wearing all day. One of his own.

The evening was warmer than the day had been. Night-blooming jasmine had erupted everywhere, its juicy perfume ambushing us as we trudged up 20th Street to Dolores Park. We sat on a bench at the crest, Ian dropping himself between Jed and me. I was adrift in the high, absorbing the gentle psychedelia of the view: dots of office light outlining tall buildings downtown, the slender ribbon of approaching cars on the Bay Bridge, a bone-colored rising half moon. As Jed started up one of his talking jags, all big plans for the future, I voiced out loud my recent idea that it might be time to leave San Francisco. "I was thinking about LA, New York, another city," I said.

"Because you want to go somewhere or because you want to get away?" Ian asked.

"I'm ready for Baja," Jed said. "Hot sun, cheap weed, sexy Mexicans."

"Would that be sexy señors or señoritas?" Ian asked.

Jed scowled at him. "Don't box me in, Party Nurse."

"Sorry," Ian said, not sounding sorry at all. I could usually keep up with his conversational aggression, but he had an unfair advantage: He was sober.

"Check this out. I was just reading about Mexico." This was me talking. "About Kerouac and Burroughs and Ginsberg crowding into this dumpy apartment in Mexico City."

"Mexico would be better off if the bohemians had left it alone. All they did was open the door to free trade and pollution," Ian said. *"White boy finds the meaning of life in the Third World. Sells memoir to First World publisher. Throngs of tourists follow."*

Jed said, "Is Kerouac the one who wrote *Queer?*"

Ian gave him a sidelong glance as I answered, "That was Burroughs."

Jed nodded. "That professor leant it to me. That's a fucked-up book."

"What would have happened if my father actually made it to Mexico?" I wondered out loud. "I might never have been born."

"Or you'd be born half-Mexican," Jed said. "That would be rad."

"This is about Woody dumping you," Ian said bluntly. "It's a no-brainer."

Jed stretched his torso across Ian to address me: "Dude, we'd have a fucking blowout in Baja, and we wouldn't need a lot of bank."

Maybe the leaning across, the exclusionary gesture, was the final straw, but I could feel Ian stiffen even before he spoke. "You guys can plan your honeymoon without me. I'm taking off." He faced Jed and said, "Listen, Junior, you be nice to my friend Jamie. He's not to be toyed with." The sentiment was sweet, but I could hear the warning it contained to both of us.

I walked a few paces with him, out of Jed's earshot. Ian threw an arm over my shoulder. "Jamie, this kid is seriously hooked on you. Or else he's using you. Either way, it's a bad idea."

"Maybe I shouldn't have fucked him this morning," I said, expecting to grab Ian's interest. But this information only deepened the crease on his forehead.

"His body, his attitude—I know how this works. I used to be a go-go boy, remember."

"You weren't a go-go boy for that long."

"I know what it's like to be rewarded just for being young and butch," he said.

"He just needs guidance."

"What about what you need, Jamie?" When I didn't answer him, he gave me a hug and wandered off. I watched him stride across the very plot of grass where I'd first spoken to Woody.

A fuzzy wave of stoned intelligence: *My friends are worried about me because I don't know what I need.*

I had habits, but no organizing principles. Always, my life had been like this. My father's needs were always terribly clear—order, regularity, a controlled environment—but he never spoke in those terms. I remembered a morning not long after my mother died, his first day back to work since her funeral, when he announced to me on his way out the door, "I expect you'll have dinner ready by six," which meant, *I'm hungry when I get home from work, and I'm used to having a meal waiting, and the woman I love isn't around to cook it, and I need you to help me, my son, my eldest child.* Life kept throwing him off balance, but he only grew more rigid. His dead wife, his gay son, his pregnant daughter, none of these things made him more flexible, more open. The opposite occurred: years spent suing the hospital, entrenched in a sense of injustice, netting him next to nothing. His needs were so strong they overwhelmed my own, replaced them even, leaving me with only one way to define myself: against him. Against everything, really. A life lived in the negative.

Another wave, another memory: in the shower, age five, my hand reaching out to touch. *What's wrong with you?* I remembered not only the original moment but the terrifying return of it on the mountaintop, naked with Jed. This time I did not repel the memory, did not break down under the power of it. This time I massaged it like a mound of clay, hoping to mold a concrete form with my unskilled hands. What emerged was a two-faced figure: the me who had, ever since, kept reaching out, waiting for a definitive *yes*. And the me who became just like him, the agent of countless rejections.

19

I woke to the insistent ringing of the doorbell, a drill invading marijuana-thick sleep. I scrambled out of Jed's dream-heavy clutch into yesterday's underwear, banging my shin on an open dresser drawer. Limping into the hall, I pushed the intercom but got no reply. The bell sounded again—it wasn't the street buzzer but the one outside my apartment door. Someone was in the hall. Maybe it was Eleanor with one of her typical, busy-body dilemmas, the transgressions only an old lady in the building has the time and inclination to discover: *There's a big bag of trash stuck in the garbage chute! Is that your microwave blocking the storeroom door?*

"It's Leon." Not Eleanor, but my landlord, Leon Hook, standing in the hallway. I opened the door to his weathered face, all thick whiskers under the brim of a Giants cap. Despite his pirate-captain name, Leon was possibly the least menacing landlord in San Francisco. So unthreatening, in fact, that I'd managed to forget I hadn't paid this month's rent. He got right to the point: "You're three weeks late."

"I've been meaning to call you," I said. "I've been waiting for a freelance job to pay me."

"You know I'm not a stickler about *on time*, but this is pushing it."

"I'll cut you a check right away. Do you mind if I postdate it?"

He frowned. "After thirty days I can legally evict."

I thought of all the visitors to my apartment who'd commented how lucky I was to have a rent-controlled one-bedroom in the Mission; of all the times I glibly replied, *Yeah, but I'm stuck here until the day I die*, never conceiving that this place could slip through my fingers. An apartment this size, in this neighborhood, could be rented for twice what I paid. I thought of myself at Seventh and Market alongside

Anton. Or across the Bay, trying to secure an apartment in Oakland without a car, without a job, with bills in collection.

Leon followed me to the kitchen while I dug out my checkbook, his eyes scanning the dishes piled in the sink, the brownie pan on the stovetop, the trash can full of pizza cartons acting as a dam against a treacherous mound of garbage. My rumpled appearance matched the disarray of the place. Without knowing exactly what time it was, I guessed it was too late for any regularly employed person to still be sleeping.

He said, "I called first, but your phone doesn't seem to be working." He pulled out his address book to double-check the number.

"Strange," I said, feeling my pulse speeding up—the kind of anxious, adrenaline-fueled surge that, lacking an outlet, quickly dissipates into defeat. The spot where I'd whacked my shin throbbed.

Once he left, I picked up the phone and got three digits into Deirdre's number when a recorded message intruded: "I'm sorry. Your service has been temporarily interrupted." On my desk I found three months of unpaid phone bills and a disconnect warning.

I walked to the Roast, where there was a pay phone, occupied at this moment by a younger guy with a pager in hand and a skateboard against his leg. The only silver lining to this cloudy morning was that Jed had slept through Leon's visit; Jed would have been one signal too many that something wasn't quite right in Apartment Two. I looked at this kid on the phone and imagined him answering a drug deal, a call from a john. I thought of the days Jed had spent paging his way through the city before I let him in, and instead of worry I felt resentment, like this was his fault. I heard my father: *Trouble finds trouble.*

A very sympathetic Pac Bell representative verified that, yes, $158.73 was ninety days past due, and, yes, I would have to pay a $295.00 deposit to reinstate service, plus another $13.00 fee, just to drive home the point that I was an idiot, though all I had to do was walk a check down to a payment center—"You've got one right there at Mission and 16th, James, just a few blocks from you"—and I'd be good to go within four hours. She asked if I had a cell-phone number, "Some way for us to get messages to you." If I'd had a cell phone I could have avoided making this embarrassing call in public. *If you had a cell phone it would have been shut off by now, too.*

I dialed Deirdre's number collect. Andy accepted the charges. "Hey, what's going on, Jamie?"

The benign sound of his voice threw me into a rage. "What's going on is that you owe me nine thousand dollars and I'm out of money and my phone's been turned off and my rent is due."

"Whoa, take it easy."

"I've been taking it easy, Andy, but I can't figure out why, three months later, my money hasn't gotten here."

"I thought your sister explained. I've been managing your father's portfolio—."

"And losing it all in bad investments."

"Aw, hold on." I could hear his mood shift, harden. "That's not fair."

"I want that money tomorrow. Do you understand me? I wrote a rent check to my landlord today and I do not—repeat, do not—have money in the account to cover it."

He cleared his throat. "That's not really my problem."

I unleashed a cascade of insults and accusations that didn't stop until Andy held his checkbook up to the phone so I could hear the sound of a check being ripped from it, a check he assured me I would have by ten a.m.

I had burrowed so deeply into the confrontation it was a shock to turn around and see the café spread out in front of me, like snapping awake for the second time. I saw familiar faces from the neighborhood, several staring frankly in my direction. One woman I recognized from my building looked at me and then blockaded herself behind a newspaper. I would have done the same thing myself.

Spewing blind fury at Andy had been a rush, a release. But the next day, when I deposited his $9,000 and was informed that a personal check from a New Jersey bank would take *up to five business days* to clear (as opposed to, say, a money order or cashier's check), I realized I should have been thoughtful and strategic instead of intimidating. My phone would stay disconnected and my rent check would bounce. I had only a handful of bucks to my name and no fury left to spew.

What followed was a string of empty, broke days during which Jed went to work—I'd given him Woody's set of keys—and I sat around waiting for something to happen. Nothing happened. Nothing could: I was cut off. No e-mail, no voice mail, no channel of connection in an age of connectivity. I chipped away at the batch of magic brownies, small steady bites flattening my life into abstraction. The high became like the hum of a refrigerator—always there, disrupting the silence, even when you forget about it.

My actual refrigerator was empty of almost everything but condiments. I ate three mustard sandwiches before I ran out of bread. I ate mayonnaise off a spoon. The cabinets held only random baking supplies and items that had occupied the far-back corners for years, stuff I couldn't remember purchasing in the first place but that I was now serving up for dinner: a can of honey-baked beans, a tin of smoked oysters, a bag of garlic bagel chips (expired). Jed came home from Starbucks with his pockets full of day-old pastries. The low-fat cranberry-orange scone went pretty well with the beans.

That's a joke, actually, meant to cover up the argument we had. Spitting out a mouthful of beans after discovering animal fat on the label, Jed announced, "We should sell that dried-up weed, dude." I thought he was joking. He wasn't. "I could pack a bunch of dime bags and sell them to these kids I work with. Or have Bethany sell them in the Haight."

"I'll have money in two days. I'm not getting involved in selling drugs."

"*Pot's not a drug,*" he mocked. "You wouldn't even notice if I took some."

"You steal from me, your ass is out of here."

"This is bullshit," he said, smacking his plate, splattering more beans on the table. "Sitting around without money."

"Go somewhere else then."

For the first time since he'd moved in, I went to bed alone, and he stayed on the couch, where he was supposed to have slept all along. Through the wall I heard the underwater warble of television voices, the abrupt jumps of his channel changing, the frequent flick of a lighter. With my nose in a pillow that smelled of his scalp, and the empty half of the mattress calling out for him, I willed away the impulse to invite him back. Nothing allowed me to sleep—and then I was waking up to a silent apartment, to the fragment of a dream, Jed's face diminishing like the dull bumper of a retreating car. My alarm clock read 3:11. I went to the living room. No sign of him or his backpack. I checked the marijuana stash. I suspected that he'd taken some, but as he predicted, so much remained in the bag that I couldn't be sure. I slept for a few more hours, and when I awoke I paged him. No response.

It was now the fourth day since Andy's uncleared check had arrived, and I literally had not a dime available to me. Jed was right; this was bullshit. I threw on clothes, gathered up a box of paperbacks and CDs and walked into the Castro. A couple hours of lugging my belongings among used bookstores and used-record stores netted me a whopping $32.14. I bought myself coffee and a bagel ($3.00), the *New York Times* ($1.08), a pack of cigarettes ($3.50). I spent $8.25 on a movie, *Erin Brockovich,* which momentarily warmed me with the sentimental belief that underdogs do indeed triumph—*Sue the bastards; win millions!* But back in the cold, gray air, slipping two quarters into the palm of a ravaged junkie, I recalled my father's lawsuit, a testimony to all the false hope placed in the hands of the legal system. I wasted another $1.50 on a large chocolate chip cookie that was meant to be some kind of self-reward, for what I couldn't tell you. I went back home with $14.31 in my pocket.

Adding up what I owed—multiple credit cards, several months of phone bills plus fees, a month's rent plus the one coming up, unpaid medical bills including emergency-room charges from when I was knocked off my bike, interest on the student-loan payments I'd deferred, money I'd borrowed from Woody—I saw how quickly I'd deplete my checking account of that $9,000. The remainder would be gone in another month, two at the most.

What if I didn't pay up? I'd be evicted, my checking account seized, my credit rating obliterated. I'd be a vagrant with nine thousand dollars and a social security number. When the money ran out, I'd discover what was left of the welfare state, or I'd enter the underground economy, selling discards on the street, peddling dried-out dope, asking for change with a cardboard sign in my hands . . . Or I could leave San Francisco with Jed: hitchhike, take odd jobs and handouts, exploit the hospitality of strangers. Unless I'd seen the last of Jed.

I was alone. An aloneness more extreme than Woody's enforced time-out, which was pressurized by a kind of hope: a problem to be solved in a finite amount of time. I had not solved it. Now I did not have a lover to fight for; I had a substitute lover I fought *with.* My friends had shifted their loyalties to Woody. My sister had shifted her loyalties to her husband. Death had stolen my mother. My father had hijacked my mother's death and turned it into a cause. My father had aborted his youth and buried it in shame. My father had called out my desire and buried it in shame. My desire to know him, my glancing desire for him, was destruction itself.

Why not just simplify everything: stand at the edge of a cliff above the fogged-in Pacific and drop into the colorless void. Disappear. I could do it today.

I went walking. I wanted to cover distance—not only get out of my apartment, but out of my neighborhood, my routine, my familiar traps. It was too cold for the rushing air of a bike ride. Afternoon fog had settled, thick and wet. I wrapped myself in an old overcoat and threw on a wool cap. My head is the first thing to get cold. It gets colder when I'm stoned, as I was again. I put the collar up. A disguise.

I bound through the Mission taking streets that I didn't usually take. Coming on an intersection from a new direction changes your understanding of a place; that alley you think of as a side street is now the main thoroughfare. I saw a painted billboard—an ad for cigarettes—I'd never seen before, the image chipped away to show the brick grid beneath. I noticed small businesses that had been around forever—a printing press, an auto body shop, a storefront crammed full of kitchen appliances—places that usually shrank from my awareness amid the bright placards and designer lighting of new restaurants, clothing boutiques, yoga studios. Looking past the gay guys in their snug jeans and the hipster boys in their saggy pants, I saw how many women made their way through the neighborhood doing the business of daily life. Central American mothers loaded down with laundry, kids at their heels toting detergent and bleach. Chinese grandmothers in floral headscarves wheeling produce in carts. An elderly white woman and her more elderly mother, their Irish faces set inscrutably, like Nana's on her way to mass.

I pushed onward to South of Market, where wide, one-way streets were obstructed every few blocks by utility trucks ripping up the pavement, laying down fiber-optic cable or copper wire, whatever it took to increase the pace of commerce. On Sixth, which was to my day what Third had been to my father's, the down-and-out crowded the sidewalks in front of single-room-occupancy hotels and bodegas, interrupting each other to hit me up for handouts. I meted out loose change and cigarettes but didn't stop to talk. I felt the dread of knowing that this part of town was my only affordable option if I lost my apartment, not missing the hypocrisy that allowed me to romanticize the poverty of the Beat Generation while being terrified of the poverty around me today. Not missing the delusion that I wanted to align myself with beatnik poets, with starving artists, when I wasn't one myself—wasn't even a *Sunday painter.* I crossed Market, where a handful of once-glamorous theaters still lured in busloads for road shows of Broadway musicals, and crossed the invisible border into the Tenderloin, where the backstage doors of those same theaters reeked of piss. My distance from both worlds—the bland suburbanites clutching purses and playbills, and the staggering crackheads fouling the parking lots where those purse clutchers paid to leave their cars—left me nowhere. Not independent but isolated.

I wanted a gulp of whiskey—truly, a craving—but the first corner store I approached was hemmed in by a crowd of guys done up gangsta-style gesturing wildly in some kind of argument: "Where's my fucking money?" "I told you, nigga, I gave it to your bitch." "She ain't my bitch, bitch." I weaved off the sidewalk, crossed the street toward a sex parlor. The eyes of the big-titted woman on the faded poster had the grim detachment of a kidnap victim's in a ransom video, assuring loved ones she's been well treated, *just pay them the money*.

I found a store where I spent five of my fourteen bucks on crappy whiskey and chugged half the bottle in a doorway. It hit my brain in a warm, defenseless wash. I was sweating under my cap, chilled from the air hitting my face, but my shoulders relaxed just a bit. I could lift my head again, let my eye find something to appreciate. There: the beauty in a sputtering neon bar sign tracing a scarlet halo out of the fog. Beneath it, a rough-looking guy standing, staring, thumbs hooked in his jeans. He had salt-and-pepper hair; a wide, unshaven jaw; a bent nose once, twice broken. I felt a flicker in my guts as he locked frost-gray eyes on me, dissecting. A start-to-finish fantasy unrolled. In it he was my savior and punisher; in it I climbed behind him to a walk-up room, guzzled his backwash from the bottom of the forty-ounce I'd bought for him at the corner; in it I let him fuck me unsheathed and unlubed on a creaky cot.

He called out for a cigarette. I lit it for him, his gnarled hands cupping the flame. On one wrist a faded blue prison tattoo, in script: *Father*. My mouth went dry until I saw the other wrist, inked with a crudely rendered crucifix. Oh, right, *that* Father. I lingered to light my own smoke. His gaze again held me fast. He couldn't have been more than ten years older than me, but I saw two lifetimes of stories in his eyes. I'm guessing he saw panic and curiosity in mine.

He went inside with the cigarette still lit. The door was so nondescript it seemed to defend a clubhouse you needed a membership to enter. Familiar music played—a song from the same Radiohead album Jed and I had listened to a few nights ago. I'd sold that CD today. I stepped inside. Momentarily blinded by the darkness. Afraid. The kind of fear that's its own high, that means anything can happen.

Four people: a grizzled bartender with motorcycle hair; two old black men, one in a brimmed hat, the other in a baseball cap, sipping beer at the bar; and the guy with the tattooed wrists, sitting at a tall table to the side, hunched over a notebook, a pen in his hand. A lefty. I ordered a beer, a Bud, took a bar stool, swiveled to face him. I lit another cigarette. The snap of my lighter drew his attention. He registered my presence, but went back to his writing. What was he recording there? The incoherency of a madman? The poetry of an authentic experience? He might have been writing a to-do list, a complaint to the city, a promise to a girlfriend.

The beer went down cold and quick. It cost only $2.50. I could afford another and still have bus fare home. He looked in my direction, pen in hand, hand covering mouth, perhaps composing his next sentence. Perhaps considering me. My overcoat had fallen open. I adjusted myself in my pants. I nodded at him slow enough that he could make of it what he wanted.

That was the last look I got from him. I was ready to leave when I saw him go into the bathroom. I waited a moment, then followed.

The narrow room had the moldy-bread smell of dried urine. He stood at the trough, leaning forward, his pen marking the wall above, adding something to the mess of scrawls already there. I could hear his flow hit the porcelain. I stood next to him, pulled my cock out, bobbing like a rubber tube, too stiff to piss. I'd gotten this far but was now afraid to look at him or even at what he was scribbling. I heard a *clank,* a splash. Heard him grumble, "Fuck."

I looked down into the wet trench, where his pen had fallen in the space between us. I looked at him. He was staring me up and down. His thick cock was getting thicker.

I reached into the trough. I grabbed his pen between my fingers. I flicked droplets from it. The corners of his mouth were turning up, even as he shook his head in disbelief. Holding his gaze, I wiped the pen dry on my pants. Now he laughed. Lines around his eyes. "How low can you go?" he asked.

I dropped to my knees on the damp floor and opened my mouth. He squared his body to mine. One hand on his cock, one hand on the back of my head, he held my face against his nuts and told me to lick.

The side of his hand knocked my forehead as he jerked himself. He stank, the way men stink down there. I bathed him with my tongue.

I gave myself over, let myself find the glory in this act. Time ceased to pass; this moment was all. I forgot where I was, literally couldn't remember. This was somewhere in San Francisco. How did I get here? I couldn't see past this scrim of skin and hair and dirty denim. I couldn't see past his wrist that said *Father.* I couldn't see past my father, who no longer existed. My life that no longer existed. My life that was entirely this: me kneeling on moist concrete in front of a gasping stranger, a stranger repeating, "Yeah, boy," a stranger yanking on my hair, a stranger now filling my mouth with a pound of flesh. I could take it. I wanted to. Wanted to prove something I couldn't name. I'd followed him out of some life I couldn't remember into this dark closet of San Francisco where everything was sharp-edged as a silhouette. I could go this low. I could go lower. His calloused palms pressed my face. My mouth gave everything it could until the thick, bitter taste of him flooded my tongue.

I stood up, swallowing. He leaned back, shuddering, but quickly pulled himself together. A moment at the cold-water sink. "All right," he said, as if we'd just agreed on something. He did not sound unkind. When he left, I looked up at the wall to see what he'd written, but it was indistinguishable from all the other marks left there.

He was no longer at his table. I stood unsteadily at the bar, catching my breath, ordering another beer. I left the bartender a two-dollar tip. He raised his eyebrows and said, "Drink up, Red." I swished beer in my mouth, telling the alcohol to kill the germs.

One neighborhood ends and another convenes in the distance of a single block. The sidewalk rose toward the hotels on O'Farrell and Geary, the pre-war apartment buildings, a smattering of Asian restaurants. A rental-car garage, a drugstore, a theater with a revival of *Hamlet*.

I climbed up to Nob Hill, the crest of old-money San Francisco. There was Grace Cathedral, more mighty than it had been in 1960, when Teddy spent Christmas Eve watching Don bowed down in prayer. Teddy had sat here after mass, looking across the street at the church, getting angry with God, the ultimate punishing father. He'd sat here feeling loneliness set in. Missing Ray. Missing Danny. Confused by Don. *Not just independent but isolated.* Not just alone but lonely.

That was it, wasn't it? Missing Woody. Missing my father. Missing what I never had and now never would.

I climbed the sweeping cathedral steps; deep in my coat pocket the whiskey bottle sloshed. I stepped into a vast dimness framed by pillars thick as redwoods. My eye traveled up to the Gothic ceiling. *You look up into those pointy arches and then you think about your own puny life down here.* Music was playing, amplified harp and keyboard, as a man and a woman harmonized an unfamiliar, eerie chant, strangely New Age in this Protestant fortress. In the open area ahead, between me and the pews, a handful of people moved in an odd formation. When I got closer I saw that they stood on a circular carpet, maybe thirty feet in diameter, into which was stitched a maze, which each of them traversed at his or her own pace. It seemed an unlikely activity, a trick: you're in a church, trapped in a maze.

Curious, dubious, my head hot with liquor, I went to the place on the carpet that marked the entry. I walked forward on a long straightaway, needing a couple of steps to secure my balance, then turned left and went straight again for a shorter distance. I wobbled at each turn, and it was all turns. Ahead of me on the path was a white-haired old man. He seemed to know what he was doing, probably wouldn't make any wrong turns. I slowed to his pace. Slow was better for balance.

Step by step I saw the pattern click into place: there were no false turns or dead ends in this maze. It was one long, winding path, folded back and forth like an intestine, that took you all the way to the belly of this beast. No tricks, no dead ends.

The other walkers, more women than men, were mostly middle-aged, almost all white and plainly dressed. A few stood apart: a pretty, hippie-ish girl in a peasant skirt; a gawky, Eurasian teenage boy, who led the way for his white mother; a smartly dressed Latina, who prayed with her hands apart, palms up. I guess I was supposed to be praying. *Hail Mary full of grace,* can't remember the rest of it. *Our Father who art in Heaven,* I don't believe, I don't believe. What's the one they say in AA? *God grant me the courage to change the things I cannot accept*—something heady like that. There were only three basic prayers, anyway. *Dear God: (A) Thank you. (B) I'm sorry. (C) Please help me.* Extra words only obscured the truth of pure need.

I caught on that the faster walkers were simply stepping around the slowpokes, and also around the people on their way out, who came up at intervals head-on. I lunged past the white-haired guy and then stayed the course, back and forth, until I got to the middle, a clover-shaped rest area. The Latina was on her feet, eyes closed, palms cupped. The hippie chick kneeled next to her, skirt tufting out. The boy and his mother were cross-legged, holding hands, her gaze faraway and his moving through the air as if following a butterfly. There was room for me next to them. I sat and saw telltale damp spots on my knees. I felt elephantine, carrying into this holy enclave the stench of booze, tobacco, semen—though I also thought it wouldn't be a bad time to break out the whiskey and pass it around, make some new friends.

I must have chuckled at this idea because the boy jerked his head. "Oh, it's nothing," I mumbled. I saw his mother's fingers tighten on his thigh. Protective, instructive. I didn't belong here, but I was tired of walking, tired of my disguise, of my fantasies and my fears. If I kept my sarcastic giggles to myself and kept the bottle in my pocket, no one would ask me to leave. I could probably stay here for hours, my life on pause, like that woman with her outstretched hands, waiting for heaven to rain down answers. I could sit here until I came up with a prayer that made sense to me. I could meditate: I'd picked up enough secondhand Buddhism from my reading, all I needed to do was keep my spine straight, count my breaths and try to do that thing they called *not being attached.* But attachment was probably what I needed. Wasn't I already drifting away from everything, like the balloon the child has let go, growing smaller in the distance?

When I closed my eyes I wondered if I might throw up.

I sat until the others had left. All but one, that old man I'd followed at the beginning. He was standing to my side. Poor guy probably couldn't kneel. I stood up, and he smiled. I could see right away he was a queen. I said hello.

"It's very peaceful," he said.

"Also kinda spooky."

Silence followed, and I thought I should fill it, though I suppose silence in a church is expected.

He put his hand out, an attempt to touch my arm, which he fell just short of. He said, "Every time I'm here I know what to do next."

"You do?"

"You just have to walk back out." He stretched his hand to close the distance, his fingers landing on my wrist, light as a moth. "And I already know the way."

I watched over my shoulder as he began the slow shuffle of his return voyage, like a minimalist dancer whose performance consists of a single walk across the stage. I was relieved to see him go. White-haired strangers dispensing wisdom have always freaked me out.

Nausea bubbled in my esophagus, threatening to erupt. I rushed across the carpet, negating the bounds of the labyrinth—which, after all, was just a suggestion woven into a rug. I fled the service, the music, the church. Traded the dark interior for the darkening air outside. Sat on a bench until I felt stable enough to make my way home.

The light was on in my kitchen when I returned, the air blue with the haze of a recent cigarette. I called out Jed's name. No response.

On the table, *Desolation Angels* lay face down. I flipped it over to reveal the chapter called "Passing Through Mexico." Beneath it lay a handwritten note:

> Jamie,
>
> I can't stay here, this city is full of shit. We got to go to Baja together. You and me.
>
> Don't get mad, but I found out I can unload that bag of pot for a few hundred bucks maybe five hundred. Let's split the money and do it! I waited for you but I gotta go. I'll be back in a few days. Page me.
>
> Jed

Darth Vader lay toppled and empty. The only evidence of the contraband stowed inside was a Ziploc baggie on the coffee table half stuffed with the dry shake. The baggie rested next to an unopened pack of cigarettes, a stronger blend of the brand I smoked. A gift. Another note beneath it: *Don't be mad, OK?*

I wasn't mad, but I wasn't not mad; I was too wiped out to declare an emotion. From the pay phone at the Roast I paged him, though it was nearly nine o'clock, the café's closing time, and I got kicked out before I heard back from him. I put in one last call, telling the story to Ian's voice mail, asking, "Does it sound to you like he's coming back? Should I care?"

If Jed didn't return, would it matter? And if it did matter to me—if Jed himself mattered to me—and if he returned in a day, fists crammed with dollars, as promised, would I go away with him? *You and me.* He'd underlined it. I saw myself in that dingy Tenderloin men's room, reaching into some rough trade's puddle of piss. Is this what San Francisco held for me after Woody?

On my bed I found the T-shirt Jed was wearing the night before, when I last saw him. A souvenir from a 1983 Police concert, the *Synchronicity* tour. It no longer fit me, but it had enfolded him like gift paper. His sweat still clung to the cotton.

I collapsed on the mattress, depleted, and masked my eyes with the shirt. His smells rose into me—tobacco and unwashed hair and something like milk. Glimpses of him disturbed my sleep: an eyeball tattooed on his forearm, winking; his lips parting to show the space between his front teeth; the fly of his boxers parting to reveal his uncut cock. I woke sensing that he'd been here during the night, in the flesh, and I searched my apartment for signs that he had. Darth Vader was standing again. I couldn't remember setting it aright, though it must have been me.

Five business days had passed, but the next morning, when I went to the bank, I was told that I had a negative balance in my account. Andy's check had not cleared. "Insufficient funds," the teller said. I dropped my head in my hands, my elbows on the counter, and I stayed that way long enough for him to prod, "Is there anything else?"

"God, I hope not," I replied, an involuntary giggle breaking through. I turned and walked away, and this laughter enlarged, fed by the stunning amazement only excess misfortune can bring. *This isn't happening,* I told myself. But it was. *Hahaha.*

I biked to a place called Buddies, which sounds like a gay bar in a comedy sketch but was actually an Internet café full of coffee sippers standing at tall tables, checking their e-mail. My in-box revealed a series of messages from Deirdre, her anxiety cresting with each one: *I'm worried about you. I can't get through on the phone. Andy said you never wanted to speak to us again. Get in touch with me. Are you OK?*

I typed her a reply that began, ARE YOU FUCKING KIDDING ME? and continued with an all-caps scorcher that I sent without rereading. I didn't feel any better when I was done. I wasn't laughing anymore, not even bitterly.

There was an e-mail from Brady with TRYING AGAIN in the subject line. I didn't read it.

There was one from my cousin Tommy: COMING TO SAN FRAN FOR BUSINESS. I skimmed it quickly, wrote down his cell-phone number.

The rest of my account was a pileup of spam and political petitions and group invitations from friends I was no longer speaking to. I marked everything for deletion.

And then I noticed one message near the end of the queue that I actually wanted to read: a reply from the literary agency I'd contacted about Dean Foster.

> Mr. Foster is no longer represented by the Schwartz and Fields Literary Agency. Inquiries should be directed to the author himself.

They provided a phone number and address in North Hollywood, California. The street name sounded familiar.

Back at my apartment I flipped quickly through the contents of my QUEST FOR FATHER folder, my eye running down the list of the Dean Fosters I'd contacted. Sure enough, I found the North Hollywood address, attached to a Dean Foster I'd mailed a letter to: the angry guy with the barking dog, the one who phoned and threatened to sue for *invasion of privacy.*

That man was Danny Ficchino.

DOWN TO YOU

20

When I finally spoke to Deirdre, I didn't tell her I had found Danny Ficchino, even though I was buzzing with pride. (After months of misfires, I had actually accomplished something. *I'd found him!*) But Deidre was managing a crisis of her own. She had literally wrenched Andy's laptop from his hands, had brought in an outside financial advisor, *someone Carly Fazio said was really smart,* had forced Andy to itemize their finances. She was not yet sure how much money they had on hand. She promised to wire a portion to me, but the rest would have to wait. I took this news more calmly than I would have thought possible a day earlier. What choice did I have? My sister was afraid she would lose her house. I was embarrassed I'd e-mailed that tirade.

Our conversation took place at Ian's. I had gone there to page Jed, after I'd sketched for myself a loose plan of action: take the money from Jed and the money from Deirdre, pay off my rent and my phone bill, use the remainder to get myself, and my recorder, to Los Angeles. To Danny Ficchino. Maybe Jed could come along. After I got my interview with Danny, I'd be free to go wherever I wanted, with whomever I wanted.

I thought about calling Danny first. I thought about writing another letter, this time trying to hook him with a more detailed description of my search and what I'd discovered about Teddy, but after the inflamed response I got last time, I put no faith in this. I forced myself to think strategically, as if this were an assignment; I had tracked down plenty of slippery people for interviews. The key was to choose a tactic that intuited the subject's psychology. All I knew about Danny Ficchino was that he wanted to be left alone. So my best bet was to catch him unawares, the element of surprise on my side. Which meant showing up at his door.

After listening to Deidre's bad news, after a few hours waiting for Jed's call, which didn't come, I felt my buzz fading. "This is ridiculous, going to LA now," I said. "I've bounced my rent check. I'm about to lose my apartment."

"You're not going to wind up homeless," Ian said.

"Does the word *eviction* mean anything to you?"

"If you get evicted, you can move in with me."

He spoke so matter-of-factly, his words filtered through a long exhale off a cigarette, that I wasn't quite sure I'd heard right. "Move in?" I asked. "Like, roommates?"

"I'm not going to ask for credit references," he said. "Though you will be forced into servitude for my website."

"Sounds like a no-brainer," I said, sunny again.

He held his palm out, and I slapped it, brother to brother. "Go to LA," he said. "Strike while it's hot."

Late that night, as I laid in bed, open eyed, cycling through the disorder of my life, it came to me. Los Angeles. Colleen.

Colleen, my oldest friend in the world. Colleen, who I was still avoiding. A few days before, a black-haired woman about Colleen's size had breezed past me on the street wearing something right out of Colleen's closet—a multicolored, patchwork-leather midi-coat, very seventies, very hippie-chic—and the resemblance was so close it ignited a flurry of stomach nerves that nearly brought my morning coffee back up. Colleen, who had always been my comfort.

If I erased the fact that Colleen had told Brady I'd screwed around behind Woody's back—which, after all, is what friends do when asked to keep secrets: unburden themselves on other friends—I saw that my anger toward her was a fortress made of sand. My behavior the night of Ray's opening washed up over this fortress, melting it to a muddy stream. I opened a file on my computer, the one that held a month of transcribed voice mails, and I found the message Colleen left me after I'd nearly shoved her, the one that ended, *Maybe you should figure out what your hostility and internalized homophobia is all about.* I had responded with a joke. Stupidity on top of stupidity.

Years ago, when Colleen had begun dating a man after having previously been only with women, she hid it from everyone, including me. She dropped out of contact, and when I finally cornered her she was curt and defensive. *Well, that's that*, I'd thought. But a short while later, she surprised me with an unannounced visit, an apology, a bouquet of flowers. What had seemed like the end was just something we got through.

Remembering all this, I got on my bike and headed toward the boutique where she worked, detouring first past a flower stand on Market. I had borrowed a couple of twenties from Ian. The vendor's offerings were standard-issue—red and yellow carnations, pink-tipped lilies with their maroon pollen-pods stripped away, purple tulips that would probably droop in a day. I went into full-tilt queen mode, annoying the proprietor by insisting I assemble my own bouquet, one stem from this cluster, a couple from that. "I need something elegant enough for a reconciliation," I told him, shooing away his fistful of baby's breath.

Through the flashy storefront, I saw Colleen and waved. She buzzed me in from her spot behind the counter. She looked uncharacteristically frazzled, dressed in a shapeless sweatshirt and old jeans. Her black bob was growing out, natural brown roots lining her scalp like weeds.

"Hi," I said, pulling the flowers from behind my back. "I've been a retard."

She beamed and buried her nose in the bouquet.

"They don't have much of a smell," I said.

"You went to the guy on the corner?"

"Yeah. They're kind of a mess," I said.

"In a sweet way," she said, smiling. "They mean well."

I held my arms out and shrugged, summoning up humility with a sheepish half-smile. We moved in for a hug, both a bit theatrical in our approach. The awkwardness of returning to a friendship that has been put on hold. Our embrace a clutch of relief.

Her boss—the manic half of the team, who we called Up—appeared. "Collee-een," he hummed, "the delivery?" He frowned suspiciously at my flowers, as though I had wheeled in a shopping cart full of cans.

"This LA trip is killing me," Colleen said after he spun off to the back room. "I can't believe I'm going to be living 'round the clock with these two drama queens."

"When do you leave?"

"I'm driving down in a couple of days."

"Want company?" I asked, making transparent my ulterior motive. "I have an interview there. For a story."

"You have a place to stay?" she asked dubiously.

"Do you have space in your hotel room?" Neither a yes nor a no was clear in her eyes. "I could be there at the end of the day to give you foot rubs and peel you grapes and bitch with you about—." I gestured toward the back, where at this moment Up was cursing and knocking around boxes in a petulant fury.

"It might be just what I need," she said. "Let me think about it."

A whine from the back: "Collee-een. Today, please."

We made a plan to see each other that night.

I went to Ian's expecting Jed's call. I was sure it would come this afternoon. There wasn't much else to do at Ian's but wait; his computer was still dead, so we couldn't work on the site. I played CDs from his collection, sad that I'd sold off most of my own for so little in return.

Finally the phone rang. Ian went to the other room and came back carrying the cordless. "It's for you." I leapt to my feet, and he shook his head. "It's not . . ."

"Oh." I took the phone. "Hello?"

"There he is!"

It took me a moment to recognize the voice through the dropouts of the cellular connection. My cousin Tommy Ficchino. "Where you been?" he roared. "I called, I e-mailed. I've been in San Fran half a week and I'm leaving in two days."

"My phone service has been interrupted."

"Yeah, your sister told me."

"She gave you this number?"

"You can run, but you can't hide, Jamie. Look, you need a loan?"

"No, I'm good." I bit my lip, unsure.

"Well, tonight everything's on me," he said.

"Tonight? I've got plans with a friend."

"Great, I'll come along," he said enthusiastically. "I'm supposed to meet the other account manager for a drink, and I'm thinking, I spend all fucking day with him, why am I spending every fucking night with him, too?"

Nothing I said—*I need some one-on-one time with my friend*;

we've got plans to settle; *we're probably meeting in a gay bar, you wouldn't like it*—discouraged him. My excuses were no match for the full thrust of his salesmanship, which was motivated, I was guessing, by whatever red flags Deirdre had sent up.

Colleen and I met at Uncle Bert's, one of the few Castro bars not given over to a wall of monitors cycling through music videos and comedy clips, the kind of place that sponsored its own softball team, where the regulars drank just a little too much and were quick to chat up strangers. I was already into my second drink when she arrived, flustered from last-minute arrangements at work and a hair appointment. She was leaving for LA the next morning, a day earlier than planned. Her bosses wanted to fly her down, but Colleen, who needed sedatives to get past her fear of flying, was sticking to her plan to drive.

I sensed that she was open to taking me along, but she insisted that *we have to work some stuff out first.* And we did, or at least started to, until Tommy walked through the door, booming a greeting and clamping my hand in his meaty grip. I introduced them to each other. Colleen reminded me that they had met over ten years before, when I'd dragged her to a Garner family party.

"I remember your face," Tommy said to her. "You turned into a real stylish chick. Back then you were in Army boots."

"And you had hockey hair," she fired back.

"Short in front, long in back." His hands gestured from forehead to neck. "You know, a *shlong,*" he said with a suggestive smile.

"You've been here a minute and we're already talking about your dick?" Colleen asked.

"Sorry, I usually wait ten minutes," he joked.

She smiled despite herself, shaking her head.

Tommy ordered us a round of drinks, his unmistakable New York accent cutting past every other voice in the place. Colleen tried to decline, claiming an early night, but he wouldn't hear of it. I sensed her misgivings—the sudden largeness of his presence and, worse than that, the fact that I hadn't warned her he was coming, a definite fuck-up on a night designed to restore her confidence in me. I suppose I had counted on him not showing.

Tommy was dressed like what he was, a businessman after-hours: pleated suit trousers, leather loafers, dress shirt opened at the collar revealing a plane of matted hair. Definitely not the norm in this queer dive, and he was sexier because of it. If you were on the make for someone who wasn't just another Castro clone, he might be your target. I suspected Tommy had been hit on by men before, not only for his swagger, but for his good humor, the instant familiarity that made every conversation an occasion for teasing.

He talked with his hands—bare hands. No wedding ring. After he made mention of one of his kids, Colleen noticed this, too. "Are you divorced?" she asked.

"I'm on vacation," he said, eyebrows raised to let her in on his misbehavior. I remembered his stories of hiring call girls; I wondered what that was like, sliding the ring on and off to ready yourself for sex. You couldn't tell yourself that your cheating was a *slip*.

"So your wife is home with four kids," Colleen prodded, "and you're sneaking around pretending you're not even married."

"Hey, I got enough Catholic guilt already. Don't call the Pope on me."

"It's not a moral issue for me," she said between sips, "but the situation doesn't seem very fair to her."

"She's happy being a stay-at-home mom. That's all the fun she asks for. That and a few goodies from Neiman Marcus."

"Whatever works for you," Colleen muttered.

I shook my head. "If Deirdre heard this conversation she'd freak."

Tommy reached an arm over each of our shoulders, marking our alliance. "Whaddaya say we just drop the subject and have ourselves some fun, huh?"

I thought about Tommy's oldest kid, Brian, the one on the porch with us after the funeral. Did Tommy think of him when he was philandering? Maybe so; maybe Tommy had picked up his behavior from his own father and would one day pass it down to Brian. Though I couldn't imagine Uncle Angelo taking such a casual attitude about his own marriage, not because his love for Aunt Katie was so consuming, but because he had always held himself up as exemplary, a right-and-wrong guy. Tommy had some of his father's man-of-the-house attitude, but Tommy was looser about it; I suspected he saw the comedy of his role. Education might have accounted for his vaguely liberal upward mobility; he'd gotten the first master's degree of anyone in the family, an MBA that had vaulted him to a new class, a more expensive house, kids in private school.

It was Tommy's idea that we move on to another place, "Somewhere we can shake it a little."

Colleen again tried to say no but had less conviction in her voice this time; perhaps it was the booze, perhaps Tommy's amiability was getting under her defenses. "Fuck it," she pronounced, coaxing the last of her cocktail through a slender red straw. "Who cares if I'm tired for the drive? I've given these guys my every waking hour for weeks now."

"I'll help with the driving," I said.

Colleen met my eyes and nodded—enough agreement in her expression to let me know that she had finally confirmed my ride to LA.

We headed to the Café, a small club marked by a long line of trendily dressed boys waiting to get in, quarts of hair gel dispersed across their fashionably spiked locks. A decade earlier this place was a lesbian hangout with a couple of bustling pool tables at which Colleen and I had killed a lot of time. Tommy threw his arm around her as we made our way up Castro Street, saying he was also going to LA for business—maybe the three of us should get together for more fun. I fell behind them, their flirtatious body language like a branch snapping back in my face.

He turned to ask me, "What are you doing in La-La Land?"

"A radio interview."

I could have told him the truth, that I'd spent the past two months tracking down his Uncle Danny; I'm not completely sure why I didn't. My plan had taken on the cloak of privacy, as if I'd be intercepting classified documents. Special Agent James Garner on a Top Secret Mission. Maybe I was afraid I would fail? Or that I would succeed, and in doing so tear away whatever dusty curtain enclosed this estranged member of our family?

They took to the dance floor immediately, *shaking it* to a new Janet Jackson song that sounded exactly like an old one. During a break, Tommy sidled up to me and asked if Colleen was available. "Why don't you stick to hookers and leave my friend out of it?" I suggested.

"Aw, lighten up, I'm only kidding," he said. "But seriously, she's very attractive."

I waited outside the rest room and cornered Colleen as she emerged patting sweat off her forehead. "We have to get you out of here. Tommy's hot for you."

"I know. It's very flattering," she said, all drunk giggles.

"Don't encourage him."

"Did you notice how big his hands are?" she asked. "I know you did."

"If you sleep with him, my sister will accuse me of plotting to destroy the family."

"How would your sister find out?" she said. "If he was just some random guy I met, and he wasn't related to you, you wouldn't be on a high horse about it."

"Are you actually attracted to him? Or is there some other—."

"We're just *flirting*." She twirled back to him, a cocktail already waiting for her in his big hand.

I left before they did, and went home to pack.

I woke up hungover, my throat raw from too many cigarettes—or else from something I'd picked up on my knees in the Tenderloin. In the bathroom mirror, mouth gaping, I peered down my throat, expecting a sore, a syphilitic warning sign.

Colleen pulled up in her Plymouth, clutching a cup of coffee. Dark glasses couldn't mask her lack of sleep.

"You look like you've been up all night fucking," I said.

"No comment." The trunk held her luggage, a nearly bald spare tire and a container of antifreeze. I added to this my backpack, my recorder and a boxy gray valise containing nearly everything I possessed of my father's: the original items from the attic, the letters he'd written to Ray, the sketchbook, the journal from the woods.

She steered out of the Mission onto 280 South, and I switched on public radio. The news show that had replaced the one I used to produce was in mid-report, telling of a San Francisco city supervisor who'd evicted an elderly tenant and her son, sick with AIDS, so that he, this elected official, could move into the unit. His aim was to establish residency in a new district in time for reelection—the kind of heartless scheme that had become regular news in the city. I waited through the report to hear from the sick son, but he wasn't interviewed, and my producer's instinct kicked in. *Interview the son! Talk to other people with AIDS! Talk about how the rental crisis is affecting people with AIDS!*

Just past the San Francisco city limits, where the car dealerships and cemeteries of Colma brought to mind the drive from New York to New Jersey—urban and congested without being cosmopolitan—Colleen asked me for a cigarette.

"You quit a long time ago," I said.

"All bets are off on a road trip."

"Is this something you're going to regret? That you're going to blame on my bad influence?"

"Light it for me," she said.

I watched her inhale and exhale, balancing the cigarette in her lips and the coffee between her thighs as she rolled down the window. "Head rush," she said.

She flicked off the radio and popped a CD into a portable player plugged into the dash: Joni Mitchell's *Court and Spark,* an album that was our morning-after standby when we first knew each other in New York and had been introduced to Joni's music by older friends at the restaurant where we worked. "Down to You" was the album's anchor, a hymn to strangers brushing up against each other on the street after fleeting, sexual nights. We used to sing along over coffee and cigarettes and the *Times.* I think she put it on as an invitation to broach the subject we were avoiding.

Might as well get this over with. "So. You and Tommy?"

Something resembling affirmation passed across her face.

"I honestly don't get it," I said.

"Do you know how long it's been since I've had sex?" she asked.

"But you didn't exactly approve of Tommy's missing wedding ring."

"That's between him and his wife."

"Promiscuity is the new monogamy?"

"Very funny."

I let Joni's melancholy voice fill my ears: words of loss, change, conviction. Colleen and I were going to be together for the next two days. I needed to de-escalate this conversation. "Okay," I said. "The least you can do is dish up some details."

She actually blushed as she geared up to speak. "Well, the first round was a little fast and furious—."

"The first round? No wonder you look so hagged out."

"He came fast."

"He's used to paying at an hourly rate."

"Round two was for me." The tone of her voice had dropped. Her eyes darted to me and away. "When it was over, he asked me about you. How you were doing."

"Please tell me you didn't say anything."

"I said it was difficult to know."

I sighed so loudly it was a whimper. "Colleen, you cannot keep gossiping about me."

"Well, if you told your friends what was going on in your life, they wouldn't have to ask each other for updates." When I didn't respond, she said, "Don't be mad."

"Don't be mad," I repeated with an ironic snort. I pulled another cigarette from the pack—the very pack Jed left for me so that I wouldn't *be mad*. I'd written him a note that morning on the flip side of the one he'd left on my kitchen table: *I'll be back in a few days. Wait for me.*

Outside the window, suburbs had given way to the green slopes of San Mateo County. We would soon be approaching the turnoff for Skyline Drive, the route to the woods—Teddy's woods, Jed's woods. The site of these trees against this wide sky, the particular curve of the interstate here, the tinny sounds of early-seventies music, all of it transported me to the last time I'd been on this road, not as a passenger but in the driver's seat.

"I should tell you a story," I said and took her all the way from the pages that Deirdre had sent to Jed showing up in San Francisco and moving in with me.

She asked, "Have you fallen for this kid?"

Fallen? Maybe. But into what? "There have been moments when he seems exactly what I need. He brings out something real in me. Something I held back with Woody."

She frowned. "You never gave Woody enough credit."

"Woody gave me too much," I said. "He gave me credit for being more together than I am. More like him. More sane."

"Is that a pose?" Colleen asked.

"Is what?"

"Because I've known you a long time, and I've never seen you as insane." She kept her eyes straight ahead as she added, "Deluded, self-destructive, irresponsible, obsessive—."

"You can stop now."

"But not insane."

"The point is, Woody and I—." Actually, I didn't want to make a *point*. "Look, it's over. Let's change the subject." It was over. It was. I told myself again, knowing I had to make myself believe it. It. Was. Over.

We merged onto 101, passing through garlic and cherry country into the arid Salinas Valley: wide agricultural fields dotted with bent-over migrant workers; scattered towns, which at seventy-five miles an hour were little more than uniform subdivisions wrapped around gas stations and strip malls; the distant, burnished peaks that yoked the landscape. The batteries powering her CD player had died. The radio offered only evangelical fulmination and the music of an old-world fiesta. Fear and cheer.

"Read me something," she said. Reading to each other was another of our New York pastimes. Back then we read mostly women authors: Toni Morrison, Adrienne Rich. We once stayed up all night finishing off *The Handmaid's Tale.* "Read me some of your father's journal."

She pulled over at a gas station, and I retrieved *In the Woods* from the trunk. I took the pages in hand and began. " 'Don brought me to this place because he needed to getaway—'. Wait, that should be two words: *get away*. 'And I needed to see something of California beyond the sordid Frisco city limits.' "

She laughed lightly, repeating "Frisco" with mockery and wonderment.

Took me a few pages to harness my father's rhythm; I had to ease into all the funny spelling and unpredictable punctuation. But soon enough I heard Teddy speaking before I spoke his words. His voice became mine, or mine became his. Hunks of clay mashed into something larger, subsuming the original pieces.

When I finished, she said, "He reminds me of you."

"Come on."

"Very black-and-white in his opinions. He puts these people on a pedestal, then the next day he's denigrating them."

"I hope he doesn't remind you too much of me," I kidded.

She fell silent—uncomfortably so for me, as I could have used reassurance—then said, "His macho posturing seems pretty familiar, too."

"You're talking about that night after Ray's. About the way I acted." She nodded. "I've apologized for that."

"I know. I know. Just beware of who's influencing you. That's all."

21

We hit Los Angeles during evening rush hour. The roads were packed to the point of stagnation, stretching our seven-hour journey to eight and a half. With the sun already down, we made a few wrong turns and lost our bearings. By the time we checked into our hotel, on Sunset in West Hollywood, we were cranky, achy, desperate for a bathroom. Colleen jumped into the shower; she was already late for a planned dinner with Up and Down.

I thought about calling Dean Foster, but the knots in my stomach let me know I wasn't ready, so instead I walked to Santa Monica Boulevard and entered the first gay bar I found. In my wallet was a twenty-dollar bill that I'd discovered in a coat pocket before I left home. Expecting that Deirdre's wire transfer would come through today or tomorrow, I figured I could afford a well drink.

"How's it going?" I asked the bartender, a perfect specimen of style and musculature, but he didn't answer, just waited for my order. This quickly became the pattern: I'd try for small talk with some guy, who would simply pretend I wasn't there. *Simply* is a stretch; ignoring someone who has spoken to you requires a complex mechanism of detachment and dismissal. I looked out of place in this crowd, my shirt and my jeans too loose and grungy, my face in need of a shave. Fine for the Eagle, but not for WeHo.

I wandered into a gay bookstore, where most of the stacks were uninhabited but a crowd of guys stood shoulder to shoulder along the magazine rack near the back, their noses pressed up to skin photos. On a whim I searched under *F*, wondering if Dean Foster's representation by a literary agency meant that he was a published author. Nothing. My gaze shifted left, toward the *G*s, where I found an edition of Allen

Ginsberg's journals, dating back to before he was a famous howling poet, to when he'd been Kerouac's best friend and, as I quickly deduced from scanning the pages, Neal Cassady's lover.

At the register, an androgynous, waify boy was serving up a retro-eighties look—asymmetrical, color-tipped bangs, a Duran Duran T-shirt with the sleeves cut off, a stack of black-rubber bracelets. He glanced at the cover and uttered, without inflection, "Ginsberg."

"I'm studying the period," I said. "Late fifties–early sixties."

"Oh, the Beats," he said wearily. "Total misogynists."

"They broke a lot of ground for men bonding with each other." I felt an almost animal need for some bonding of my own; he was the first person who'd acknowledged me in the last hour.

As he rang up the sale, he shrugged, unmoved, which I decided to take personally. "In 'Howl,' " I insisted, "Ginsberg wrote about getting fucked up the ass by motorcyclists and sailors. No one was depicting that in 1955."

"Have you seen *Queer as Folk?*" he challenged. I stared back at him coolly. "That'll be $18.39."

I had eleven dollars in my wallet—and no ATM card. Had I lost it? I remembered all at once a moment earlier in the week when, with no money to withdraw, I'd removed the card from my wallet and flung it at my desk. I could picture it banging against an ashtray and landing next to my computer keyboard, where it no doubt still was. For the benefit of Duran Duran, I patted down my pockets with a dopey grin before walking back to the shelf.

I slid the Ginsberg book into its proper place alongside Genet's *The Thief's Journal.* Genet, who had been a book thief. Ginsberg, who was once arrested for carting around stolen goods. Me, with eleven dollars to get through two days in LA.

I dug the metallic theft-proof strip from the binding and folded the Ginsberg volume under my coat. I exited the store with a brazen wave to Duran Duran. Behind him, a co-worker was flashing the overhead lights, ready to close up shop. I caught a snippet of the two of them debating who would straighten up the magazine rack.

My heartbeat had quickened in the rush of shoplifting. I walked a couple blocks trying to maintain composure, finally stopping under a streetlight outside a darkened art gallery. The prints in its window were full-color blowups of homo-pulp-fiction titles—*A Hardened Criminal*, *He Burns Through the Night*—suitably framed for contemporary décor. I smoked a cigarette and read a few pages of the journals, letting my nerves calm. All around me, gay guys in expensive jeans strolled and gawked, trailing cologne, while in front of me Ginsberg documented his creeping insanity, his pornographic dreams of making love to Cassady, his grimy hallucinations. I found myself wondering why I'd devoted all this time to Kerouac's prevaricating prose when here was the openly gay Ginsberg blazing a trail for genuinely queer outlaws.

I looked up to see Duran Duran at the curb, unlocking his yellow, old-model Volkswagen Beetle. Our eyes met and he gave a faint nod of recognition. Then he cocked his head with curiosity, noticing the book in my hand, and his smile disappeared.

"Stealing from a community bookstore is fucked up," he shouted across the domed roof of the car. "Why don't you steal from a Barnes and Noble?"

A handful of passersby stopped and stared at him, and then followed his verbal harangue toward me. I darted my head around as if I, too, wanted to know what the fuss was about.

"Yeah, you," he said. "You know who I'm talking to."

My pulse raced again. Los Angeles was a foreign country, its cops notoriously rough. Getting busted here would be a trip to a Turkish prison. Duran Duran remained outside his car, shouting accusations with a jabbing finger. I tucked the book under my arm and strode away, up a side street that grew darker the farther I got. Then I broke into an adrenaline-fueled run.

Colleen—sitting on the bed with paperwork spread around her, a laptop open, a pen tucked behind her ear—greeted my sweaty-faced arrival with alarm. I tried to evade her questions with jokes, but she kept pushing. "I needed this book for research, but I stupidly left my ATM card at home," I told her. "So I took it. And ran back here."

"Christ, I can loan you money; you don't have to steal," she said.

"I guess I wanted to," I said. Her mouth fell open. "It's part of my midlife crisis."

"You're too young for a midlife crisis."

"My father died at sixty. I'm more than halfway there."

She grabbed her purse from the table and pulled out two twenties. "Here."

"You don't have to."

"For tomorrow? Don't you have an interview to do?"

"Thanks." I folded the bills next to the ten and the single in my wallet and asked her, "About tomorrow? Any chance you could lend me your car?"

Her eyes expressed something like amazement. "Aren't you here to give me back rubs?"

"Never mind. I was just asking."

I went to the circular table in the corner, which had a phone on it, and dialed Dean Foster's number. I hadn't prepared my speech, figured I'd just wing it. His answering machine picked up: "Solicitors should remove this number from all lists. Professional inquiries may be left after the beep." The voice was terse—neither the defensive tone of the man who'd replied to my letter nor the theatrical bellow of Robbie the Greek. But even without a barking dog in the background, Dean Foster's desire to be left alone was clear. At the beep, I hung up.

Colleen watched me from the bed. "Who are you calling?"

"This guy I'm trying to meet. He lives in North Hollywood."

A gentle sigh escaped her lips. "I'll know in the morning whether I need the car. If I don't, you can use it. Do you have your driver's license on you?"

"Of course."

"Do us both a favor," she said. "Double-check."

I stayed up late soaking in the tub, reading my pilfered book, while Colleen slept on the other side of the wall. I heard her call out in her sleep, a sharp, wordless moan. I waited for more, but that was all. A passing disturbance. For a moment I fantasized us as roommates again, back in our tenement apartment: one of us in the bathtub (located in the kitchen) and the other breathing the heavy air of dreams just a few paces away.

When I awoke, her car keys were waiting for me on an end table, along with a note reading, "Carry on bravely!" I smiled in recognition, remembering the elderly British woman who had been our upstairs neighbor in New York. She used to stop us in the hall to chat, a scarf over her head, her hands clutching at the buttons of her raincoat; every encounter ended with her chipper imperative, "Carry on bravely." She had survived the Blitz in London, and this phrase always echoed with the ingrained fear of walking out the door into an assault from the sky. Colleen and I had made this salutation our own, though it had been years since either of us used it. Perhaps she felt some of the nostalgia that had overtaken me last night.

I phoned Dean Foster, and this time I left a message: "This is Jamie Garner, Teddy's son. I wrote you a letter a couple months ago and was still hoping to talk to you. I got your number from the literary agency. I mean no harm, but I have questions for you." I left the number of the hotel and hung up. There. It was done. If he never replied, I could at least say I tried. With a map from the front desk—a lousy map, short on details, as it turned out—I drove to North Hollywood, but could not locate the exact street on which Dean lived. I asked directions, got even more lost, and eventually found myself on a freeway, pointed toward the ocean.

Preparation is half the battle, my father liked to say. *The other half is what you can't prepare for.*

I scanned the radio dial, unleashing a horde of obnoxious DJs provoking their listeners into arguments and commercials rife with faux-ironic humor and stiff, scripted repartee. My driving was as skittish as ever, and the regular updates on accidents and traffic delays didn't help; I didn't know the city well enough to avoid them. I finally landed on the commercial-free radio station, which eased my nerves and allowed me to see that Los Angeles indeed held some appreciable culture.

The day took me to Venice Beach, where I circled for nearly an hour trying to find a parking space that wouldn't cost me. Even with Colleen's money, I was pinching pennies, knowing full well that I could blow through fifty dollars without even trying. Venice was weekday-empty. Haze filled the sky. Intermittent gusts of wind kept the temperature too low for lying around on the sand. I'd imagined I'd see surfers, or at least some enticing flesh, but even the shirtless dudes bore a shifty street demeanor. So soon after my encounter in the Tenderloin I was leery of eye contact with strangers. Venice seemed to exist somewhere between New York and San Francisco: vaguely hippie like Haight Street, but with a more bruising energy. In that 1960 tourist guide sent to my father by Aunt Katie, the author had claimed that San Francisco's *Beatnik Land* was in the process of relocating to Venice. No sign of the counterculture here, where the promenade featured little more than T-shirt kiosks and bootleg CDs at a discount. I watched a basketball game, fast-moving black and Latino boys who were graceful and intimidating all at once; their physical assertiveness as they barged past each other instigated in me the exact mix of fear and desire I could trace back to my first furtive glances at male flesh in the middle-school locker room.

A loose-limbed woman—tanned skin hanging like paper off her jaw, hair sun streaked and split at the ends, open mouth revealing lost teeth—sidled up to me for a cigarette. I make it a point never to say no to a fellow nicotine addict. After I gave her a light she remained at my side, peering through the fenced-in court, asking me questions—"Where you from? What are you doing here? Where you going next?" Finally she moved closer, her dry lips hissing in my ear, "Are you looking to score?" I didn't know if she meant drugs, which seemed likely, or sex, hinted at in the way her collarless black sweatshirt drooped over a prominent clavicle, bony shoulder, the hint of flat cleavage. With little more than a grunt I walked away. From behind me I heard her agitated voice, saying something that sounded like, "You ain't been a brother to me."

I turned around, feeling a fight pulsing in me. "I just gave you a cigarette, bitch."

She repeated herself. This time I heard it clearly: "You ain't any better than me."

I threw up my hands, surrendering. She followed me halfway back to the car, twenty paces behind, a frail, ghostly hellhound muttering recriminations.

Colleen returned around eight p.m., hours before I expected her. She threw her coat on the bed and announced, "I just quit my job." She wanted a cigarette and didn't care that we were in a nonsmoking room; the room was rented to her bosses. "Fuck them," she growled. What had happened: An important delivery had been messed up—it might have been the very one she was working on when I stopped by the boutique—and though it wasn't her fault, she took the blame because Up, who'd actually addressed the label, insisted she had given him the wrong address. They wanted her to drive across town to retrieve the missing garments, but I had her car and they'd rented a five-speed (Colleen couldn't drive stick), so Up had to go himself. He spent his entire traffic-clogged trip screaming at her from his cell phone, calling her a saboteur. Meanwhile, back at the fashion show, Down was popping pills, growing steadily more slurry and absent-minded. The fashion show's lineup had to be rearranged to accommodate their delay, which put them in a bad light with the organizers and other designers. In the end they got all their outfits on stage, to great applause, and in fact the later slot proved to be an advantage—a more high-profile point in the program, right before a local favorite.

"There's this press luncheon tomorrow," she concluded, "which we weren't originally invited to but now are, and I'm supposed to work all night to make alterations for a new set of models. That's when I told them I quit."

"Are you sure?" I said. "This could be big, right?"

"Who cares if they get famous?" She puffed away. "Next job I get will be working for women. Not gay men who think they're in touch with femininity but are just as sexist as straight guys." She shot me a look. "No offense."

"Guilty as charged," I said, thinking of the woman in Venice—how the *bitch* I'd tossed at her had soured the air.

Colleen went to the bathroom to flush her cigarette. When she returned, she said, "So let's get the hell out of here."

"How about dinner? I'm starving."

"No, I mean let's go home." She must have seen me deflate. "How did your interview go?"

"Nothing yet."

"We can't stay here. They're paying for the room."

"It's paid through tomorrow, right?"

"Yes. But they'll be here any minute to raise hell."

We decided to go out on the town, get dinner and drinks, stay up late enough to avoid the fashionistas. Colleen broke out her credit card, and we grew tipsy and bold, making extravagant plans for the next step in her career (designing her own line, starting her own business) and mine (documenting her new venture for a radio segment, maybe even for a film: the birth of the next hot designer). It was the giddiest fun we'd had in months, though there was something vaguely histrionic about our conversation. We were trying too hard. Under the surface, our separate pressures were barely held at bay.

"Wanna go for a ride?" I asked her.

"Where to?"

"North Hollywood."

We piled back in her car and bought a new map at a gas station. I found Dean Foster's street and navigated us in that direction. We cruised the block twice before I settled on which house was his—the one masked by an overgrown front lawn, a couple of wild palms and a row of flowering bushes that bore the sign of long-ago landscaping abandoned to the elements. A Spanish roof, its curved terra-cotta tiles cracked and missing in places, peeked above the fronds. Only one light shone, at the foot of the driveway, its bulb aimed toward a sign: BEWARE OF DOG.

"He's not exactly sending out a welcome," Colleen said.

"I should just go ring the bell now," I said.

"Jamie, it's midnight."

"Right." But I continued to imagine it. The knock on the door. The surprise.

"So are you going to tell me who this guy is?" she asked.

I took a deep breath. It was time to tell her. "Remember that box I brought back from New Jersey? The guy in the head shot, my father's old friend?"

Back at the hotel room, the message light on our phone sent out rapid red blinks. The automated voice announced, "You have six new messages."

"I think these are probably for you," I told Colleen. She took the phone, frowning through a series of emergency requests from Up and Down, who, of course, couldn't do half of what had to be done without her. As she erased the final message, the phone rang again. "They'll keep calling until I answer," she said with a groan.

"Let me." I grabbed the receiver. "Hello?"

"This is Dean Foster."

"Oh." I flashed wide eyes at Colleen, pointed to my chest. "This is Jamie Garner. Thanks for calling back."

"What's this all about?"

I scrambled to compose myself. "I'm in LA—."

"You work in show business?"

"No. I got your name from your agent—."

"So you're in publishing?"

I remembered his outgoing message addressed to *professional inquiries*. "I'm a radio producer in San Francisco. Mostly public radio."

"That's not show business, that's government. I got no time for the government. I'm a busy man, lot of stuff in development."

"Well, do you have any time to meet tomorrow?"

"What I'm saying, kid, is what's in it for me?"

"Mr. Foster, I've done a little research on your career, watched some of your films, and I'd be interested in talking to you. You could call it research and development." I paused, not wanting to pretend this was all business. "You do remember that we also have a family connection?"

A deliberative gust of breath pushed through the phone. "What hotel are you at?"

I gave him the name; yes, they have a bar, I assured him, and a restaurant.

"But I'd happily speak with you at your house."

"No, no. The landscapers are coming."

"I see. How about in the restaurant at noon?"

"Have a Bloody Mary waiting for me. Extra Tabasco."

"You got it."

"Ciao."

I said good-bye, but he'd already hung up.

Colleen took the car to meet a friend for brunch. I put on a clean shirt, loaded my recorder in my backpack, and went down to the restaurant, where I grabbed a small table. I told the waiter I wanted a Bloody Mary to arrive when my companion showed up. I emphasized the extra Tabasco. His face took on the stultification reserved for problem customers.

I had nearly finished the Bloody Mary I'd ordered for myself when Dean walked in, a half-hour late.

He was Robbie the Greek plus twenty-five years and a few dozen pounds around the middle. His hair remained thick and black—too black; the curls twisting from the V-neck of his turquoise-blue sweater were more salt than pepper. I wouldn't have been surprised if somewhere under his sweater and the high-waisted, cream-colored trousers was a girdle. He didn't wear a gold medallion, but it would have fit the look.

I stood and waved. As he made his way over, I couldn't help but wonder if his eyes were scrutinizing me behind his dark glasses; I remembered how Ray had been struck by my resemblance to Teddy. But Dean gave no such indication. We shook hands, exchanged names. I thanked him for his time.

"Where's the waiter?" he asked gruffly, eyeing my glass of tomatoey melt-off.

"I've ordered one for you," I said.

"I like them with extra Tabasco." He scanned the room impatiently, without speaking, until the drink was placed in front of him.

"I'm so glad you agreed to meet me," I began.

"Tell me about this radio show." He was leaning forward on his elbows, his hands clasped. I noticed a pinky ring with a heavy, cobalt-blue stone.

I embellished, telling him about my past assignments and how I was gearing up for a return to radio, looking around for story ideas, most likely something on San Francisco history, as I'd been talking to people who had come of age in the forties and fifties.

"I was never in San Francisco," he said. "Hollywood, that's my turf."

He adjusted his sunglasses. I noticed that their frames were the same shade of blue as the stone in his ring.

"I was under the impression that you'd visited San Francisco before you moved to LA? Back around 1960?"

"No way. Never liked that city."

"There was something in one of my father's letters, or journals, that made it sound like he went to San Francisco because you'd gone there first."

At *my father,* his posture shifted. He glugged his drink without replying. Perhaps I was charging in too quickly. I shifted gears. "Tell me about your movie career."

"I made pictures for twenty years. And got ripped off every step of the way."

"You had great screen presence," I said, mentioning the titles I'd seen, offering inflated praise. I asked him about his literary ambitions.

"I've been working on my memoirs for decades," he said, his voice swelling, "but they're so hot no one will touch them. I've got dirt on every mover and shaker in this town. You don't spend your life in show biz and not learn a thing or two."

"I would think there'd be a big market for gossip."

"I'm not talking gossip," he barked. "I'm talking scandal! I'm talking sensational stuff! They ran me out of town for it. I made five pictures in Italy before I came back."

"What do you mean, ran you out of town?"

"And you're damn right there's a market for it. It's just the gatekeepers you can't get past." He leaned in closer. "You talked to those shysters at Schwartz and Fields? Don't believe anything they told you."

"All they did was send an address."

He leaned back, assessing. "You tell them you're in radio?"

"Yes, but I don't want to create a false impression, Mr. Ficchino. I think you know, from the letter I sent you—"

His forehead went white. "The name is Foster."

"I'm sorry. Of course, my mistake." I felt my skin heat up, and I spoke faster. "Actually, I brought my recorder today. I thought we might consider this a pre-interview."

He crossed his arms. "You got a contract?"

"I'm not sure we need one. At this stage, this is mostly personal for me."

"Order me another beverage," he said. He sat with his arms folded, silently intimidating, while I placed the order, including another for myself even though I hadn't eaten breakfast and was already buzzed from the first. After the waiter left, Dean opened his hands wide. "Who are you, kid?" he demanded. "What are you up to?"

"I'm Teddy Garner's son. I want to know who he was. And I think you can help me."

"That's it? That's your pitch?" He swelled with annoyance and, no doubt, with vodka; I heard in his voice the menace of *The Criminal Kick*. Two women at the next table paused their conversation to gawk at him. "You call me out of the blue, drag me from my house at a very busy time and expect me to take a fucking stroll down memory lane? You better try harder than that."

"Okay, how about this: I want to know if you had sex with him."

He fell back in his chair. The clatter of the dining room filled the vacuum. I was glad to see I'd unnerved him. I hadn't come all this way to be bullied.

Through chugs of his cocktail he snarled, "You got balls, you know that?" He drained his second drink. The ice was still rattling in the bottom of the glass and already he was looking for the waiter. I had no idea what this place charged for a Bloody Mary.

I reached into my bag and pulled out the letter Teddy had written to Danny, the first one I'd found, stuck in the binding of that *10 Perfect Days* book. "He wrote this to you. For some reason he never sent it."

He removed his glasses and cocked his head back to scan the page.

"I recognize the scribble," he said, with a glance at me. His eyes were rimmed by dark lashes and still held a hint of his youth beneath age-heavy lids. It was my first glimpse of the Dean Foster whose glamorous picture I'd been staring at for months. An almost weary gesture seized his upper torso. A sway of disbelief. "Jesus Christ. Rusty fuckin' Garner."

"I wouldn't ask if you weren't family."

"Family? Don't fucking insult me." A gallows laugh, bitter. "Did my brother put you up to this?"

"Angelo? No, Angelo is—." I stopped myself from completing the sentence, but he was waiting, clearly curious. "He passed away six years ago."

A shadow fell on him, his eyes losing their furious spark, his lips bleeding of color. He put his glasses on again. I started an apology, but he held up his hand to shush me.

Over his shoulder I saw the waiter approaching. I couldn't get away with putting this tab on Colleen's room; she'd already checked out. Maybe I could put it on her bosses' room; she probably wouldn't mind sticking them with the bill.

Dean Foster pushed back his chair and stood up. "Without a contract I can't talk to you," he said.

The waiter asked, "All through?"

I looked desperately at Dean, who had risen to his feet. "Stay for another," I pleaded.

He turned to the waiter and said at full volume, "This is the worst Bloody Mary in the whole fucking city. Weak and bland."

The waiter stammered an apology that went ignored.

Dean's eyes were on me now. "I don't know what the hell you're up to, kid, but I got nothing for you. *Nothin'.* You can take your nosy questions and your public radio and your friggin' family, and stick it where the sun don't shine."

With that, he walked away, disappearing through the lobby and out the glass door, swallowed up in bright light. I called after him, to no avail.

The bewildered waiter was still hovering. "Sir?"

"I have to follow him," I said, grabbing my backpack and hopping up from my seat. Something—the bag swinging in the air, my leg knocking against the table—jostled a glass and sucked it into my lap, flooding my groin in scarlet. He held out a napkin, but I backed away. "I can't deal with this now."

"What room shall I charge this to?"

I pulled a number out of the air—415, the SF area code—and hurriedly traced Dean's path to the street. Air conditioning gave way to the asphalt's chafing heat. I felt the cold spill soak through to my underwear. The sidewalk was cluttered with porters loading luggage in the hotel's curved driveway while patrons on phones stood idly by. Dean couldn't have gotten far, but I saw no sign of him. I didn't know where he would have parked, what his car looked like. I rushed to the nearest intersection, looking in every direction but finding nothing.

I couldn't believe how badly this had gone. But it was about to get worse: When I gazed back at the hotel—a three-story hotel, no fourth floor, no room 415—I saw the waiter pressing through the front door, a security guard at his side, their heads swiveling like predators.

I saw myself return to them, apologize, explain the situation. *I gave you the wrong room number? An honest mistake. Here, why don't I pay cash?*

I saw all this unfold, but I had already reacted, I was already sprinting away at full speed, controlled by an impulse that said, *You don't owe them nothin'.*

A fugitive dash through oncoming traffic, brakes squealing nearby, angry horns punctuating my every step. I looked over my shoulder, saw the security guard in pursuit. The recorder in my backpack banged against my spine. I cut onto a side street lined with dappled West Hollywood homes, turned a corner, then another. Unsure where I was going. Certain I would be trapped. Respectable gays lived here with security signs staked into lawns, SUV's waiting in driveways. You can hide behind a big car like that. The true purpose of a monster car: concealment. Me hiding behind an SUV. Dean Foster hiding behind dark glasses. Danny Ficchino after all these months. Ranting at me. His story still a secret. Now I'd never know.

I'm running south, or east, I can't tell; I'm all turned around. How long do I have to run before I'm sure they're not after me? Why am I running? Why did Dean flee? What I said: Angelo is dead. And Teddy is dead. I'm the Angel of Death. I might as well be dead myself.

I blast out of this maze onto Santa Monica Boulevard, panting, heaving, *these fucking smoker's lungs*. I'm at the same corner where I was confronted by the guy from the bookstore. I hear a siren. Did they call the police? I am an easy target, a pale redhead drenched in criminal sweat. I have a baggie of pot in my pack. I should call Colleen. Are there still pay phones in LA? Over my shoulder, a blur of blue in the distance: a big man. My predator, still searching? *All this for a bar tab I could have paid.*

The light is red, but I dash onto Santa Monica, leaping without looking. I pause to let a car whiz by, but there's another and another coming right at me. One swerves, passing so close I feel the vibration through my backpack, and I stumble and I can't recover. My balance is sucked away like the trick floor of a carnival ride. Eight lanes to this street, and I'm now stumbling across three of them, falling onto my hand, my shoulder, my hip. *Ow, fuck, ow!* I'm down.

Oncoming headlights, diamonds of light in the bright sky—they keep their lights on during the day in LA? You should get up, you should get away, but for what? Your quest is over. Fifty dollars in your pocket, marijuana in your bag, Teddy's letter in your bag, Danny's voice in your head. *You got balls*. Yes, you do. The balls to stay down on the pavement as this car drives straight toward you. Who cares if you get up? If you get up, you're still running. Diamond light coming. Tires screaming. Car horn angry. Danny angry. Teddy angry.

Burning ground holds you down; you let it.

Close your eyes don't watch it happen.

Bile in your throat *extra Tabasco*.

Jesus Christ Rusty fuckin' Garner.

Stick it where the sun don't shine.

An outcry of brakes, scorched rubber on blacktop, a gust of heat like a knife to the throat, like strangulation. You're floating through the charred air. Are you free now?

A voice emerges, then another. The angry voices of men, voices that have always been there. Anger is the fear of men unleashed.

I opened my eyes. A car was pivoted not two feet to my right. The one that almost hit me. A woman was stepping from it, heels on pavement.

Onlookers looking, mouths open. But no cops, no security guard, no waiter.

"I'm okay, I'm okay." I waved a hand to anyone who cared before noticing the abrasion, seeping blood down my wrist. On the ground my stuff was scattered: my bag with the zipper gaping; my recorder, batteries ejected; Ginsberg's journals, splayed. An extra T-shirt—I would need that now; there was blood on my sleeve. Teddy's letter did a flip-flop on the asphalt.

"You could have been run over. I came so close." The woman from the pivoted car stood in front of me: stylish in a blinding white dress, ageless with a halo of blonde hair. A smooth face and concern in her eyes. She'd collected the remainder of my spilled belongings: cigarettes, lighter, pot. "Put this away," she advised.

It seemed that I knew her. "Do I know you?"

From behind us, the guy in the other car: "Get out of the road, fucking asshole!"

The woman shouted back: "A little compassion here!" Then softer, to me: "Which way are you going?"

I looked around. There was an answer to this question.

She guided me to the curb. "I think you're in shock, honey."

I did know her: a soap-opera actress, *Days of Our Lives.* Summers during high school, I watched the show with my mother, religiously. The character had two names—no, they were twin sisters. The evil one plotted against the good one, but the good one killed her instead, though not before she'd lost her mind, was dumped by her husband, had her fortune swindled.

"Do you need a lift to your car?" she asked.

I sent her away with muttered thanks. She'd abandoned her chariot in the middle of the road, hazards flashing. Other drivers were laying on their horns. I watched her soar on slender heels, hair radiant in the light, a white dress gleaming. My Hollywood vision.

I heard a siren. Maybe not for me, but still. Up ahead I saw a movie theater, ten titles stacked on the marquee. I jogged toward it, pausing at a mirror in an antique-store window. My shirt was untucked, soaked in sweat and torn where the arm was bloody; the stain on my khakis had set; my shoulders trembled. My face was distorted, eyes wild, skin hot pink under damp copper hair. A sputtering flame fighting for air.

I bought a ticket to the biggest blockbuster advertised, a John Travolta action movie. I thought, I can hide in a crowd. In the bathroom, I washed up, packed paper towels on the gash, changed my shirt. A guy came in talking on his phone and steered around me and my mess. He continued his conversation from the crapper.

At the snack bar, I spent four dollars on a small popcorn, suddenly ravenous. The theater held ten empty seats for every one patron. I slunk low, still expecting arrest. The cool, carpeted darkness promised the relief of a hermitage, but the film was violent and militaristic and false, full of shooting without wounding, killing without dying. People die every day, but Hollywood doesn't know how to show it. Travolta was uttering his every line with smugness, like a man who'd never actually feared for his life, who'd remained above it, protected by money and fame. He'd once been twenty and beautiful; I had tacked his poster inside my bedroom closet. Recently I'd seen him promoting this movie in a magazine, posing with his perfectly constructed family, talking about what he called religion.

I couldn't stay here, but I was afraid of the street. I could still feel the heat of the road beneath me. Why hadn't I gotten up? I'd waited in my fallen position. The actress's swerve made the difference. The good twin to the rescue. I had been saved.

I had not saved myself.

The streets were a maze, but there was no other way. I had to return to the world.

What had that white-haired man in Grace Cathedral told me?

You just have to walk back out.

22

Colleen yelled at me on the phone, then yelled at me in person, outside the movie theater, where she picked me up. She'd been driving around for half an hour. Our original plan had been to meet at the front desk, where we'd stored our bags, after I was through with Dean. When Colleen returned, she was met by the head of hotel security, who, collaborating with the waiter and the front-desk clerk, had deduced that the guy who cut out on his bar tab was the person who had stayed in her room. "They wanted your name," she told me. "They wanted to bring in the police." She lied and charmed her way through the interrogation, telling them that she didn't know me, that I was a guy she'd picked up in a bar, that we hadn't exchanged personal information.

"Thanks for not giving them my name."

"Thanks for the fucking humiliation, Jamie. Four guys ganging up on me in this tiny office."

"Those fuckers," I said.

"What about you, *fucker*? You left me to the wolves."

"I wasn't thinking. I had to go after Danny Ficchino."

"You could have paid the damn bill."

"I was so confused," I muttered. "I wanted to die."

"You don't get to die, asshole. You get to sit here and listen to me tell you to get your shit together." And she told me, again and again. She was mythic, volcanic.

When she finally fell silent, I asked, "Did you tip the waiter?"

She reached over and slugged me in the arm, her fist hard as steel.

"Sorry!" I cried, flinching. "Really, truly, truly fucking sorry."

I tried to explain myself—not myself so much as my awful meeting with Dean Foster, his transparent bombast, the way he freaked out when I mentioned his brother, Angelo's death.

"Angelo, your uncle?" she asked. "Tommy's father? This guy Dean Foster is Tommy's uncle, too?" Some computation passed across her face, shaking off the fury she'd been draped in since she picked me up.

"Where are we going?" I asked.

"I got a room for tonight. A different place. I'm not sure I even want you there."

"We're not going back to San Francisco?"

"Not today."

I saw that unreadable look in her eyes again. "There's something you're not telling me. Is this about work?"

"No."

"Then what?"

"Nothing."

Another night in LA, another chance. *Just walk back out.* "I should try to talk to him again."

"To Danny Ficchino? He doesn't want to talk to you."

"Probably not, but I've got nothing to lose. I've got to make this right." I squinted at Colleen and said, "Maybe I can borrow your car?"

"You're unbelievable."

"I've got balls."

"I'd like to cut them off."

The hotel was downscale from the last one; a motel, really, left over from the 1950s but not revised for the kitsch entertainment of the new moneyed class. The bathroom showed signs of wear—seams of mold in the tub corners, a drizzle of rust under a window frame—though it smelled piney clean. I took a necessary shower, standing in the cleansing flow for a long time, conversing with Dean Foster. Various scenarios played out: the one in which I show up at his place and he doesn't open the door; the one in which he opens the door and his ferocious dog attacks me; the one in which he invites me in and I fuck it up again. The one in which he apologizes, telling me he forgot to take his medication that morning, and we share an all-forgiving laugh.

I stood at the sink, shaving my face with a disposable razor from Colleen. There was a knock on the bathroom door. Before I answered, in walked Tommy Ficchino.

Startled, I let the edge of the blade nick my skin. I wrapped a towel around my waist. "What the fuck are you doing here?"

"I been waiting for you to finish up, but I really hadda piss." He stepped past me, planted himself in front of the toilet, unzipped. "Keep your eyes over there."

"Why, if I look you'll turn gay?" I dabbed toilet paper on the cut.

"I just don't want to make you jealous."

I heard the force of his stream begin churning the water. I looked. Through the folds of his pleated pants, a few thick inches dangled out, the glory previously hinted at by Colleen. "So I'm assuming Colleen called you?"

"Actually I called her."

"Why are you calling Colleen in LA?"

"Why do you think?" He zipped up and flushed.

"You're playing with fire, Tommy. Since you last saw me I managed to destroy things with Woody."

"Yeah, I hear you've been a real big problem for everyone." He crossed his arms, parted his legs. His jokiness, never far from the surface, was notably absent.

"You've got nerve coming in here with your big swinging dick to lecture me."

"What are you fucking talking about? I'm your fucking pal! We're family."

"Except you don't know anything about my life."

"You think I woulda messed around with Colleen if I didn't trust you?" He uncrossed his arms, threw them wide. "So show me a little in return, okay?"

I pushed out of the bathroom. Colleen was sitting on the bed, listening, waiting. "He was in town on business," she said.

My back to both of them, I dropped my towel. *Kiss this white ass.* I pulled on underwear, jeans, the last clean T-shirt I'd brought. I could feel the air touch the slit of blood expanding on my chin, so I blazed past them, back to the sink.

Tommy called after me, "Why didn't you tell me you were gonna see my uncle?"

I watched a dot of crimson bloom on the tissue. Danny was linked to Tommy and Tommy to me, me to my father to Katie to Angelo and back to Danny. A chain of blood, each link weak. "I didn't know you'd care."

"So what happened? Who is he? What's he like?"

I looked away from the mirror. Tommy and Colleen stood side by side, framed in the doorway. He had a hand on her shoulder, but they looked not so much like lovers as long-time friends, already to a stage where working as a team came naturally. The space between them, filled with early evening light, orange and blue, glowed like a lattice.

"I can take you to meet him," I said.

Anxiety always works like this: You imagine every scenario but the one that comes to pass. Yes, the bungalow was unlit as Tommy and I crossed the empty street, passed the BEWARE OF DOG sign and the jungly growth, and made our way up toward the front door. Yes, the dog roared as if from an engine in its bowels, the sound of bared fangs, wild canine eyes, claws scratching the wall waist-high. Yes, we had to ring and then knock and ring again before the door sighed open the width of the chain that secured it. Yes, when Dean faced us—his breath fumey with booze, the Doberman behind him growling—he was unwelcoming, as expected.

But when I said, "I've brought my cousin, Angelo's son," Dean's eyes, framed this time by clear reading glasses, went wide. He commanded the dog to shut up.

We waited as he scrutinized Tommy. "Which one are you?"

"Tommy. I'm the youngest," he said, reaching out for a shake. The dog let loose a bark so loud I scurried back a step, but Tommy held fast, his hand suspended between the hard surfaces of door edge and jamb.

"You've got no business here," Dean said, but his voice wavered.

Tommy said, "I've come to pay my respects."

"Jesus Christ," Dean muttered. I watched him mull this over. For a moment it could have gone either way. Then he said, "I better put Victor in his room before he eats your kneecaps."

We walked into a space identifiable as a living room only by the TV set and two armchairs on either side of a coffee table, upon which sat a half-empty vodka bottle. The rest of the room was a homespun workplace, cluttered with the fits and starts of whatever vast, disarrayed project Dean occupied himself with.

My eye went directly to a reel-to-reel tape machine the size of a car windshield, set up in the far corner. A soprano's aria filled the air, though it came from some other source, because the tape was frozen on its spools. A microphone on a stand had been patched into the console. The room's longest wall was lined with file boxes, crooked as old brick face, each marked with a month and year going back to the 1980s. Down a darkened hallway I spied more boxes, the big kind for files and the thin ones for tape reels. Two long folding tables on metal legs blocked a sealed-up fireplace; each table was piled high with three-ring binders that sandwiched the lettucey edges of newspaper clippings. He must have subscribed to twenty or thirty publications; magazines were scattered everywhere. The room smelled like old paper, dog food and dust.

"Are these the movies you did?" Tommy asked. I had filled him in on Dean's career, and Tommy stood now facing a row of framed movie posters with titles in English and Italian. There were other framed images, too: signed photos of Lana Turner, Natalie Wood, and Ingrid Bergman, who'd penned, "To Dean, un ragazzo bello! Good luck."

"I was big in Italy. I had a part in a Rossellini film."

"Which one?" I asked.

"My scene got cut. I coulda been big as Warren Beatty in this country, and I woulda been, too." He left the room and returned carrying a plastic jug of concentrated orange juice, which he set down beside the vodka. "I don't know how strong you take them," he mumbled. He folded into an armchair and motioned Tommy to the other.

I fixed myself a screwdriver, then approached the reel-to-reel. "You've got quite a setup here."

Dean said he'd done some voice-over work in the seventies and later bought the machine from a recording studio. "Hit PLAY and RECORD," he commanded, and I did, sending the slender magnetic tape snaking through the gears. "Turn the mic around, facing us. You know how to work the levels, Radio Guy?" he asked. I said I did. He intoned a sound check: "Dean Foster, eleventh of April, the year 2000. I'm here today with some unplanned visitors—." He interrupted himself to order, "Turn it up. Up! Strong!"

"You're pushing into the red."

"That's right, I want to see a little red!"

I upped the needle into the squawk zone, dangerously tempting distortion. But, hey, it was his machine. He'd obviously run it a million times.

"You want me to leave it on?" I asked, unsure if this was just a demonstration.

"That's right. It's for the memoirs."

"You got a contract?" I joked.

He grumbled and flapped his hand at me, dismissing the technician from the set. His pinky ring glinted—a different ring, with an amber stone. Once again the stone perfectly matched the frames of his eyeglasses and corresponded as well with the orange sweater he wore.

Tommy cleared his throat. I didn't know if he was improvising or had scripted this on the way over, but he launched into a speech, his elbows on his knees, his hands conducting the air in front of him. Tommy the salesman, pitching a product: the family. He said he'd always wondered about his uncle Danny, always wanted to meet him; he was surprised that I had tracked him down; he was *truly honored* to be here. "I feel it's never too late to start a relationship," he said.

Dean's eyes drifted across Tommy like a spotlight scurrying to catch an actor, overshooting the mark, inching back. He landed on the expensive gold watch that flattened the hair on Tommy's thick wrist. "Is that a Rolex?" He waved his glass toward Tommy, who straightened up to avoid a splash. "You get an inheritance from your father?"

"Nothing much. My brothers got the business, and my mother—."

"They made sure I never got a dime!" Dean shouted. I watched the needle spike; from a dark chamber of the house Victor howled. I knew that the Ficchinos had started out immigrant-poor; I assumed whatever money Nonno Ficchino left behind went to his widow, who remained in their cramped Hell's Kitchen apartment until the day she died. But Dean was now recounting the *fourteen-carat jewelry, the Cadillac they sold that was supposed to be mine,* various *treasury bonds* in specific dollar amounts, as detailed as a list of this morning's groceries. "I had some legal trouble. I told them I needed some money. It was entrapment; it wasn't even my fault. But they used it against me—Angelo, Katie, and Rusty with his big mouth, who couldn't keep a secret if you paid him."

I'd been biting my tongue, but the mention of my father made me bold. "Aunt Katie's still talking about how you didn't go to her wedding," I prodded.

"I can't answer for my parents," Tommy jumped in. "But for myself and, you know, the younger generation, we like to think the past is the past, and let's move on."

Danny wasn't moving on. The past was the present; the curtains had parted and the ghosts were on stage. "How's I supposed to go to their wedding with this one there?"

"You mean my father," I corrected.

"Like father, like son," he said. Slurred, really: *like shun.* His anger had lit the fire of his intoxication.

"I'm not like him," I protested.

Tommy spoke up again. "Jamie had a rough time with his dad. Uncle Teddy didn't understand him."

"You got Rusty's same hair," Dean said, "and that mean face of his." From his chair he aimed a stare at me so intense, so hostile and belligerent, it could have sent a wild animal to flight. And it had, hadn't it? Sent me running into the street that morning. I hated him right then—but only as far as I'd failed to make him understand.

He was pouring himself another drink. I stepped to his side with my empty glass and leaned forward. Our faces hovered close, close as they'd been since the restaurant. In a directed, hushed voice, I said, "You're not the only cocksucker in the room, you know."

He lurched, slivers of ice tinkling in his glass. I waited for whatever condemnation would follow, but Dean remained speechless, mouth agape.

Tommy shifted in his seat, looking helpless. He'd bought a ticket to the wrong show; the ghosts were invisible to him. I had told him earlier that I thought Dean was gay, and surely the signs were evident—the pinky rings, the framed divas, the opera music soaring to the heights—but I hadn't given Tommy many details.

Dean regained his composure. He focused his stare on me, asking, "You ever had your heart broken?"

"I guess."

"If you gotta *guess*, then you ain't. I'm talking *the rug pulled out*."

"It's complicated," I said. Was my heart broken now, after Woody? Can you throw love away and still wind up with a broken heart—the boomerang of rejection? The thought of Woody brought an unexpected flush to my neck; or maybe that was the vodka, as I sucked down a mouthful, *gulp,* and felt it rise back up, *bam.* The boomerang of hard liquor. "I guess I'm usually the one pulling the rug."

"So you're as bad as your father."

"I wish you'd stop saying that."

"Your father broke my heart," he said.

"He broke mine, too," I shot back.

Tommy hopped to his feet, saying, "I gotta step outside to make a call." I watched him leave, fists swinging, gold wedding band on his left hand, chrome cell phone in his right, ready, no doubt, to dial Colleen.

"I don't trust any son of my brother's," Dean said.

"He's the best of the bunch. I wouldn't have brought him here if—."

"I don't trust you, either," he said.

"From the first time I saw your picture, I knew I had to meet you," I said, trying for a language he might understand. "I had to hear your side of the story. If I could just have an hour to ask you my questions."

Tommy returned before I got a response. "Colleen's wondering if we're gonna go meet her for that drink we talked about. Whaddaya say, cuz?" His eyebrows lifted, broadly telegraphing his need to be excused from this stifling room.

Dean was pouring himself more vodka. He glanced at me over the top of his specs and wiggled the bottle.

"You go," I told Tommy. "I'll take a cab back to the hotel."

"You sure about that?" I nodded. He approached Dean Foster's upholstered throne. "I'm very glad to have met you, Uncle Danny, and I hope to stay in touch."

"It's *Dean*," he said.

"If you need any help with anything, call me." Tommy presented a business card, offered a handshake, clasped his second hand onto their mutual grip.

He let himself out, and then it was just me and Dean, a couple of drunk drama queens arranged in an unlikely proximity on Teddy Garner's scorched earth. "It's ironic, you being homosexual," he said to me. "Because otherwise he got what he wanted."

"What do you mean?"

"A son! He wanted a son."

This sounded like a cue: I pulled out my tape recorder, set it between us. Dean looked at the machine with curiosity. He had questions about it: How it worked, what it cost, where was the tape? We were inching towards an interview. "Let's do this," I said.

"Aw, hell," he muttered." You're gonna ask me again? If I had sex with him?"

"There's a lot I want to ask you. But sure, for starters: Did you?"

"Yes. Once. The worst mistake of my life."

I didn't get that on tape. But he said it. Word for word, I'm sure of it. I remember the stupefied silence that followed as I went rigid from this admission. Forgetting to press RECORD. Forgetting, it seemed, to breathe.

Finally, composing myself, telling myself, *This is it, don't blow it,* I started the recorder and began.

Near as I can figure out, we're talking about June 1961. When my father came to visit you.

I came to Hollywood in, what, '59 or '60. Probably Rusty showed up with his suitcase about a year later. He wasn't going back to Frisco. We didn't have phones, see? You just drop by, leave a note if I'm not there. I have a definite memory of his note slipped under the door, because he had that scribble.

I've gotten pretty good at deciphering it.

He shows up, no money, no job, trying to impress me with this and that about San Francisco—the artistic types, beatniks, what have you. But wearing the same clothes from a year ago in New York. I said, "You look like a bum." Look, I'd done pretty well for myself right away, got an agent, met some showbiz folks. Six months in, I had a screen test for *The Roman Spring of Mrs. Stone*—which went to Beatty but shoulda been mine. I was a kid, but they saw I had *it*.

What did he tell you about his time in San Francisco?

Sounded to me like he spent a lot of time getting drunk by himself. And was always broke. And I got the feeling he might have made a few bucks hustling. You know the phrase "rough trade"?

Sure. But he wasn't—.

I suspected it, because he'd come to LA with a couple of homosexuals. I'm thinking he let one of those guys blow him in exchange for the ride.

I know about them. A guy named Don and—.

All I remember is something happened to get Rusty's knickers in a twist. "Can't trust these queers," and so forth. But in a way that made him more attractive.

I don't understand.

Because the thing you wanted was a real man. If you were a homosexual, you didn't want to have an affair with a pansy; what was the point of that? With "trade" you got someone who's masculine but also lets you blow him.

But was a guy who was "trade" considered straight or gay?

Trade was its own category, though many a time the trade turns into a fag himself. "Trade for a week, gay for life," was the joke.

Did you two ever have anything physical before this? Back in New York?

We dated girls, but it was more talk than action. Tell each other about your date, make it sound good and sexy, and meanwhile we're, you know . . . with ourselves. Next to each other on the bed, but not touching. Kid stuff. All guys do it, right?

I guess a lot of guys do. I did.

Rusty was my best friend. He took care of me. This was the West Side; they grow 'em tough there! *West Side Story*—that was our neighborhood, with the gangs. It's all gone now. They knocked it down for that place, the opera place—.

Lincoln Center?

Exactly. When I met Natalie Wood, I told her I shoulda been in *West Side Story*, because I *am* the West Side! Plus, I had my looks. Not to say anything, but most of those guys in that movie, they got nothin' in the looks department. I don't care how high they can kick.

You guys weren't part of a gang in your neighborhood, were you?

Rusty could have been; he had the temper. And his dad was a famous drunk. Once, I saw him throw Rusty down the stoop onto the sidewalk, arguing about who knows what. Did it right in front of all of us. Never forget it. And my brother, Angelo, was another one. What you'd call macho. He'd swat you on the head in front of your pals. Rusty wasn't like that, though he had a temper. So the tougher fellows would leave me alone because of him. The thing is, he was an A student. He got a prize once for an essay in high school, on the subject of citizenship, I think. We'd go to the museums or an art gallery or a foreign film. Not too many from our neighborhood went down to the Village for a foreign film.

So why'd you go to California?

I went for Hollywood! I had the looks. Me and Rusty argued about it, because he said San Francisco's the place. Not for me. Plus I figured, put some distance between us. I was pretty hung up on him.

It seems like he wrote you a lot of letters, but you didn't write back much.

He sent me pages of that chicken scratch. I burned them all.

You burned them?

Look, kid, don't get upset. I was crazy about him, but there was no point with a guy like Rusty. He got bent outta shape because I took him to a bar—it was an actor's bar, but he looked around and saw a lot of homosexual clientele. He said he'd had enough of that in San Francisco. "You better not be one of those fruits, too." And so forth.

Were you "out" at the time?

Well, discreetly. You didn't just walk around like today with your so-called pride. What are they proud about? Because their ass is hanging out? You didn't talk about it—but that's Hollywood. Always been that way, and still is today. I met Henry Wilson, the famous agent. He had Rock Hudson, Troy Donahue, all of them. Let Henry blow you, and he gets you a part. I had talent, but they can't see your talent; first thing they see is the face. Any pretty boy who's made two pictures in Hollywood can fill a book, because the casting couch ain't just for women. Which is the title of my memoir, *The Casting Couch Ain't Just for Women.* If you catch my drift.

I catch it.

So there's Rusty saying, "I'm gonna stay with you in LA." "Okay," I say, "but you gotta give me some privacy." "For what?" Which is when I let him know.

So how did he respond?

First the temper. "No way, you can't be one of them, Danny," and so on, as mean as his father. Then he calms down and gives me the theory he'd come up with. He had some name for it—"The Theory of Three." A guy was a one.

A worm?

A *one*. A guy was symbolized by number one. Like a stick. And a woman was symbolized by number two, because, I don't know, she had two tits, or two sides to her twat, or something. Pardon my French.

> *This was a concept he came up with himself?*
>
> I've never fucking forgotten it. One plus two equaled three, which was the baby, and that was the Law of Three. But one plus one equals two, see? Two guys together make a woman out of both of them. He had it all worked out, psychologically speaking. So after we make it, he's telling me this theory.
>
> *After you "make it"?*
>
> Yeah. Since you're dying to know, that's what wound up happening.
>
> *What wound up happening?*
>
> What you'd call a quickie. Like with trade. Jesus Christ, you're a ballsy one!

All through this, he'd poured a steady stream of vodka down his throat, and here he swept his arm wide and lost his grip on the glass, which crashed into pieces. The noise set off a volley of muffled barking from the Doberman. Dean raised himself from the armchair, calling out, "I know, Victor, I know," as if the two of them were in telepathic agreement on some familiar subject. When I rose to help, Dean told me to sit. He kicked the shards under a table and left the room without explanation.

As I waited through the sounds of Victor's howling and Dean's shuffling feet, I phrased and rephrased my next question, searching for the right words to ask what he meant by *a quickie*—what Teddy, for all his theories and protestations, permitted himself. This was not prurience. I had accumulated so many words about my father, but together they clouded the truth. I wanted the specificity of an image, of an action, even if it came from the drunken memory of Dean Foster. I knew I would never hear it from Teddy himself; Dean had burned the letters.

But when Dean returned, already in mid-sentence, my tongue, swollen and sluggish with booze, betrayed me. I couldn't force myself to demand the gory details. I wasn't as ballsy as he thought me to be.

—so I wake up and he's gone. The next day. Not even a note. I kept thinking I'd hear from him, because he was the writer, but—nothin'.

Did you ever see him again?

One time in New York, when I went back for the movie. The beach picture—you saw that one. He showed up, and afterwards we did some drinking at my hotel. Come to think of it, maybe that's when he gave me the Theory. And he said some nasty things to me; I should get help, I was sick.

Is that why you didn't go home for the wedding?

I had a picture to shoot. Did you see *Encounter in Tijuana?* We had Ava Gardner on that one, but it did lousy box office. I played one of the cops. I had a scene with her where I say, "A lady like you might want to remember what she was doing on the night in question."

You didn't skip the wedding on purpose, but because of work?

They said I should squeeze in the trip, and maybe I could've, I don't remember. I woulda had to stand up there with Rusty, in the wedding party, two groomsmen, after the thing he'd said to me. No way. Katie says, "If you don't come, your brother'll never speak to you again." No one ever let me forget it. Angelo, Katie, no one. Like I said, biggest mistake of my life. Don't fall for a straight guy.

So you think Teddy was straight?

Not as straight as they come, but yeah, in the end. Straight. And then here's the kicker: He tells my brother that I'm in Hollywood with a homosexual crowd, and my brother tells me he wants me back in New York, to keep an eye on me. Let me tell you, there was no respect, not from a one of them. Then I was on my own, and my career would have taken off, but because of the arrest.

This is the arrest you mentioned before?

That was entrapment. By the police. And they never had proof of anything!

Entrapment?

Sure. You're in a public toilet just taking a leak. And the police used to do that—they'd go into a john, and the stinkin' guy would be undercover, right? And he'd have his, you know, hanging out at the pisser—not hanging, at full mast, gettin' himself aroused on the taxpayer's dime. Good work if you can get it! All I did was give it a look. What're you supposed to do, ignore it? But they arrested me for lookin'. Then they tell your employer, which in my case was the studio, and then your agent can't get you work. And the kicker is, my agent was dabbling with all the young actors who had good looks and wanted a career. If you let him suck you, you got a part. The casting couch ain't just for women, which will be the title. And I got all the names. You listen to these tapes, you'll hear every one.

Did anyone back home know about this?

The word got out. I had no work in Hollywood after that. I said, "Angelo, send me some money," and he said I had to come to New York to pick it up, but no way. I couldn't have a career in New York. And I was supposed to get the Cadillac and split the bonds and the jewelry, and Angelo said only if you come to New York. "I'll come for the funeral, but I'm not staying." And they didn't give me any of my inheritance, not even after the funeral.

Your father's funeral? Did you see Rusty there?

> I think he was in the Army. I don't remember. I'd crossed him off. But I never forgot. You don't forget. He said he was taking care of me by trying to get me out of the homosexual lifestyle. Sure, and tell my brother and steal my inheritance? Every step, someone stole from me. Now you tell me, what kind of love is that? Even in Italy, I was a big star—made five pictures, with my face in the European magazines—and they took it all. And Hollywood has a short memory. You get a couple of breaks, that's it. They'll see, though. The research I've done. I've got every newspaper clipping put together, and I know where the money flows and who's sleeping where, and I'll get the last word. They're going to remember Dean Foster. When I'm through with them, they're gonna know my name.

There was more, but it was increasingly less coherent, and at some point I stopped asking questions and let him exhaust himself. He eventually drifted away in his chair.

When I stood, the room spiraled away from me. My brain was a disturbed sea sloshing behind my eyes, my stomach queasy: vodka for breakfast, popcorn for lunch, vodka for dinner. I fumbled my way to the bathroom—painted and tiled in a late-sixties aqua, which under the low-wattage light seemed the very hue of nausea. Within a minute I was letting loose one, two, three, four explosive blasts of vomit, so powerful they seemed to be emptying not just my stomach but my mind, my senses, my emotional reserves. The heaving was so violent that I entertained the thought I was dying, but it left behind an immediate calm, and within moments I felt cured, a citizen of a new, cleansed world. I washed up to the sounds of the still-growling Victor, poised behind one of these closed doors.

I discovered the kitchen at the back, strewn with even more newspapers. The fridge held only orange juice, tonic water and old condiments encrusted around their lids. An enormous trash bag filled with vodka bottles slumped against the wall like a giant, sad stuffed animal. I found a box of glazed donuts in a cupboard and shoved a few into my mouth. The healing comfort of sugar. On the wall above the Formica kitchen table was a rotary phone. I pictured Dean standing in this very spot after he had received the letter I'd first sent him, ranting into the mouthpiece about his privacy. I dialed Colleen and got her voice mail. I told her, "I'm through here. I'm ready to go home."

In his armchair, Dean remained unconscious, head drooping, mouth open. I hit STOP on the reel-to-reel. I snooped in a couple of those dated boxes; nothing more than news clippings inside. I found no manuscript, no Proustian prose epic in the making. I suppose the memoir existed only in oral form—decades of recordings, a treasure trove of magnetic tape. What would he do with it? Was any of it transcribed? Perhaps that was why he'd been dropped by his agency—failure to produce anything on the page. Or maybe it had been his personality, careening between its twin poles—sober and intimidating, and bombed and melancholy—all that was left of the optimism that had once allowed him to boast, a year into his Hollywood dream, *You can say you knew me when.*

It was time for me to go. I found a broom and dustpan and cleaned up the broken glass. On a scrap of paper I penned a good-bye note; my hand was shaky enough to rival Rusty's infamous scribble, but it was important to acknowledge this night, these confessions, and not simply skulk away. At the front door, I turned back one last time to see if he would wake. He didn't stir. In the morning, what would he make of all of this? When he played back his recording, would he regret having spilled so much? Would there be a new angry message waiting for me when I got back to San Francisco?

Outside, the humid air was a cool, damp towel, a balm for the hangover I felt coming on. I wasn't quite steady on my feet, but I'd be okay. Either Colleen would come looking for me or I'd flag down a cab or I'd stumble my way back to the hotel. Whatever happened next I would handle. If it took until dawn, I'd handle it.

ECSTASY

23

My apartment hummed with emptiness when I got back, more so because there were signs that Jed had been here: a pizza box in the trash, a CD in the player that I'd never seen before, a dialogue box cautioning that my Mac had been *improperly shut down*. In the bathroom I watched gray water drain at the speed of melting ice, the pipes clogged, I guessed, from another arm-shaving session. I could picture him here, back from whatever trip he'd taken, expecting to find me waiting, dispersing his excitable energy into rooms that were stale with cigarette smoke and years of inertia—a picture that left me hungry to see him and unsure what I wanted when I did. This delayed plan, this escape to Baja—what if he was ready to go? I'd gotten to the end of my search; did that mean I was free to leave, too?

First things first. My bank card was on my desk, where I'd expected it. I walked to the nearest ATM, touched the key for my balance and crossed my fingers, waiting through one of those unnaturally elongated moments during which doom and hope spin past like slats on a wheel of fortune. Where would it stop?

AVAILABLE BALANCE: $9,000.

Thank you, Deirdre. I don't know what it took, but I thank you.

I walked to the check-cashing vendor on Mission and 16th to pay my phone bill. There, under a cold fluorescent glare, I eavesdropped on a conversation between two women standing on either side of me in the slow-moving line. They had some shared history between them, the specifics of which I couldn't quite figure out; this seemed to be their first conversation in a long while. One of them wore sunglasses, dark as her skin, shuffling in place as she sipped from a paper bag. The other was tall and straight spined; when she flicked her long, cornrowed braids, she was positively regal. She wore a MUNI uniform and talked with great pride about her regular paycheck, her religion, her sobriety. "Girl," she said to her friend, "I gave it *all* up."

"I only have a little now and then," Sunglasses mumbled, washing down her words with a chug from the paper bag.

Braids told the story of bringing her *babies' daddy* to court to collect child support. "That asshole had the nerve to stand before the judge saying he can't pay for our children because he's got a *fungus* on his foot. He takes off his shoe right there and waves his ugly warts around."

"Stop! What'd all you do?"

"I said, 'Oh, no. I am a child of God. Do not bring your voodoo to me.' "

She was deadly serious, but I had to look away to suppress a smile.

When I got home I broke out my checkbook and went down the list of what I owed. Landlord—pay him. Utilities—pay them. Even if I went to Mexico with Jed, I would need somewhere to return. Dentist—sure, they'd been nice about everything. Collection agency—yes, get them off my back.

And Woody? I owed him nearly two thousand dollars. I could probably get away with not paying; he hadn't been bothering me for it. But *getting away with it* was, I saw, my own brand of sneaky voodoo. I was not a child of God, was not about to *give it all up*; still, I went ahead and wrote this one last check. I enclosed a note:

> *There are things I would do differently, if I had the chance. Maybe this will begin to clean the slate.*

I labored over each measly word, each possible misinterpretation. I signed it, "Love, Jamie." This seemed important, this "Love." Not open to interpretation.

My phone line reactivated later that day. My voice mail was at capacity, and most of the messages were from Deirdre, updating me on her money situation, wondering where I was, wondering why she hadn't heard back from me, worrying some more, and finally announcing that she'd booked a ticket to San Francisco for herself and AJ. They'd be here in a week.

"I don't know if that's such a good idea," I said when I called her back. "I'm not even sure I'll be here. There's this trip to Mexico."

"You're broke, and you're planning a vacation?" There was a sharpness to her voice.

"It's not a vacation. More like a retreat. A getaway."

"You stay put until I get there."

"What is this, some kind of *intervention?*"

"It sounds like you need one."

"Everything here is under control."

"Good. Then it's a perfect time to visit."

I made more excuses—*my apartment smells like cigarettes, there's nothing for AJ to do*—but she knocked them down one by one. The tickets were purchased. They were coming.

"Dude, we should be leaving *yesterday,*" Jed said, digging into his pocket to pull out a wad of what appeared to be twenty-dollar bills. "Mission accomplished on the herb. *Vamanos, amigo*."

He had reappeared as I was pillaging my kitchen cabinets—pulling out the remaining expired products and tossing them in the trash—and he unspooled his tale of traveling to San Jose to unload the pot, which involved a series of mishaps, including getting sucked back into the drama of his mother, stepfather, and the Stanford professor. It was vintage Jed: sounding true enough to earn my sympathy, without erasing my doubts that I was being played. "I can't change my sister's plans," I told him.

He asked if they would be staying here, and when I said yes, he said, "Which means I'm not, right?"

I paused, a half-spent, years-old jar of popcorn kernels in my hand. "Where have you been staying since you got back to the city?"

"With Bethany. But her boyfriend's coming back today."

"Maybe you can stay at Ian's. He has an empty room."

"Maybe I'll just leave without you."

"No!" I sucked in air, surprised by my own vehemence.

He stretched, drawing up his shirt, then dropping a hand to his exposed abdomen. He rubbed there, as if polishing an apple: pink skinned, juicy, maybe poisonous. Until that gesture, I had breezed past my sense memories of his flesh. Now his physical presence, so knowingly flaunted, lit the flame again. *Don't fall for a straight guy*, Dean had said, and though Jed wasn't exactly straight, I recalled the warning like a slap, and I turned my eyes away.

"Can't you just give me a week?" I asked.

"A week," he said. "But that's it."

Jed went to Ian's. I forgot to ask him for my share of the money. I forgot even to ask for my keys back.

I spent that week alone in my apartment, cleaning. *Deep cleaning* was what they called it at the bed-and-breakfast, a twenty-room Victorian mansion, where I'd worked when I first moved to the city; once a month the maids would be scheduled by the inn's portly owner, who spoke in New Age platitudes but was really a petty tyrant, to *deep clean* the premises. The phrase summoned up an extra-powerful vacuum sucking grime from the depths of the carpet and streams of concentrated ammonia sluicing along the mildewed grouting beneath clawfoot tubs.

With Deirdre and AJ coming, I charged ahead, cleaning not just deep but also high and wide. I got down on my hands and knees in the kitchen with a soapy, hard-bristled brush, laboring over every dingy streak on the pale linoleum; and I reached from a chair with the vacuum's extension wand, targeting the dust-caked picture rail. I did it with only coffee for fuel; the pot pipe stayed in a drawer, no wine sat waiting on the counter. I wasn't even smoking cigarettes. I'd run out in LA, and rather than borrow one more dime from Colleen, I rode all the way home without a single puff. This was surprisingly easy at first. I'd developed a slight but persistent head cold that last night in LA, trudging through the damp, smoggy air in my vodka delirium. Now the very idea of taking smoke into my lungs hurt.

For a week, my dreams were vivid, upsetting, embattled. Inspired by Ginsberg, I started leaving my journal, much disused lately, next to the bed in order to record what went bump in the night: *Chased on foot by malicious figures, can't see their faces, their bodies are sharp, angular, like shadows in expressionistic art, but goofier, more like Spy vs. Spy in Mad Magazine . . . Woke sweating cornered by monstrous face, horned, bloody—the devil? Seemed to be trying to speak to me but I wouldn't listen, wouldn't respond . . . In an old movie palace all the seats have bad views and I can't see the screen no matter where I sit. I find a seat near Woody but I fall and am kicked in the head by people in the aisle. I fight back kicking and swinging and finally bite into someone's skin, but I don't want to be so cruel. I wind up in the back of the theater, it looks like a stadium, big wide halls wrapped around. A young skinny guy in an old-man's sweater approaches. He looks me in the eyes and says "All cru-alities are relative."* I remembered this last one vividly, the epic search of it, the violence and remorse, the strikingly odd face of the guy in the striped sweater—wizened but youthful, a boy-witch—and his strange phrase. *Cru-alities:* Was that supposed to mean *cruelties? Dualities*? *Cruel realities*?

Each dream was a confrontation in which I remained mute. Only on the night before Deirdre arrived did I speak: I stood facing a crowd in what was supposed to be Jerusalem but looked a lot like the Tenderloin. Again I had been chased, but now my pursuers stood at bay, willing to listen. Like bile churned up from within, what was to be communicated began to rise, hot as steam and thick as custard, from my loins into my stomach and throat. It burned and choked, but I knew it had to come forth. As if pregnant, I was at its mercy until the end. Freed from the cage of me, the words finally erupted into creatures of flight, bats and birds and fish with wings, and I heard my voice, the voice of a deaf person who has never known speech, say, "Ecstasy."

As I left my apartment to meet Deirdre and AJ at the airport, I ran into Eleanor, who, while shushing Dinky, told me I had woken her from sleep in the middle of the night. She said, "Honey, you were shouting."

"I'm having crazy dreams this week," I admitted, and then added, "I'm quitting smoking." As soon as I said it, I wanted a cigarette, and in that moment—the illumination of the craving—the decision was made. I was not just taking a break, I was quitting. I was done with it.

Ecstasy isn't just a drug, but what the dream brought back were memories of drug trips. There was the most recent, with Jed, the frightening climax of which I now saw as inevitable, given that I'd been faking my identity when I swallowed the truth serum. There was the first occasion I ever took E, with my ex, Nathan, who had spent the whole time delivering an aggressive, gloomy monologue about decay and apocalypse—which also now seemed inevitable, given the degraded state of our relationship at the time. Unlike those couples who slowly stagnate, our excessive passion had been a dying star growing bigger and more fiery as it approached its demise.

And I remembered the visit Deirdre and Andy made to San Francisco a couple years before they married. For a week I took them to the usual tourist stops, all the while complaining how *touristy* everything was. I wasn't trying to act superior; I truly didn't know what else to do with them. My own routine was limited to a handful of bars and cafés in the Castro and the Mission, places I didn't think they'd like or that I'd decided they shouldn't see lest they gawk or feel uncomfortable around the fringe dwellers who made up my life. This was before the mid-nineties, when the fringe became fashionable.

On the second-to-last night of their visit, we went to a party at Colleen's, where we all took ecstasy and—no gloom meisters among us—swelled toward the expected declarations of love. Expected for the drug, though not for Dee and me. We had never spoken to each other in those terms, and even the artificial inducement of the moment didn't detract from my sense that we made a breakthrough that night: We'd demonstrated that we were capable of purer feeling. As for Andy, he wore a fool's grin throughout, unable to form words. When I gushed to him, "It's so great the way you're looking out for my sister," he struggled to respond, finally coming up with, "What me and Deirdre have is above average." Thus, for the night, he became Above-Average Andy.

After that party, Dee and I had joked that she should smuggle a capsule of E home and break it into Dad's nightly glass of milk. It was tempting to think that a single magic bullet might have punctured my father's steely membrane; hadn't ecstasy first been produced for clinical purposes? Dee and I hadn't spoken "I love you" more than a couple of times since then; ours was a breakthrough deferred. *Purer feeling* was no match for the family structure that positioned her—a new wife and mother—at the center of things while forcing me into self-exile. Maybe ecstasy was no match for the *crualities* of all relatives.

That trip was seven years ago. The truism is that it takes seven years to regenerate every cell of the body. Deirdre and I were new beings now, at least physically. That was my hope. Like in the old saw: *Together again for the first time.*

I took BART to the end of the line, then transferred to an airport bus. I got there on time, gifts in hand: a pink Gerber daisy for Dee and a kid-size soccer ball for AJ. The first thing I noticed as she came through the gate was how her hair, pulled back from her face, had reverted to its natural muddy brown. As she craned her neck to look for me, I saw the last of her frosted highlights tied together like a shaving brush at the back.

Then I realized she was alone. We hadn't even pulled out of our hug when she launched into the story of how AJ had pitched a fit as they were packing—a marathon of tears that lasted all the way to the ticket counter. "Finally I said, 'I'm going, and you're staying here,' and he calmed down. Andy said I should go without him, and if AJ regretted it later, too bad. His own fault for being such a brat."

"Is it possible for a five-year-old to need space from his mother?" I wondered aloud.

"I've never left him alone for this long." She was already digging into her purse for her phone. "I almost called home from the plane, except it's like five dollars a minute to use that thing on the back of the seat."

I squeezed the soccer ball, which felt puny and inadequate in my grasp. I'd been nervous about AJ coming, worried that I didn't know how to be an uncle to a five-year-old, especially on my own turf, so I'd made preparations, searched the guidebooks for activities for kids, bought a few videos I thought he'd like.

Deirdre's thumb was skating atop the keypad. "Hi, it's me . . . Yeah, it was fine. How is he? . . . He didn't say anything? . . . Okay, let me talk to him . . . Hi honey, it's Mommy. I'm with Uncle Jamie. Are you okay? . . . Really? . . . You're sure you're okay? . . . Mommy loves you a lot."

She hung up as I was mouthing that I wanted to speak to him. "Sorry, he had a friend over," she said.

"Rejected by yet another male in the Garner family!" I swooned, touching the back of my hand to my forehead. The sting of my nephew's absence surprised me—for God's sake, the kid was five—but it was real, just the same. Still, I didn't want to increase Deirdre's anxiety, so I added quickly: "We'll just have to figure out how to have fun without him."

At baggage claim I asked about Nana, who was starting to walk again, her spirits finally lifting, and Deirdre asked about Woody. I told her a version of our breakup so vague it must have been obvious I was editing out the unflattering stuff. The last time I was at this airport I'd stood at this very carousel with him, and I could visualize now his face as I'd reacted to his question about the stain on my shirt. Exiting the airport in the car Deirdre had rented, I sat in the passenger seat, as I had that night, just three months ago, when Woody had driven me back to the city. I had felt then that something new awaited me, in the form of the box I'd carted from the attic. What I hadn't known was that this beginning would also bring about an end. Or had I? Had I provoked it? I saw him in the driver's seat, headlights moving across his face. Even in the darkest moments of that ride there was still a gossamer glow upon him—the orange light of the city at night—and he wore a patient smile, the kind you reserve for someone in whom you've placed your trust.

I snapped back to attention, to Deirdre at the wheel asking me if I could recommend a hair salon. "I cut my own," I said.

"You do?" she deadpanned. "I couldn't tell."

"Very funny. We'll ask Colleen," I said. "She'll know." I told Dee about Colleen quitting her job, about how she was going to follow her longtime dream of designing her own clothes, starting with classes in pattern making and tailoring. She wasn't going to waste any time, would turn the situation to her advantage.

"You haven't told me about going to LA," she said.

"It's a long story."

"Well, we've got all week." She patted my thigh. "Just you and me."

At the touch of her hand, I felt an unexpected lightness: I'd have her to myself, adult to adult, our time not dictated by the needs of a child. Then the chime of her cell phone, that wireless umbilical cord, tolled again.

When we walked into my apartment, Jed was visible at the far end of the hall, sitting at my computer, bare chested.

"I can't figure out how to work your modem," he called out. Behind him, in the living room, stood a girl with short, mangled hair, a black hooded sweatshirt, black Dickies cut off below the knee, and lace-up boots. She looked like Colleen ten years ago, a *riot grrl*, possibly lesbian, with a pretty face and a stance like a wrestler.

"That's my Bethany," Jed said, his thumb arcing toward her—though what I heard was, "That's my Bentley," as if he was instructing a valet to park his car.

She said, "Hey, 'sup? I'm Bethany," and flagged her hand at us. "Nice crib."

"This is my sister, Deidre," I announced.

Jed popped to his feet and charged down the hall with his tattooed arm extended, his every muscle taut. I flicked on the overhead light and his nipple piercing twinkled. He had never appeared more sexual than he did at that moment, gripping my sister's hand, then backing far enough away to afford us both a prime view. Deirdre's eyes roamed frankly across his skin, like he was a gigolo I'd hired to surprise her.

"Your brother's awesome," Jed said to her. "He's totally helping me out."

Deirdre nodded, looking confused, and excused herself to go to the kitchen for a glass of water.

I stepped close to Jed. "Why is your shirt off?"

"I was gonna borrow one from you."

"Dude, you need to go," I said.

"This won't take long. We can stay out of your way."

"Why can't you use Ian's computer?"

From down the hall, Bethany spoke up. "We're not, like, *into* Ian right now." Jed sliced his hand across his neck, twice, a gesture directed at Bethany but done broadly enough to ensure that I saw him reining her in. This annoyed Bethany, who grumbled, "It's no secret he's on a power trip."

Jed turned his full attention to me. "Everything's chill. No worries."

The phone rang. I moved past Jed, down the hall. "Hello?"

"Jamie? Ian. Is he there?"

Jed had joined Deirdre in the kitchen. I could hear her voice questioning him, though the question itself was obscured. Bethany had plopped on the couch and was sagging forward, her knees knocking together. There was a blanket of neutrality about her: She could have been annoyed or embarrassed or just plain bored.

I asked Ian what had happened—what *was* happening, right now?

"Did he tell you about the broken window?"

"What window?" I looked around the living room.

"At my place. Never mind. Tell him to wait there. I'll be right over."

"No, Ian. Deirdre's here."

"Jesus Christ." I heard him flick a lighter and inhale. "Put him on," he said through the muffle of smoke.

Jed answered my summons by marching halfway down the hall and then pausing abruptly, his head dropped, his hands on his exposed hip bones—a pose meant to indicate some necessary collecting of thought, or maybe he was just pouting over whatever he'd done to piss off Ian. He and Bethany were an army of nonverbal gestures, dramatic but open to interpretation.

I walked out of earshot as soon as he took the phone. Whatever this was, I didn't want to know. Back in the kitchen, Deirdre asked, "How old is he?"

"Nineteen." Seeing how poorly this sat with her, I added, "I'm helping him out," before realizing this line was Jed's from a moment ago.

I heard the phone bang onto its cradle, followed by the amplified sounds of the modem beeping and hissing. With a deep, weary breath, I trod the hallway once again, coming up behind Jed and Bethany, who were hunched over the keyboard, complaining in turn about the slow connection.

"I need you to clear out, dude," I said. "And I need the keys."

Jed looked stung. "My keys?"

Bethany muttered, "What did I tell you?"

"What *did* you tell him?" I asked.

"You're not gonna go to Mexico," she said.

Jed forced a laugh. "Bethany's a trip, right?" I could see distress gathering in his eyes; I remembered the story of that Stanford professor shipping Jed out before the faculty party.

I said, "This has nothing to do with Mexico. I just need keys for Deirdre while she's here." He pushed away from the desk and stood facing me, clearly agitated. "Please," I said.

He reached for my shirt, his fingers gripping a clump of material above my heart, and tugged, pulling me off balance. "I miss you, bro," he said. His head fell humbly forward and his eyes rolled seductively upward. Then his lips covered half the distance between us and, magnetized, mine traveled to meet him: a full, wet lock that I let continue too long. *I could kiss him like this in Baja*—a thought that produced no image, no warm anticipation, just a question: *But what would I have to give up?* I pulled away, tasting tobacco in our spit.

After he left—grabbing a shirt and taking Bethany with him—Deirdre asked, "Is he why you broke up with Woody?"

"No," I said hurriedly. And then, sighing, "But it's related. It's all related."

We stared at each other, grappling for words—she obviously trying to form another question, me tossing around exactly what I meant by *all*. When it came to what went wrong with Woody, how far-reaching was the web of circumstance?

Finally she said, "I should take a shower," and the subject was dropped.

After showering, she napped, and I paced the apartment, desperate for counsel. Ian was the obvious choice, but Jed might be with him. The only other person who knew anything about Jed was Colleen. I called her at home, prepared to blurt out the one question on my mind: stay or go?

But Colleen preempted me, saying, "Speak of the devil."

"What's that mean?"

"There's someone here who wants to talk to you."

She handed off the phone before I could protest. My stomach lurched violently, expecting Woody.

"Hey, dude, long time no anything." Not Woody—Brady.

"Wow. Yeah, it's been a while," I said. "What are you doing there?"

"I was telling Colleen about a rad warehouse party this weekend. There'll be bands and DJs, and Annie's showing some of her new artwork, too. You should come."

"My sister's in town."

"Bring her along. It'll be amazing."

"Maybe."

He cleared his throat, a sharp sound that I recognized as distinctly his, calling up an image of his face: dark eyes, straight hair, slightly soft chin. "Jamie, I've sent you like a hundred apologetic e-mails. You gotta talk to me."

"I know. We're due." I smiled at how genuine he sounded. "I just needed some time, I guess."

"So what's new?"

"Where do I start?"

"Colleen told me you tracked down that guy you were looking for, the one your father knew."

"It was pretty intense. I haven't quite absorbed it." He wanted to hear details, so I sketched him a portrait of Dean Foster: the reclusive B-movie actor with decades of audiotaped memoirs in his home, the movie career blunted by entrapment, and his—my—family's homophobia. I could tell Brady was impressed. Laying out the story so succinctly, I impressed myself. "I haven't called him again, but I should."

"Hell yeah! You've got to get ahold of those tapes, man. Don't you get it? This is what you've been looking for. Dude, you've got your *angle*."

In an instant, I understood what my future held. Here, in San Francisco.

* * *

"I have something to show you," Deirdre said. From her suitcase, she retrieved a photo album, its binding cracked and its cover so rippled with age I immediately knew it had come from the attic.

"Dad's?" I asked.

"It was Mom's. There's so much stuff of hers up there. I've been digging through it, trying to figure out who she was." She added shyly, "I've kind of been inspired by you."

She flipped the album open to a grid of images from our mother's childhood in Germany. There was Shirley, a bright, fair girl in plain clothing, standing in a vegetable garden, green beans snaking up poles in the background; and again, proudly displaying the hens she helped her parents raise on their few acres of land in Bavaria. My mother was born in 1945, just after the end of the war. Her father had fought briefly for the German army, was quickly injured and went back to his village to take over his family's land. Even in the aftermath of the war's devastation, my mother's childhood seemed more placid than my father's in New York, where everything was a struggle for the Garners. They met each other in Germany. He was in the US Army, and she was a teenage waitress at a restaurant run by one of her uncles, down the road from the base where he was stationed. The final pages in the album featured pictures of them together.

Deirdre said, "Mom used to say that the soldiers were like boys playing dress-up. But Dad already seemed like an adult, because he took time off after high school."

"She always said he stood out," I recalled, lingering over a handsome shot of Teddy in his khaki uniform—sturdy, though not yet the imposing block of granite he would become. Black-and-white photography turned his copper hair a gleaming silver. Under the brim of his cap, his serious face was anchored by two impossibly pale eyes, notably without expression.

He was only in Germany for a year, but by the time he left she was wearing his ring. The following year she got a student visa, came to the States and lived with the family of a cousin in the Bronx. Here Deirdre filled in some details, things she'd recently learned. At City College, Mom took science classes, hoping to be a veterinarian. Dad was in school back then, too, working on a bachelor's in literature. (I remembered that he wrote his final undergraduate paper not on Kerouac or Camus, but on *The Great Gatsby*, a book he reread every year.) They married after school was over. It was very simple, the whole thing: Meet, fall in love, set up your future together. Much simpler, I now knew, than what came before for Teddy.

"Look what else I found," she said. She pulled a tiny object from her purse and handed it to me.

A gold band. His wedding ring, the one I'd searched for and failed to find, the one he was to have been buried in.

"I got rid of Dad's bedroom furniture," she explained, "and there it was beneath the dresser, half stuck under the rug."

"I looked there," I said, though in truth I couldn't remember how thorough I'd been. There were gaps in my memory of that week in New Jersey—the funeral itself was almost gone, as if I'd had a fever the entire time, half-asleep while the world spun around me. Until I entered the attic.

I tossed the ring from one palm to the other. It weighed less than expected. I suppose they hadn't had the money for something more expensive, more solid. On the inside was an inscription, a single word: *Always.*

Deirdre said, "I think you should have it."

I blanched. "What am I supposed to do with it? Find a wife?"

"Right, like I've come all the way out here to tell you to go straight." The look on her face told me I was being rude, ungrateful, that this was meant to be a gift. She tried again in earnest. "You might want to exchange rings with a guy one day. I read in the paper they're doing these civil ceremonies in Vermont now."

"I could never give a guy this ring," I said. "It's a symbol of something I don't understand."

"They loved each other. You understand that."

I let it drop to the table. It bounced—three rapid, hard sounds without reverberation. She stared at it, at me, at it, at me.

"Why don't you save it for AJ?" I asked, hoping to appease her, and when that was met with further silence, I returned to the album.

The last pages were from their early years of marriage. Square-format snapshots in faded colors, framed by yellowed edges. Beaches and parks and mountains. The two of them dressed up for a night out with Angelo and Katie. Shirley was a fast learner, an American girl with a Marlo Thomas flip, Capri pants and canvas sneakers. Teddy kept his military haircut all through the sixties. There was a shot of them moving into our house in Greenlawn, a truck backed up to a path bordered by the same purple azaleas that bloomed there every spring. Another of the tree at the foot of the driveway, the one that fell into the street onto the Angry White Lady. And one of Shirley showing off the new living room wallpaper, a ghastly web of metallic blue curlicues. "Remember that?" Deirdre asked. "It was awful."

"I'd kill for it now. A San Francisco apartment in those hideous sixties patterns would be flawless."

"You can't wallpaper a rental," she said, perhaps innocently, though I took it as a dig.

"Some of us didn't inherit enough to buy a house."

"Please tell me we're not going to fight about money," she said.

I breathed deep and relaxed my shoulders. A flash of Dean Foster ranting about gold jewelry. In forty years I did not want to be griping about my inheritance.

You wouldn't know from these pictures that Teddy and Shirley's generation was about to explode, that in San Francisco the hippies were already wearing flowers in their hair. But what use did a girl from a German village have for an American revolution? The album ends in 1966, the year before I was born, when Teddy *got what he wanted*, a son. Though not the son he wanted.

I'd seen nothing like this photo album among Teddy's San Francisco artifacts, no pictures of him with Ray, with Don, with Chick and Mary. Those few images of Danny had been buried, not displayed. Teddy had sketched and poeticized his Frisco days, but a couple years later, in the light of Greenlawn and Shirley and the routine he would lock himself into, he put away his notebooks and loaded up the camera. *This is what we show the world,* was the message. *The permanent record.* I scrutinized the photos for some trace of the identity he'd claimed and abandoned in San Francisco, some glimpse of remorse or disconnection.

"What's that look on your face?" Deirdre asked.

"With everything I know about him now, all this . . ."—I swept my hand across the evidence—". . . feels like a betrayal."

"What are you talking about? This was the happiest time of his life!"

"But he had been on track to have another life, in San Francisco. If he wasn't so freaked out by what was inside of him, he could have been artistic and unconventional. Instead of playing house with his perfect wife."

"That wasn't *playing house.* That was our family." She slammed shut the album, pulling it away from me as if I might do it harm.

"I can't help it, Dee. I'm still so angry with him."

"Apparently you're angry with *her,* too."

We began to argue, another version of the argument we always had, the one about how neither of us understood the other. It ended with her pushing away from the table, the album hugged to her chest, her footfalls trailing the carpet to my bedroom—which was her bedroom for the week, her door to slam.

I stood up and went to the counter, where I kept my cigarettes. But they were not waiting for me.

Apparently I am. Angry with my mother.

My mother, with her love for my father, who did not love me. My mother, with her English so perfect she might have been schooled in Britain. With her blonde hair so perfect. Blonde beehive, blonde shag, blonde 'fro, blonde perm. *Don't take my picture, I haven't set my hair.* With her eye shadow to match her dress. With her apron at the stove. With her gold cross on a chain around her neck; with her prayers to the Father who did not listen. With her hand on his shoulder as he's about to blow. With her eyes on me, *Don't push him.* With her arms around me, saying, *I'll talk to him.* With invisible blonde hair on her upper lip. With a razor for me, *You're becoming a man.* With her smell of tea rose (I dab some on in the bathroom). With tears in her eyes (I forgot Mother's Day). With tears in her eyes (I'd yelled, *He can go to hell*). With tears in her eyes (I'd saved Deirdre from a bully). With cotton soaked in alcohol she cleans the scratch on my face. With hand twisting in mine we dance to the radio. With a hand white with flour, *Can you turn down that noise?* With face stricken in worry, *Were you smoking tobacco?* With perfect English slipping, *Vat if your father found out?* With arms wrapped around him, with checkbook balanced for him, with meals waiting at six, with excuses for him at the ready. With stoked fireplace, with sewing machine buzzing, with fondue bubbling. With chest pain, *It's nothing,* with not answering the phone all day, *Something's wrong.* With blonde hair matted on hospital pillow, with surgery in an hour, with last words, *Go wait with your sister.* Without good-bye.

She says, *He had a hard day at work. Don't let it bother you.* She says, *He's just mad. Don't let it bother you*. She says, *He only wants the best for you. Let me talk to him for you*. Did you talk to him, Mom? What did he say? But that's not what I meant. Should I talk to him now? Later? Never? But I don't understand. But he doesn't understand. What do you mean, it's nothing? It never gets better. What do you mean, I know he loves me? He never shows it. What do you mean, your heart hurts?

What do you mean, her heart stopped?

He says, *I expect dinner at six*. He says, *There's nothing to talk about*. He says, *Don't be mad at God, be mad at the hospital*. He says, *I can't be there. I'm meeting the lawyers*. He says, *It's not an excuse for your grades to suffer. I expect to see an improvement. I expect the student-loan paperwork filled out by tomorrow.* He says, *Jesus Christ, what were you thinking?* He says, *Jesus Christ, are you wearing her perfume?* He says, *I don't want Eric in this house again. I don't care what you feel. It's sordid. I know where it leads. It's sordid. If your mother was here to see this, my God.* He says, *Alcohol is poison*. He says, *I ever catch you doing drugs, so help me*. He says, *Most people who think they're artists just want to goof off. What makes you think you know better? What makes you think I don't know what you're up to?* He says, *When I make mistakes, I learn from them. Responsibility breeds respect. You show me one, I'll show you the other*. He says, *You show me another woman as good as your mother*. He says, *She's turning over in her grave.*

Yes, apparently I am. Angry at them both. This anger like an album of photos, frozen in time. Frozen before I had figured anything out. Orphaned in a house of ice.

Apparently I have been walking through the Mission looking for cigarettes. As if storming out of my apartment could remake the past. As if this cigarette between my lips could soothe the pain. The burn of tar in my throat does not; pulverizing the half I don't smoke does not; giving the rest of the pack to a homeless guy does not. Sitting on a bench avoiding Deirdre does not soothe the pain.

Nine thousand dollars in the bank will not purge grief from my body.

A box of keepsakes from the attic will not purge the grief.

Danny Ficchino's secrets will not.

Teddy himself in the flesh, age twenty, a cigarette in his mouth and booze on his breath, traveling with me to Mexico, not asking, *What's wrong with you*, when I reach out my hand—Teddy himself might purge the grief.

I am orphaned. Deirdre and I together, orphans. Orphans who cannot change the past but can grieve it. Must grieve it.

When I got back to my apartment Deirdre was still locked away. The wedding ring sat on the kitchen table. I picked it up. It was too big for my ring finger. I slid it on my thumb instead.

I tapped on the bedroom door, waiting to be asked in. This must be what a parent feels with a teenage child: It's my domain, but I need your permission to enter this corner I've ceded to you. She was propped up in bed, reading what I immediately recognized as Teddy's writing. *In the Woods.* "I glanced at these pages before I mailed them," she said. "But I didn't notice how much he sounds like you."

"Colleen said it's his obnoxious attitude." I sat next to her on the bed. "That seems to be something everyone can agree on."

"Not obnoxious." Her eyes squinted into the window light behind me. "Opinionated. Saying things to get a rise out of people."

I nodded, ready to get a rise out of her. "I found Danny Ficchino."

She said, "I was wondering when you'd mention it."

This caught me off guard. "Did you talk to Tommy?"

"He called, right before I came here. He didn't paint a very pretty picture."

"We have Dad to thank for that."

Her eyes narrowed, as if in doubt. I began to fill her in on what I'd learned—Danny and Teddy's sex, Teddy outing Danny to the family, Danny's arrest and ostracism—and little by little her hardened expression went slack. When I was through, she asked, "Did you believe him?"

Did I? It hadn't occurred to me not to, though he might have said anything, for any reason. His tongue might have been just another bleeding wound, spurting. But no, no. That wasn't fair. He'd come around to trusting me. He'd been waiting his whole life to tell someone this story. Someone in the family.

"I do believe him. Though I was a little afraid of him. He was drunk and bitter. Very isolated."

"I worry about you, Jamie. That you'll become like that. Cut off." I started to protest, but she charged ahead. "Tommy told me about you in LA. He thought I should know. It freaked me out to hear how broke you were, and that you'd been drinking a lot. And something about running out on a restaurant bill—."

"Did he tell you what he was doing in LA?" I spat out defensively.

"He was there on business."

I came close to ratting out Tommy's fling with Colleen—if Deirdre wanted to sit in judgment I could give her plenty to judge—but a vision of Tommy with his hands clasped around Danny's, Tommy the Ambassador of Reconciliation, stopped me.

She said, "To be honest, I was afraid what I'd find when I got here."

"Is that why—?" I was going to ask, *Is that why you planned this trip so quickly?* but then another suspicion took shape, this one more damning. "That's why you left AJ at home, isn't it? Because you didn't want him around me." She averted her eyes. "That's fucked up, Deirdre."

"For all I knew, the place would be a mess, you'd be drunk, or evicted—."

I jumped to my feet angrily, talking over her. "So you're here to save me?"

"—and then I get here, and there's this half-naked teenager who you're going to Mexico with."

"You may not understand my life, but I've always made it work."

"Not lately," she insisted.

"No, not lately. Lately, I've been unhappy. I've been sad. I'm just starting to understand that. But you've been unhappy, too."

"I'm not unhappy!" Her voice cracked. We both heard it.

"You ever think you might have something to learn from me?" I shouted. "Or that AJ might like it here, might need a change from the routine you and Andy lock him into, trying to keep him from harm at all costs? Ever think you don't have all the answers?"

"I know that," she yelled back. Walking through her adult life, Deirdre held the reins on the very air around her, but in this moment she appeared vulnerable and unguarded. She looked, for a change, like my baby sister.

"When Danny Ficchino was in trouble," I said, stepping closer, "everyone turned away. Aunt Katie still denies what happened. She acts superior about her family while she's cutting off those of us who don't fit the bill."

"I'm not Aunt Katie." Her voice fell, hushed. "I've always made an effort."

"Not when it came to Dad. You took his side."

"I didn't take his side, Jamie. I just took care of him." She held out her hand. I followed her curled fingers back to the bed and sat down, facing her. "I tried, Jamie. I did. I'm sorry I failed. But at a certain point, I understood that I couldn't make him love you. Not the way you wanted."

She took my hand. Her hand was small boned, like our mother's. Her palm was dry and warm; mine was damp with nerves. She squeezed. I didn't pull away.

There was nothing for me to say. I believed her. She'd tried, but he'd been impossible. And then he'd lost his mind.

He hadn't loved me, not the way I wanted, not the way a father is supposed to. If he had, I wouldn't have spent months trying to find some version of him that, in my grief, I could relate to, maybe even learn to love—some Teddy I could imagine loving me back.

Deidre and I stayed in that night. I cooked dinner, and we drank wine, three bottles between us. I had stories to tell her, stories recent and long-buried, and she had years to recount to me. We didn't raise our voices to each other again, didn't fall into the same old argument. That argument was unwinnable. The man at the center of it was dead. He'd been dying for years, while we'd raged on.

Before bed, we made each other promises, which we swore to keep.

In the morning there was a shyness between us, an emotional hangover that compounded the actual hangover. Standing in the kitchen, quietly sipping coffee, each of us wearing the clothes we'd slept in, we were like a new couple after a date that wasn't supposed to have ended in a sleepover.

She'd already been up for an hour and had put a call in to Andy. "I've got news," she told me. "Aunt Katie's going to take Nana for a few weeks. So they're coming."

"Who's coming?"

"Andy and AJ. In a couple days. They're going to spend the rest of the week in San Francisco. You're right, Jamie, I shouldn't have kept them away." As I tried to imagine the four of us in my apartment, the walls shrinking even as I pictured it, she added, "Andy reserved a hotel room."

"With what money?"

"We didn't lose everything," she said. "We won't be moving into our dream house, but we're not going to be homeless, either."

"Are things between you two okay?" I asked.

"They've been better," she said, her voice surprisingly calm. "But we've been together long enough to get through shit like this. Plus, what's the alternative?"

"Couples break up over less."

She shook her head firmly. "I don't believe in divorce."

Looking at Deirdre in the morning light, I felt a peculiar longing for her company, as if she'd already checked into a hotel with her husband and son. For all the flare-ups of the day before, she had been mine, all mine. I couldn't remember any previous time like that, couldn't imagine something this rare happening again any time soon.

"So what did you want to do before they show up?" I asked.

"It's up to you. I don't want to interrupt your schedule."

I laughed, trying to conjure up anything resembling a routine in my life. "Usually I'd be stoned by now," I said.

"This early?"

I shrugged. She concentrated on her coffee cup and after a moment said, "Okay."

"Okay what?"

"Get me stoned."

I asked her several times if she was sure about this, then I made her call home once more before turning off her cell phone. "Rule number one," I pronounced. "Don't talk to anyone who's going to make you feel paranoid or guilty because you're high." I packed a very light bowl; a little goes a long way for someone who isn't a regular imbiber. She coughed her way through one puff, then a second, then guzzled a glass of tap water and disappeared into the bathroom. A few minutes later I found her pressed up to the mirror, studying her skin.

"I'm getting old," she said. "I have little wrinkles here, and here. But I still get blackheads. How is that possible?"

"No mirrors for stoners," I said. "Rule number two." I was playing a version of Party Nurse, more psychological than pharmaceutical.

"Mom was so pretty," she said. "I got the worst of both of them. His big head and her overbite. His peasant legs and her ears."

"You don't have any of those things!" I said. "I got the worst of their personalities. His stubbornness and her superficiality."

"You're not superficial," she said. "People who are materialistic drive you crazy."

"But that's just a pose, isn't it? I have all these rules to make myself better than anyone else."

"No, you have principles," she said. "The only thing I believe in is getting AJ to school on time."

"You're loyal," I said. "That's the most important thing."

Flush with the morning that had risen from the long, hard night and warmed into new intimacy by the pot, we'd slipped into a little love-me game: I'll tell you what's wrong with me, and you reassure me that everything's fine. To play the game you have to know ahead of time that it will go well. Allowing ourselves to dive in was an act of faith.

We walked into my backyard, which once upon a time was a cultivated garden but had long been left untended. Even wild it showed the seasons, such as they are in San Francisco: wet, green-grassed winter; a spring full of dainty white wildflowers and California poppies, the most orange of flowers; and then the dry, yellowed summer, the dirt gone to dust until August fog brought back moisture and sent an old rose bush into early-autumn second bloom. Two metal chairs, their webbed rubber seats cracked with age, rested in the center of a concrete island too small to qualify as a patio. An enormous flowerpot, lopsided and chipped, sat there, too, stuffed with cigarette butts, most of them my brand. I could shovel them out now, erase the toxic evidence; or I could leave them, a reminder of all the foul air I'd let myself breathe. I thought about telling Deirdre that I'd quit, but to say so seemed like a jinx.

At Colleen's recommendation we called a salon on South Van Ness that turned out to be staffed mostly by drag queens out of drag. Deirdre described the highlights and cut she wanted. The stylist, Stefan—an androgynous, lanky European in perfectly snug, low-slung jeans and a pink Izod cropped high—immediately began lobbying for something completely different: "Let's go dark, with chunky blonde strips, and bring it up shorter in the back. It'll be flawless with your heart-shaped face."

I could see the panic in my sister's eyes. "I'm a soccer mom from New Jersey," she said.

"Girl, you are going to feel ten years younger when I'm done with you, and all those other soccer moms are going to be mad with jealousy, not to mention copying you a year from now."

They haggled and came up with a compromise—shorter and darker, yes, but make those blonde chunks blend in, please. I watched him go to work, my eyes drawn to the exposed strip of his hairless belly, which was soft without being flabby, like a teenager's, and so at odds with his adult face, which bore the permanent expression of someone who'd seen it all. I complimented his hair, which from forehead to neck rose to a center ridge, like a Mohawk but without the sides shaved. "We're all about the faux-hawk right now," he said, and sure enough, I would see this style everywhere within two months. "I can give you one," he told me, and even though I protested that my hairline was too high, the hair I had far too wispy, he assured me he'd make it work.

"I'm kind of going for a more down-and-out look lately," I said.

Stefan was having none of it. "You keep letting this red mop of yours grow, honey, and the only look you'll be working is Bozo the Clown."

Deirdre, hair gooey and wrapped in foil, piped in, "I'll pay for it, Jamie," and that sealed the deal.

"You're going to clean up nicely," Stefan purred at me.

Afterwards, we met Colleen at the Orbit Room, drank elaborately garnished electric-blue cocktails, and soaked up her praise. It was important for Deirdre to hear; she'd been worrying that she was somehow ruining her image with a hip hairdo.

I think it had been a while since she'd felt good about herself.

24

Andy and AJ were scheduled to arrive the next evening. I felt an impending panic, as if my brief spell at the ball with Deirdre would end at the stroke of midnight; tomorrow it would be pumpkins and cinders. Colleen had invited us to join her at the big party she was going to that night, the same one Brady had mentioned on the phone. It would be held in two connected warehouses, one space featuring a dance floor with different DJs, the other a stage where local bands would play. The warehouses were slated to change owners, and the artists who'd been collectively renting there for years had already begun to relocate to Oakland. This would be their farewell blowout. When I checked my e-mail that day I found a note from Ian about the same party, saying he was thinking of going. *I'll bring Junior,* he wrote. At first I thought this was a code for some new drug until I realized he meant Jed.

I floated the idea to Deirdre, warning her to not get her hopes up, that it might not be her scene. "Are you kidding?" she said. "I never even go to the movies anymore."

We went shopping for clothes that afternoon. I bought my first new pair of jeans in years, the first in a very long time that weren't standard-issue Levi's. Jeans were being reinvented: lower at the waist, higher in the crotch. The *relaxed fit* days, thank God, were over. Still, I complained that they were too trendy—they belonged on fashionistas like Shane, the temp transcriber who took me out with his friends, not on secondhand types like me. But Deirdre told me they made my ass look good. "Isn't that what you gay guys want?"

We took a taxi to a street the driver didn't even know, in a no-man's land on the far side of Potrero Hill, almost invisible for the way it was squeezed between overlapping freeway ramps. We had to wander through a row of unmarked industrial buildings on foot before we found the parking lot and then trek down a wide alley to get to a back-door entrance, shielded from the road to distract the police, no doubt.

I'd been worried that we were getting there too early—it was only ten o'clock—but the crowd was already gathering. Deirdre paid for our entry, ten dollars each, and we made our way through a dimly lit corridor, which opened on a three-story cavern with walkways and decks built-out overhead. We found Colleen with one of her girlfriends, a regular at this space who explained that people were showing up early in case the party was shut down, but that if it went all night we'd see *some amazing things.* "Everyone's coming," she said. "They've got DJs from every scene in town. Total cross-pollination." I left Deirdre with them and made my way to a bar set up under a wall of monitors flashing cartoony animation. Unlike at an actual nightclub, everyone was patiently waiting their turn, chatting with strangers in line.

A slim guy in a fancy, deconstructed red sweater—all seams and pulled threads—and a pair of jeans not unlike my own, though definitely a few inches narrower at the waist, stood in front of me, the overhead light playing on the shine of his dark hair, turning black to almost blue. He was swaying to the trancey house music filtering in from the dance floor, his head tracing circular patterns, like an eraser on a wipeboard. I developed an entire fantasy based on this limited glimpse: Instantly I had this guy showing up at my clean, smoke-free apartment, flowers in his hand, a dinner I've prepared for him already in the oven, those German knives sharp and gleaming on the counter. I cast him as a *wunderkind* architect, artistic but financially solvent, who wanted nothing more than to take care of my debts and bring me to gallery openings and offer me his ass every night, his face in the pillow, that black hair in my fist . . . I had inched my way forward for a better look, but when I got next to him I felt a palpitation in my stomach that snipped my fantasy in mid-fuck: I recognized him. He did a double take, and I watched his eyes try to determine how he knew me.

"What's up?" he said, with a cautious smile.

"Ready for a drink," I replied.

"If I get there first, I'll order for you."

"I need three."

"That's okay. I can hand them back."

"Um, okay." He still hadn't put it together. "You're Roger, right?"

"Yeah, where do I know you from?"

"Jamie."

"Oh!" Alarm in his eyes as it clicked. "You're Woody's, um . . ."

"Yeah. He introduced us at that lounge."

"Right." He returned his attention to the bar line, craning his neck like a driver trying to determine the cause of a traffic jam. He saw Woody every day. He probably knew every terrible thing about me.

For weeks I had thought of him as my rival, though that was never true. I said, "Sorry I was an asshole that night we met."

"I was kind of tacky myself."

"Don't mention it," I said, though I was glad he had. "How's life at Digitent?"

"You didn't hear?"

"No."

"The Magoo deal is off, so Digitent is over. The official line is: 'scaling back to a core staff to re-vision the corporate mission.' That's a quote. Today was the last day for most of us. We've made this our unofficial pink-slip party."

"So, is *everyone* here?"

"Woody's coming," he said, understanding my question.

I started to ask if Woody had also lost his job, but Roger had reached the bartender. He passed back drinks in plastic cups. I dug out my wallet. "Don't worry about it," he said. "Severance pay."

I watched him maneuver away, three drinks pressed between his two hands, pausing to air kiss a woman in a tight denim jacket with a white fur collar. Someone else from Digitent? I lost sight of him before I could see if his path might lead to Woody.

Deirdre and Colleen were not standing where I'd left them. I looked around and spied them off to the side, in an area set up as a gallery. Through the thickening crowd, I saw Colleen introducing Deirdre to Brady and Annie. Brady wore an untucked cowboy shirt, one of his party staples. His arm was over Annie's shoulder, his head nodding along with whatever small talk Dee was making. I had known they would be here, but this first sighting after so long set my nerves aflutter.

Annie spotted me before he did. With a forced smile—clearly she was nervous, too—she said, "I can't believe you're here."

"Brady told me about it," I said.

"But I can't believe you're here," she repeated.

"Hey!" Brady beamed. He slid away from Annie and pulled me into a hug that was a near calamity, as I still had three drinks in my hands.

For once in my life, the moment didn't end in a crash of cups and spilled liquid.

"Your sister's awesome," he said.

Deirdre took her drink and toasted me. "We were looking at Annie's art," she said.

Annie's art consisted of drawings sketched with thread on fabric, usually of San Francisco cityscapes—houses, telephone poles, parked cars. I'd always liked the way her handmade technique remade the solid world, the structures we take for granted, into something delicate. Two new pieces, sewn onto colorless muslin, hung on the wall. The imagery was the same, but her treatment of it had gotten looser: threads were left hanging, the ends matting together in tangles as if the subject matter was decomposing, these familiar sights no longer sustaining their form. It was almost mournful.

"Does this have something to do with you guys looking for a place to live?" I asked her. "A feeling of displacement?"

She turned to study her pieces as if she'd never seen them before. "Sure. Why not? I never know what I'm doing until someone else looks at it."

"I haven't told you," Brady said, "but I've totally hooked up with the folks who are throwing this party, and I'm getting in on their new digs."

"What do you mean *getting in?*" I asked.

"We're moving to Oakland."

"I'll get a studio out of it," Annie said.

"No," I cried. "Don't go! Don't leave San Francisco!"

"It's gonna be awesome, dude," Brady said. "The place is basically a radio station, with webcasts 24/7. It's mostly been music, but we're talking about expanding that. You should get in on it, man. They need content people."

I hadn't seen them in months; I'd nearly written off Brady as a traitor. But now the idea that I could lose him to the other side of the bay was crushing. I think he read my mind; he tried to assure me it wasn't that far.

"Without a car, it's not that close," I said. "I need you to help me edit this new piece. The one we talked about."

"Definitely. That one's going national, dude."

He held up his hand for a high five. It was as good as a contract.

I leaned toward Annie and said, "I heard Woody's coming." She nodded. "Should I talk to him?"

"Sure, if you run into him." Her response was guarded enough to sound like discouragement.

With Deirdre, I began exploring the upper levels—an intricate, teeming compound. Wooden staircases rose up to mezzanines with views down to the stage; catwalks connected to decks where kitchens, bedrooms and studios had been fabricated. On the eve of abandonment, most of it had been stripped of possessions; a few couches, futons and little tables cluttered with cups remained. Here and there we saw a computer screen flashing patterns. I smelled Nag Champa incense, spilled beer, skunky pot, an occasional cigarette, what might have been poppers, what might have been Earl Grey tea, occasional perfume, a faint hint of mildew. Conversations rippled along snaking lines for the unisex toilets.

Deirdre and I checked out each nook and cubicle, searching faces, eavesdropping here and there, noting body language when the noise was too strong. The crowd was mixed—not like in Teddy's day, when mixed meant mostly gay with enough women thrown in to ward off suspicion. Today *mixed* had more to do with style: postpunks in black anarchist gear, gay party boys dressed up tight and shiny, glam women with startling hairdos, ravers in fake fur brandishing glow-in-the-dark toys, the pagan-faerie-Burning-Man crowd in anything. Hipster fashion was changing. Child of the seventies (ironic T-shirts, wide collars, polyester pants) was giving way to Fashionable Rag Doll (stripes and patterns paired together as if nothing could ever clash). In our new retail outfits—my ribbed black sweater, her satiny blouse—Dee and I looked too dressed up, though I can't imagine anyone cared but me.

"Are you okay?" I kept asking her, and she kept saying yes, her fate in my hands as we wandered, until someone sloshed a drink on her open-toed shoe and all at once her frustration seeped out.

"Are we going anywhere in particular?"

I'd been roaming with such efficiency, I realized I could only be looking for Woody. Understanding this, I grew terrified that I'd find him. I saw his face concentrate, his lips tighten, his eyes narrow under their expressive brows: his unhappy reaction to my sudden appearance. The camera closed in, soap-opera style, both of us staring meaningfully. What would I say to him?

"I just wanted to investigate," I said.

"Can we stand in one place for a while?" she pleaded softly.

"Good idea," I said, espousing fail-safe party philosophy: "If everyone keeps moving, no one finds anyone." Choose a well-positioned spot and let him come to you. If you're lucky, he will.

"How about we watch the bands," she suggested.

We climbed back down and entered the second, attached warehouse. On stage a six-piece band called the Cubby Creatures was performing a song that went:

You should always know your own diseases
You should always take care of them.
You should always know your strengths and weakness
You should always want to be my friend.

It sounded like gypsy music, with a violin, a clarinet, a bass line like a sitar's, a keyboard like an organ and some kind of Tibetan bell dinging at the beginning; halfway through the drums kicked in and the whole thing transformed into a lover's argument, the lead singer turning against the one he'd beseeched. I couldn't imagine what Deirdre made of it, but she swung her body as though she listened to this kind of thing every day. Maybe it was because the band was having so much fun she could only catch hold. Or maybe it was the little puff of pot she indulged in when Brady joined us. I waved away his pipe, a swirl of colored glass. I'd already downed my drink too fast; my instincts blared a warning about getting fucked up. Not my plan tonight.

The audience thinned out after the set, but we lingered in place. Brady and Deirdre had gotten enmeshed in a stoned dialogue about marriage. She'd asked him if he and Annie planned to get married, and he'd responded with, "Why would we?"

"Marriage keeps you honest," she said.

"But married people lie to each other all the time," he said.

"But they know when they're breaking their vows, which makes a difference."

"Vows are cool, but the institution—it's just a social pressure."

"You can't make a life with someone," she insisted, "until you make that commitment. Then you have a history together."

"Does the couple make the commitment," he asked, "or does the commitment make the couple?"

I still had my father's wedding ring encircling my thumb. His commitment to my mother had been honest and true, but I was plagued by the notion that he had broken some commitment to himself. Could he have loved her with the same unwavering bond, and set up a life with her in the same structured fashion, but still found a way to admit that in his past was another kind of man, the disordered soul of an artist and writer who sought intimacy in less traditional ways than marriage, who had once conducted an affair with a married woman, who had given his body, briefly, to men? Does a marriage vow let you disavow whatever came before?

Or was I trying to mold him into the man I wished he had been, as he had done to me for years?

Standing in that room, aware of the revelry surrounding me—conversation, music, the enlarged antics of the fired and evicted—I felt all at once fragile, as if I were transporting eggs in my pockets.

I excused myself, leaving Deirdre to Brady, and went outside for air.

The alley was lined with smokers. In the shadow of a solid, corrugated-metal fence, I walked through their exhalations. I felt no craving, only curiosity: what to do with my hands—which is to say my mind—without the usual, reliable gestures, the smoke-colored illustration of what it means to pass time, breathing.

Farther along the fence I caught sight of a motorcycle and two guys talking heatedly beside it. I recognized that it was Ian's motorcycle before I recognized Ian . . . with Jed. They shuffled apart at the sound of my approaching footsteps. "Jamie!" Ian called, sounding relieved. "Junior can't get in. They're carding."

"Didn't they ever hear of *all ages*?" Jed complained, his eyes locking on mine. "I've been waiting for you," he added, his face half in shadow, making it difficult to read. More difficult than usual.

"Are there any other doors?" Ian asked. "Anyone who could bring Jed in? Maybe with a girl they'd let him in. Is Deirdre here?"

"She's here. Everyone's here." I looked from one to the other. "I'm told that Woody's here, too."

"Did you talk to him?" Ian asked.

"Not yet. But I plan on finding him."

Jed thrust himself away from us. "Fuck it. I don't want to go to this stupid boring stupid fucking party." He strode off, his rant continuing in mumbles.

"It's been mood swings for days now," Ian said, loud enough for Jed's benefit. Then he moved closer to me, confiding, "All he talks about is leaving town with you."

"I'll speak to him."

I caught up to Jed a few paces down the alley. He turned around, his eyes darting, the look of someone thinking fast, planning contingencies in anger. I reached out my hand, pulling his focus to me. We leaned against the fence together.

"What's going on?" I asked.

"Nothing's going on. That's the problem. I'm sitting around waiting for you."

"Maybe you shouldn't wait," I said gently.

"You told me to, until after your sister leaves."

"I know. But I'm not sure I'm ready to pack up my life."

He stepped closer, laying his palm on my chest, the same gesture he'd used to compel a kiss from me in my apartment. I felt that flutter in my throat again, like a bird that has spied an approaching cat. Or was I the cat, whistling the bird nearer and nearer, ready to swallow it whole?

I sloughed off his grasp. "I have to go back to the party."

He moved in again, trying to close the gap. "You got a haircut. It looks trendy."

"Every person I know is in there, Jed."

"So?"

"So, if you can get in, great, and if you can't, I'm still staying."

"Are you getting back together with your boyfriend?" His voice split on *together*.

"This isn't about Woody," I said. "It's about my life here. The life I already have."

"I don't get you, dude. I don't fucking get you." He stormed past me. In his anger he was as sexy as ever. The inverted triangle created by his wide shoulders and narrow waist was an arrow pointing to his ass. It scared me to want him, to be just one more person using him.

"I can be your friend, Jed." A used-up line, but it stopped him midstep. I tried again: "Brothers, right?" He was facing me now. "Please don't be mad," I added, a plea that I thought he'd understand, that he'd first used with me, the underlying meaning of which I finally comprehended: *You have to trust me on this one.*

I watched him think this over and then reject it. He forced himself past Ian, toward the parking lot. Away he went, among the car hoods splattered with streetlight.

"I have to let him go," I said, so softly that Ian, approaching, misheard.

"Yeah, go back inside. I'll deal with Junior." He shouted Jed's name, but got no answer. "Hey, are there any queers in there?"

"Definitely."

"Okay, I'll be back." He lifted his helmet, started to walk away.

"Ian? Tell him I'll talk to him later, okay?"

"Okay."

"And one more thing—."

"Yeah?"

"Just, thanks. For sticking with me, helping me out. All of it."

He sauntered over with an almost romantic swagger. His arm settled on my shoulder. "You're number one," he said. "Everything else is just . . . keeping things interesting."

He touched his lips to mine, and as he pulled me into a hug I recalled exactly what it had been like to first kiss him at the Detour in the light of a pinball machine all those years ago. We'd both had thicker hair and thinner waists, and what we knew about each other was pure imagination. What had lasted was this: the sense that as soon as I knew Ian, I knew everything about him, and was willing to give him as much in return. The time was always now. The manifesto was eternal.

Jed had retreated into silhouette. I had assumed he was only pouting, a tantrum fueled by impatience and jealousy. I might have done things differently if I knew I would come home that night to a voice mail from him telling me he had left—off to Mexico, or wherever the road would take him. His raspy voice forced back emotion, saying, *You should be coming with me*, while I stared at that goddamn Darth Vader head, entertaining the thought that he might be right. If I had known all this, I would not have let our last words at the party be angry ones. I would have tried harder to explain to him what he'd given me, which was different than what I'd simply taken. I would have offered him my blessing for his trip. *You have a lot of living to do*, I might have said, as Ray had written to Teddy when she set him free.

Ian's bike gunned, its light snapping on—a roaring brilliance cracking open the darkness, parting stragglers from its path. I watched as the distant figure of Jed assumed shape in the headlight. Words I couldn't hear flew between him and Ian, with aggravated gestures to match. For an instant, Jed turned his face my way. I waved, and he sent me a nod so deliberate and grave it looked like a signal. I had read it as *Later, dude,* but he'd meant good-bye. He took Ian's extra helmet, swung a leg over the bike and was carried from my sight.

* * *

I had avoided the dance floor. There were gay guys circled together in groups, with shirts off or with shirts on tight, accentuating the armature beneath. For years I'd let this breed of peacock bother me, but now I thought, Maybe I don't care. The effort it took to be annoyed by someone else's good time was a waste of my own. So in I went, dodging elbows and arms extended with drinks, *leading with the hip*, as a queen once taught me. Getting through the crowd is a treacherous thing no matter how many times you have braved the dance floor.

I knew where to stop, at a beam of mote-heavy light, an empty disk of concrete floor waiting to be occupied. I settled in, and my arms began to piston, sending my body in search of the beat. Around me: a white chick in cool glasses at two o'clock; a dark-skinned guy with dreads and a Brazilian football jersey at four; and at six, one of the only drag queens in the house, towering over everyone. She could have been almost any race, but her hair was a white girl's pure platinum, blown sky-high as if from dynamite. With her was an adoring admirer, a handsome hipster in silver sneakers, striped pants, a sleeveless T-shirt pulled tightly over a short-sleeve button-up. He had curly brown hair, thick eyelashes, a face full of silly expressions. The kind of guy you look at and think, *My next boyfriend should be this cool.*

The beat overtook me, like a guardian angel making all my decisions. Without trying, my arms and feet were in sync. I was busting out little moves I hadn't tried in ages. I positioned myself in the direction of the drag queen, hoping her friend would peel his eyes away from her, so I could partake in the simplest kind of flirting: smiling at a stranger on the dance floor.

Then my eyes landed on Woody's face above the hopping masses.

His movement, that head bob, was so familiar it took the air from my lungs; his shorn hair still surprised me. Disco lighting, scarlet-gold-violet-blue, refracted in beads of sweat on his forehead. I had to avert my eyes just to get my breath back, and then immediately needed to see him again. His hairline, so prominent now without the curls, was like a pencil sketch of a bird in flight, a line dipping to a point, then swooping up again. Concentration tugged at his brow. I caught him counting his steps, his lips fluttering so imperceptibly you wouldn't have noticed unless you knew to look. I knew. He stood far enough away that he wouldn't necessarily see me, and each time a twitch in his cheek or a torque to his shoulders threatened to send his gaze toward me, I snapped away. To him and away. To, away. I didn't know which was worse—that he'd catch me looking or that he wouldn't notice me at all.

He was dancing with the woman I'd seen Roger air kiss, celebrating their freedom from the dot-com sweatshop. His tongue escaped his mouth and poked past his upper lip, catching a drop of sweat slinking down his cheek. His shoulders were sweat soaked under a white V-neck, overhead light carving crescents of shadow from his clavicle. *He wears those V-necks to work under button-up shirts. Did he come to this party right after they fired him?* Did he even know I was here, as I knew he was, long before I stumbled on him in the only place I hadn't already looked.

We were sharing the same room for the first time in weeks. We were breathing from the same reserve of air. Standing near enough to watch him lick his lips, I felt it like a kiss. Jed, Ian, Woody: It was a night of remembered kisses.

His dancing was still awkward, less endearing without those collegiate curls framing his manly forehead. *He'll never be a good dancer.* An unkind thought: It took effort not to be hurtful. My thoughts like spears, poisoned at the tips. He had given me his trust, and I was careless. I thought I could throw plates to the floor and they wouldn't break. I thought I could hurl the boomerang without getting nailed myself. I thought I could hate my father and not hate Woody.

I looked away for too long, and I lost him. I could stay with the beat and look again later. Or I could chase him. I had no reason to believe he wanted to speak to me. But I wanted him to know I had something to say, if he let me.

A guy stepped into my path. Shadowy eyes caught my glance. "Holy shit, it's you!" His voice unmistakably excited.

"How's it going?" I said, trying to recall where we'd met. We'd had sex, that's all I was sure of. Cornered by a trick as I tried to reach Woody.

"Do you remember?" he asked, grinning with mischief. Brown skin, close-set eyes, a prominent nose. Give him a baseball cap and a backpack and—.

"Newark Airport," we both said, a jittery release. I felt heat in my neck.

"It's Rick," he said, hand on his chest as if pledging allegiance. Or he might have said Rich. I had trouble hearing so close to the speakers.

"What are you doing here?" I asked.

"I'm staying with some friends. They said this was the best party in SF tonight."

"Are you still traveling?"

"This is my last stop before I go home. I love it here! It's so fun! I've been all the way around the world." He named countries I'd never visited, never even considered. He asked, "Did you ever finish *On the Road?*"

"You remember that?"

He smiled that smile again. "You did me a big favor, Jamie. It set the tone for a lot of my . . . adventures."

He was charming. I saw why it had been so easy to hand myself over to our instant infatuation. If I hadn't broken a pact with Woody, I would never have looked back on this with shame.

Stranded in an airport lounge, two strangers intersect, a random collision that should mean nothing but alters everything. Each proceeds on a tangent according to the force of that collision. And what if they'd never met? What if I hadn't followed Rick into that rest room? What if I hadn't been reading Kerouac that day, attracting his interest? What if that box in the attic hadn't sparked my curiosity; what if I hadn't gone into the attic in the first place? What if my father and I had spoken in the years before he died, if I'd been forgiving of him, or him of me, no matter what the personal cost?

All these influences we cannot control, bleeding into the moments when we must choose: the power we take versus the mercy at which we are placed. In the face of this, *What if* was the perpetual, imprisoning question, the one without an answer. The dead end inside the maze.

I brushed a hand along Rick's cheek, surprising myself with how tender I felt for him, which was really a tenderness for the human heart—for my own, for Woody's, for Jed's, none of which I had been tender enough with; and for my father's, the mystery of which I was implicated in, even now, after the quest, as I suppose I had always been. *You are part of me,* I might have said to Rick, as the chaos of pleasure tornadoed around us. But I chose to say, "Take care of yourself," and I kept moving.

If everyone keeps moving, no one finds anyone, but sometimes you can't sit still. Sometimes it's up to you.

Past the dance floor, in the far reaches of the warehouse, an enormous, enclosed structure had been built: a temple, woven of branches. Braided wooden walls twisted fifteen feet high toward a minaret roof. It looked solid and fragile all at once. An arched doorway opened into a womblike chill space, aglow under black lights and smoky with incense as I entered. An altar curved along the far wall under a Frida Kahlo self-portrait silkscreened on a tapestry. The altar was covered with dozens of idols, sacred and profane: the Virgin Mary, Saint Francis surrounded by animals, different versions of the Buddha (the old fat one, the feminine princely one), Barbie and Ken dolls, Transformers, Smurfs. A field of trinkets and charms spread out below all this: folded notes, photographs, keys, stuffed animals, a hand-glued collage of Princess Diana, a VOTE NADER 2000 bumper sticker. A guy and a girl crouched at the altar, adding to the devotional clutter.

My boot sent an empty plastic water bottle skittering to the left, toward a tangle of torsos on cushions. I followed it with my eyes.

It came to rest at Woody's feet.

He was watching me from a loveseat, where he sprawled in every direction, a human crossroads: long arms on the cushions to either side, long legs protecting the space in front.

I stepped to him and said, "I've been looking for you all night."

He showed no surprise. He raised his drinking cup, which held just a finger of liquid at the bottom. "I'm officially out of work, and officially getting drunk."

I had no cup to toast with. I'd drunk nothing in the last hour and felt almost completely sober. I offered my sympathy, but he waved it away.

"I'm free," he said.

"But your money?"

"The money! You were right, Jamie. The money was just . . ." —he held out a palm and blew— ". . . *Poof!* Nothing."

"I should never have talked to you that way," I said.

A burst of laughter shot in from behind, a trio of women bringing their conversation into the space. I stepped forward to make room as they passed, and Woody patted the empty half of his sofa, saying, "You've been looking for me all night."

Intoxication gave him a sharper edge than usual, a butch hardiness that seemed almost invulnerable. His damp T-shirt, lavender under the black light, coated him like liquid. His nipples poked the fabric, a reminder of the flesh I knew so well. The new black sweater I wore was already dotted in lint, every speck of it bright as radioactive ash.

The couch was so soft that I sunk backwards, as if into water, though I felt stiff with fear. We had to twist inward to converse, a simple gesture that required great effort. Our knees bumped, and we both shifted away.

He said, "Thanks for sending the check."

"Don't mention it, it was nothing," I said, instantly appalled at the tone of my voice. "What I mean is, it was a big deal for you to lend, and I'm sorry it took so long."

"You surprised me. Your note." He didn't elaborate, instead upended his cup to lure the last drops into his mouth. The sight of his exposed neck made me nearly ravenous, an acute desire quickly mocked by the exaggerated jiggle he gave the container, as if the only thing on his mind was a refill.

The women I'd let pass were now sitting to our side on a futon mattress wedged against the wall of branches. One of them waved a cigarette towards us and asked did we mind, and when we said no, asked if we wanted one.

"Not me, but this guy might," Woody said, slapping my thigh.

"I'm not smoking."

"You're quitting?"

"I'm not not-quitting."

"You said you'd be smoking 'til you lost your first lung!"

"I've said a lot of stupid things."

He patted my knee, this time almost consolingly. I grabbed his hand in mine and pulled it toward me. Our eyes met, and it could have been a moment of—well, it could have been *the* moment, the one that I so desperately wanted between us and had been preparing for since I'd learned he was here. The correct, restorative apology; the perfect summation of my remorse. The great eraser. His eyes were shot with pink spider webs, and through the boozy gloss I could see a flinch of terror. He had hoped to keep this congenial, and now he was trapped with me and my needs, my predictable cries for help and salvation. I fell into a silence that stretched beyond the point its solemnity could hold.

"Are you completely stoned?" he asked.

"Not even a little."

"Then what is this?"

"This is me at a complete loss." My throat was bark dry. Smoke prickled my nostrils. I unclasped my hands, slick with moisture, and released him.

"Is this about us?" His eyebrows lifted, a tiny hint of receptivity that gave me courage, and at last I found words.

"So much has happened, and you're the person I most want to talk to about all of it. And I know this is the wrong place and time. You're here with your friends. You just got fired. And no matter how much everyone is celebrating, you must be destroyed by this. You gave those people a lot of time."

"Too much," he said. He looked down and said, with irony this time, "I'm free."

I reached out again, my fingers encircling his forearm as if taking his pulse. "Yes," I said. "*Us* is on my mind."

He inhaled and exhaled deeply. "Why don't you write something down for me? Whatever you want to say. And then I can read it without reacting, and you won't have to react to me reacting, and after that . . ."

"After that we'll talk?"

"Yeah, sure. But no promises. This isn't about—."

I didn't let him finish. "I'll write you a letter. A long letter, on paper. I can't do this by e-mail."

"Okay, then," he said.

"Okay, then."

We had a plan, it seemed. I had a task. A letter. Where would I start? Newark Airport? The attic? Stepping off the bus in Greenlawn . . .

Our silence invited a sudden visitor, a harlequinned creature in a patchwork jumpsuit: glow sticks wreathed around its neck, androgynous face pancaked in white glitter, earlobes plugged with strobing red lights. The look was pure Scary Clown, the type that puts the dread in audience participation—but when it opened its mouth out came a feminine voice so lilting and blissful she might have been a children's librarian. "Have you made your offerings?" she asked.

Woody and I looked at each other, both of us suppressing a startled grin.

She cocked her head, waiting. "This is the Altar of the New. Put something on the altar you want to leave behind."

"Put something old on the Altar of the New?" Woody asked in a voice so sardonic it sounded more like mine than his.

"Uh-huh. We're burning everything just before dawn."

"Can I just throw myself onto the pyre?" I asked.

"No animal sacrifice," she said, unblinking. She left us with a "Blessed be," and floated like a giant neon smudge to the women on the futon. I heard her tell them, "No smoking in the temple."

Woody slid forward, weight shifting to his feet. "I need another drink."

"I'm gonna stay here a while. An altar is perfect for my penitent mood."

He nodded and stepped away. I watched him move to the altar, reach into his wallet and withdraw a card. He scanned the other objects until he found a place for his. He didn't linger. At the arched doorway, bending to fit through, he pivoted in midcrouch and waved to me. I waved back, feeling neither elated nor let down. Just relieved, from the burden that I might never speak to him again had I not gotten it right, right then.

Pillows were scattered in front of the altar, and I went to one, sitting cross-legged and searching for what Woody had left. There it was: his Digitent identification card. His face framed in curls. A mug shot from jail. A relic.

I had a credit card in my wallet I'd never use again. The slip of paper with directions to this party. A cigarette lighter.

From my thumb I slid my father's wedding band. I turned it in my hand, gazed at the inscription. It should have been buried with him. It wasn't meant to be kept as a souvenir. It wasn't meant for me. I placed it on Woody's badge. They would go into the fire together.

The band stage had been closed, the upper levels cleared. Anyone who was left was corralled and herded to the dance floor. There were hundreds of us in motion, compressed in this pounding, humid box. Sweaty faces, bug-eyed trippers, loose-limbed drunks. I'd long ago lost track of time, and Deirdre had made it clear this was her last night of freedom, brushing away any suggestion that she needed a good night's sleep for Andy and AJ's arrival. She'd undone a button on her blouse and was dancing with her hands in the air and her eyes closed while two guys, possibly sexier than any she'd ever danced with, cast all their attention on her. Colleen and Annie were all dopey smiles and dilated pupils, having each taken a hit of E. They'd offered one to me, and I almost said yes, remembering my dream of Jerusalem; then I decided the dream had not been a directive but some other wisdom requiring a clear head to decipher, and I passed. Brady was good and stoned, swaying to his own inner music. The Digitent castoffs had circled around Woody. A head above everyone else, his rhythmic stiffness transformed by hours of drinking, he looked like a counselor cutting loose on the last night of camp. Even Ian, who had returned, was doing his bearish shuffle, putting the moves on Rick, who had his shirt off, his sinewy traveler's body a vision in bronze. And there I was, too, in the midst of this throbbing soundscape, in the midst of these people who were still my friends, my family, in a place where I belonged. The DJ was wrecking us, our bodies in her power as surely as those two turntables she controlled. She crafted us a journey that thickened and intensified one layered effect at a time, building to a euphoria so great you seemed not to need your body at all; you might just transcend the very vessel that carried you here. Then she'd bring us down slowly, the music stripped to a primal heartbeat, the resting point where we would find in one another's eyes the confirmation that yes, I'm here and I feel it, too. Yes, we agree, this goes beyond individual will. Yes, we trust there will be another peak.

Yes, I surrender. To all of this, my life, I surrender.

The silvering darkness just before dawn. The air cold, colder still against bodies wet with sweat. The real club kids were ready for this, wrapped in ankle-length faux-fur and matching hats, their backpacks rigged with water bags accessed through tubes. The amateurs like me were shivering, dehydrated, in unlined jackets, heads bare, huddling together for scraps of warmth. Deirdre stood in front of me, enfolded in my arms, her head lazing back on my shoulder. Colleen, Annie, and Brady stood to our side, a blanket from Brady's truck swaddling them like triplets. Ian had left with Rick, neither aware that I was the degree-of-separation between them. Woody was gone. He'd slipped off without good-bye. The chill in the air seemed to be smacking up against the very part of me that he'd taken away. A phantom limb.

With dozens of strangers, now familiar from the spell of our dancing, we circled around oil drums in the parking lot, watching fire dancers who had already juggled and twirled their flames for too long, the breathlessness of their spectacle evolving from hypnotic to simply numbing. To the sounds of drumming, the disassembled temple of branches was carried out. A pagan eeriness descended. Two voices, both female, began a wordless, chanting harmony. No speeches were made, no prayers recited, no gods invoked. The kindling was dispersed among the metal containers. Baskets of offerings were sifted atop the wood. The dancers approached with torches. The singers held a final chord. The fire licked the branches: the slow spread of flame, the crackle of ignition. A penance of waiting.

The first pyre erupted in violent orange.

I heard the breath of a hundred mourners release.

Epilogue

TWO LETTERS

Dear Jamie,

I would have bet money I'd heard the last of you though you're nothing if not persistent. To tell you the God's honest truth, I thought you were full of bs about being a radio producer, but the contract you sent got my attention. I had my attorney look it over, he's a very powerful entertainment lawyer and says it's on the up and up, so I decided to sign. Here it is.

Like you suggested I listened to "This American Life" and it seemed to have good production quality, but I ask you, how are you going to take a career like mine and boil it down to an hour? I'm giving you a chance to prove you're not just another shyster who's all talk, no action. Don't mess up or you'll have Dean Foster to answer to.

One more thing, I pulled this letter out of a box, and figured you'd want a look at it. I thought I burned everything Rusty ever sent me so how this one survived is a mystery.

Yours truly,
Dean Foster

May 18, 1961

Dear Danny (or I guess I should say "Dean"),

Get a load of you in your new Hollywood life! That was a great surprise the news about the screentest plus the fancy picture with your "autograph" which I'll save and maybe it'll be worth money one day. I gave up on you after so long not hearing back but at long last here you are and practically famous to boot.

Now its the early early morning and I've come to this paper to recount the night as it rolled along. Hours upon drunken hours marked by wild conversation hysterical shouting running down Columbus like I owned the street then nodding off in strange apartments and at last back to my foggy attic where I have downed a bottle of Coca-Cola with extra sugar stirred into it to bring my dumb mind back up to snuff so I might write these words to you. I will attempt the details in clear order but first let me offer the main fact—which is last night I came face to face with Kerouac himself. I'll give you the whole fantastic and also terrible story.

It began at the end of my shift closing up the Hideaway when Don said there's a party, Chick and Mary are in town. I thought they were sore at me which is a long story for another time, but Don said let bygones be bygones so I went along. Sure enough the party was fullswing with jugs of redwine bottles of ale and roasting smoking meats on a backyard grill and overlording the whole proceeding was Chick who told me to take over the grill and I say no sir I'm off the clock. Mary is already three sheets into it, she's a fish in a beer aquarium standing among the hard drinking artists arguing about Nietzsche and Communism and the Negro Problem and the electric chair. Mary tells me the big news the rumor that Kerouac is back in Frisco. He is to write a new book and has been seen out and about with the City Lights crowd. So when the party wound down Don, Mary, Chick, me and some others are off on this mission. Suddenly I was sober as a church with the idea of meeting my hero.

Cafe Vesuvius was packed to the door with revelers loud voices and sounds of breaking glass. You couldn't have made your way through without getting a foot stepped on by someone even more drunken and wobblylegged than yourself. Kerouac is in the back, at the center of the loudest brawlingest glassbreakingest table in the house. The gang shoved me through the crowd. Mary knows some of the fellows in the Kerouac party. Hellos all around, Kerouac asks "Who's buying my next bottle?" Mary says "This kid came all the way from New York to meet you, this is the highlight of his life." Kerouac takes a look at me and says "Are you a spy from my publisher wondering why I'm out on a bender instead of writing the next chapter of my legend?"

Danny it was a mesmerizing moment and I could hardly speak. He looked a whole lot older than I expected and his eyes couldn't focus and half his face was sliding off his bones from the effects of too much drink. "No sir Mr. Kerouac I'm just an admirer of your inspirational book <u>On The Road</u>." He said "That happened more than ten years ago. This time I came by train." I laughed along with everyone else though it seemed like the joke was on me. I said "I also like <u>The Subterraneans</u> which I just found out was really about New York and not San Francisco" (how's that for a kicker—the very book that got me interested in Frisco to begin with!) and to this he says "I have to watch out for libelous ladies." (Which I believe he was referring to the woman he based the main character upon. She was ready to sue him for using details of their affair so he changed things around.) Then he looks me in the eyes with "Buy me a drink kid." I said sorry I'm broke and he said "A drink is the price for a piece of my soul."

These eerie words struck me dumb. I got shoved aside and I was once again your friend Teddy in a room full of folks who don't give a rats ass about me or me about them. Short while later the whole place gets even more earsplittingly loud and lo and behold Kerouac is stumbling out to the street. And behind me I hear a shouting voice calling "The King of Beats is a phony! " (It reminded me of Papa the time we saw him thrown out of The Shamrock Inn. Remember that?) Danny it was ugly to see the famous man as just another drunk being mocked. I wondered what had happened to him? I mean to the madman of <u>On The Road</u>, who had hopes and beliefs. You don't get that mushfaced and darkeyed from a single bender. That comes from years of giving away pieces of your soul. I looked around, at Don and Mary and the whole bar, all of them dipped in years of drink. And the thought of me turning out like one of them made me double over in laughter. I was hysterical with it. I went running right into Columbus whooping crazy as a chimpanzee with hornhonking taxis slamming brakes in every direction and Don chasing me down yelling "Get out of traffic you damn fool!" Later I vomited up my guts which wasn't so funny.

Now I'm thinking that Kerouac was right to wonder if I was a spy. Because I was, though not in the way he meant it. I was a spy from the people he never sees—all us dumb readers who soakup his words and put themselves in his shoes and dream his dreams with him. Only his shoes are stumbling down the pavement like any drunk.

Truly I think I've had enough of these achey daybreak mornings with too much booze in my belly and no money in my pocket and no chick to curl up with. I'm not the praying type but about a day ago I said "All right God give me a sign whether or not its time to leave Frisco" and I think this night was my sign. So don't be surprised if I show up in Hollywood to see you Danny, and I'm talking soon. Right now I'm asking myself that same question that Kerouac said in The Subterraneans. "What's in store for me in the direction I don't take?"

You don't ever know do you? Unless you jump ship mid way.

Your friend for always,
Teddy

Acknowledgments

I take great pleasure extending gratitude where it is due. First, to the Djerassi Resident Artists Program, where this novel began and where, years later, I finished the first draft. In between, my "artist's retreats" with Christine Murray and John Rossell moved the writing of this novel forward in leaps and bounds. My deepest thanks to you two, great friends and great company.

Every month for four years I have foisted chunks of this manuscript on a group of writer friends, who helped make it better than I could have done on my own, and whose collective talent continues to humble and inspire me: John Vlahides, Elizabeth Costello, David Booth, and Catherine Brady. Along the way I have benefited from the careful reading, advice, and bottomless generosity of Kevin Clarke, Maria Maggenti, Dave Hickey, Gary Rosen, Robert Kaplan, Christine Murray, Sonia Stamm, Fenton Johnson, my family, my friends, and my colleagues at the University of San Francisco.

That this book exists at all is due to the phenomenal energy, wisdom, and guidance of Jandy Nelson. Along with everyone at Manus & Associates Literary Agency—thanks for always watching my back.

John Scognamiglio, my editor: For the intelligence and care you bring to each step of our collaboration, I thank you, along with your hardworking colleagues at Kensington Books.

For sharing stories of life in San Francisco past, I am in debt to the painter Pat Sherwood, whose art provided an inspiration for Ray Gladwell's landscapes and portraits; and I blow a kiss to the late Bill Plath and Dick Rousseau. My appreciation also goes out to Mike Finn for sharing Bill and Dick's letters; to Roman Mars for educating me about public radio; to Michael Lampen, for sharing the history of Grace Cathedral; to Tucker Schwarz for allowing me to hang her fine art on my fictitious warehouse walls; and to Jol Perez and the Cubby Creatures for the perfect lyrics. The "twig temple" in chapter 24 was modeled on Patrick Dougherty's *St. Denis' Tower.* To all the inspiring San Franciscans in my life, thanks for keeping this city interesting.

Finally, this book has been greatly influenced by the encouragement, decency, and openheartedness of my partner, Kevin Clarke, and my father, Karl Soehnlein, Sr. This one's for both of you.